"Hilo ...
—Malcolm S., age 9,
Riverdale, N.Y.

"**GINA WAS MY FAVORITE** character because she's into science and soccer like me! I also liked D.J.'s family because it looks like mine!"
—Kiran M., age 7,
Carlsbad, Calif.

"*Hilo* is **REALLY, REALLY FUNNY.** It has a **LOT OF LAUGHS.** The raccoon is the funniest."
—Theo M., age 7,
Miami, Fla.

"**HIGH ENERGY** and **HILARIOUS**!"
—Gene Luen Yang, National Ambassador for Young People's Literature

"**FANTASTIC. EVERY SINGLE THING ABOUT THIS . . . IS TERRIFIC.**"
—Boingboing.net

"My students are obsessed with this series. **OBSESSED!**"
—Colby Sharp, teacher, blogger, and co-founder of the Nerdy Book Club

"More **GIANT ROBOTIC ANTS** . . . than in the complete works of Jane Austen."
—Neil Gaiman, author of *Coraline*

"Anyone who loves to laugh should read *Hilo*. It is **ACTION-PACKED** with a robotic touch."
—Breslin S., age 10,
Jackson, Mich.

"*Hilo* is loads of **SLAPSTICK FUN!**"
—Dan Santat,
winner of the Caldecott Medal

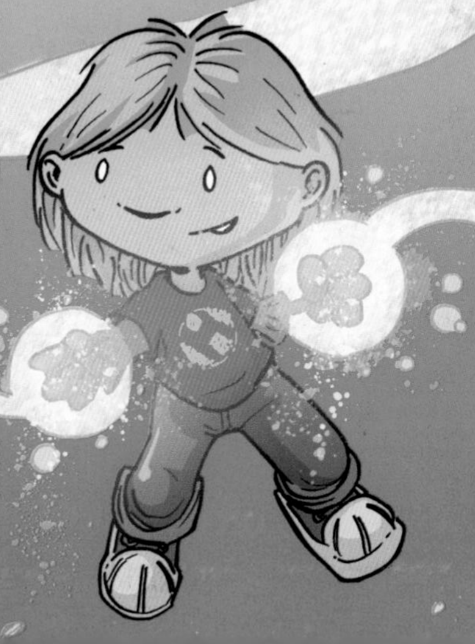

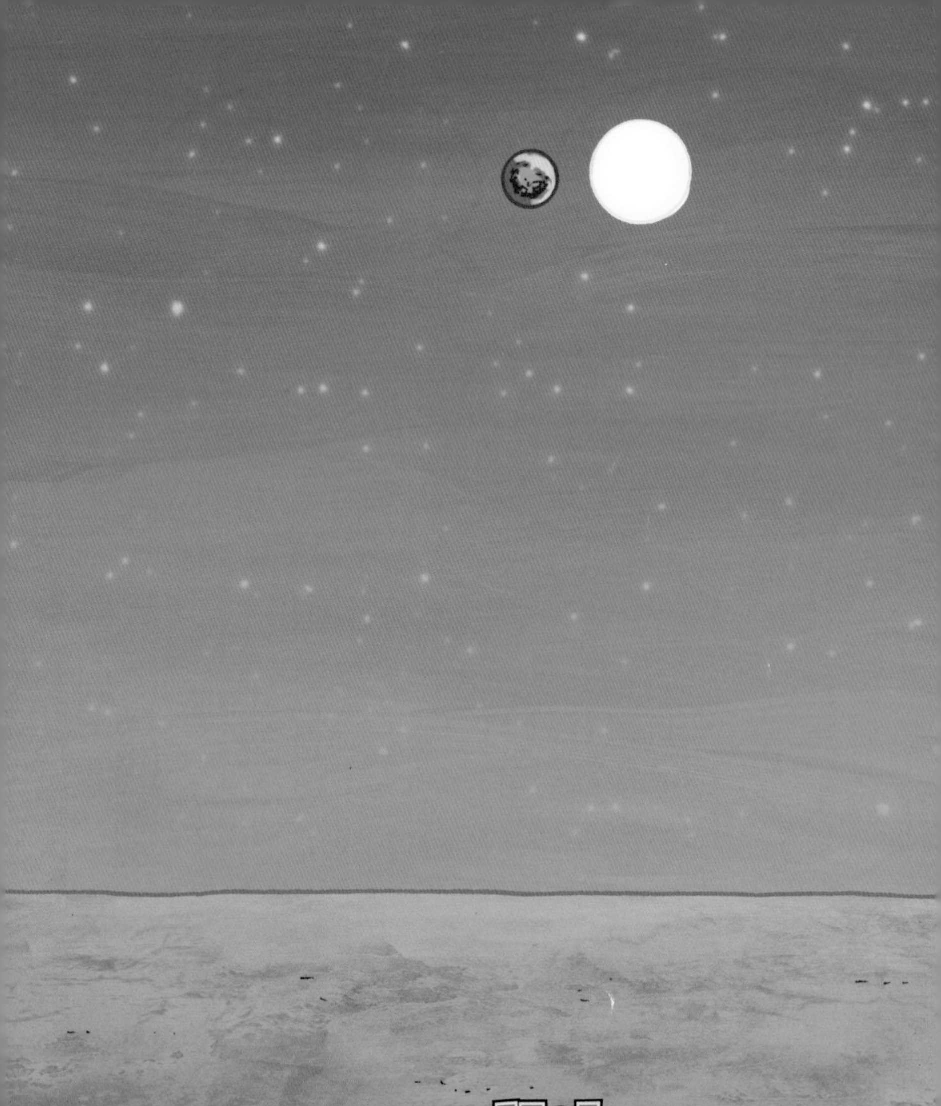

READ ALL THE HILO BOOKS!

HILO #1 THE BOY WHO CRASHED TO EARTH

HILO #2 SAVING THE WHOLE WIDE WORLD

HILO #3 THE GREAT BIG BOOM

HILO #4 WAKING THE MONSTERS

HILO #5 THEN EVERYTHING WENT WRONG

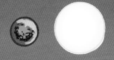

BOOK 5

THEN EVERYTHING WENT WRONG

BY JUDD WINICK

COLOR BY
STEVE HAMAKER

RANDOM HOUSE 🏠 NEW YORK

Copyright © 2019 by Judd Winick

All rights reserved. Published in the United States by Random House Children's Books, a division of Penguin Random House LLC, New York.

Random House and the colophon are registered trademarks of Penguin Random House LLC.

Visit us on the Web! rhcbooks.com

Educators and librarians, for a variety of teaching tools, visit us at RHTeachersLibrarians.com

Library of Congress Cataloging-in-Publication Data

Names: Winick, Judd, author.

Title: Hilo. Book 5, Then everything went wrong / by Judd Winick.

Description: First edition. | New York : Random House, [2019] |

Summary: "As D.J., Gina, Hilo and Izzy go on another adventure together, Hilo gets even closer to answering the questions of his past. But the shocking answers he gets are not the ones he expected or wanted"—Provided by publisher.

Identifiers: LCCN 2017034073 | ISBN 978-1-5247-1496-3 (hardcover) |

ISBN 978-1-5247-1497-0 (hardcover library binding) | ISBN 978-1-5247-1498-7 (ebook)

Subjects: LCSH: Graphic novels. | CYAC: Graphic novels. | Robots—Fiction. | Friendship—Fiction. | Extraterrestrial beings—Fiction. | Identity—Fiction. | Science fiction.

Classification: PZ7.7.W57 Hm 2019 | DDC 741.5/973—dc23

Book design by Bob Bianchini

MANUFACTURED IN CHINA

10 9 8 7 6 5 4 3 2 1

First Edition

for

SHANA and JODI

who always
light
the way

CHAPTER 1

GOING TO BE HARD

MY NAME IS DANIEL JACKSON LIM.
BUT EVERYONE CALLS ME --
D.J.!

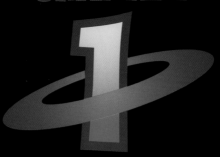

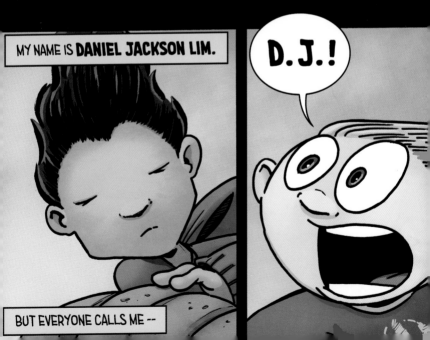

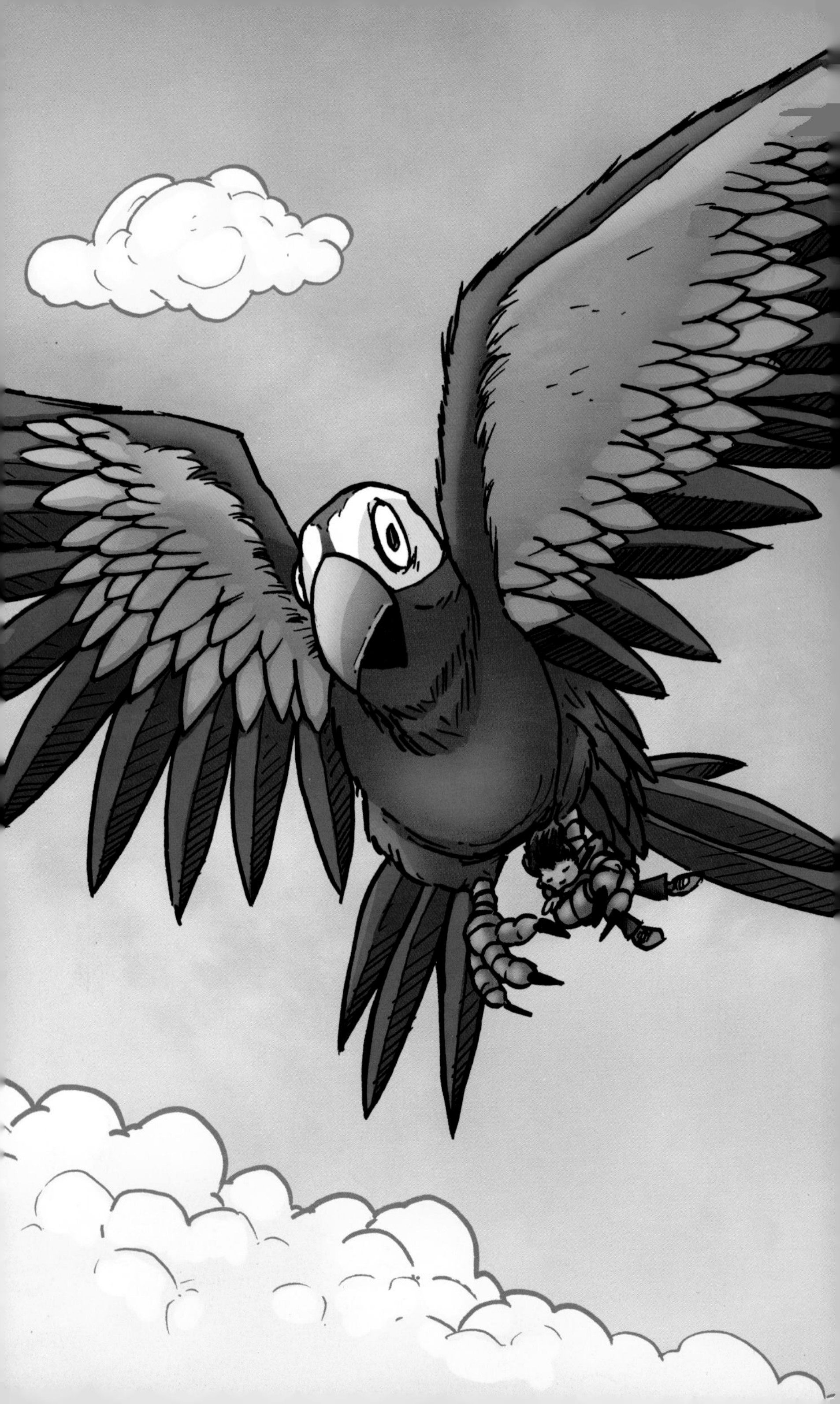

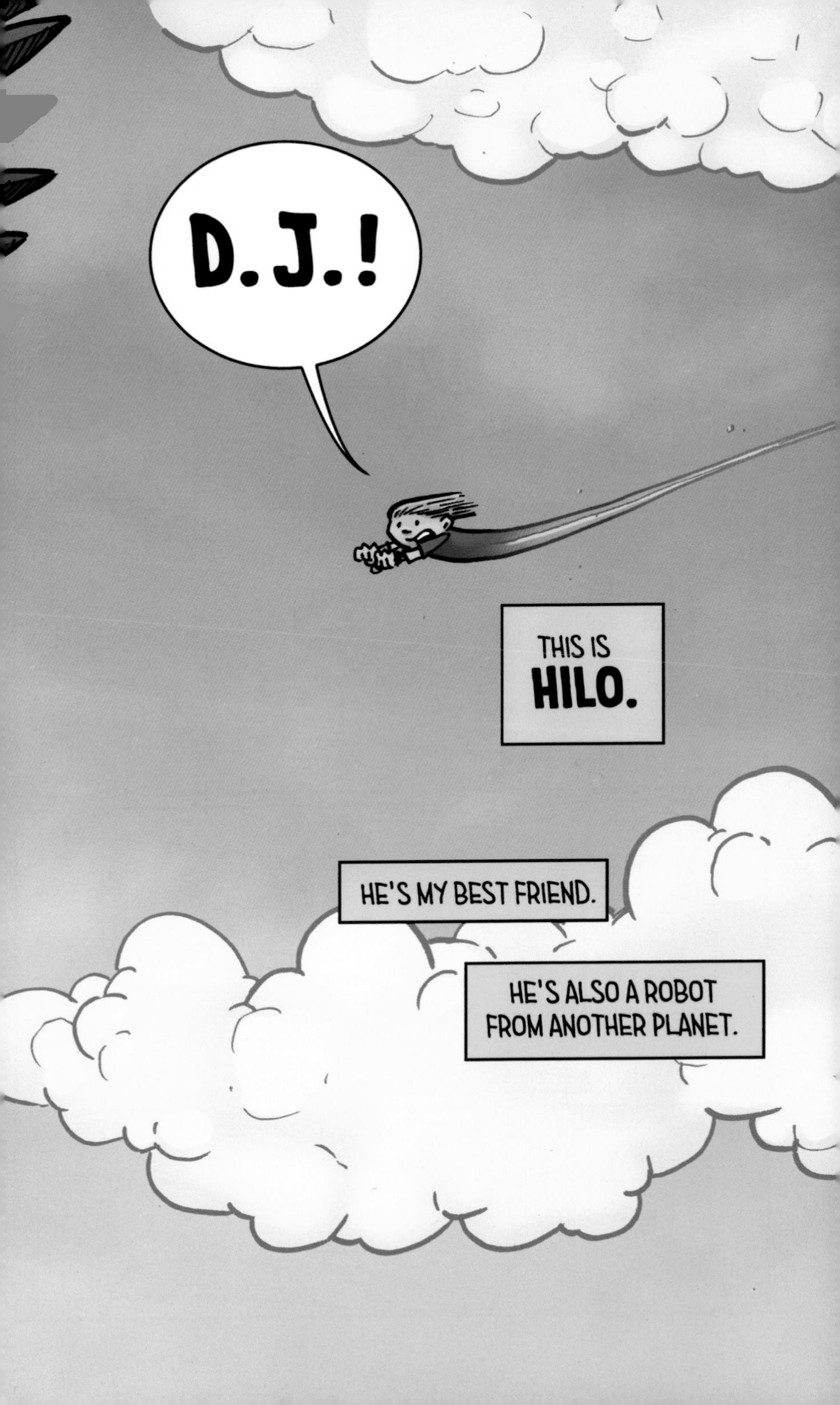
D.J.!
THIS IS HILO.
HE'S MY BEST FRIEND.
HE'S ALSO A ROBOT FROM ANOTHER PLANET.

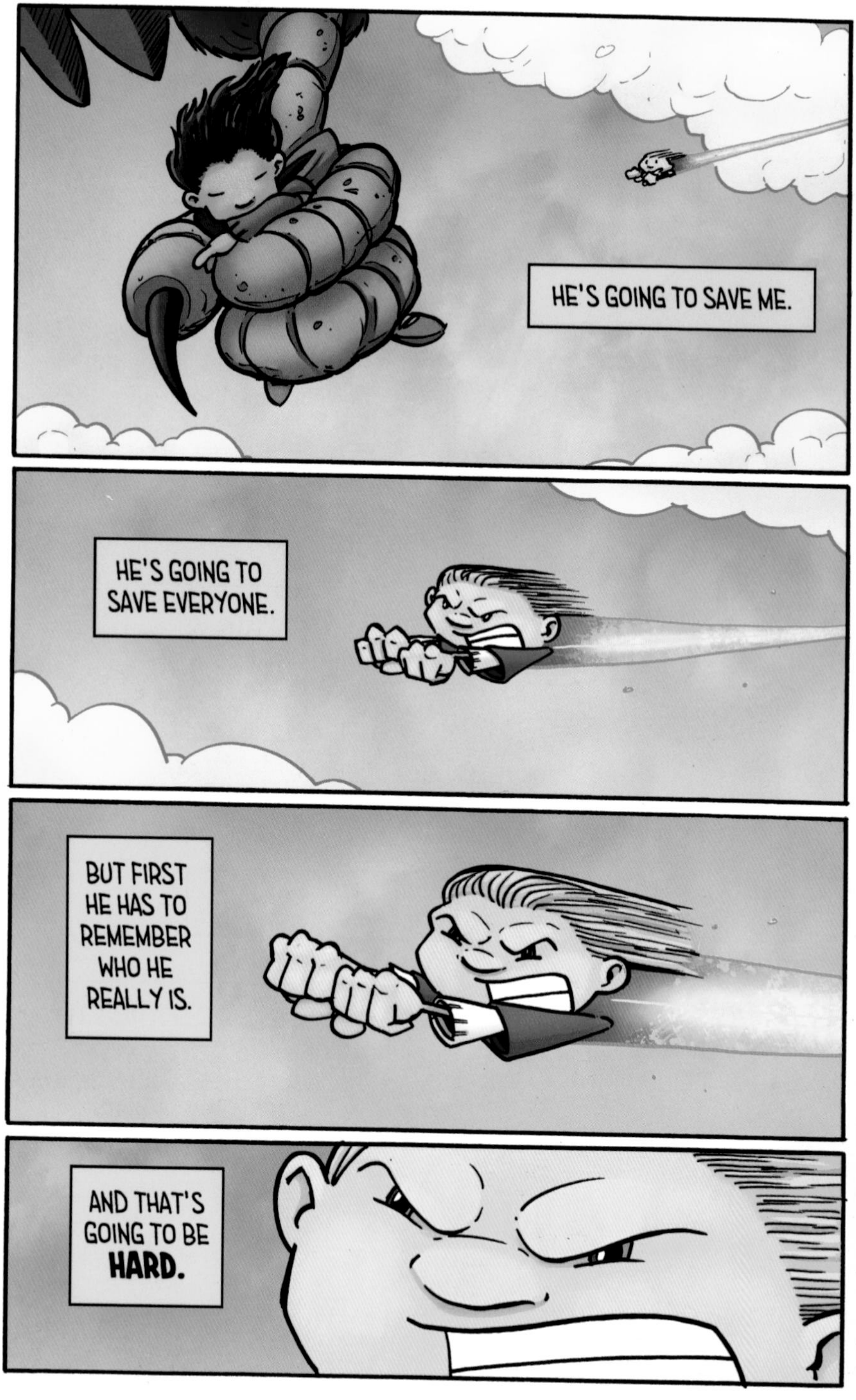

HE'S GOING TO SAVE ME.
HE'S GOING TO SAVE EVERYONE.
BUT FIRST HE HAS TO REMEMBER WHO HE REALLY IS.
AND THAT'S GOING TO BE **HARD.**

CHAPTER 2

HERE

TWO DAYS AGO.
IS THAT REALLY...?
IT **LOOKS** LIKE --
YEP.

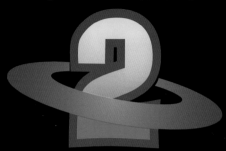

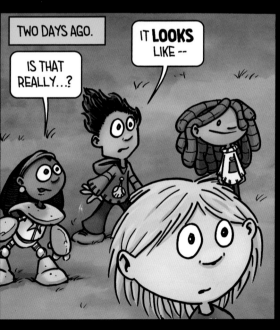

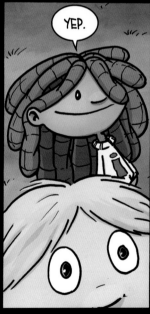

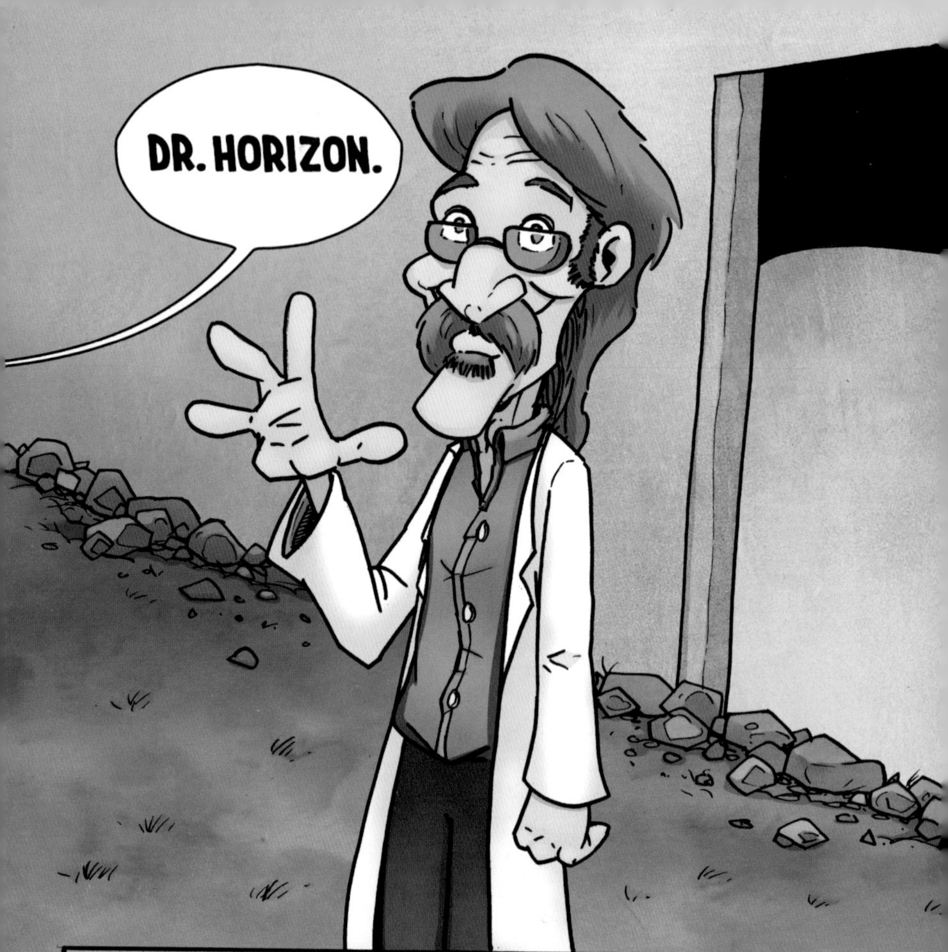
DR. HORIZON.

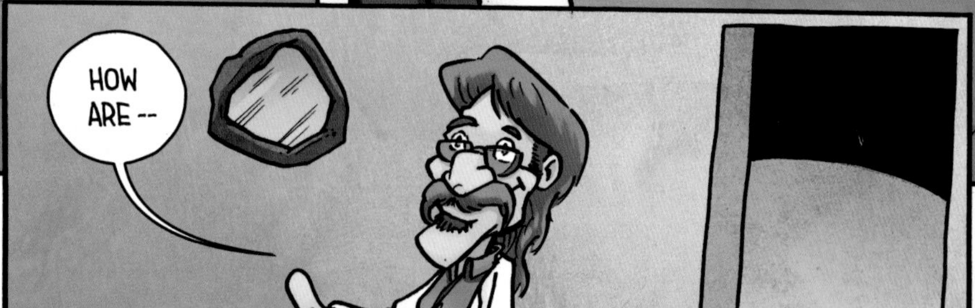
HOW ARE --

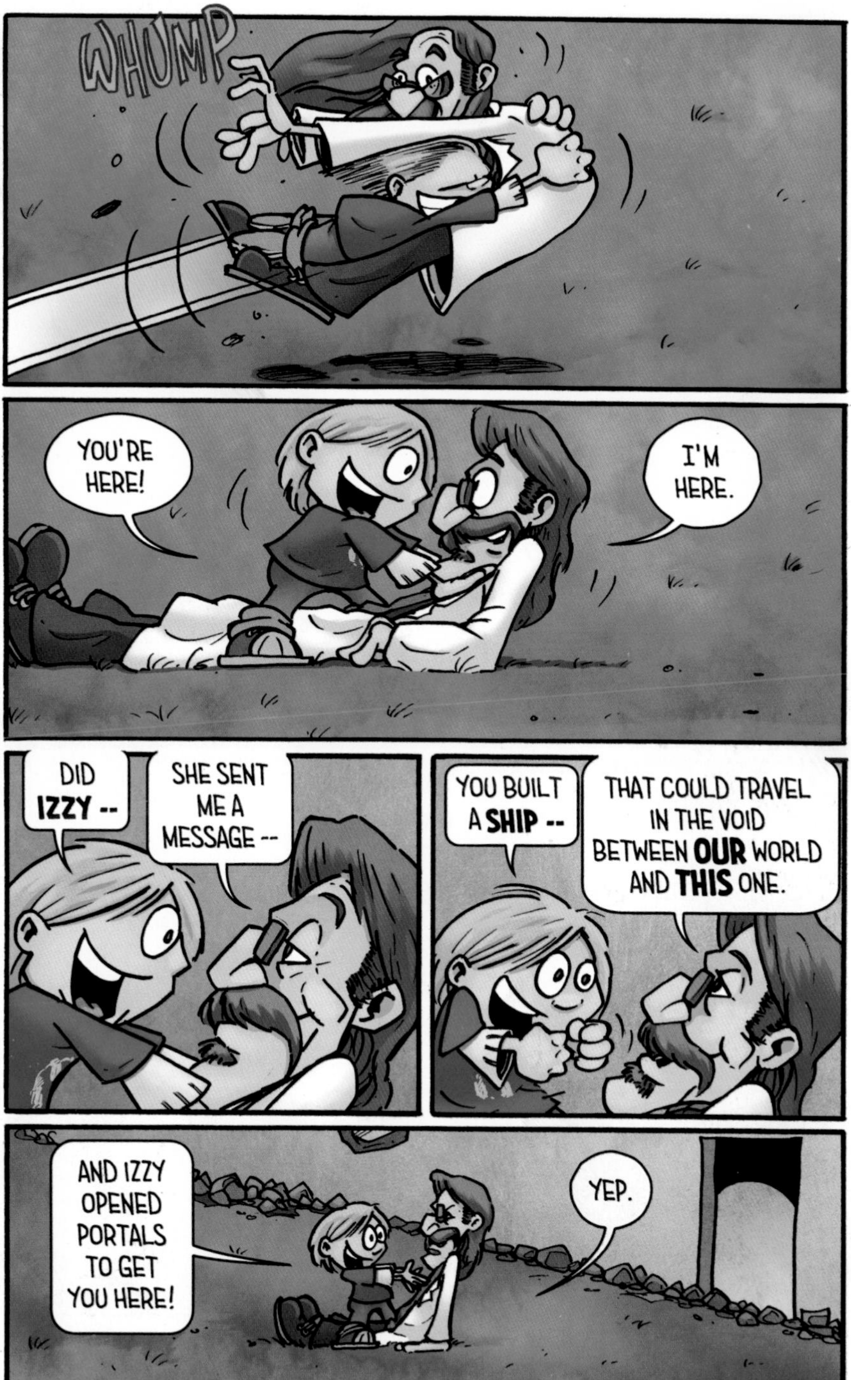
WHUMP
YOU'RE HERE!
I'M HERE.
DID IZZY --
SHE SENT ME A MESSAGE --
YOU BUILT A SHIP --
THAT COULD TRAVEL IN THE VOID BETWEEN OUR WORLD AND THIS ONE.
AND IZZY OPENED PORTALS TO GET YOU HERE!
YEP.

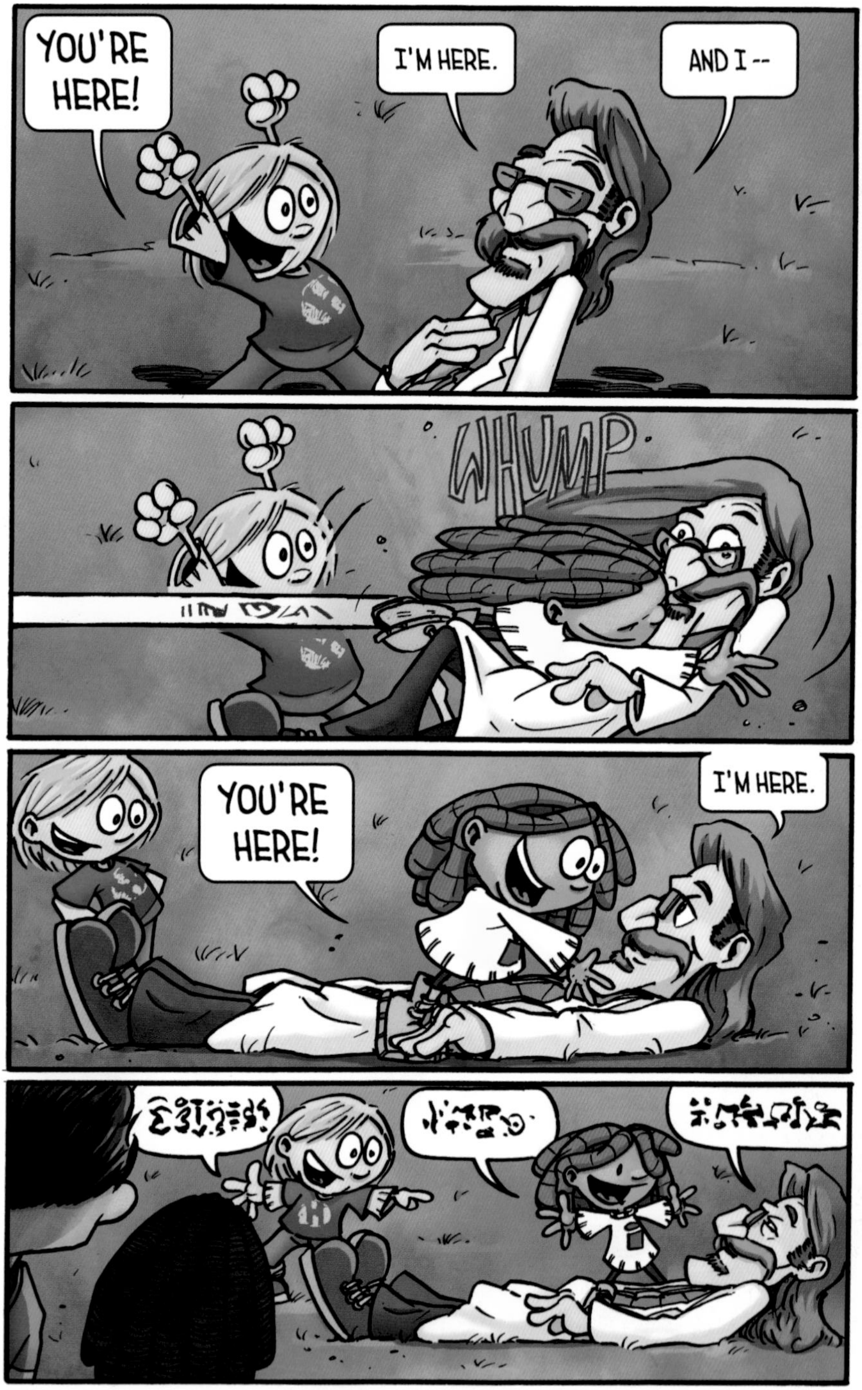
YOU'RE HERE!
I'M HERE.
AND I --
WHUMP
YOU'RE HERE!
I'M HERE.

WHAT ARE THEY SAYING?

YOU CAN'T UNDERSTAND US. WE'RE TALKING 予芳予分.

予苍芳予分.

此序示苓分.

WHAT? 予芳予分.

WHAT?

予芳予分. IT'S OUR LANGUAGE FROM OUR PLANET. HILO AND ME ARE ROBOTS. SO WE CAN ABSORB LANGUAGES FROM PEOPLE. DR. HORIZON CAN'T SO HE SPEAKS 予芳予分.

予芳予分.

OOH. YOU'RE NOT PRONOUNCING IT RIGHT.

YOU KIND OF SAID, "I HAVE A FROG BUTT."

WHICH I DO NOT.

TOTALLY DO NOT.

GUYS! WHAT ARE THEY SAYING?!

予众系序分.

此序示分.

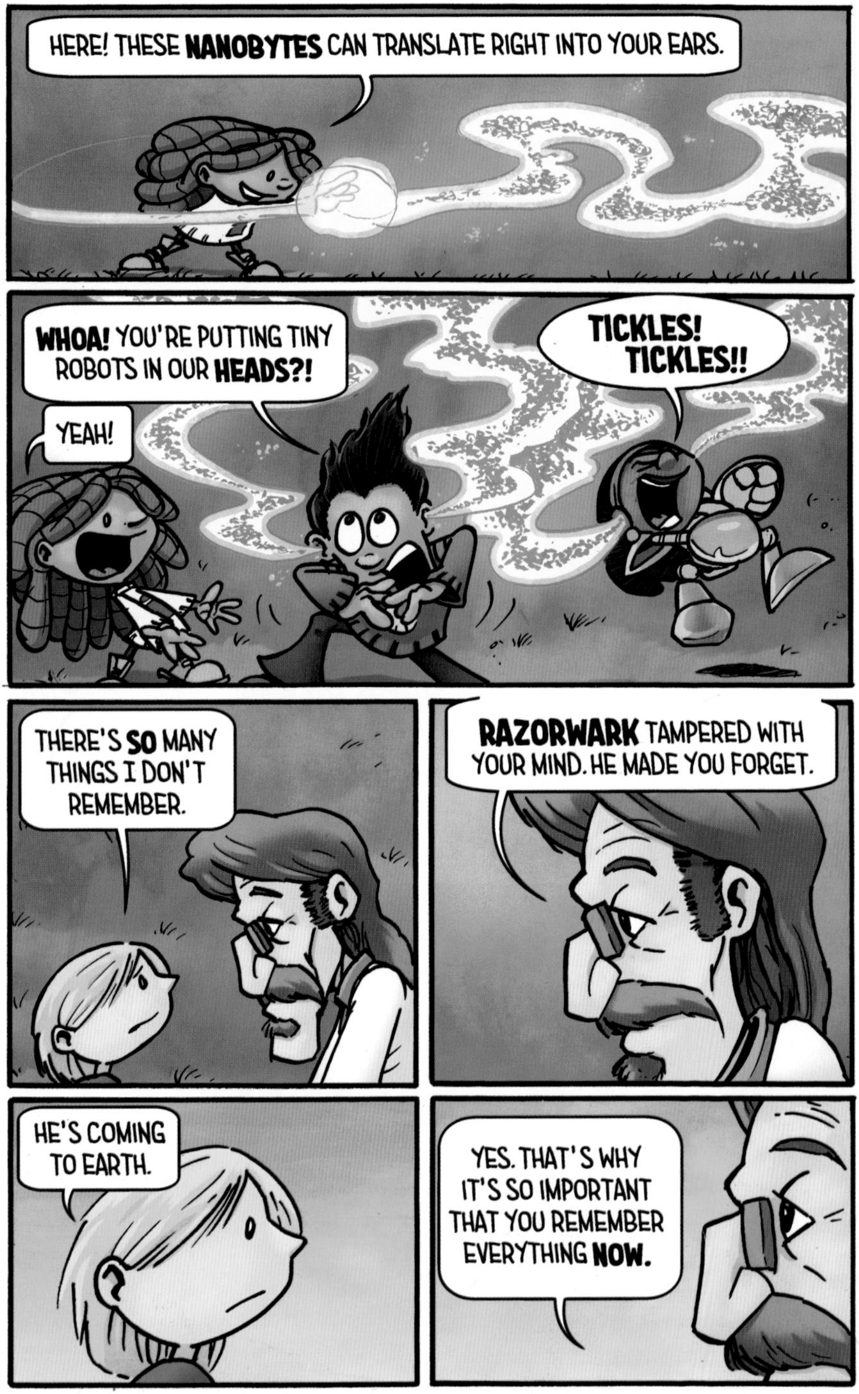
HERE! THESE **NANOBYTES** CAN TRANSLATE RIGHT INTO YOUR EARS.
WHOA! YOU'RE PUTTING TINY ROBOTS IN OUR **HEADS?!**
YEAH!
TICKLES! TICKLES!!
THERE'S **SO** MANY THINGS I DON'T REMEMBER.
RAZORWARK TAMPERED WITH YOUR MIND. HE MADE YOU FORGET.
HE'S COMING TO EARTH.
YES. THAT'S WHY IT'S SO IMPORTANT THAT YOU REMEMBER EVERYTHING **NOW.**

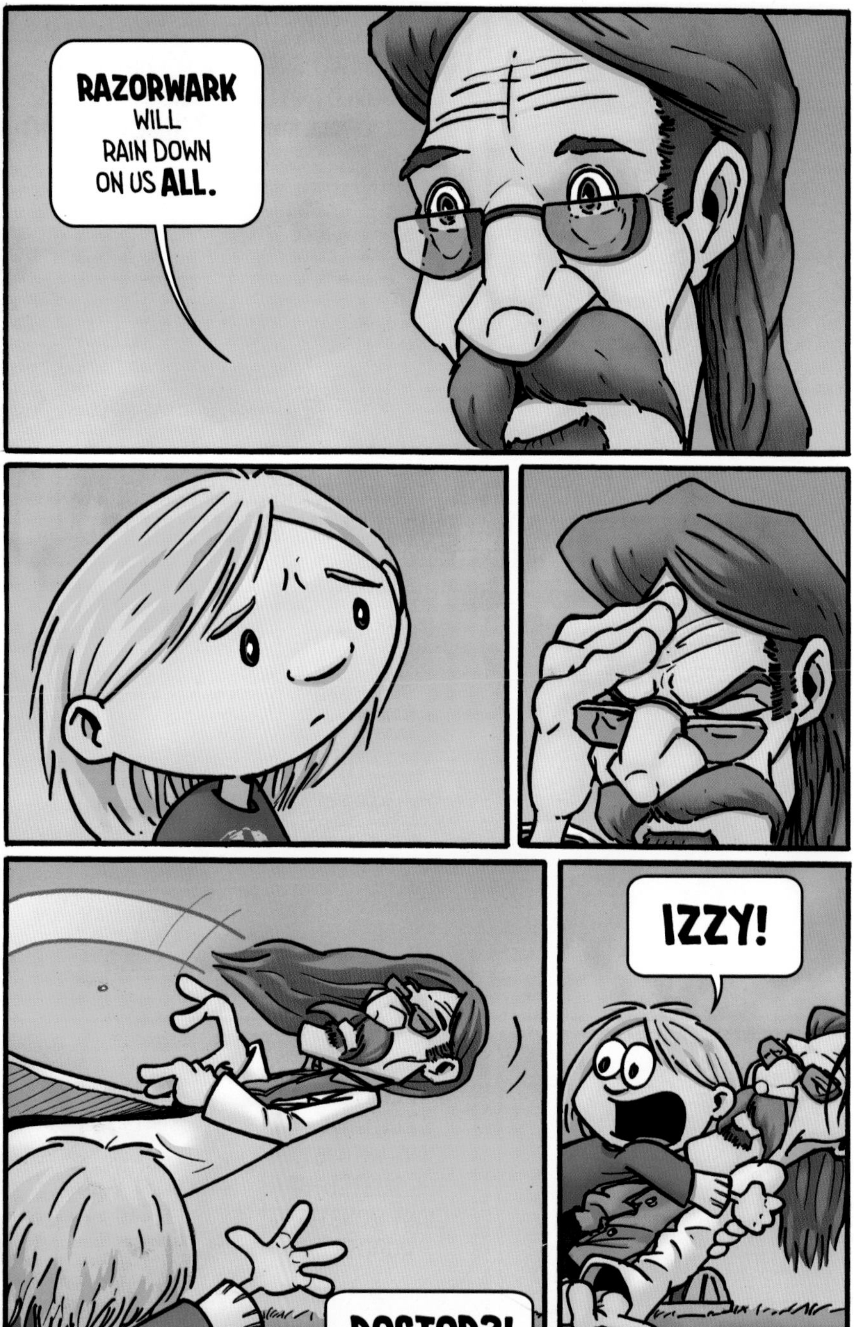
RAZORWARK WILL RAIN DOWN ON US ALL.
DOCTOR?!
IZZY!

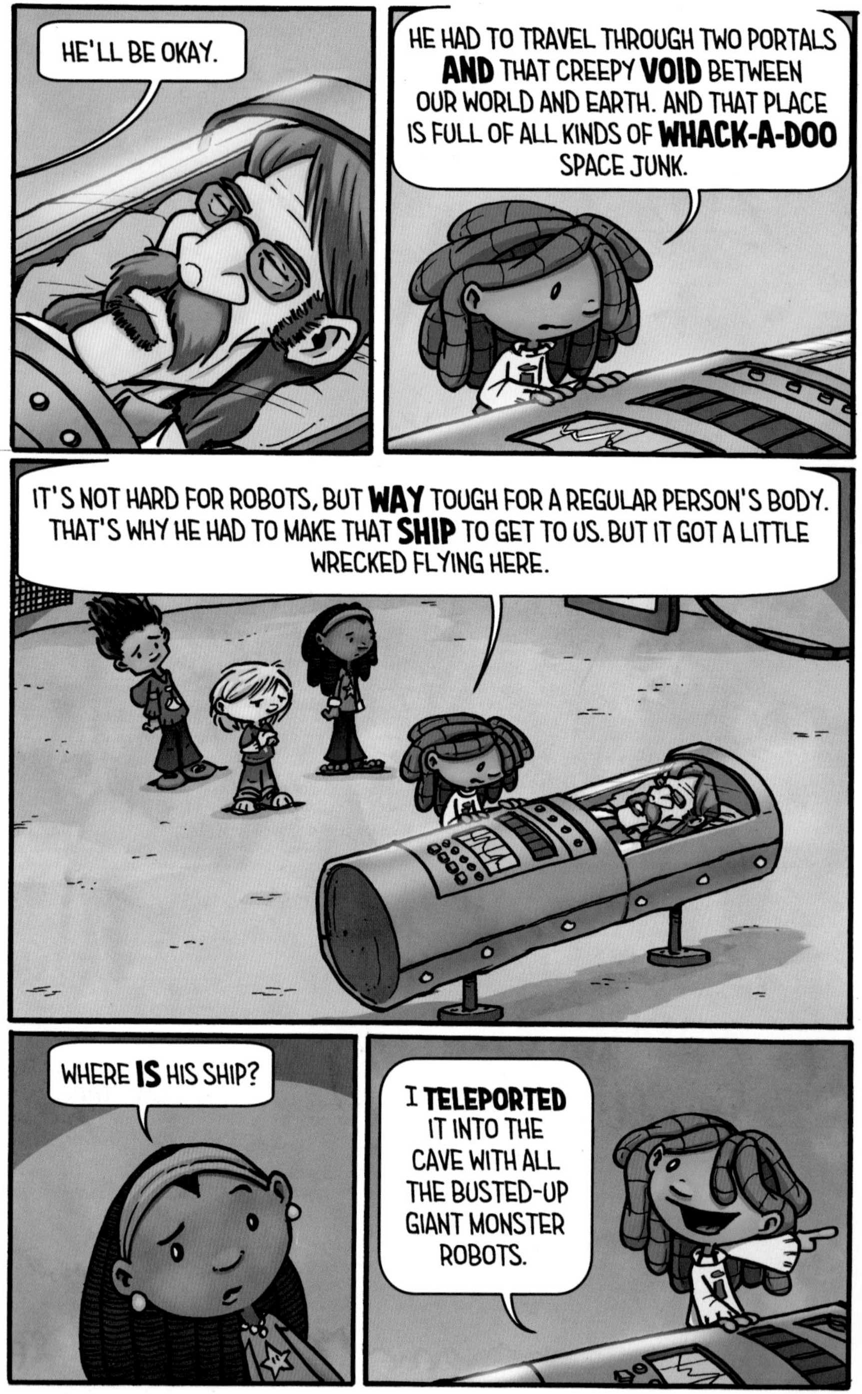
HE'LL BE OKAY.
HE HAD TO TRAVEL THROUGH TWO PORTALS **AND** THAT CREEPY **VOID** BETWEEN OUR WORLD AND EARTH. AND THAT PLACE IS FULL OF ALL KINDS OF **WHACK-A-DOO** SPACE JUNK.
IT'S NOT HARD FOR ROBOTS, BUT **WAY** TOUGH FOR A REGULAR PERSON'S BODY. THAT'S WHY HE HAD TO MAKE THAT **SHIP** TO GET TO US. BUT IT GOT A LITTLE WRECKED FLYING HERE.
WHERE **IS** HIS SHIP?
I **TELEPORTED** IT INTO THE CAVE WITH ALL THE BUSTED-UP GIANT MONSTER ROBOTS.

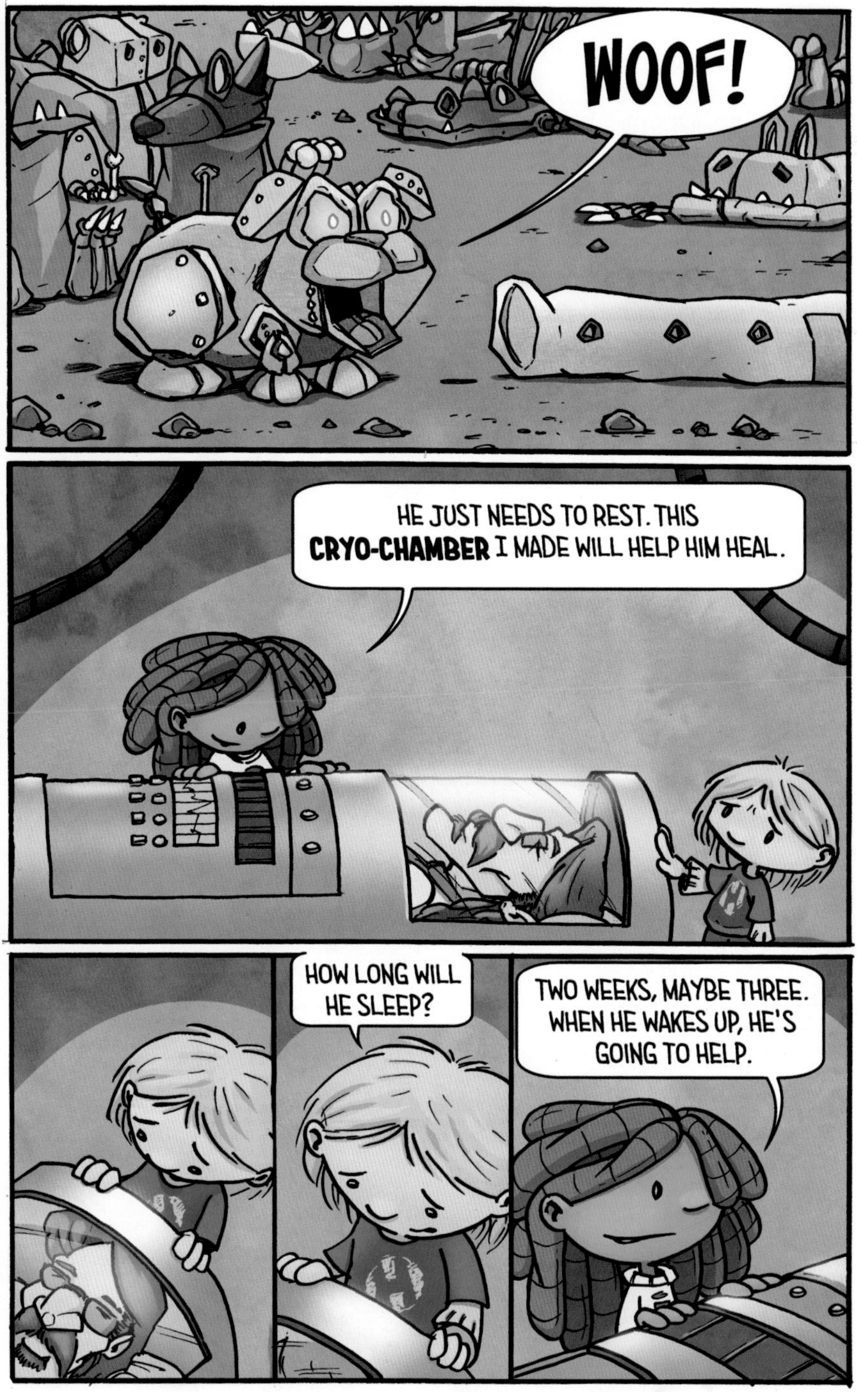
WOOF!
HE JUST NEEDS TO REST. THIS CRYO-CHAMBER I MADE WILL HELP HIM HEAL.
HOW LONG WILL HE SLEEP?
TWO WEEKS, MAYBE THREE. WHEN HE WAKES UP, HE'S GOING TO HELP.

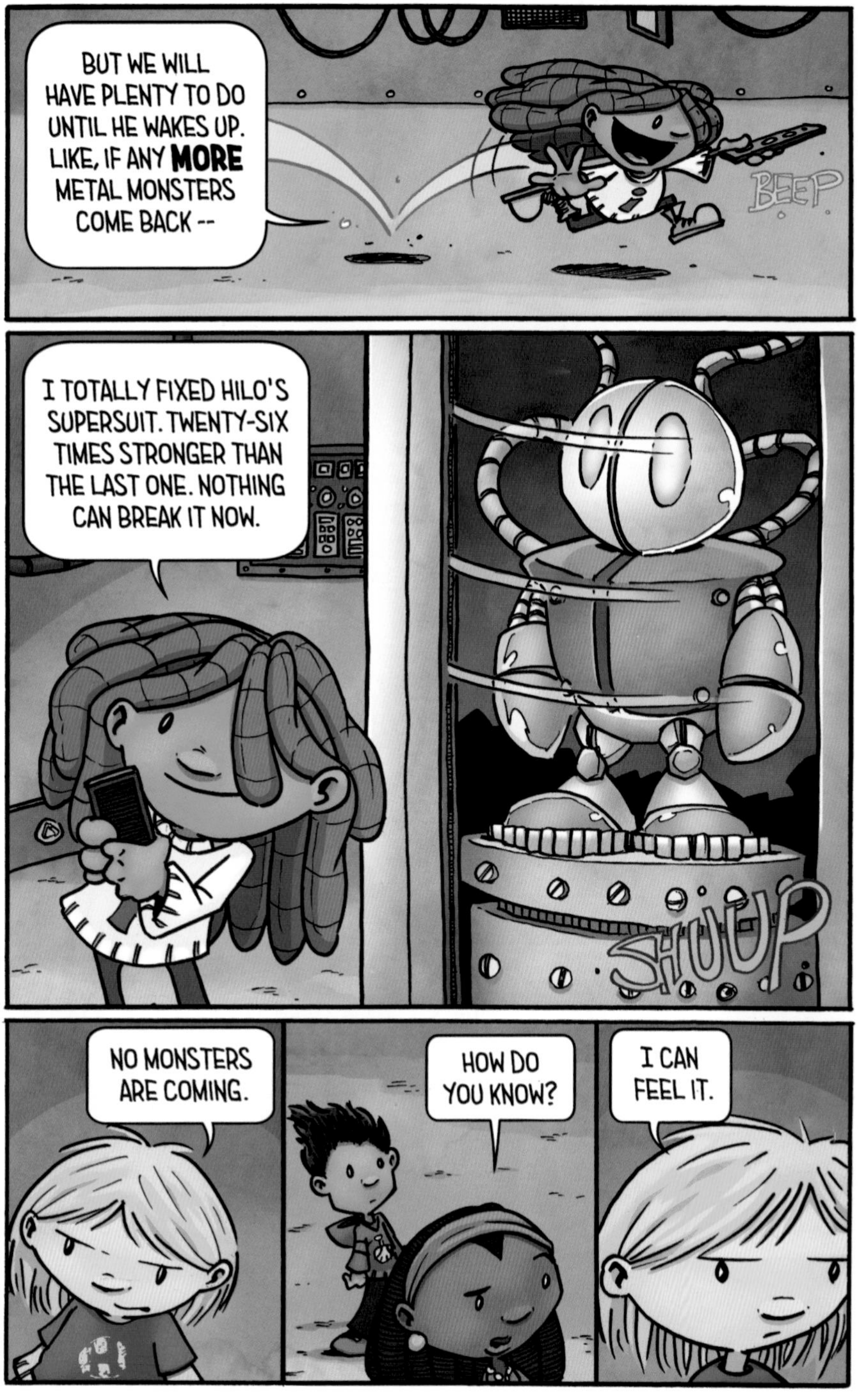
BUT WE WILL HAVE PLENTY TO DO UNTIL HE WAKES UP. LIKE, IF ANY **MORE** METAL MONSTERS COME BACK --
BEEP
I TOTALLY FIXED HILO'S SUPERSUIT. TWENTY-SIX TIMES STRONGER THAN THE LAST ONE. NOTHING CAN BREAK IT NOW.
SHUUP
NO MONSTERS ARE COMING.
HOW DO YOU KNOW?
I CAN FEEL IT.

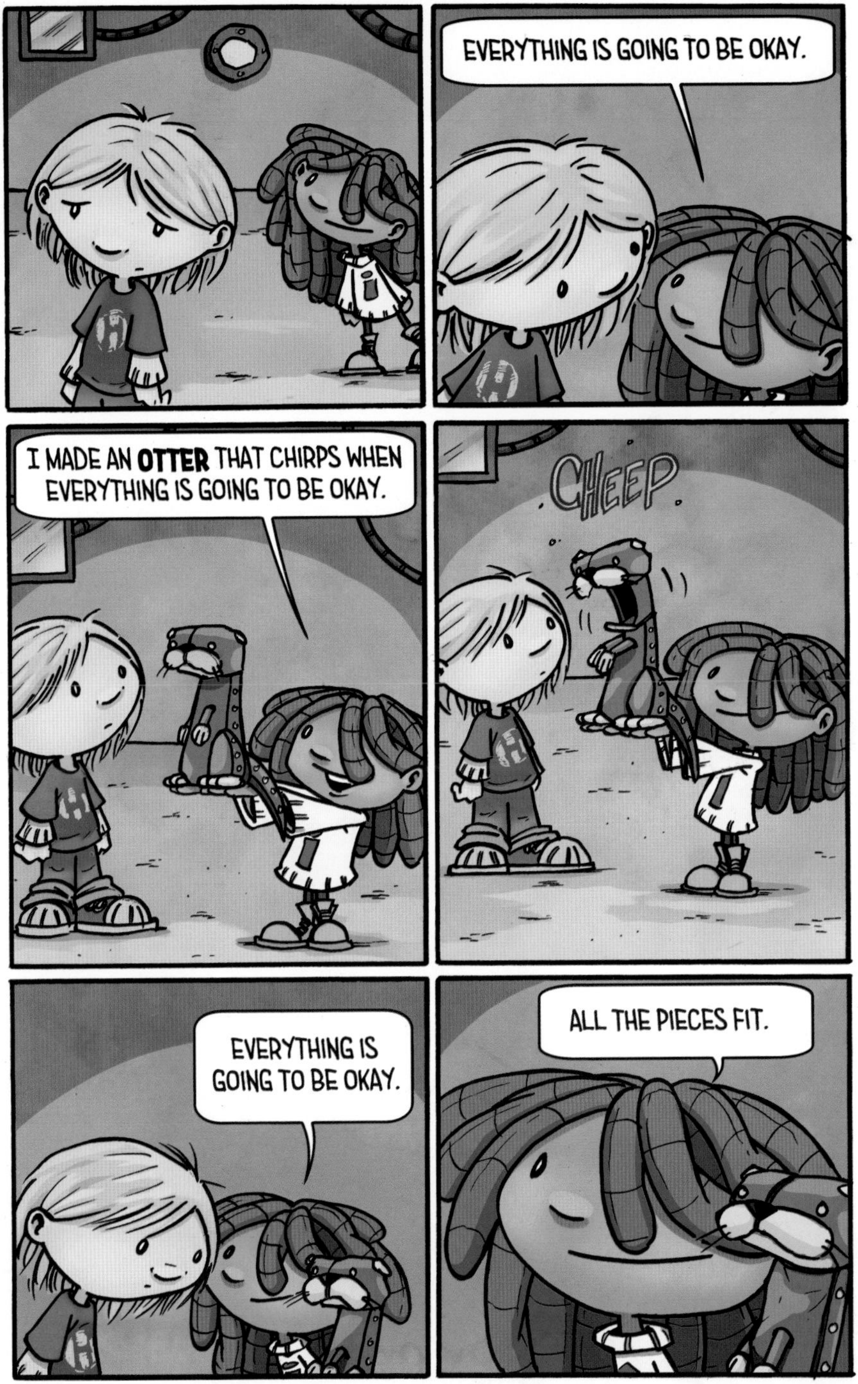
EVERYTHING IS GOING TO BE OKAY.
I MADE AN **OTTER** THAT CHIRPS WHEN EVERYTHING IS GOING TO BE OKAY.
CHEEP
EVERYTHING IS GOING TO BE OKAY.
ALL THE PIECES FIT.

3

WHACK-A-DOO

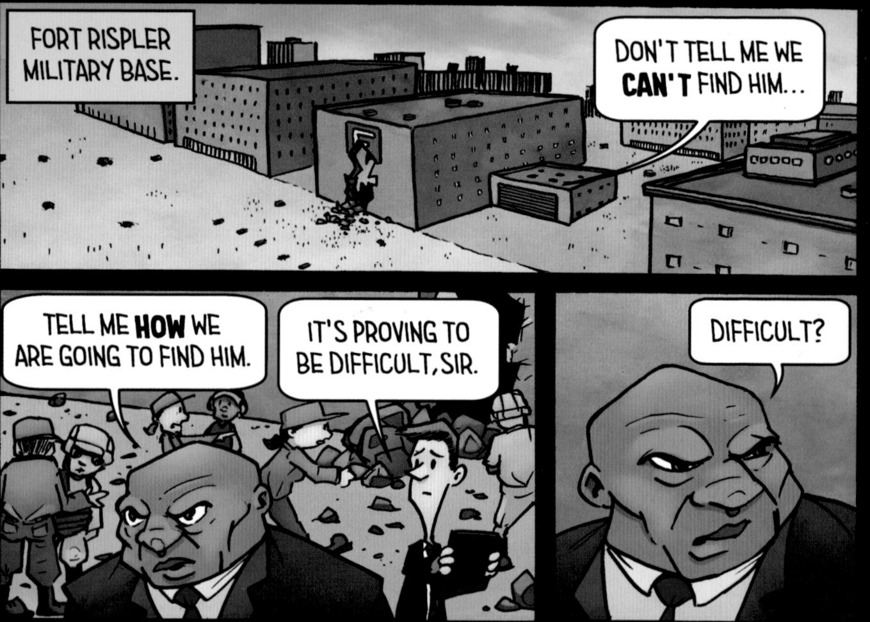

FORT RISPLER MILITARY BASE.
DON'T TELL ME WE **CAN'T** FIND HIM...
TELL ME **HOW** WE ARE GOING TO FIND HIM.
IT'S PROVING TO BE DIFFICULT, SIR.
DIFFICULT?

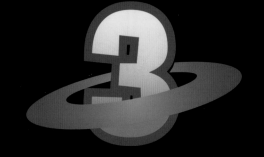

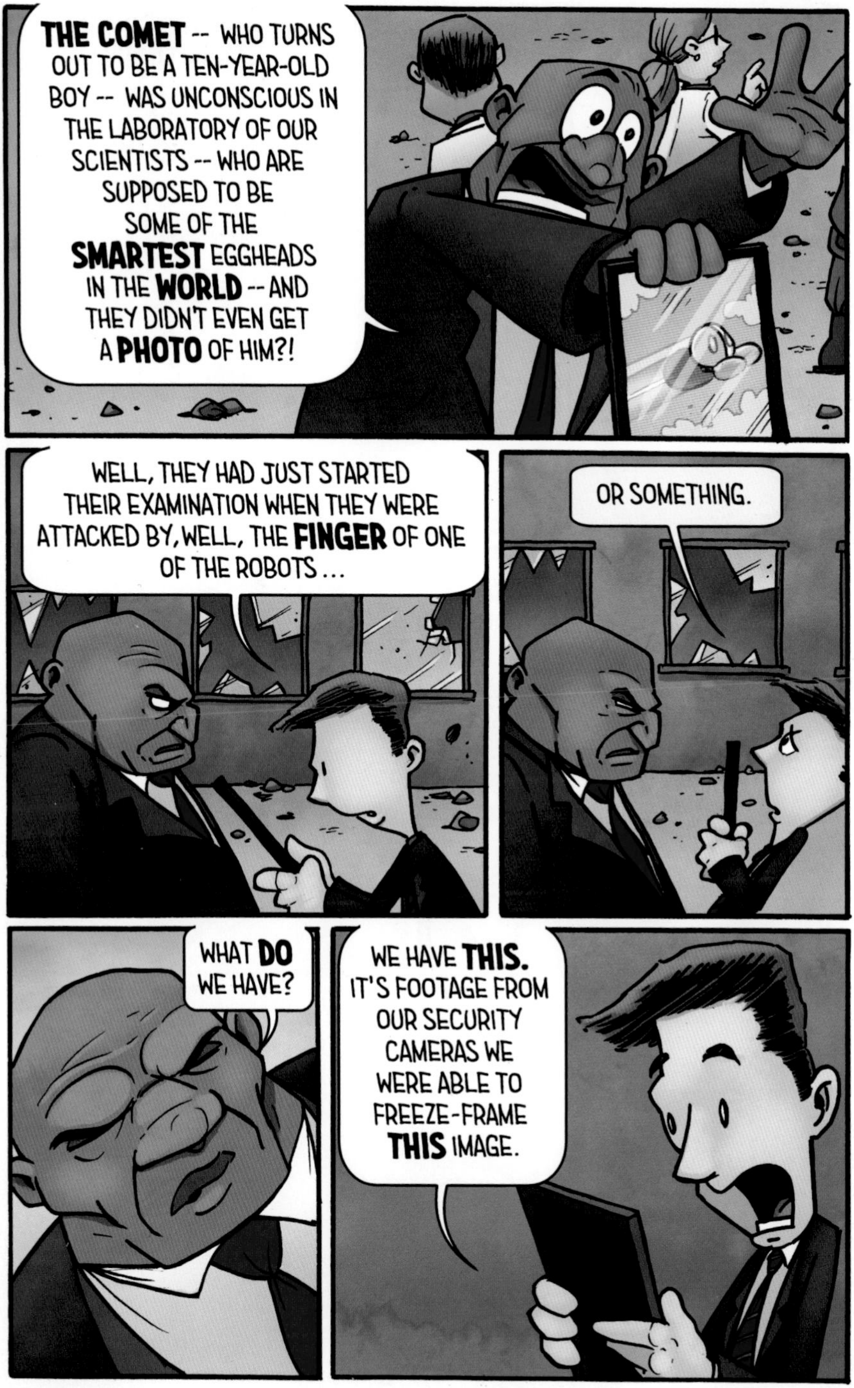
THE COMET -- WHO TURNS OUT TO BE A TEN-YEAR-OLD BOY -- WAS UNCONSCIOUS IN THE LABORATORY OF OUR SCIENTISTS -- WHO ARE SUPPOSED TO BE SOME OF THE SMARTEST EGGHEADS IN THE WORLD -- AND THEY DIDN'T EVEN GET A PHOTO OF HIM?!
WELL, THEY HAD JUST STARTED THEIR EXAMINATION WHEN THEY WERE ATTACKED BY, WELL, THE FINGER OF ONE OF THE ROBOTS . . .
OR SOMETHING.
WHAT DO WE HAVE?
WE HAVE THIS. IT'S FOOTAGE FROM OUR SECURITY CAMERAS WE WERE ABLE TO FREEZE-FRAME THIS IMAGE.

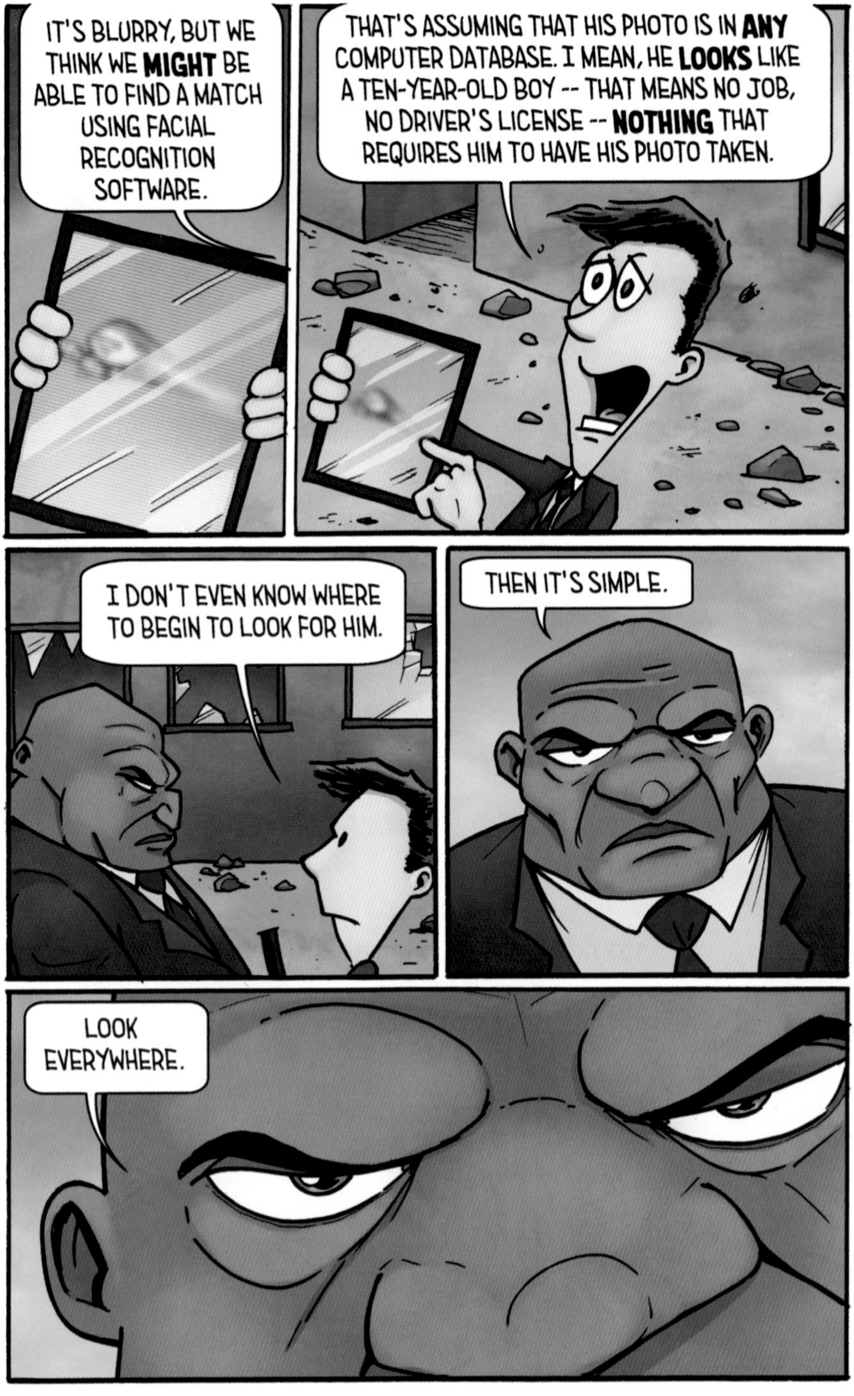
IT'S BLURRY, BUT WE THINK WE **MIGHT** BE ABLE TO FIND A MATCH USING FACIAL RECOGNITION SOFTWARE.
THAT'S ASSUMING THAT HIS PHOTO IS IN **ANY** COMPUTER DATABASE. I MEAN, HE **LOOKS** LIKE A TEN-YEAR-OLD BOY -- THAT MEANS NO JOB, NO DRIVER'S LICENSE -- **NOTHING** THAT REQUIRES HIM TO HAVE HIS PHOTO TAKEN.
I DON'T EVEN KNOW WHERE TO BEGIN TO LOOK FOR HIM.
THEN IT'S SIMPLE.
LOOK EVERYWHERE.

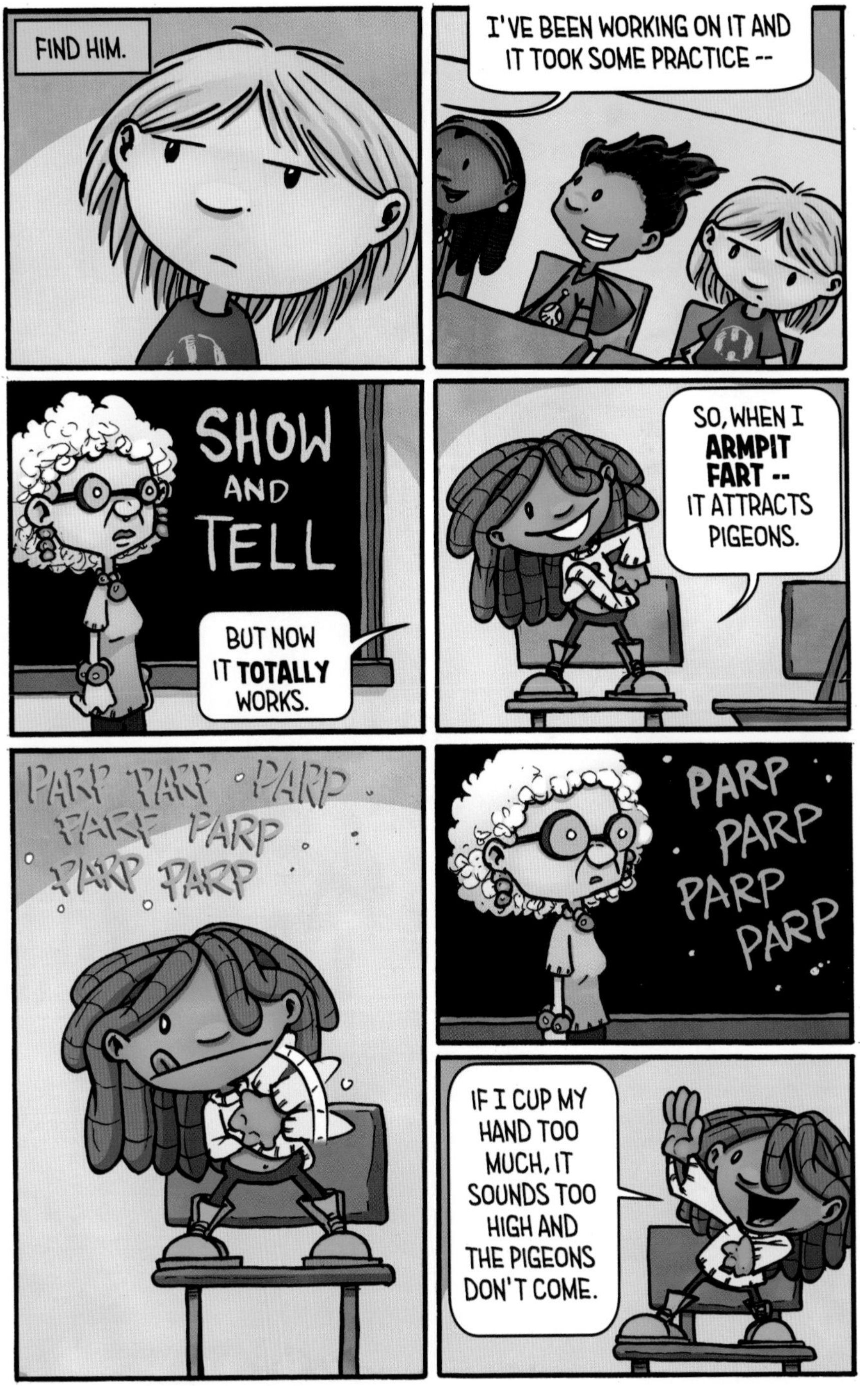
FIND HIM.
I'VE BEEN WORKING ON IT AND IT TOOK SOME PRACTICE --
SHOW AND TELL
BUT NOW IT **TOTALLY** WORKS.
SO, WHEN I **ARMPIT FART --** IT ATTRACTS PIGEONS.
PARP PARP PARP PARP PARP PARP PARP
PARP PARP PARP PARP
IF I CUP MY HAND TOO MUCH, IT SOUNDS TOO HIGH AND THE PIGEONS DON'T COME.

20

MS. POTTER, MAY I PLEASE GO TO THE BATHROOM?
YES.
KING
WHOA.
WHEN I DO MY RIGHT ARMPIT I CAN CALL SEAGULLS.
TUBMAN

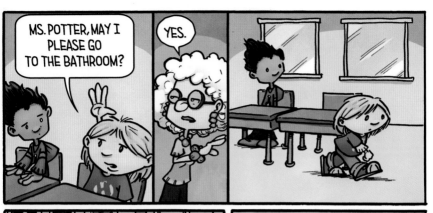

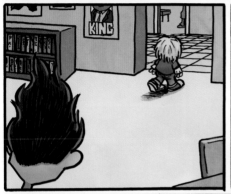

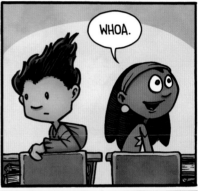

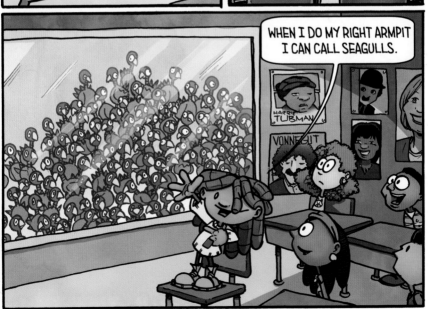

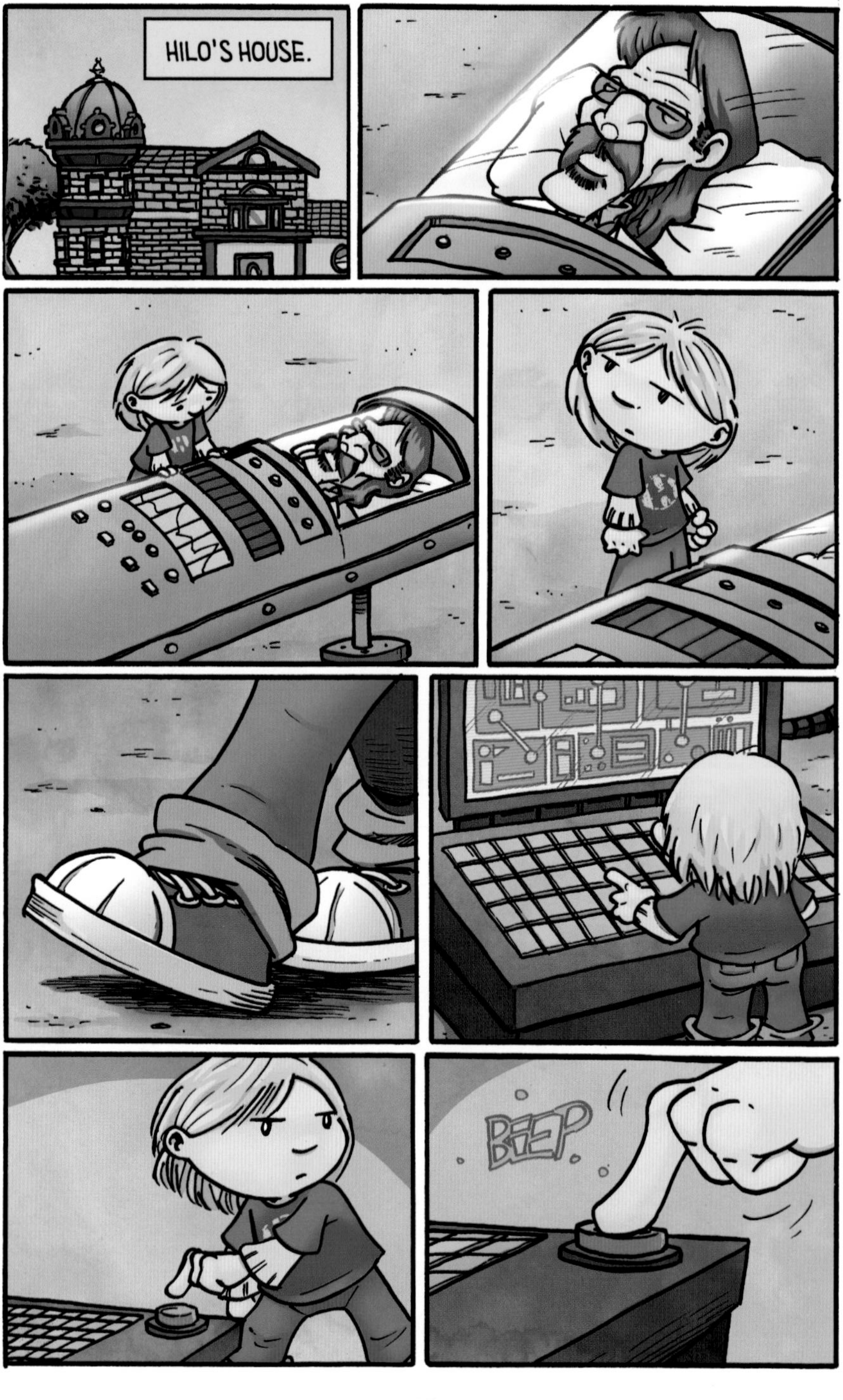
HILO'S HOUSE.
BEEP.

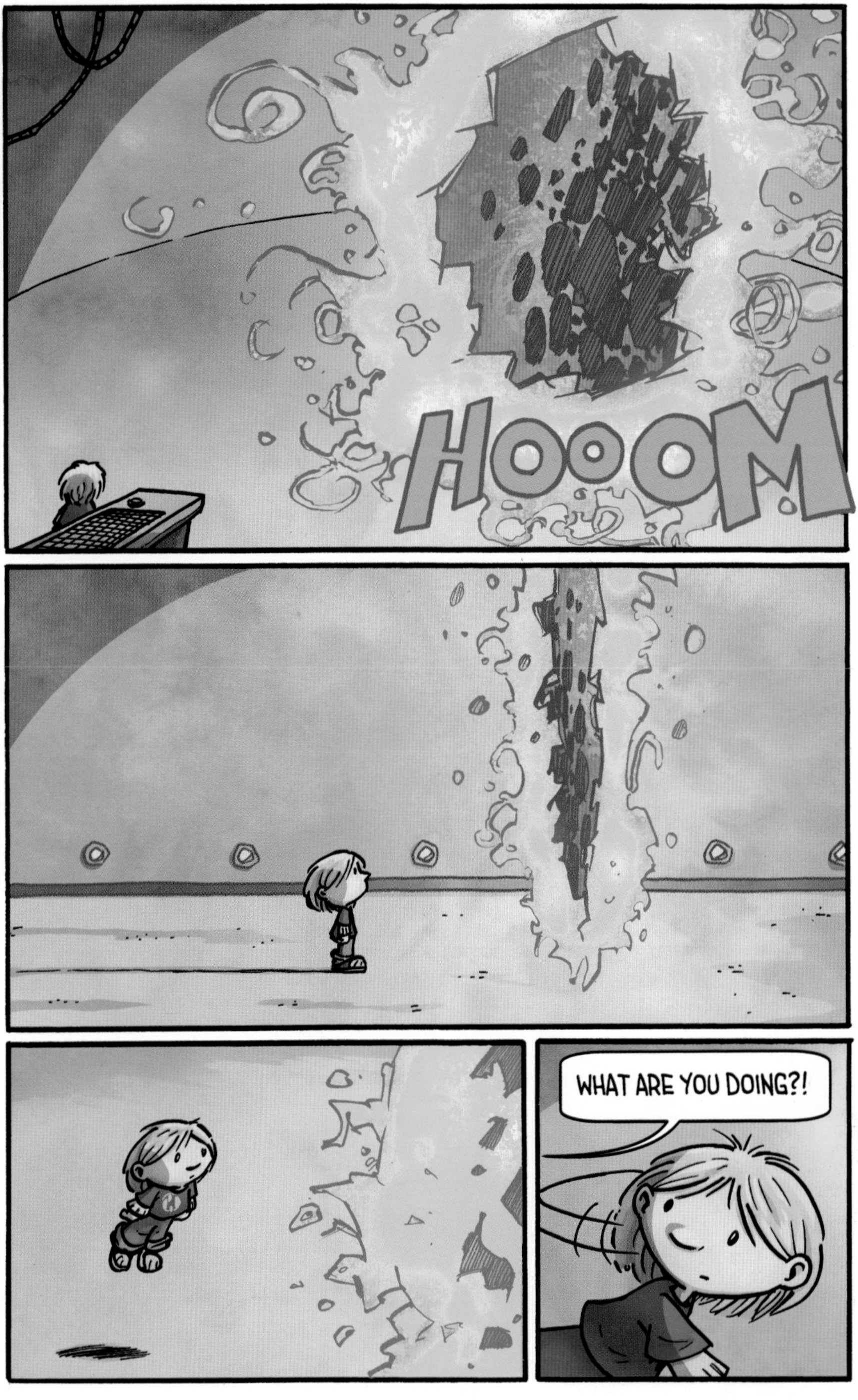
HOOOM
WHAT ARE YOU DOING?!

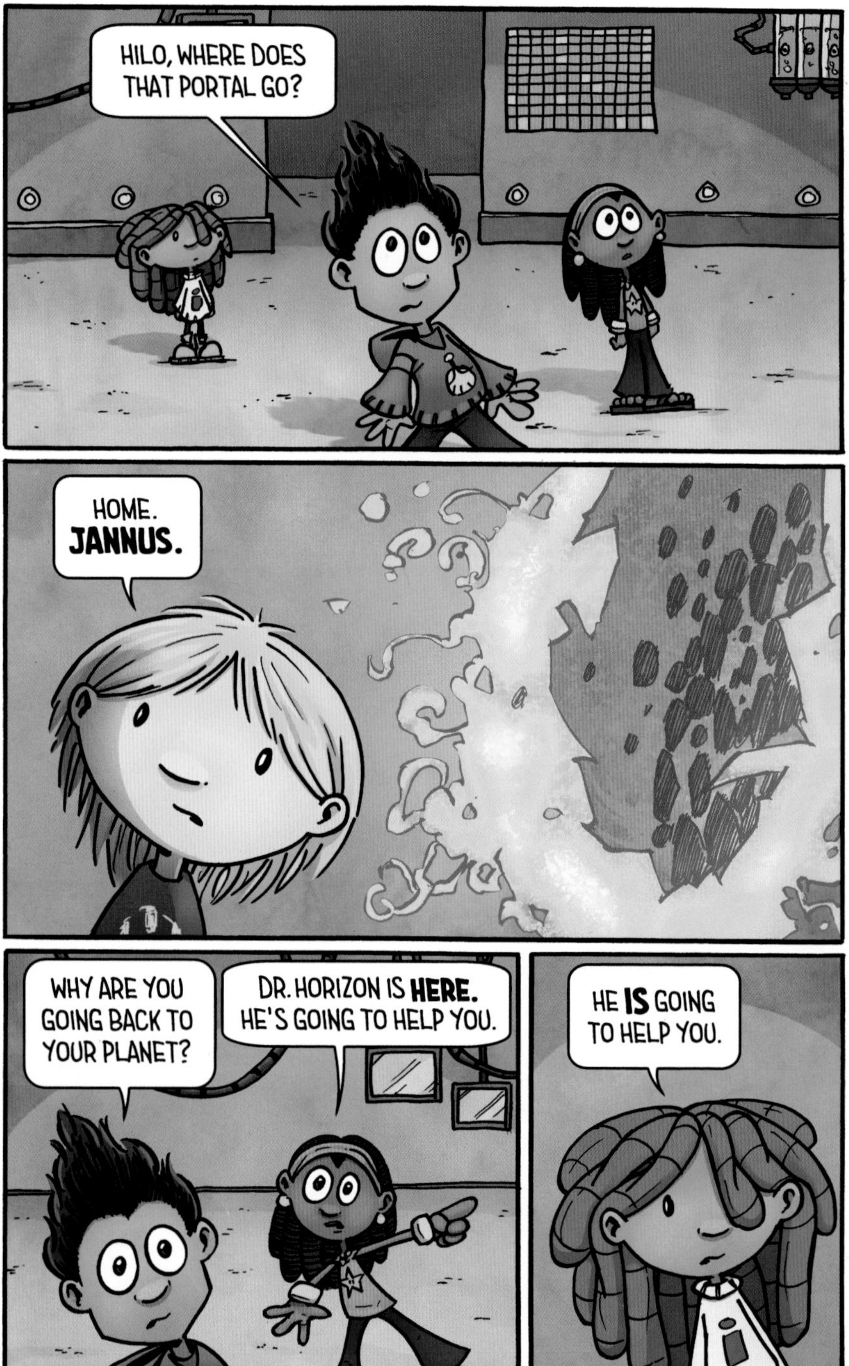
HILO, WHERE DOES THAT PORTAL GO?
HOME. **JANNUS.**
WHY ARE YOU GOING BACK TO YOUR PLANET?
DR. HORIZON IS **HERE.** HE'S GOING TO HELP YOU.
HE **IS** GOING TO HELP YOU.

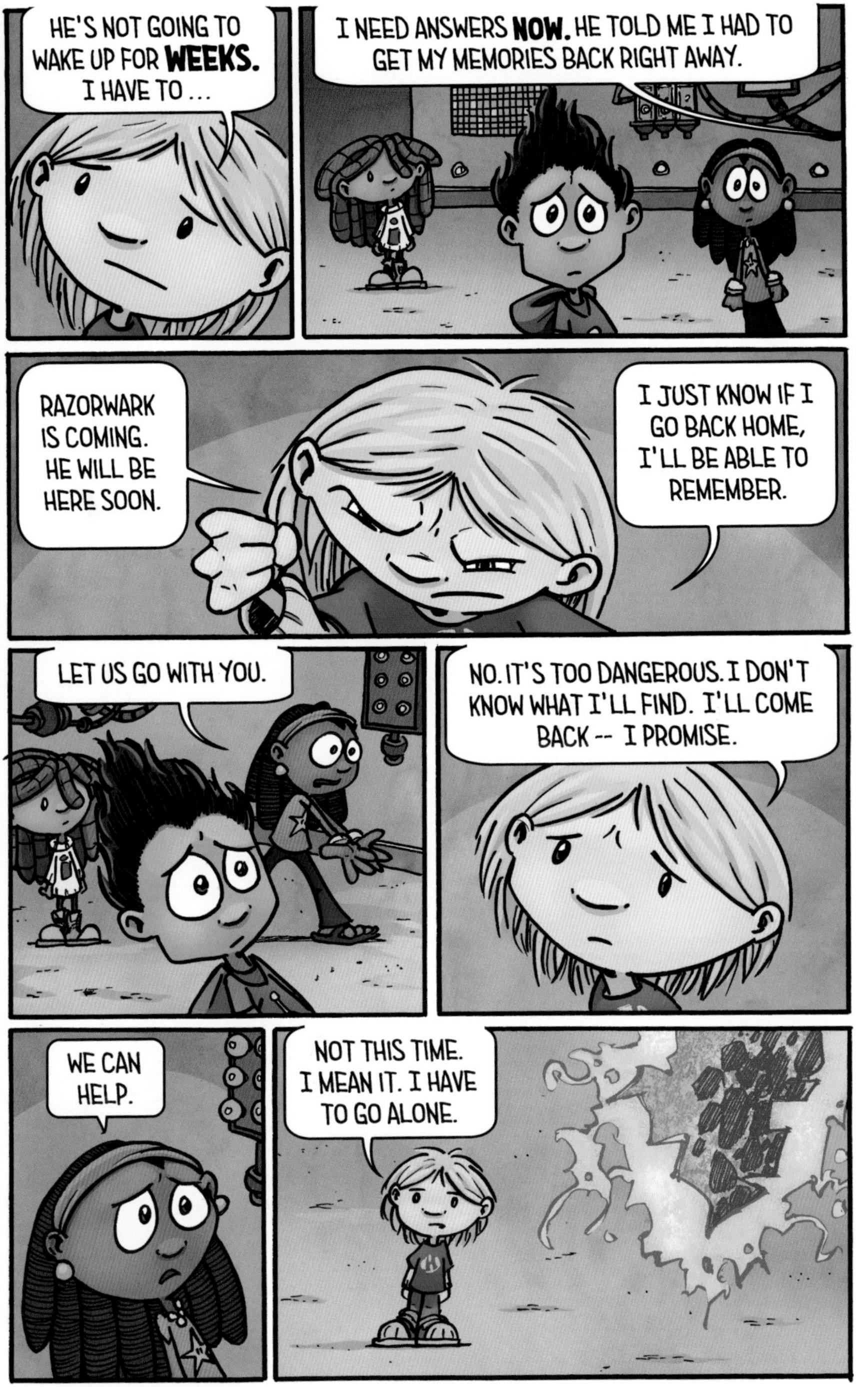
HE'S NOT GOING TO WAKE UP FOR **WEEKS.** I HAVE TO ...
I NEED ANSWERS **NOW.** HE TOLD ME I HAD TO GET MY MEMORIES BACK RIGHT AWAY.
RAZORWARK IS COMING. HE WILL BE HERE SOON.
I JUST KNOW IF I GO BACK HOME, I'LL BE ABLE TO REMEMBER.
LET US GO WITH YOU.
NO. IT'S TOO DANGEROUS. I DON'T KNOW WHAT I'LL FIND. I'LL COME BACK -- I PROMISE.
WE CAN HELP.
NOT THIS TIME. I MEAN IT. I HAVE TO GO ALONE.

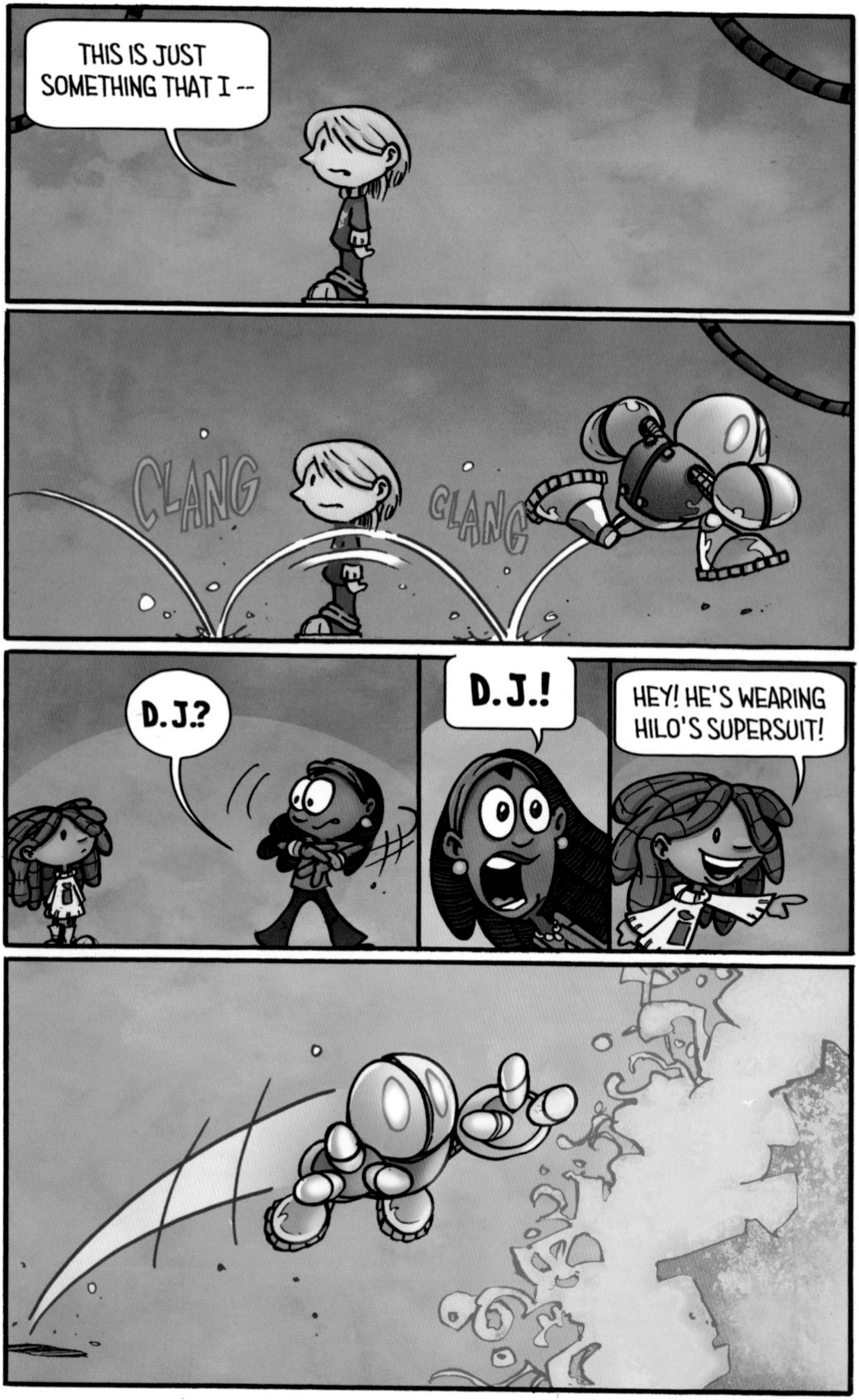
THIS IS JUST SOMETHING THAT I --
CLANG
CLANG
D.J.?
D.J.!
HEY! HE'S WEARING HILO'S SUPERSUIT!

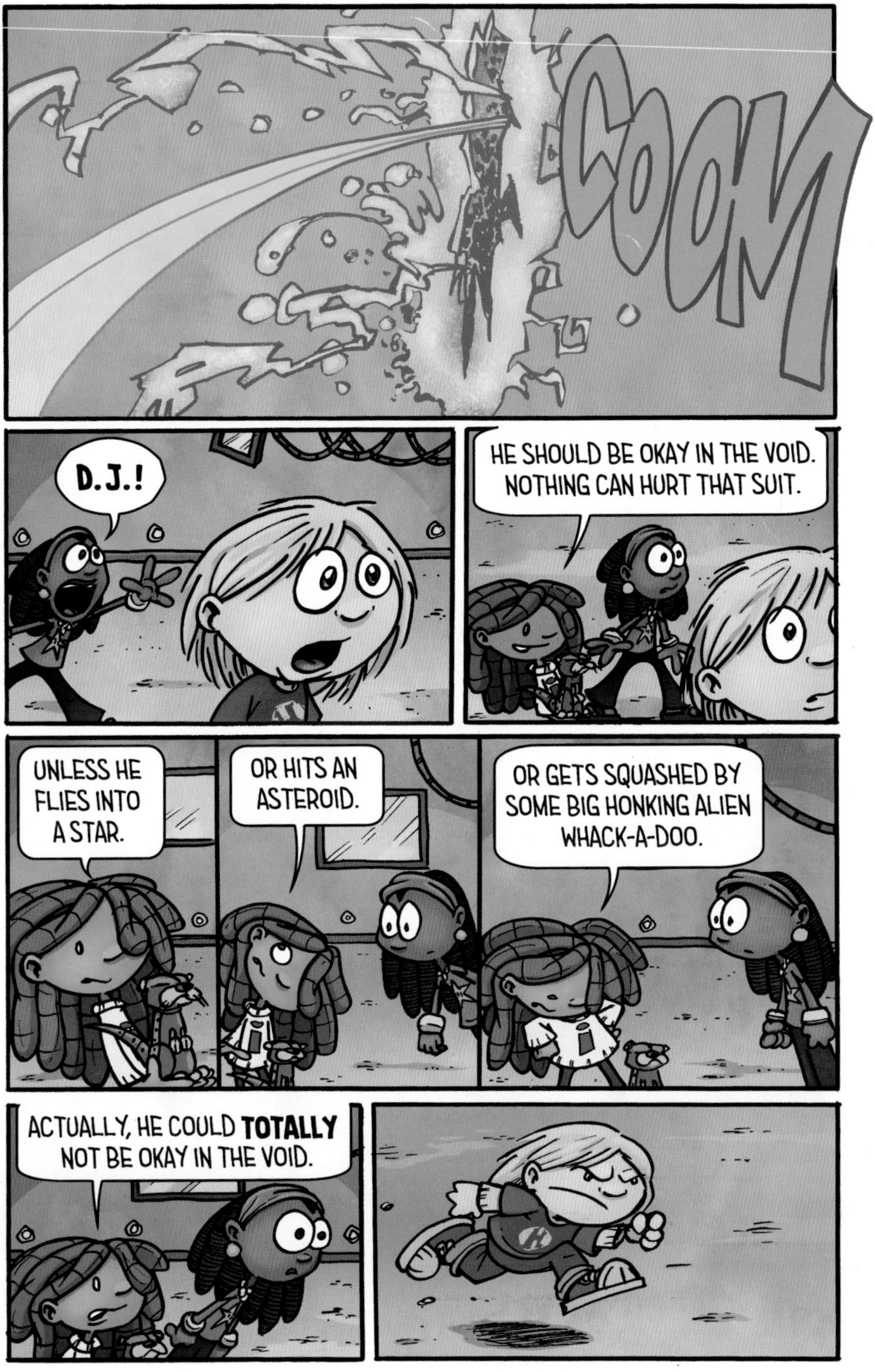
COOM
D.J.!
HE SHOULD BE OKAY IN THE VOID. NOTHING CAN HURT THAT SUIT.
UNLESS HE FLIES INTO A STAR.
OR HITS AN ASTEROID.
OR GETS SQUASHED BY SOME BIG HONKING ALIEN WHACK-A-DOO.
ACTUALLY, HE COULD **TOTALLY** NOT BE OKAY IN THE VOID.

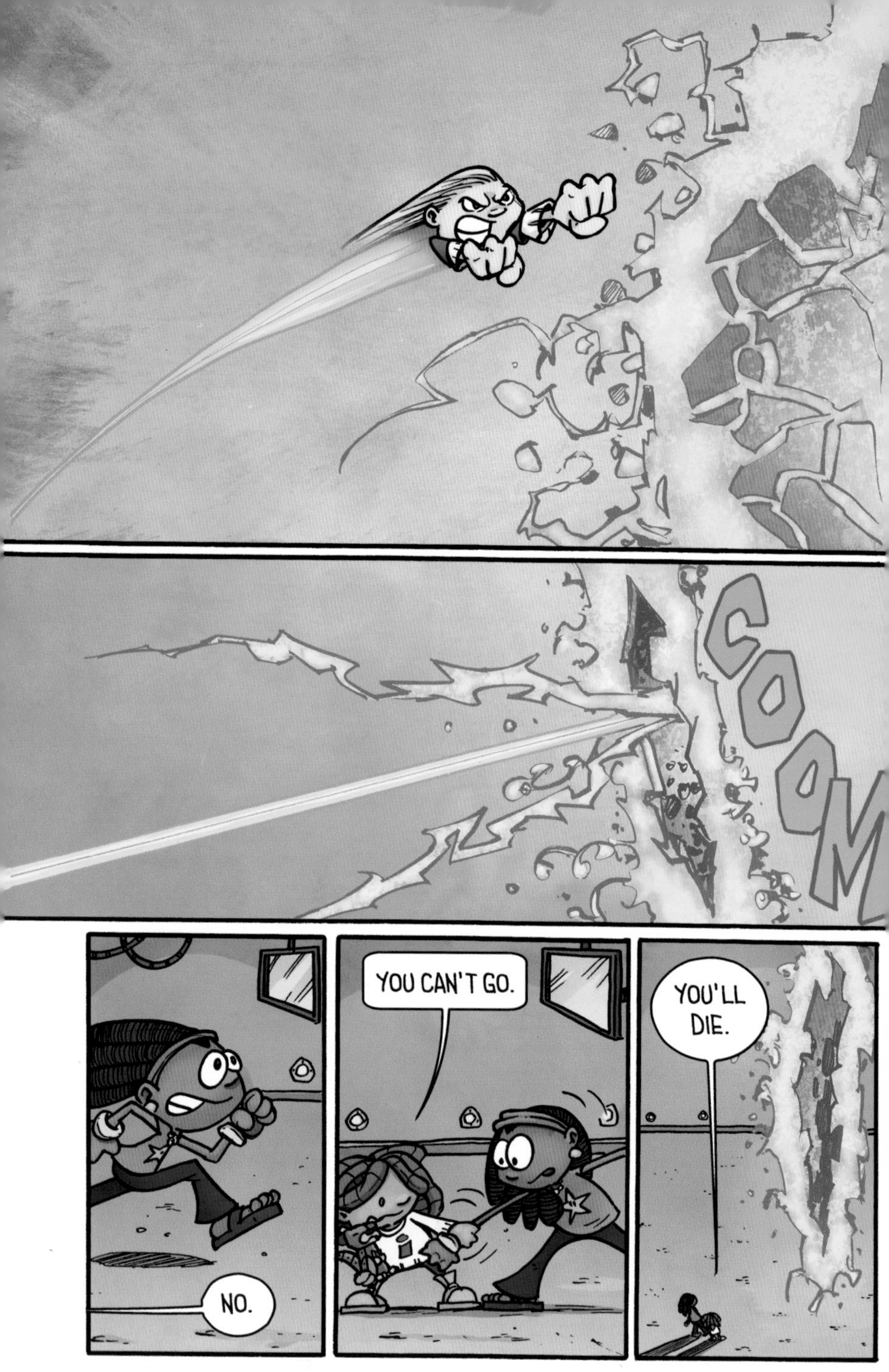
COOOM
NO.
YOU CAN'T GO.
YOU'LL DIE.

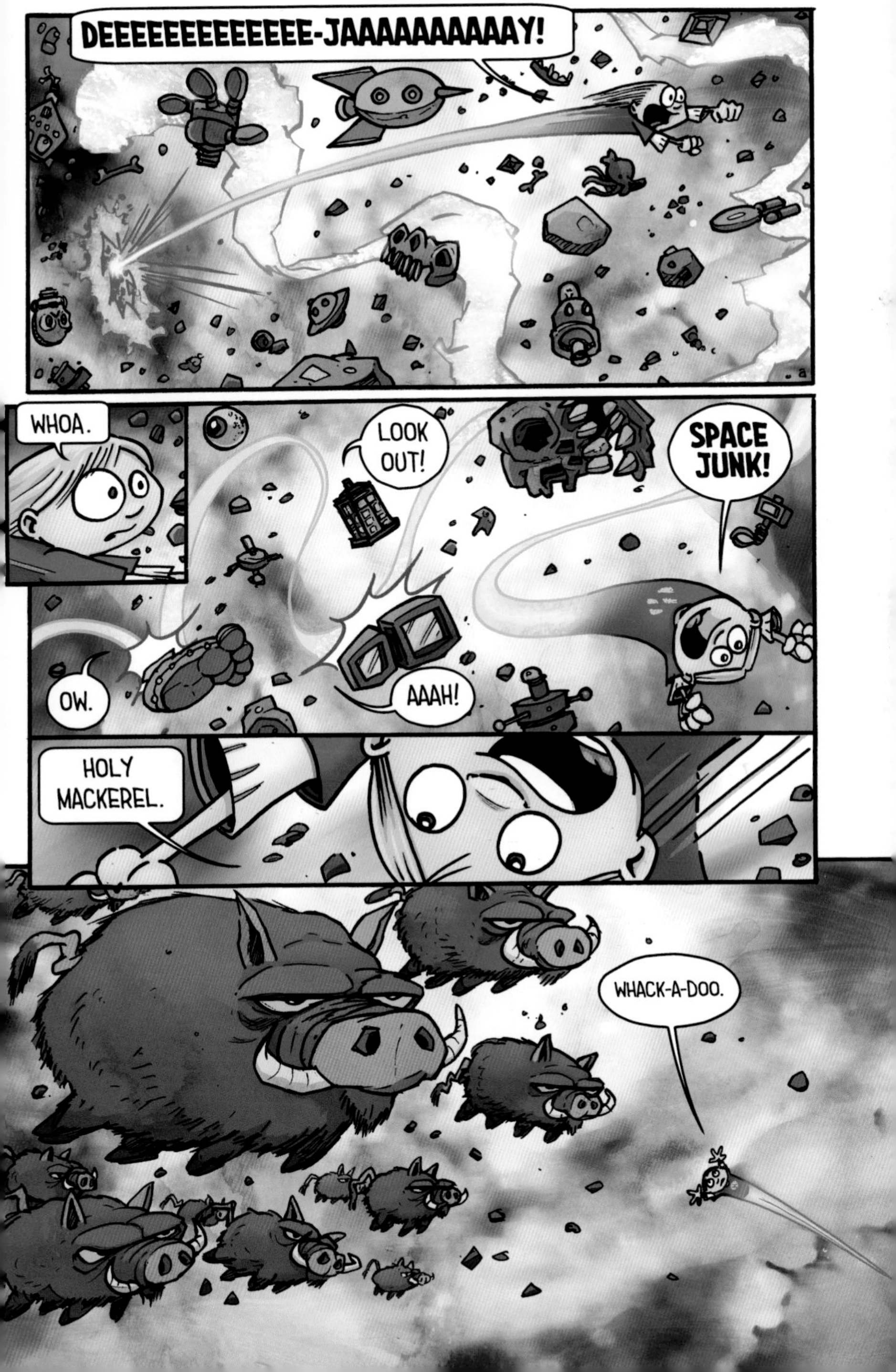
DEEEEEEEEEEEEE-JAAAAAAAAAAY!
WHOA.
LOOK OUT!
SPACE JUNK!
OW.
AAAH!
HOLY MACKEREL.
WHACK-A-DOO.

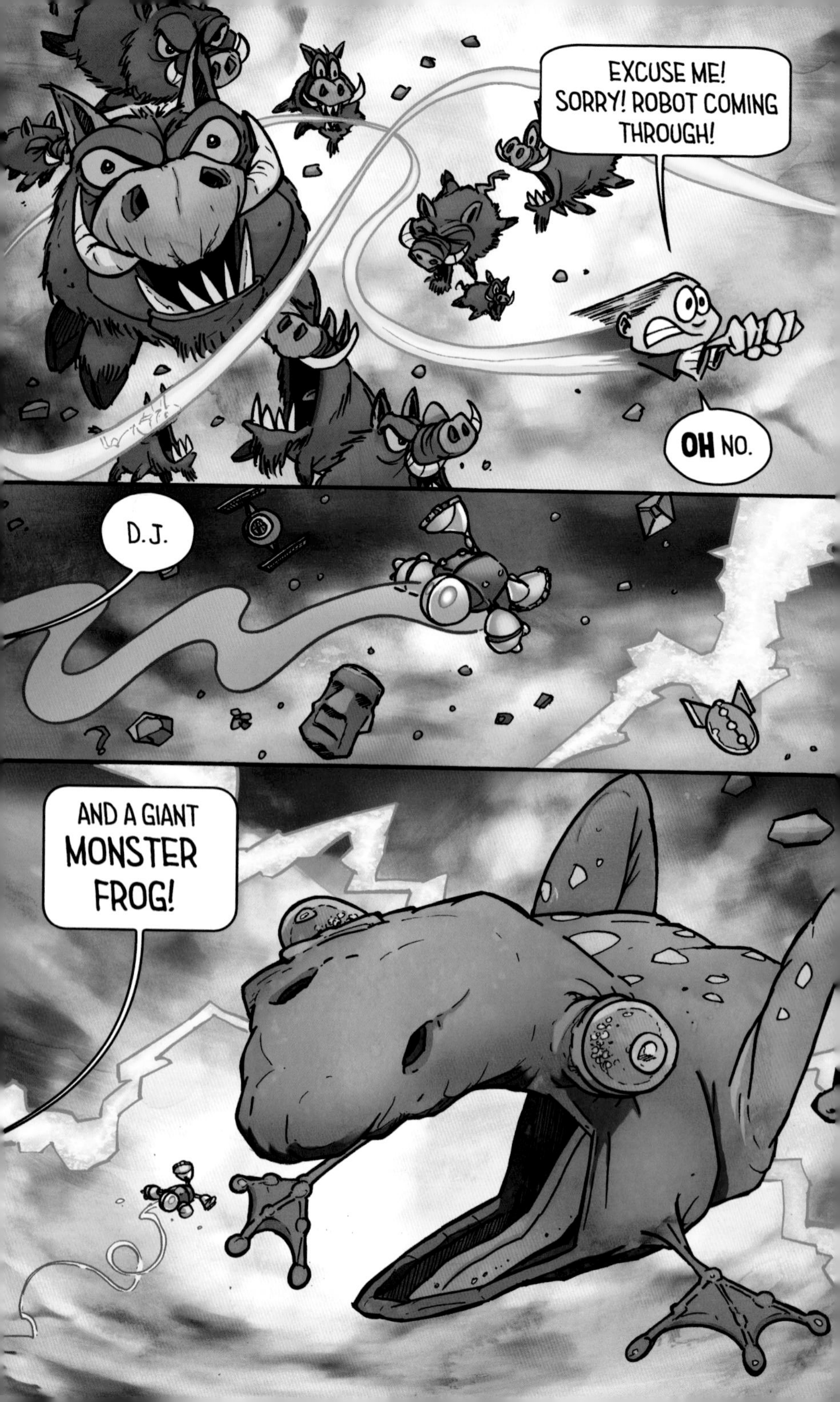
EXCUSE ME! SORRY! ROBOT COMING THROUGH!
OH NO.
D.J.
AND A GIANT MONSTER FROG!

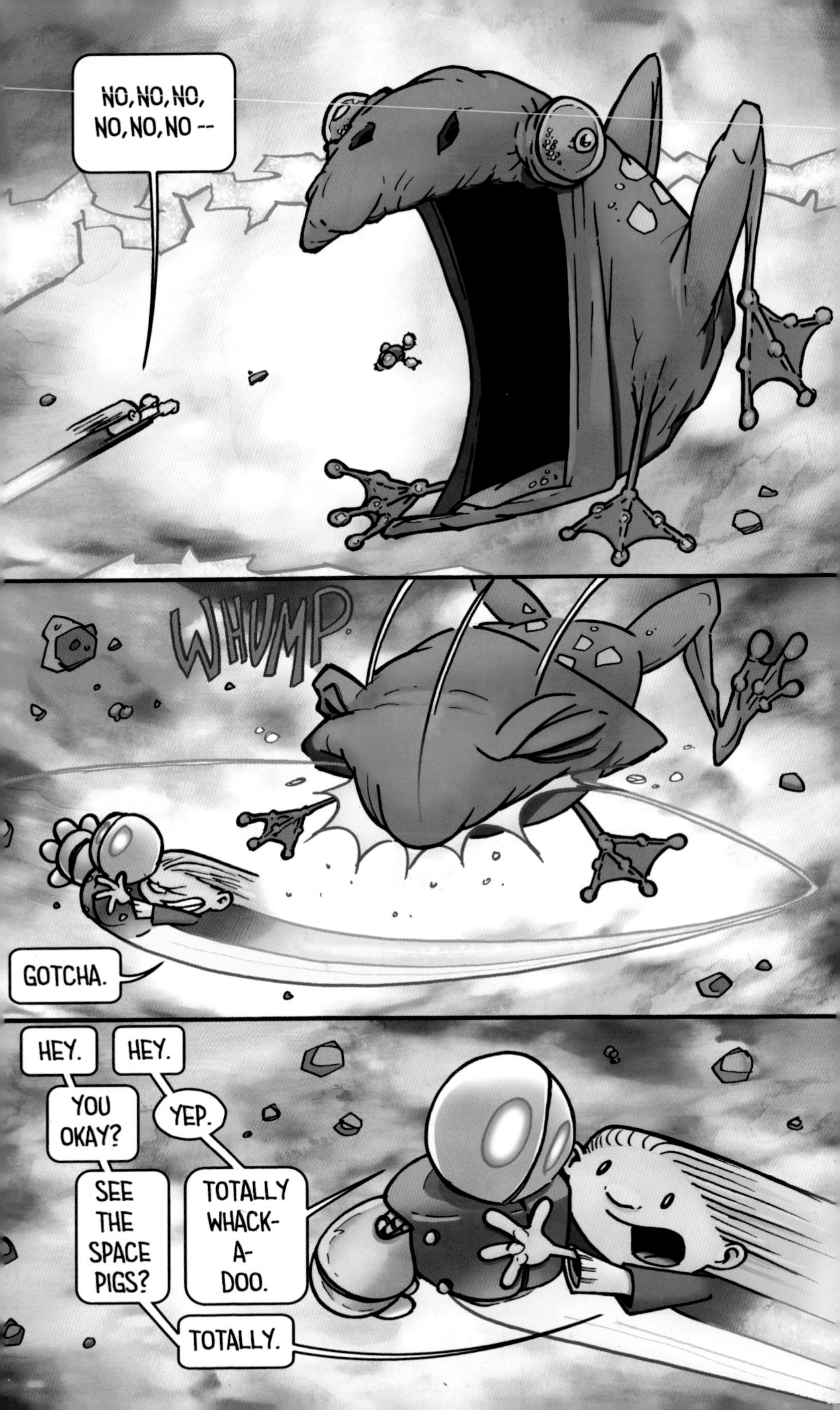
NO, NO, NO,
NO, NO, NO --
WHUMP
GOTCHA.
HEY.
HEY.
YOU OKAY?
YEP.
SEE THE SPACE PIGS?
TOTALLY WHACK-A-DOO.
TOTALLY.

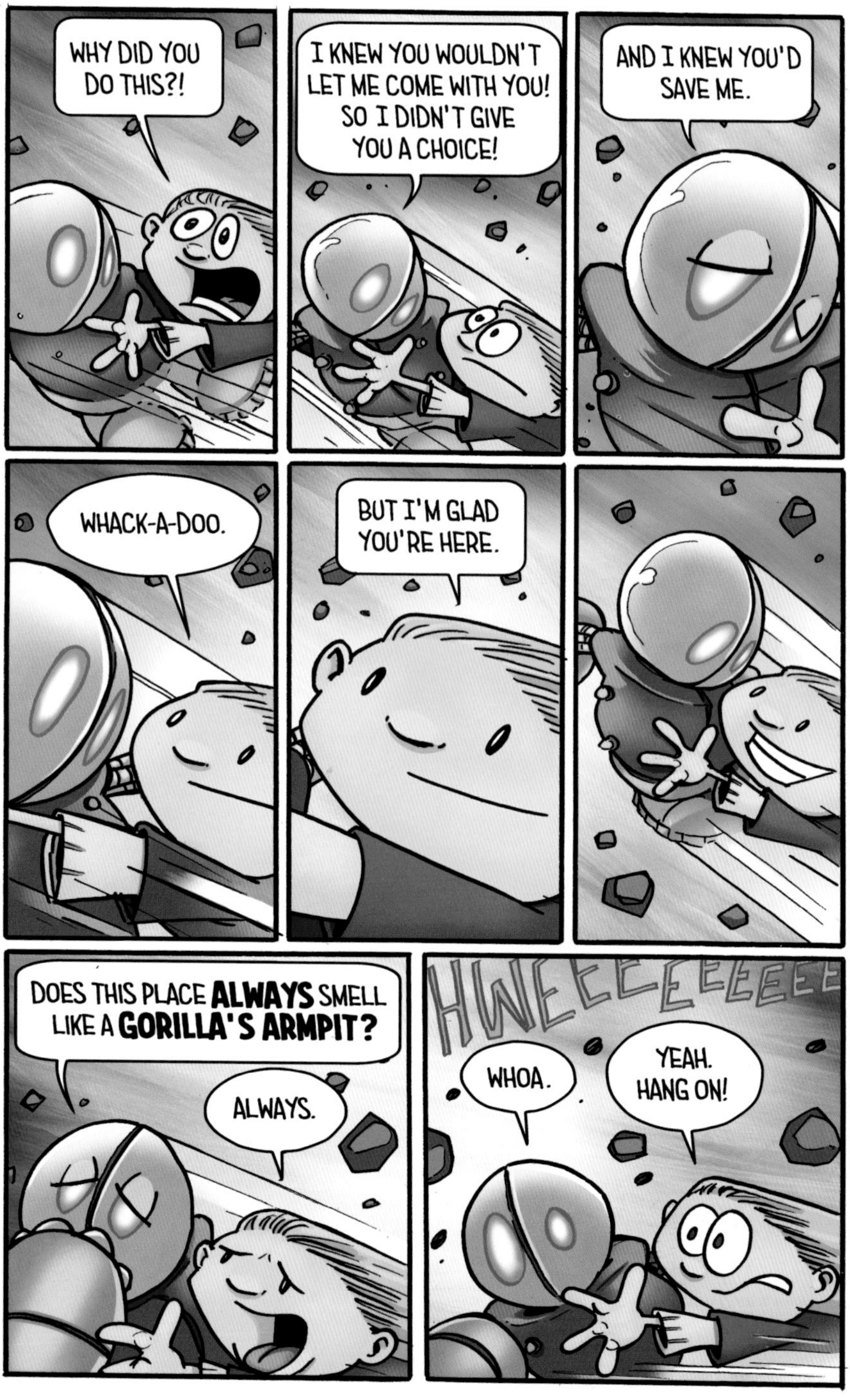
WHY DID YOU DO THIS?!
I KNEW YOU WOULDN'T LET ME COME WITH YOU! SO I DIDN'T GIVE YOU A CHOICE!
AND I KNEW YOU'D SAVE ME.
WHACK-A-DOO.
BUT I'M GLAD YOU'RE HERE.
DOES THIS PLACE **ALWAYS** SMELL LIKE A **GORILLA'S ARMPIT?**
ALWAYS.
HWEEEEEEEEE
WHOA.
YEAH. HANG ON!

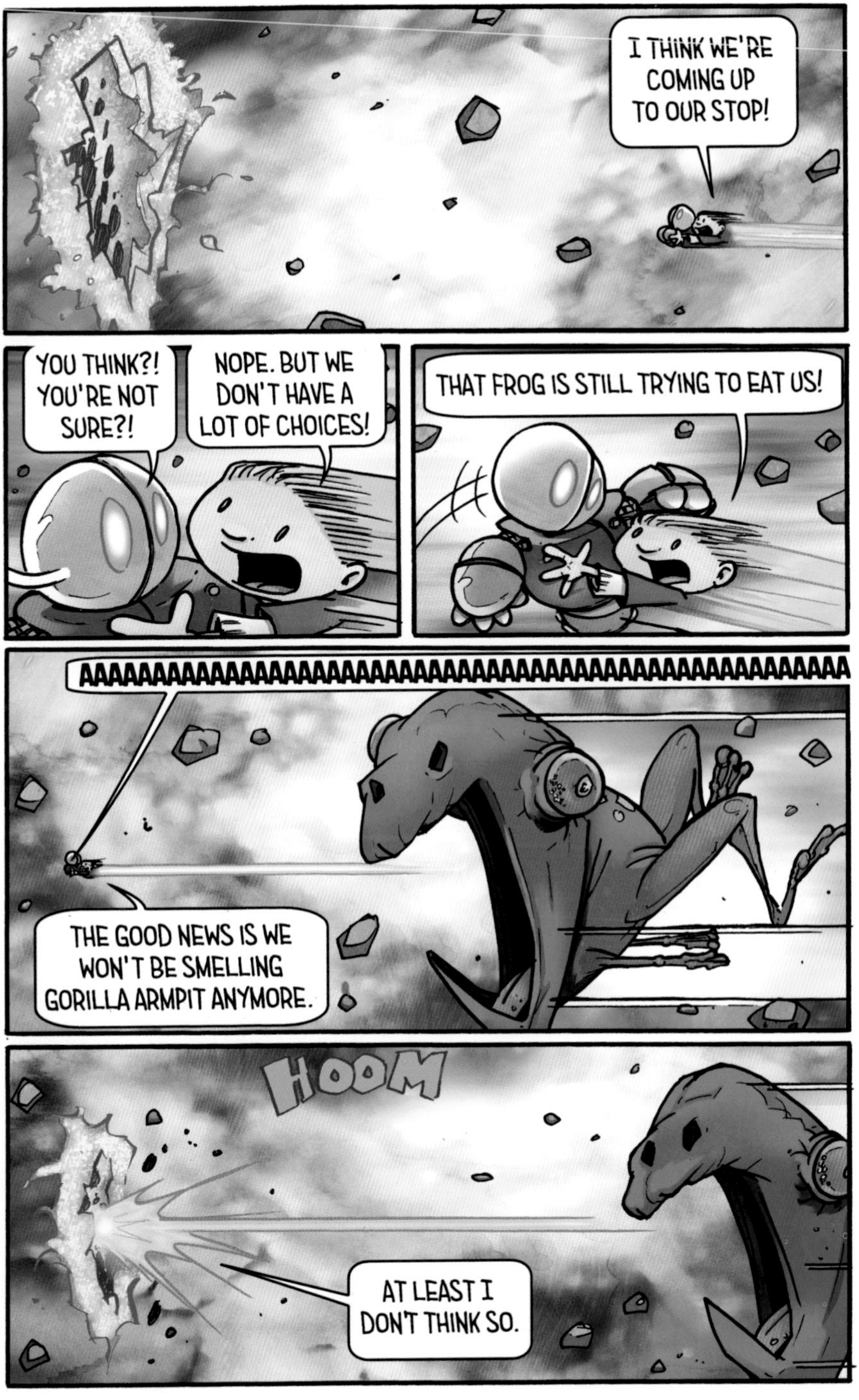

I THINK WE'RE COMING UP TO OUR STOP!
YOU THINK?! YOU'RE NOT SURE?!
NOPE. BUT WE DON'T HAVE A LOT OF CHOICES!
THAT FROG IS STILL TRYING TO EAT US!
AAAAAAAAAAAAAAAAAAAAAAAAAAAAAAAAAAAAAAAAAAAAAAAAA
THE GOOD NEWS IS WE WON'T BE SMELLING GORILLA ARMPIT ANYMORE.
HOOM
AT LEAST I DON'T THINK SO.

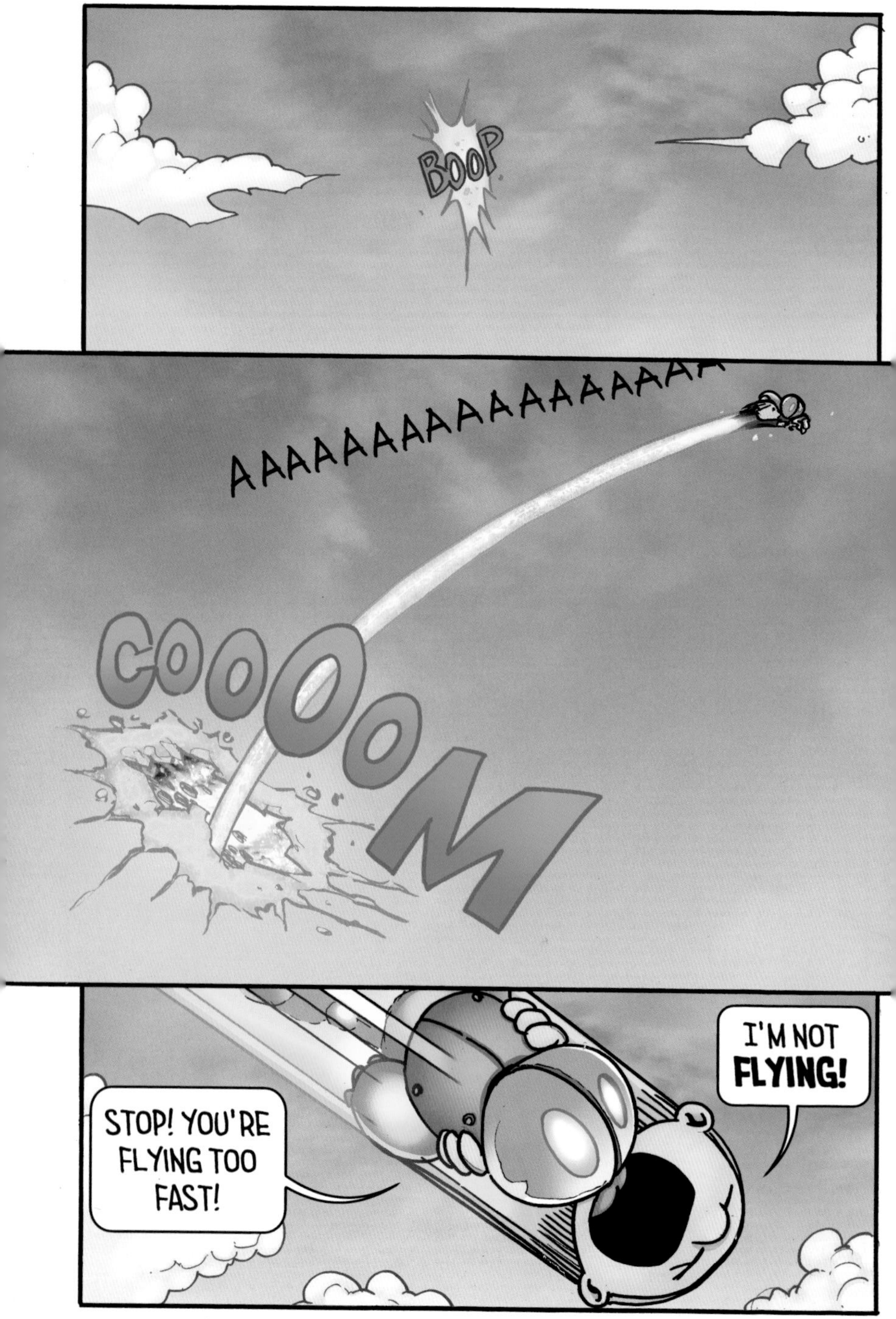
BOOP
AAAAAAAAAAAAAAAAA
COOOOM
STOP! YOU'RE FLYING TOO FAST!
I'M NOT **FLYING!**

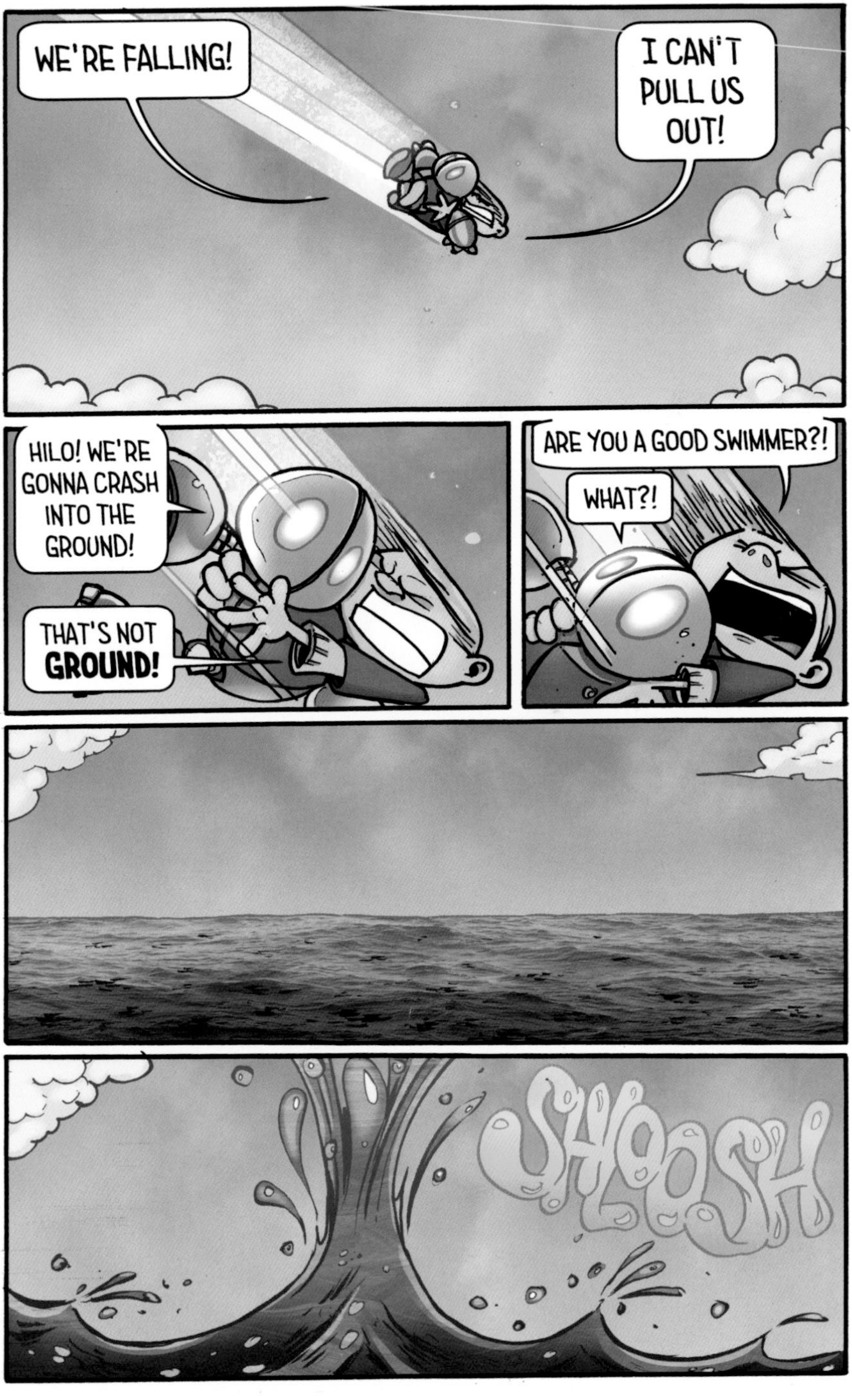
WE'RE FALLING!
I CAN'T PULL US OUT!
HILO! WE'RE GONNA CRASH INTO THE GROUND!
THAT'S NOT **GROUND!**
ARE YOU A GOOD SWIMMER?!
WHAT?!
SHLOOSH

CHAPTER 4

BADA BOOM BA!

WE HAVE TO GO AFTER THEM!
WE CAN'T.

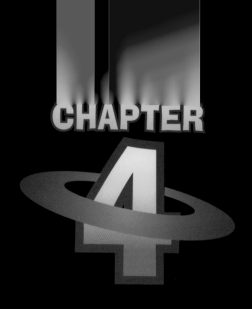

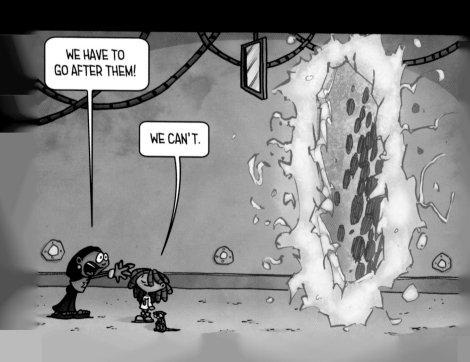

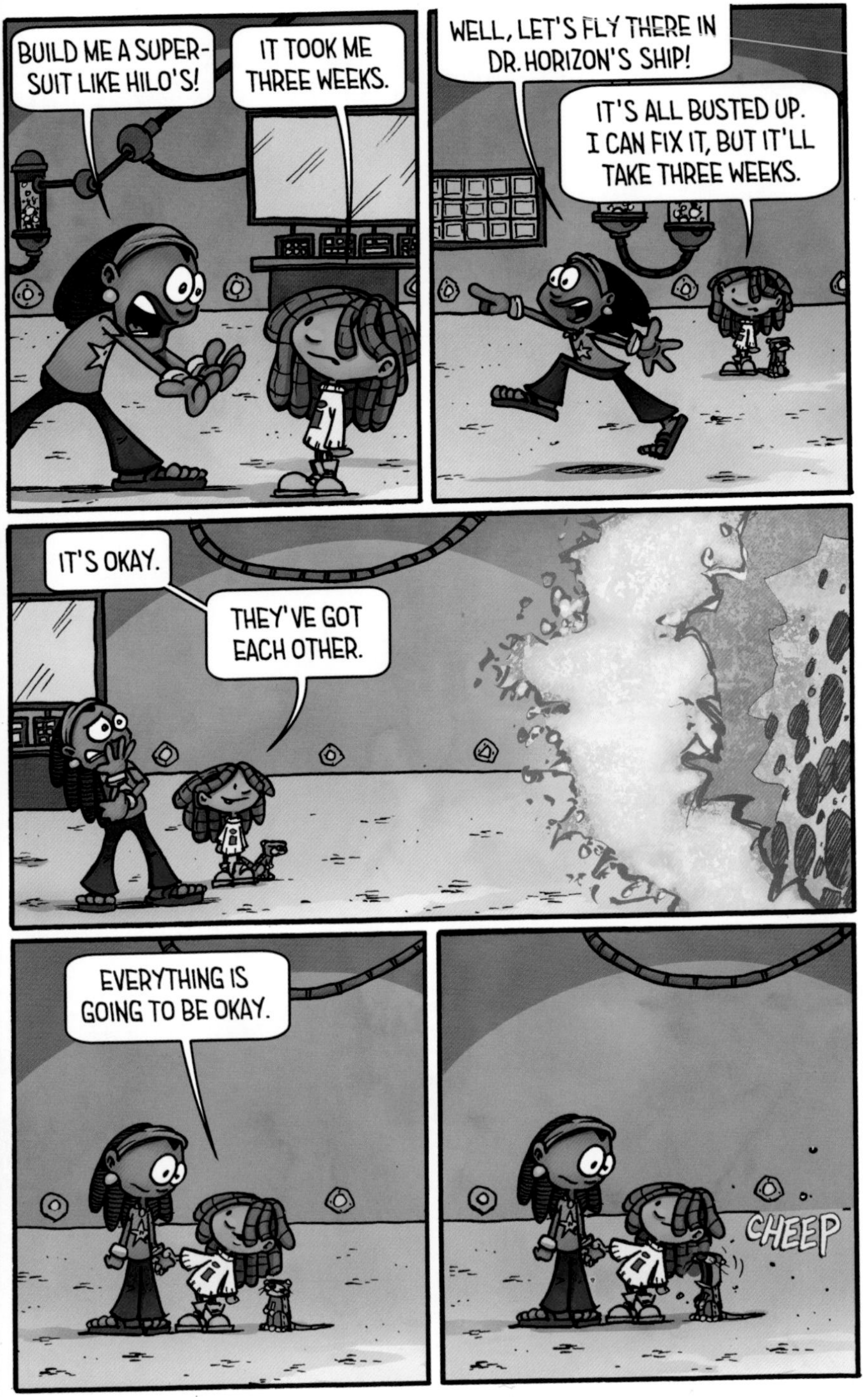
BUILD ME A SUPER-SUIT LIKE HILO'S!
IT TOOK ME THREE WEEKS.
WELL, LET'S FLY THERE IN DR. HORIZON'S SHIP!
IT'S ALL BUSTED UP. I CAN FIX IT, BUT IT'LL TAKE THREE WEEKS.
IT'S OKAY.
THEY'VE GOT EACH OTHER.
EVERYTHING IS GOING TO BE OKAY.
CHEEP

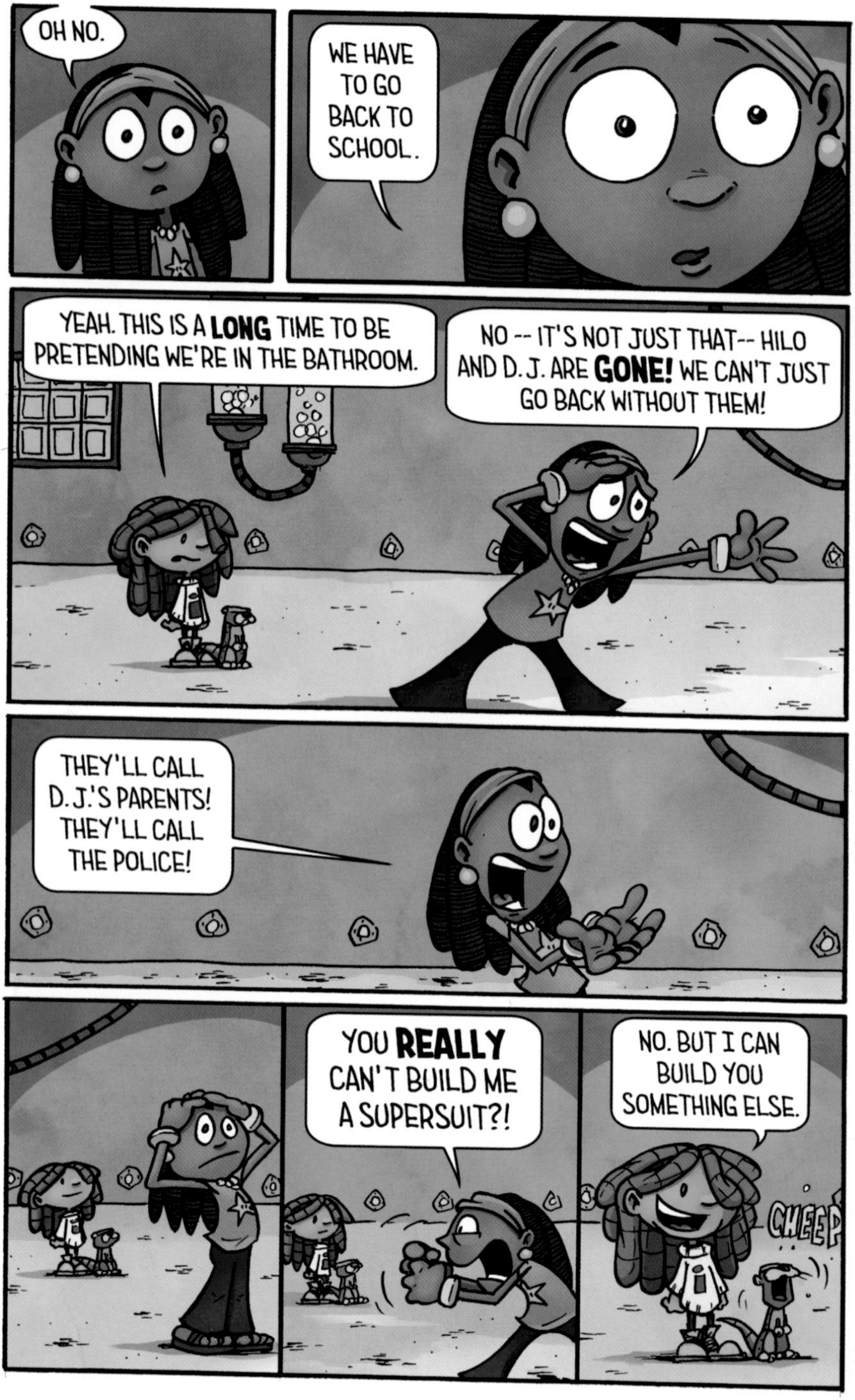
OH NO.
WE HAVE TO GO BACK TO SCHOOL.
YEAH. THIS IS A **LONG** TIME TO BE PRETENDING WE'RE IN THE BATHROOM.
NO -- IT'S NOT JUST THAT-- HILO AND D. J. ARE **GONE!** WE CAN'T JUST GO BACK WITHOUT THEM!
THEY'LL CALL D.J.'S PARENTS! THEY'LL CALL THE POLICE!
YOU **REALLY** CAN'T BUILD ME A SUPERSUIT?!
NO. BUT I CAN BUILD YOU SOMETHING ELSE.
CHEEP

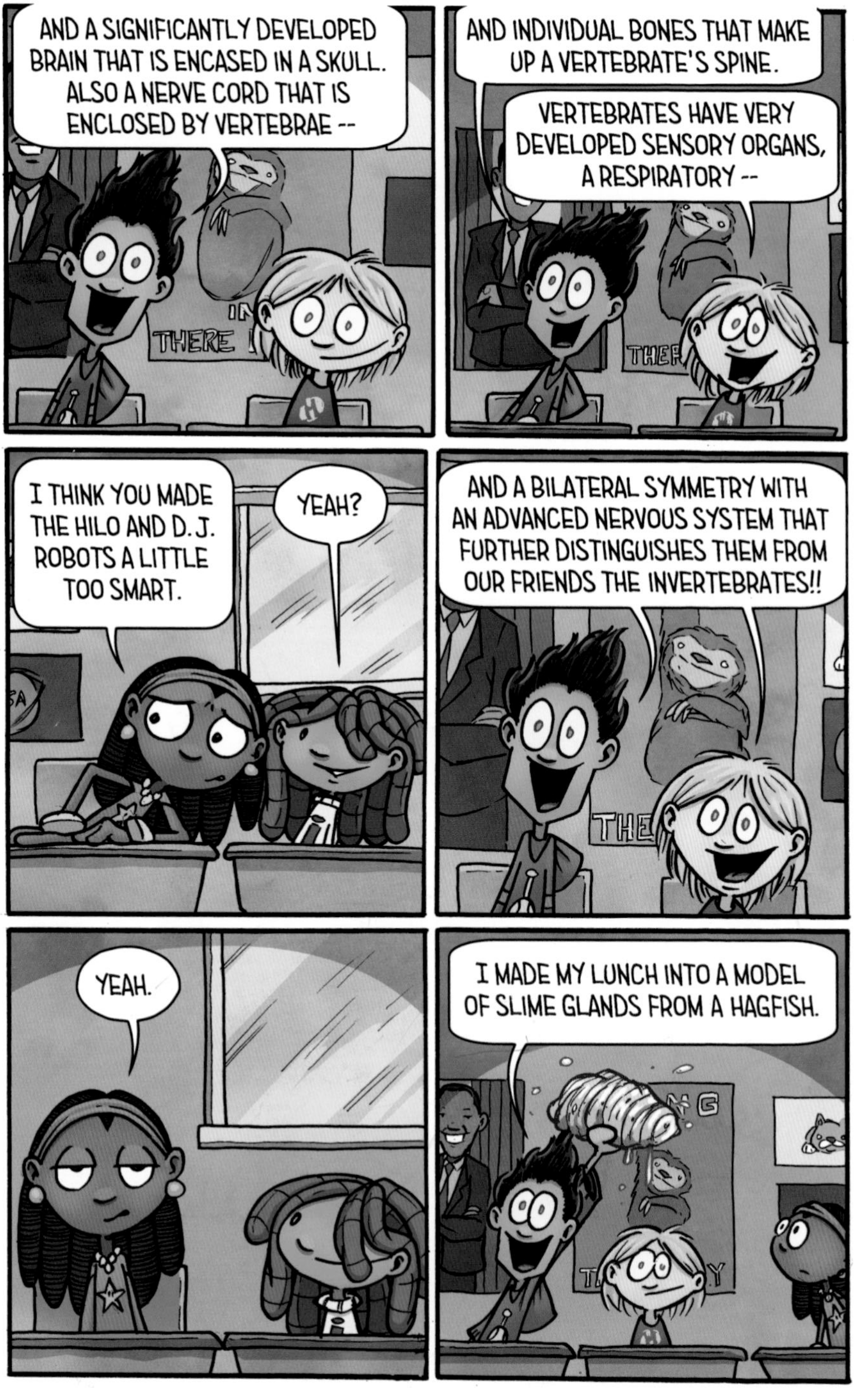
AND A SIGNIFICANTLY DEVELOPED BRAIN THAT IS ENCASED IN A SKULL. ALSO A NERVE CORD THAT IS ENCLOSED BY VERTEBRAE --
THERE
AND INDIVIDUAL BONES THAT MAKE UP A VERTEBRATE'S SPINE.
VERTEBRATES HAVE VERY DEVELOPED SENSORY ORGANS, A RESPIRATORY --
I THINK YOU MADE THE HILO AND D. J. ROBOTS A LITTLE TOO SMART.
YEAH?
AND A BILATERAL SYMMETRY WITH AN ADVANCED NERVOUS SYSTEM THAT FURTHER DISTINGUISHES THEM FROM OUR FRIENDS THE INVERTEBRATES!!
YEAH.
I MADE MY LUNCH INTO A MODEL OF SLIME GLANDS FROM A HAGFISH.

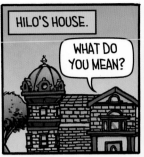

HILO'S HOUSE.

WHAT DO YOU MEAN?

WHAT'S WRONG WITH THEM?

SO MANY THINGS ARE WRONG WITH THEM!

I MEAN -- THEY LOOK EXACTLY LIKE THEM, AND THAT'S AMAZING, BUT--

I CAN SHOOT NICKELS FROM MY BELLY BUTTON!

THIIIIING

POONT

OUTSTANDING!

HOW FAR CAN YOU SHOOT A CERAMIC FISH?

41

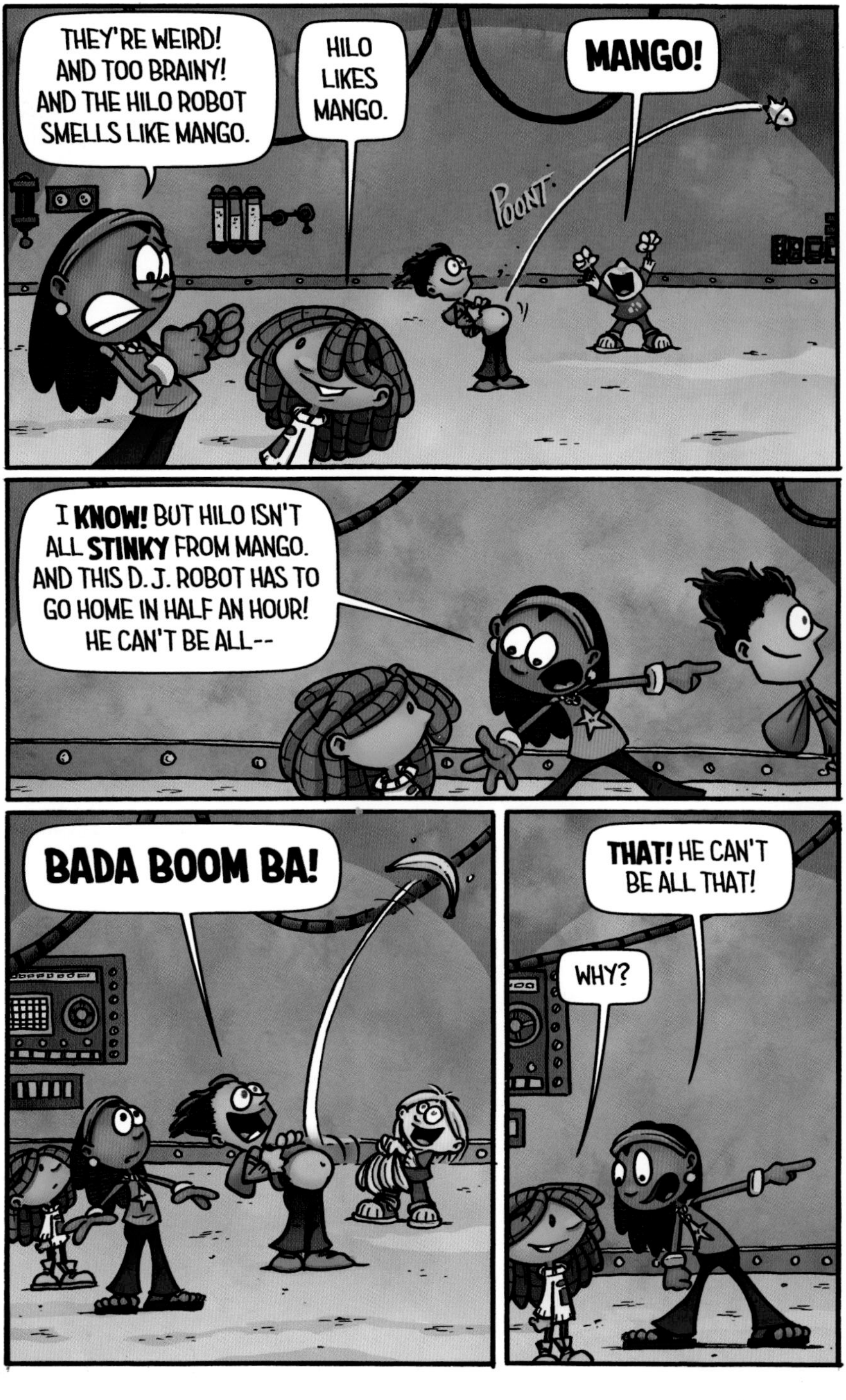
THEY'RE WEIRD! AND TOO BRAINY! AND THE HILO ROBOT SMELLS LIKE MANGO.
HILO LIKES MANGO.
MANGO!
POONT
I KNOW! BUT HILO ISN'T ALL STINKY FROM MANGO. AND THIS D. J. ROBOT HAS TO GO HOME IN HALF AN HOUR! HE CAN'T BE ALL--
BADA BOOM BA!
THAT! HE CAN'T BE ALL THAT!
WHY?

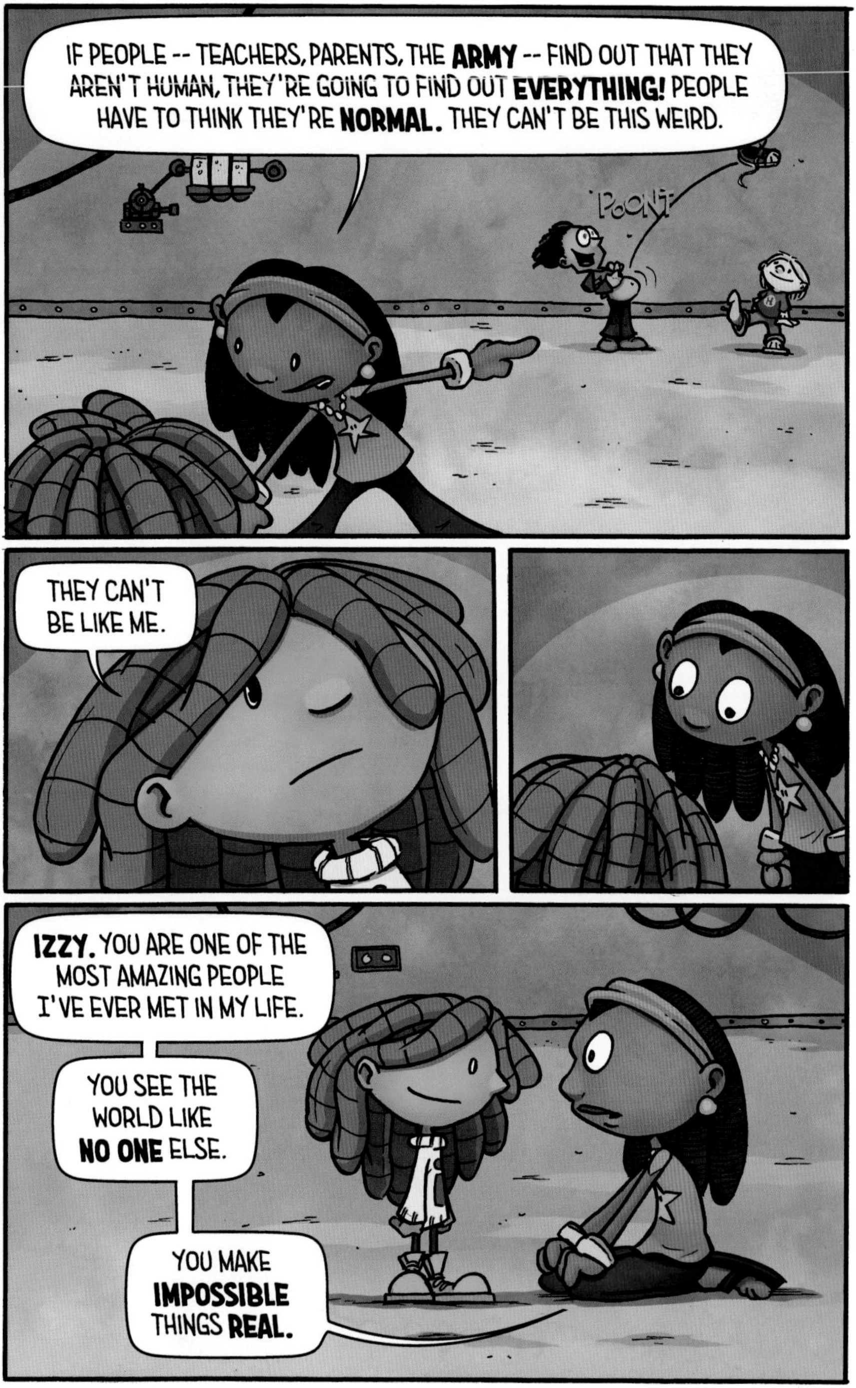
IF PEOPLE -- TEACHERS, PARENTS, THE **ARMY** -- FIND OUT THAT THEY AREN'T HUMAN, THEY'RE GOING TO FIND OUT **EVERYTHING!** PEOPLE HAVE TO THINK THEY'RE **NORMAL.** THEY CAN'T BE THIS WEIRD.
POONT
THEY CAN'T BE LIKE ME.
IZZY. YOU ARE ONE OF THE MOST AMAZING PEOPLE I'VE EVER MET IN MY LIFE.
YOU SEE THE WORLD LIKE **NO ONE** ELSE.
YOU MAKE **IMPOSSIBLE** THINGS **REAL.**

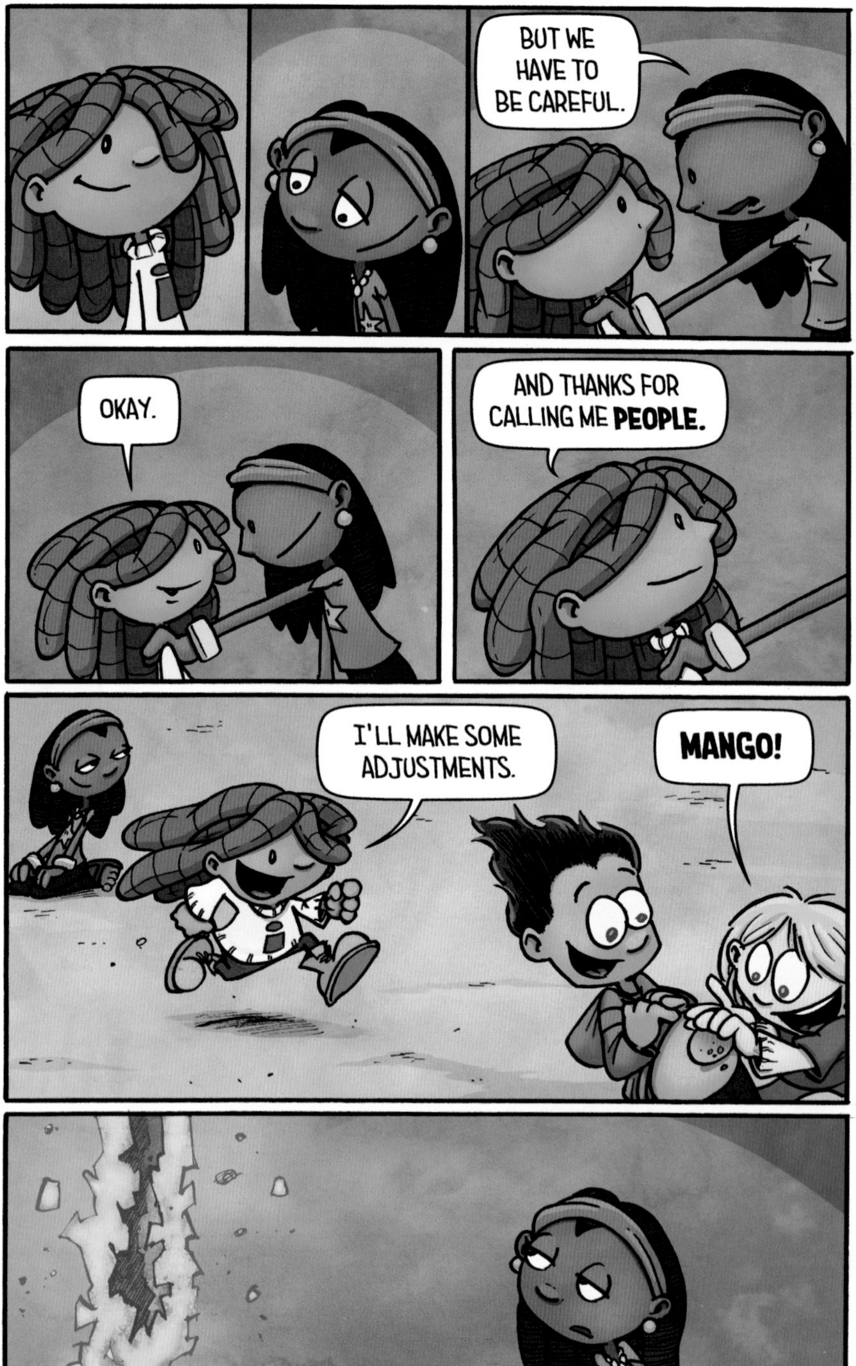
BUT WE HAVE TO BE CAREFUL.
OKAY.
AND THANKS FOR CALLING ME PEOPLE.
I'LL MAKE SOME ADJUSTMENTS.
MANGO!

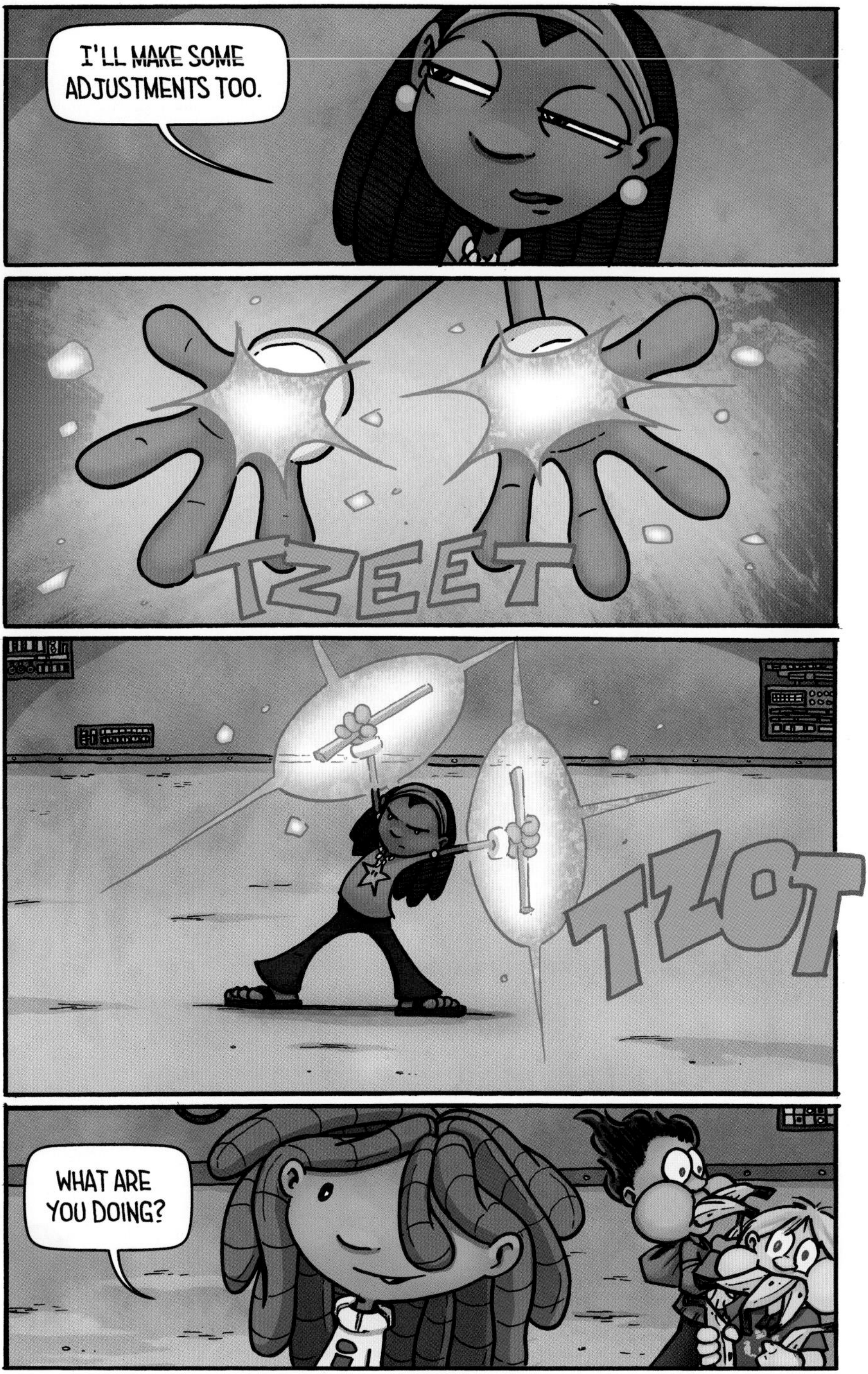
I'LL MAKE SOME ADJUSTMENTS TOO.
TZEET
TZOT
WHAT ARE YOU DOING?

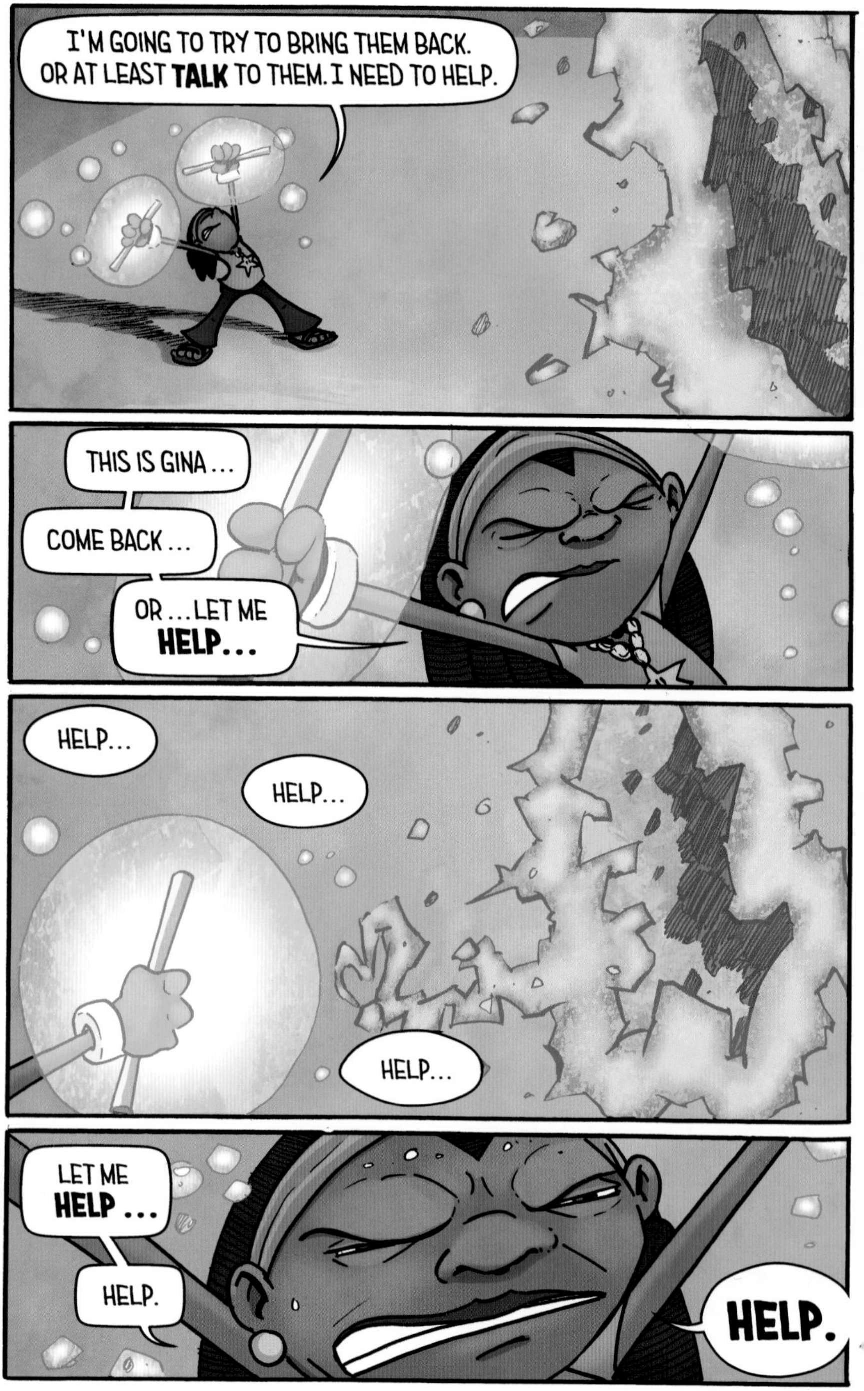

I'M GOING TO TRY TO BRING THEM BACK. OR AT LEAST **TALK** TO THEM. I NEED TO HELP.
THIS IS GINA . . .
COME BACK . . .
OR . . . LET ME **HELP . . .**
HELP. . .
HELP. . .
HELP. . .
LET ME **HELP . . .**
HELP.
HELP.

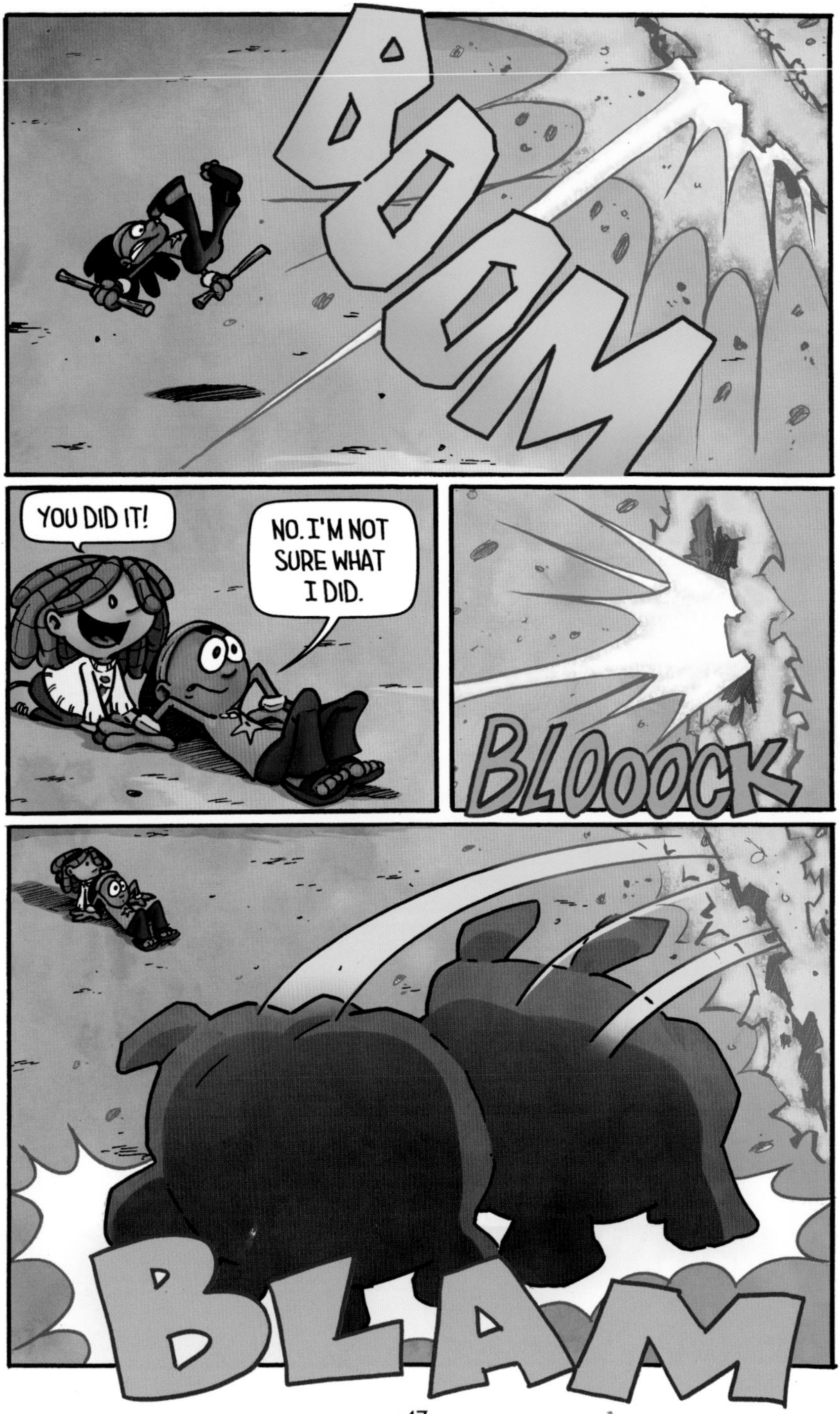
BOOM
YOU DID IT!
NO. I'M NOT SURE WHAT I DID.
BLOOOCK
BLAM

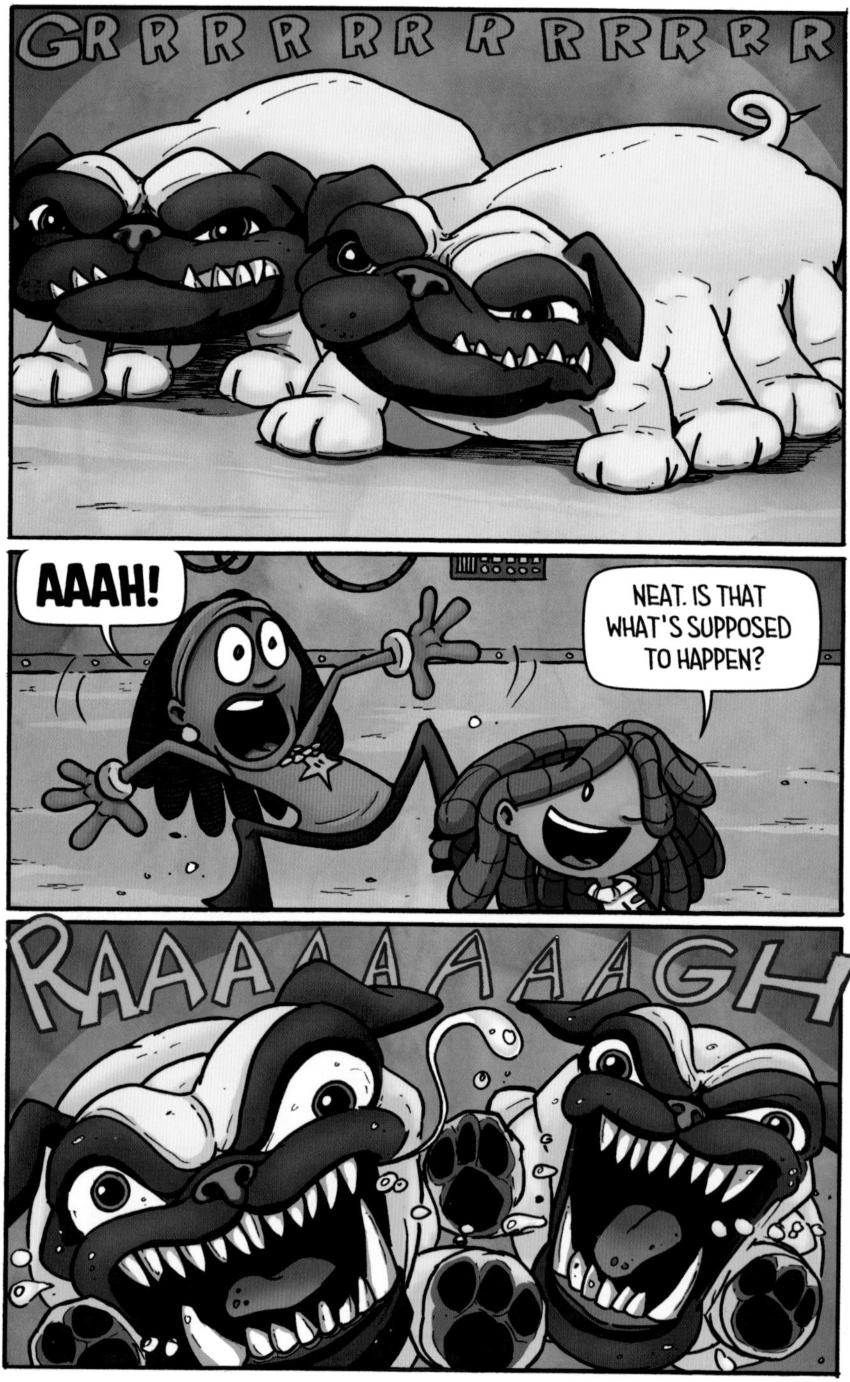
GRRRRRRRRRRRRR
AAAH!
NEAT. IS THAT WHAT'S SUPPOSED TO HAPPEN?
RAAAAAAAAGH

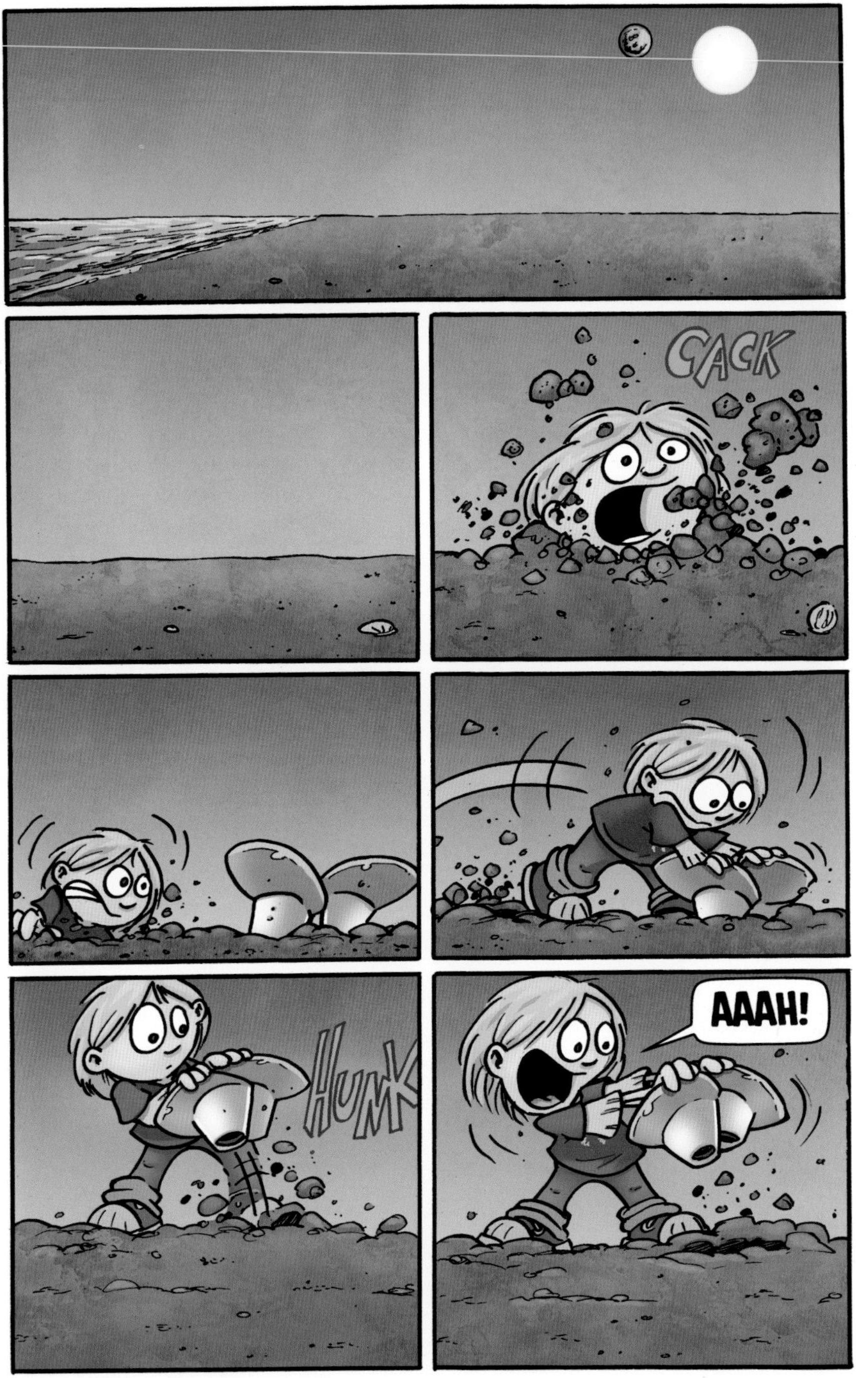
CACK
HUNK
AAAH!

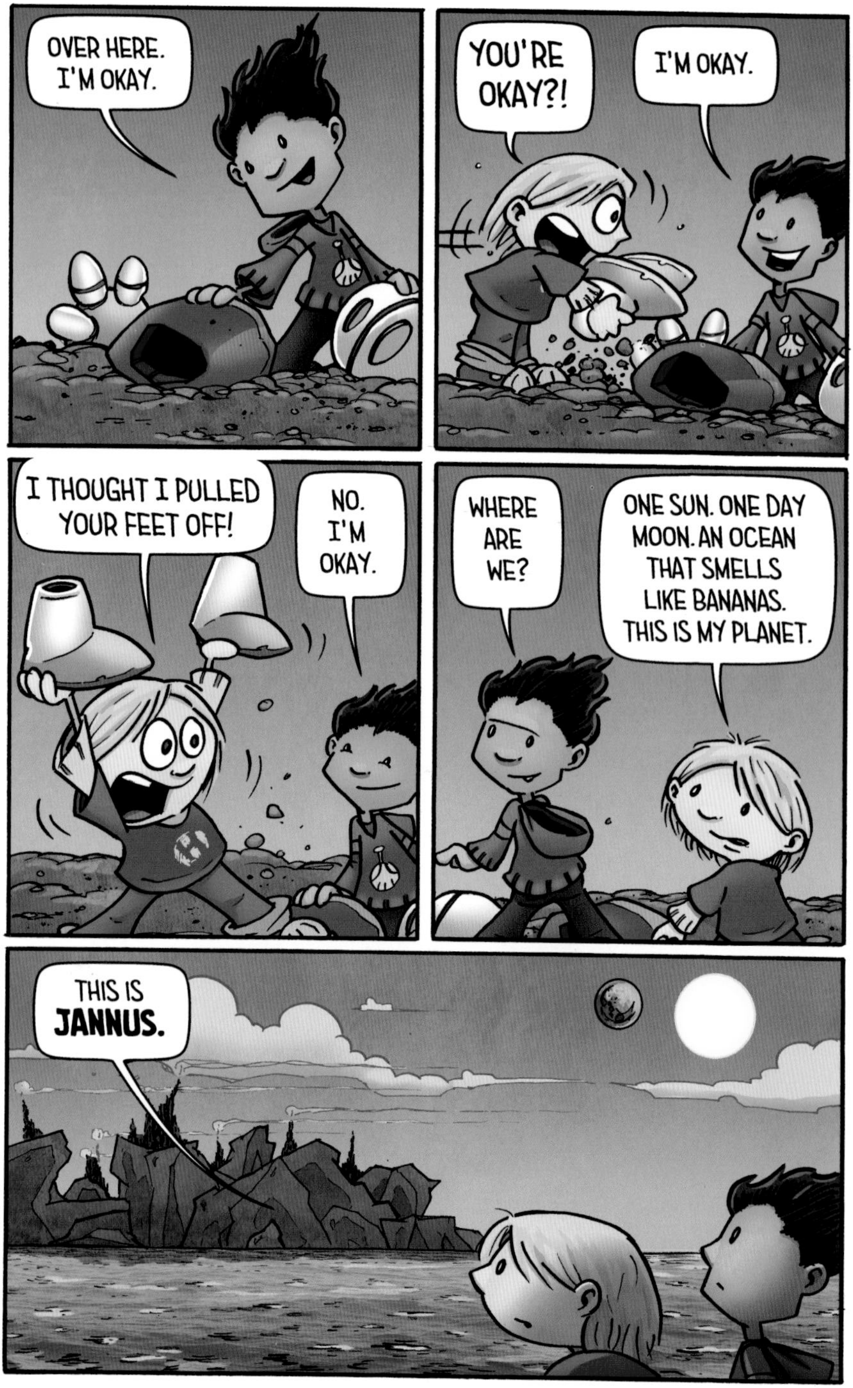

OVER HERE. I'M OKAY.
YOU'RE OKAY?!
I'M OKAY.
I THOUGHT I PULLED YOUR FEET OFF!
NO. I'M OKAY.
WHERE ARE WE?
ONE SUN. ONE DAY MOON. AN OCEAN THAT SMELLS LIKE BANANAS. THIS IS MY PLANET.
THIS IS **JANNUS.**

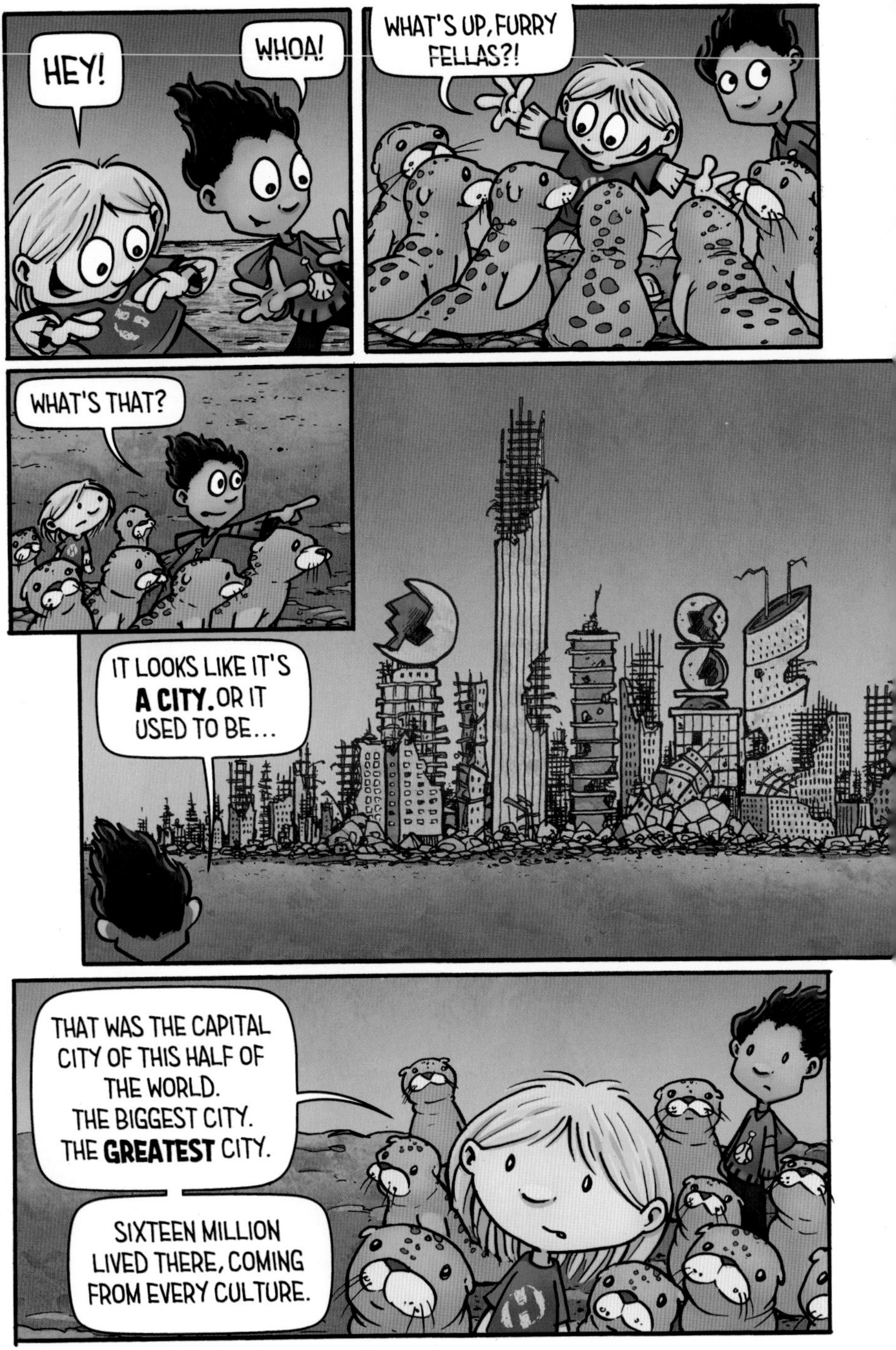
HEY!
WHOA!
WHAT'S UP, FURRY FELLAS?!
WHAT'S THAT?
IT LOOKS LIKE IT'S **A CITY.** OR IT USED TO BE...
THAT WAS THE CAPITAL CITY OF THIS HALF OF THE WORLD. THE BIGGEST CITY. THE **GREATEST** CITY.
SIXTEEN MILLION LIVED THERE, COMING FROM EVERY CULTURE.

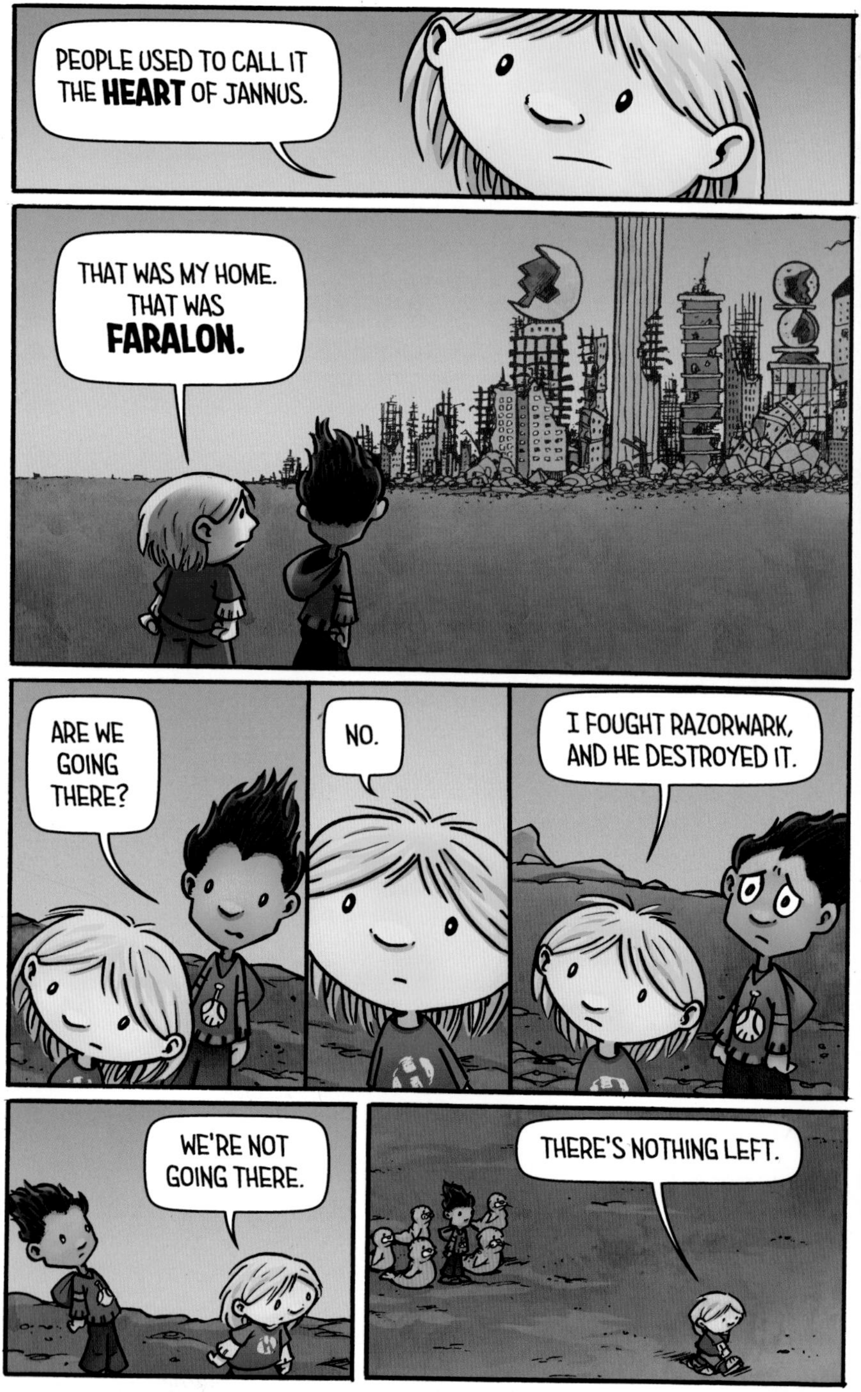
PEOPLE USED TO CALL IT THE **HEART** OF JANNUS.
THAT WAS MY HOME. THAT WAS **FARALON.**
ARE WE GOING THERE?
NO.
I FOUGHT RAZORWARK, AND HE DESTROYED IT.
WE'RE NOT GOING THERE.
THERE'S NOTHING LEFT.

CHAPTER 5

DOGS AND CATS

AAAAAAAAAAAAAAAAAAAAAAAAAAAAAAAAAA
AAAAAAAAAAA
ROWF
ROWF
ROWF

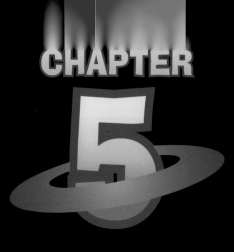

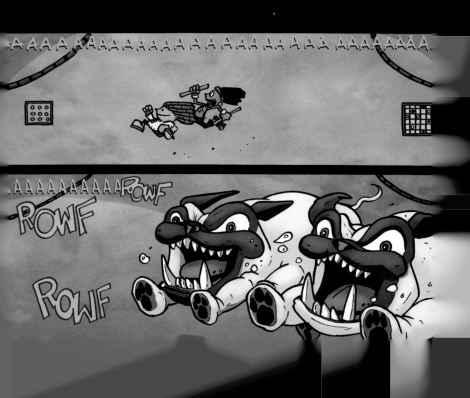

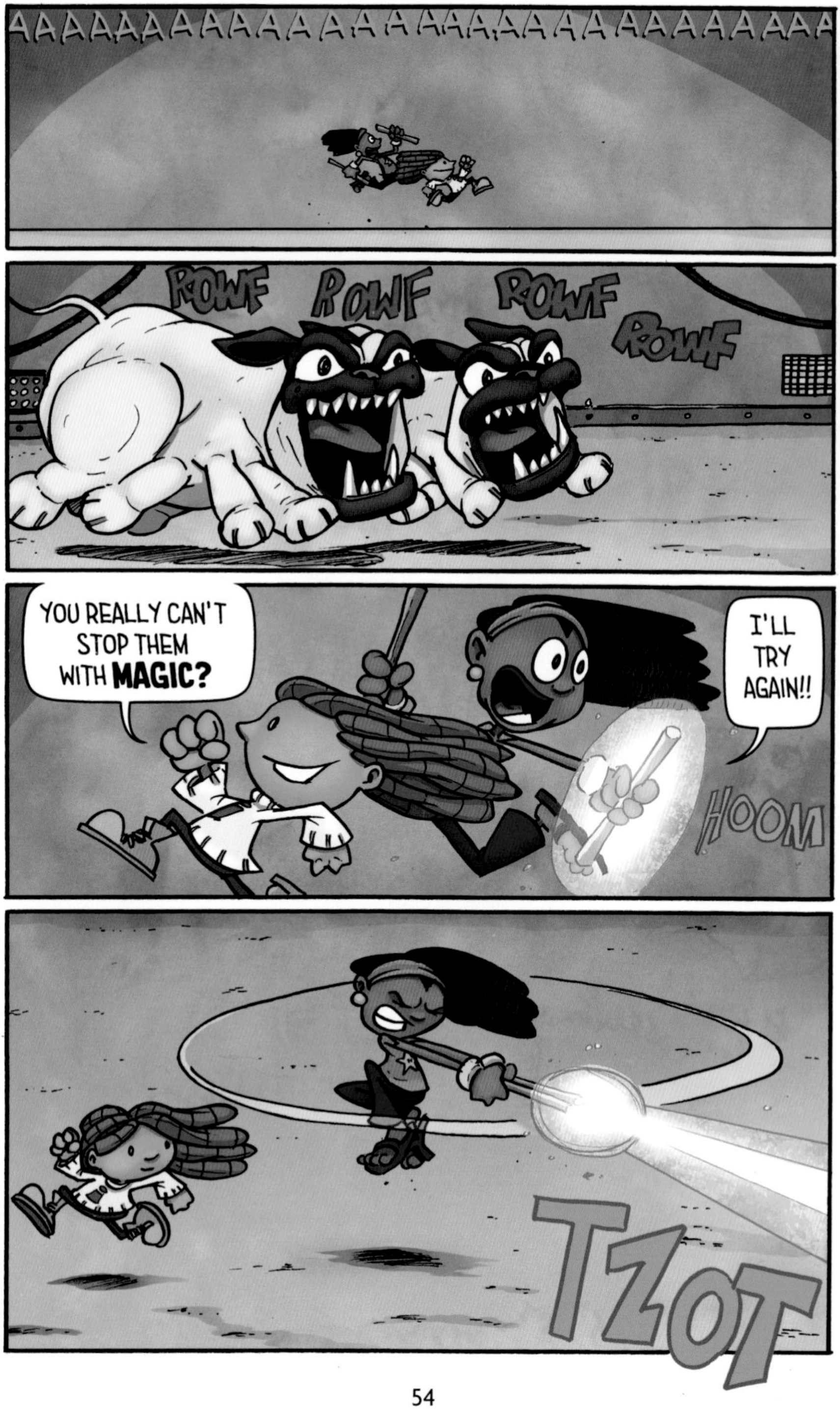

AAAAAAAAAAAAAAAAAAAAAAAAAAAAAAAA
ROWF ROWF ROWF ROWF
YOU REALLY CAN'T STOP THEM WITH **MAGIC?**
I'LL TRY AGAIN!!
HOOM
TZOT

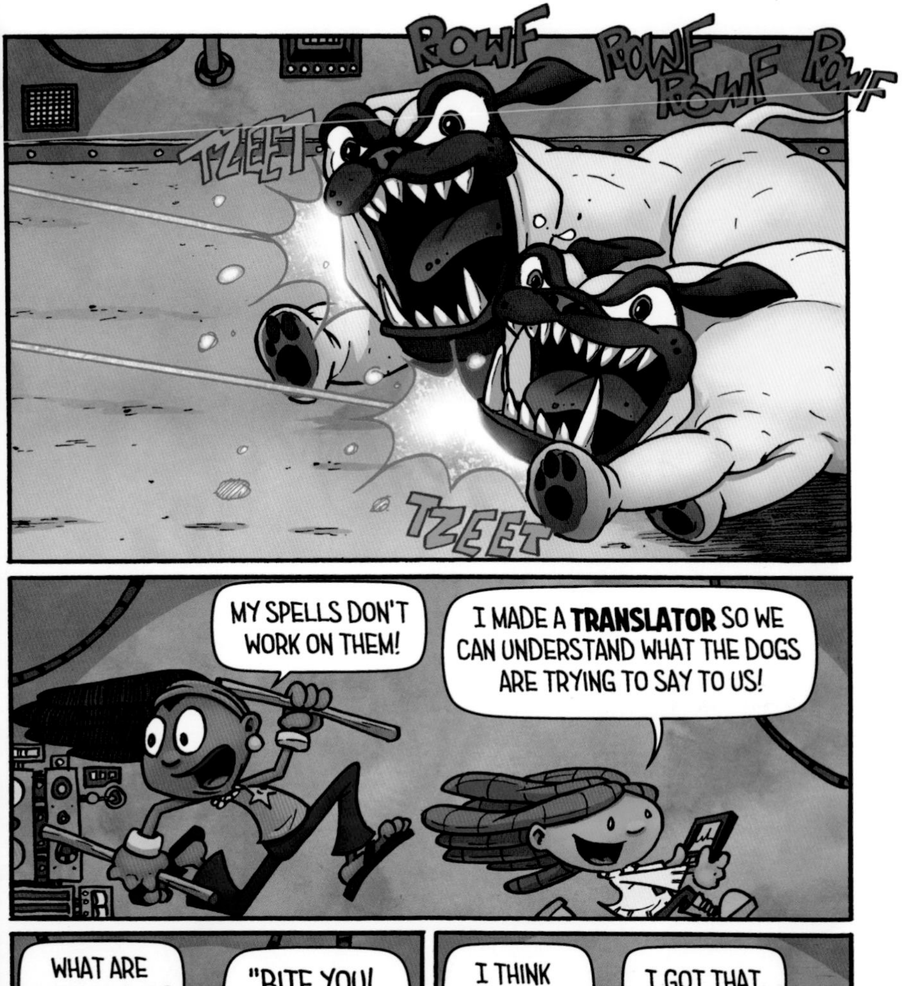
ROWF
ROWF
ROWF
ROWF
ROWF
TZEET
TZEET
MY SPELLS DON'T WORK ON THEM!
I MADE A **TRANSLATOR** SO WE CAN UNDERSTAND WHAT THE DOGS ARE TRYING TO SAY TO US!
WHAT ARE THEY SAYING?
"BITE YOU! BITE YOU! I'M GOING TO BITE YOU!"
I THINK THEY WANT TO BITE US.
I GOT THAT.

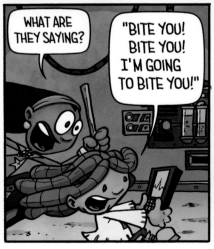

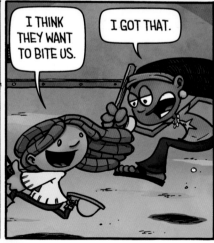

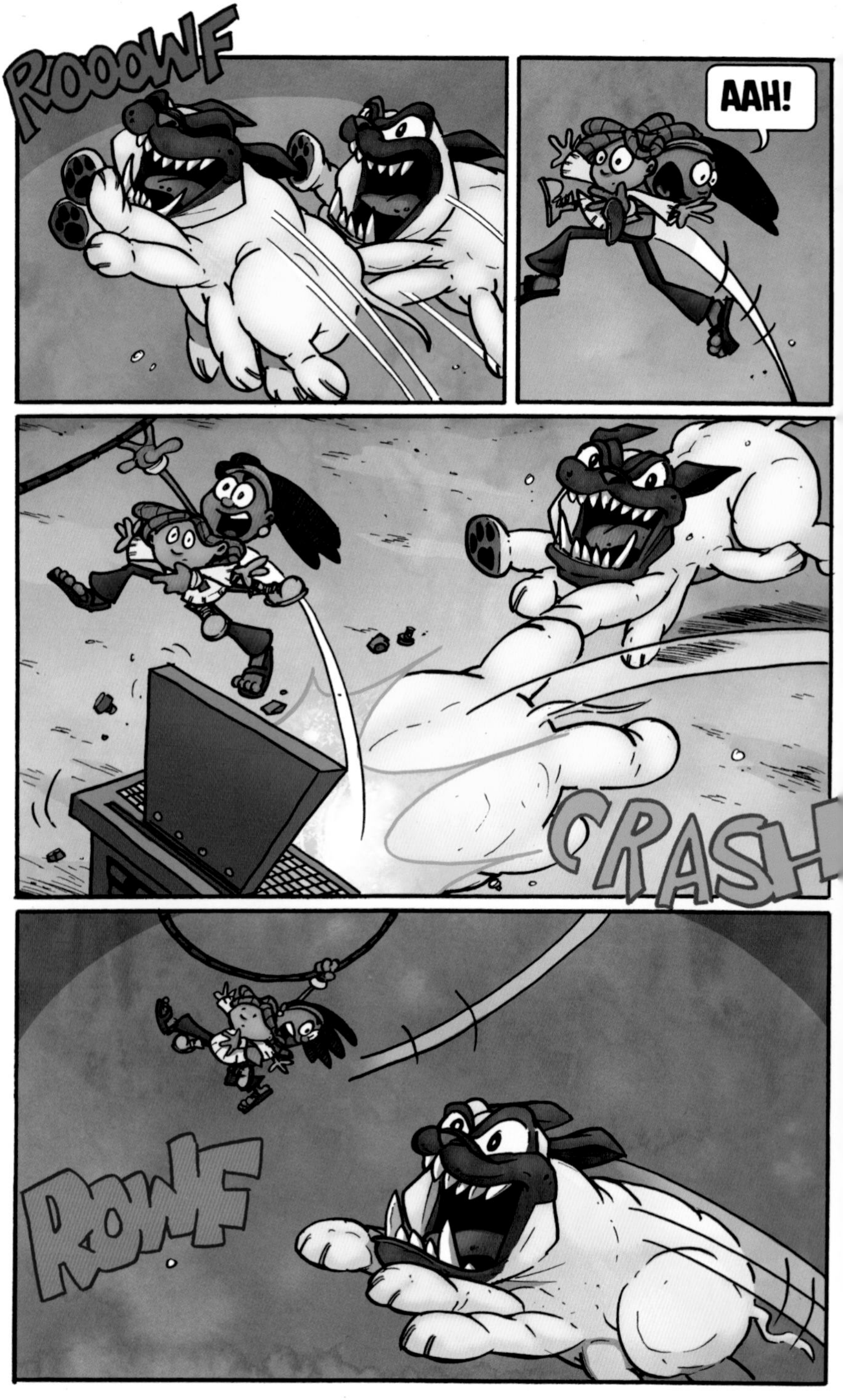
ROOOWF
AAH!
CRASH
ROWF

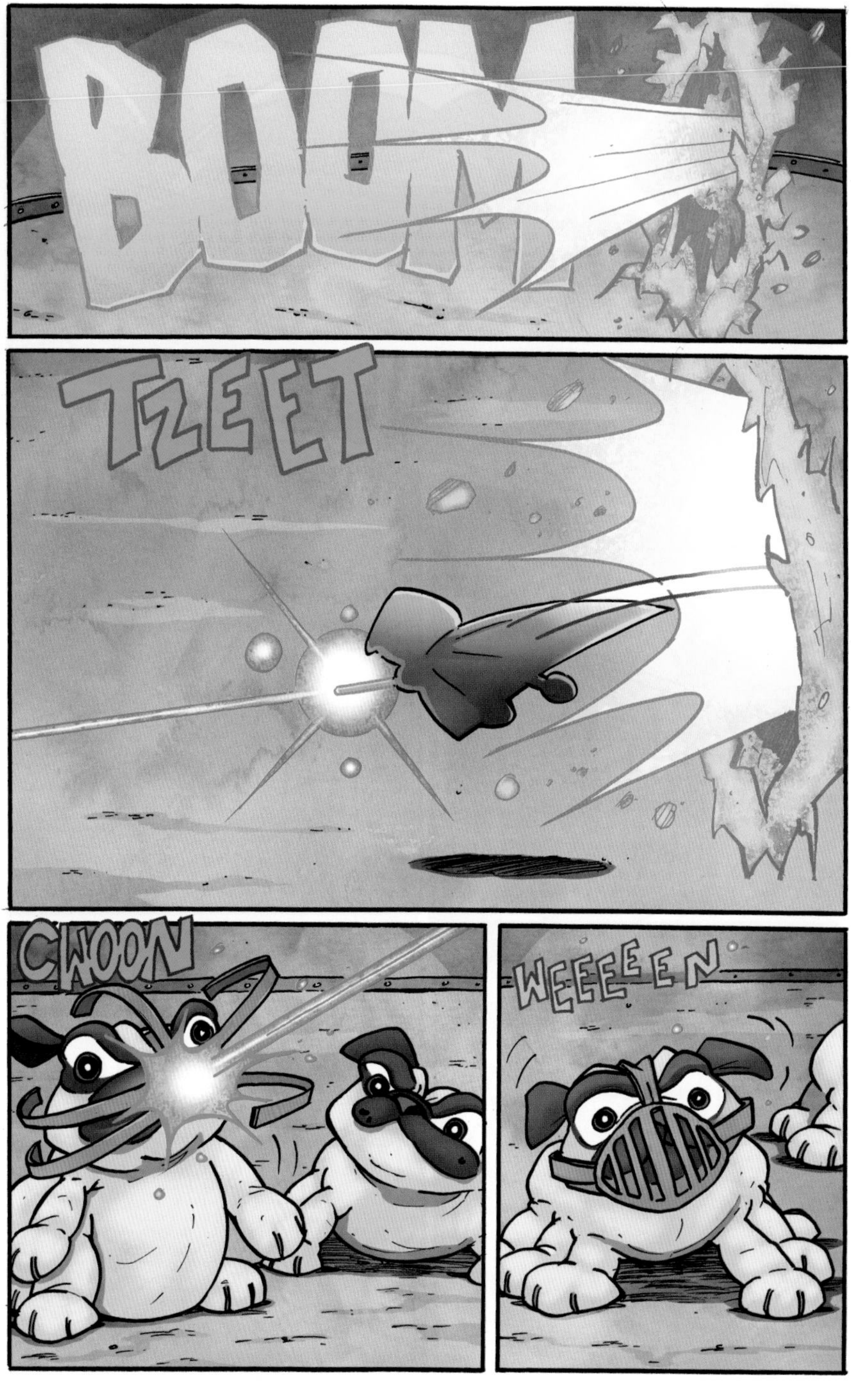
BOOM
TZEET
CWOON
WEEEEEN

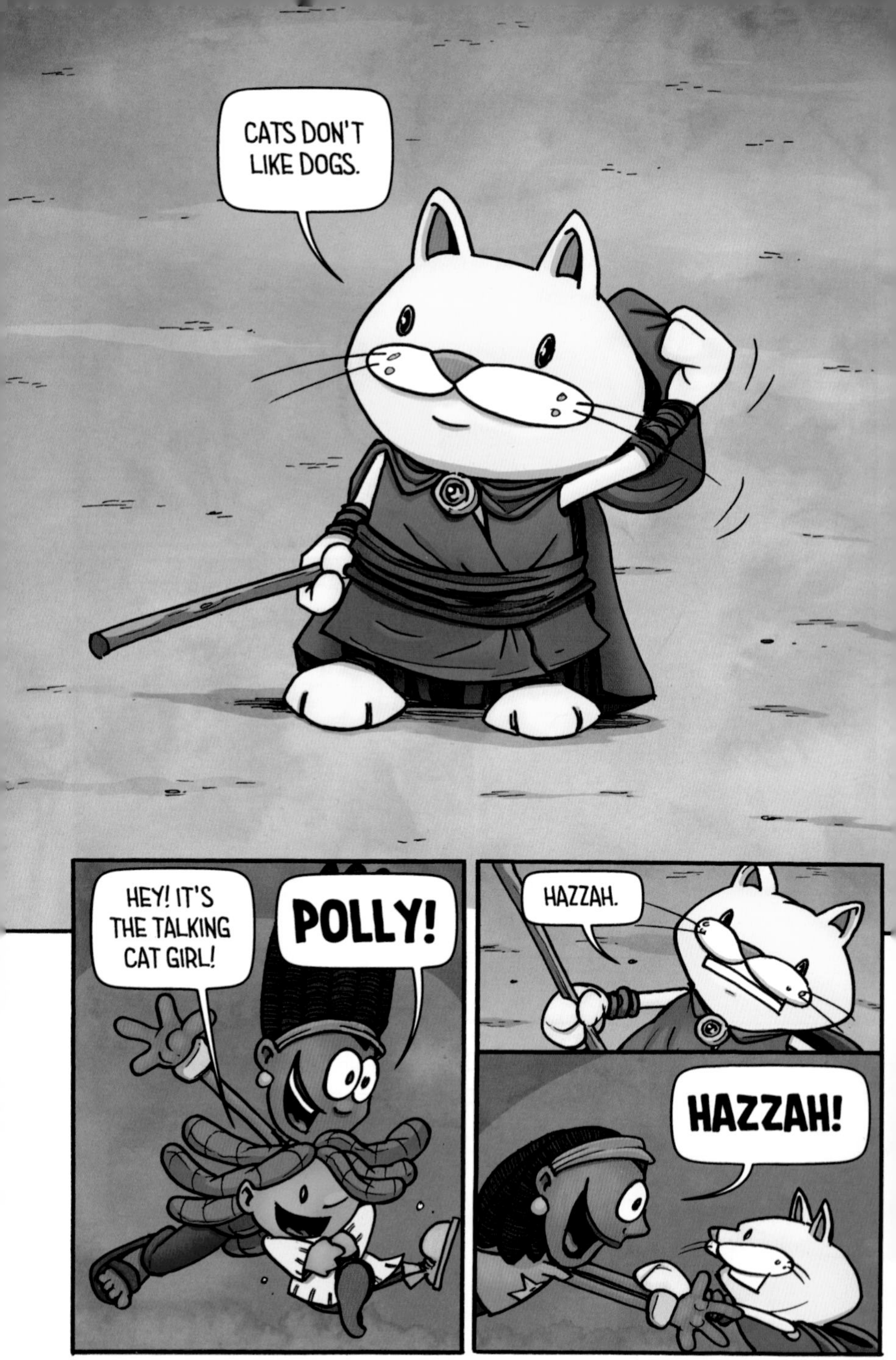
CATS DON'T LIKE DOGS.
HEY! IT'S THE TALKING CAT GIRL!
POLLY!
HAZZAH.
HAZZAH!

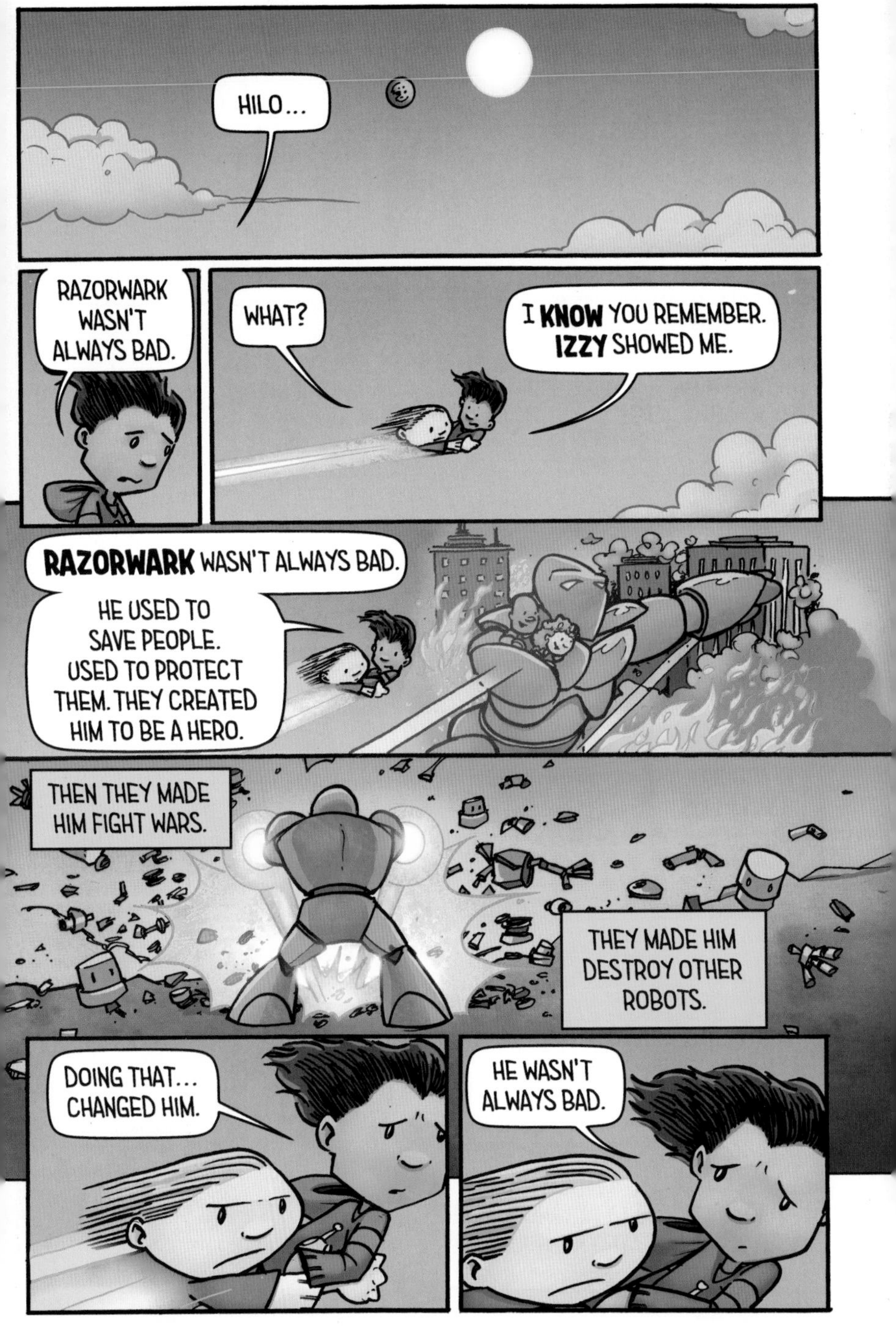
HILO...
RAZORWARK WASN'T ALWAYS BAD.
WHAT?
I KNOW YOU REMEMBER. IZZY SHOWED ME.
RAZORWARK WASN'T ALWAYS BAD.
HE USED TO SAVE PEOPLE. USED TO PROTECT THEM. THEY CREATED HIM TO BE A HERO.
THEN THEY MADE HIM FIGHT WARS.
THEY MADE HIM DESTROY OTHER ROBOTS.
DOING THAT... CHANGED HIM.
HE WASN'T ALWAYS BAD.

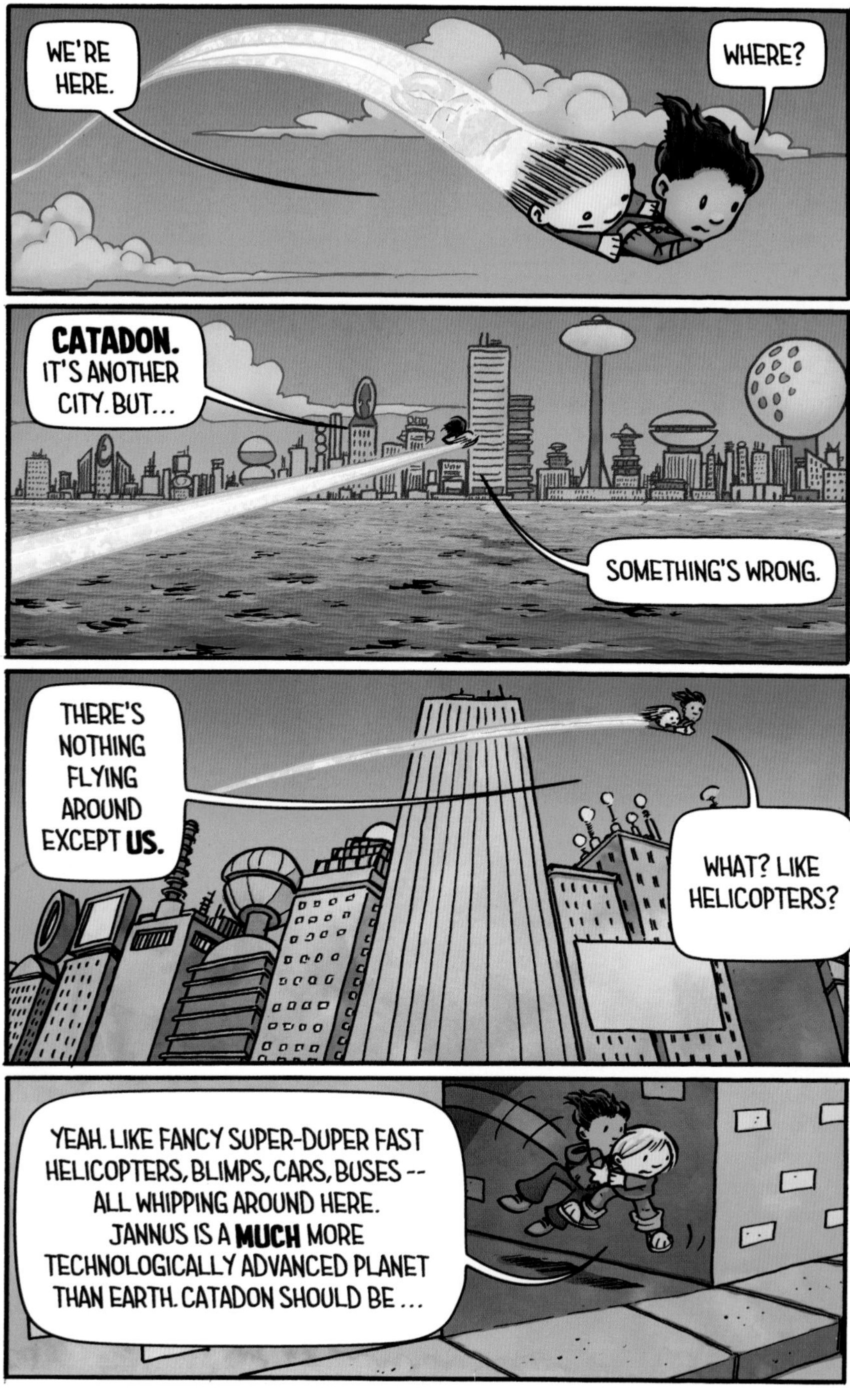
WE'RE HERE.
WHERE?
CATADON. IT'S ANOTHER CITY. BUT...
SOMETHING'S WRONG.
THERE'S NOTHING FLYING AROUND EXCEPT US.
WHAT? LIKE HELICOPTERS?
YEAH. LIKE FANCY SUPER-DUPER FAST HELICOPTERS, BLIMPS, CARS, BUSES -- ALL WHIPPING AROUND HERE. JANNUS IS A MUCH MORE TECHNOLOGICALLY ADVANCED PLANET THAN EARTH. CATADON SHOULD BE ...

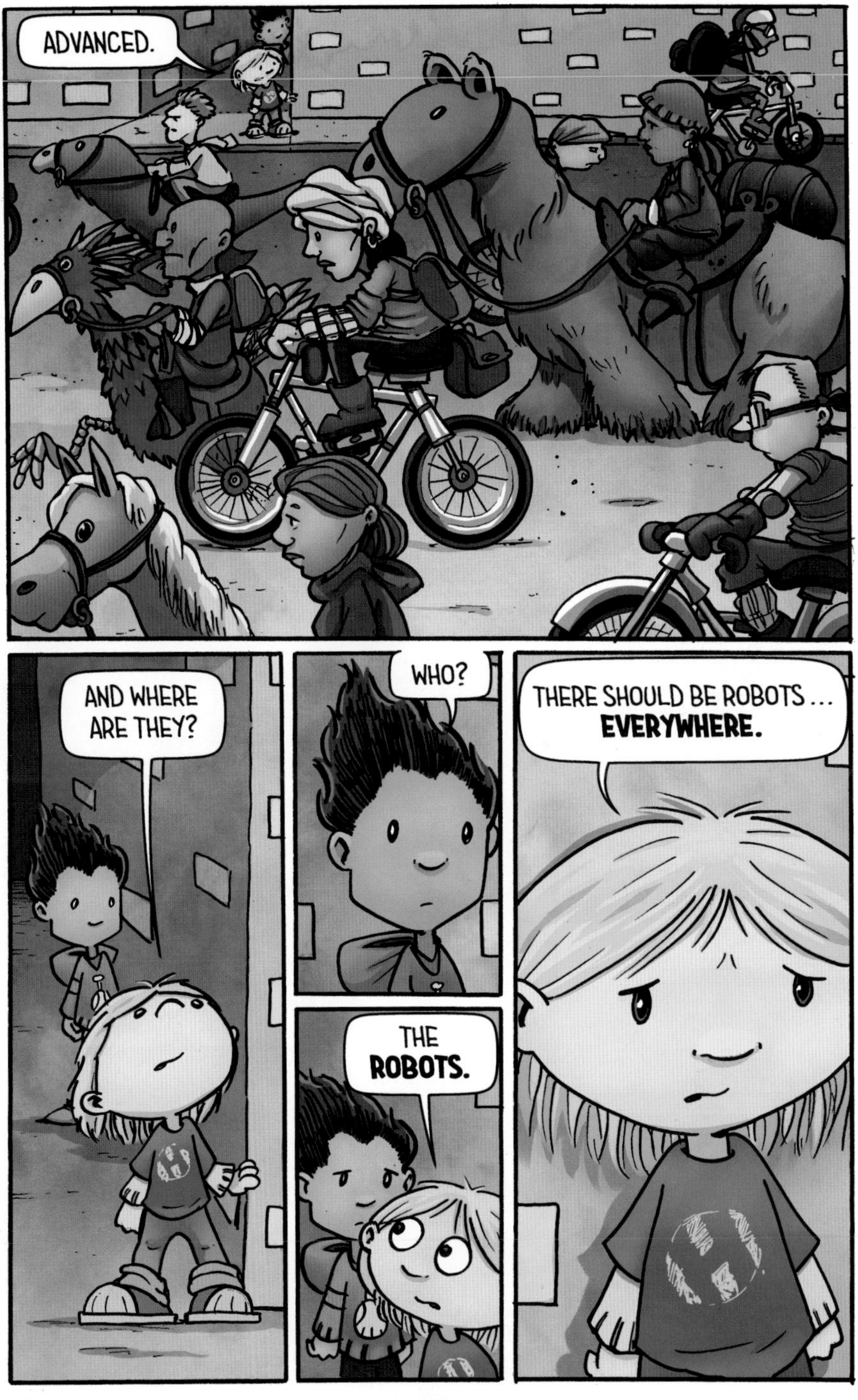
ADVANCED.
AND WHERE ARE THEY?
WHO?
THE ROBOTS.
THERE SHOULD BE ROBOTS ... EVERYWHERE.

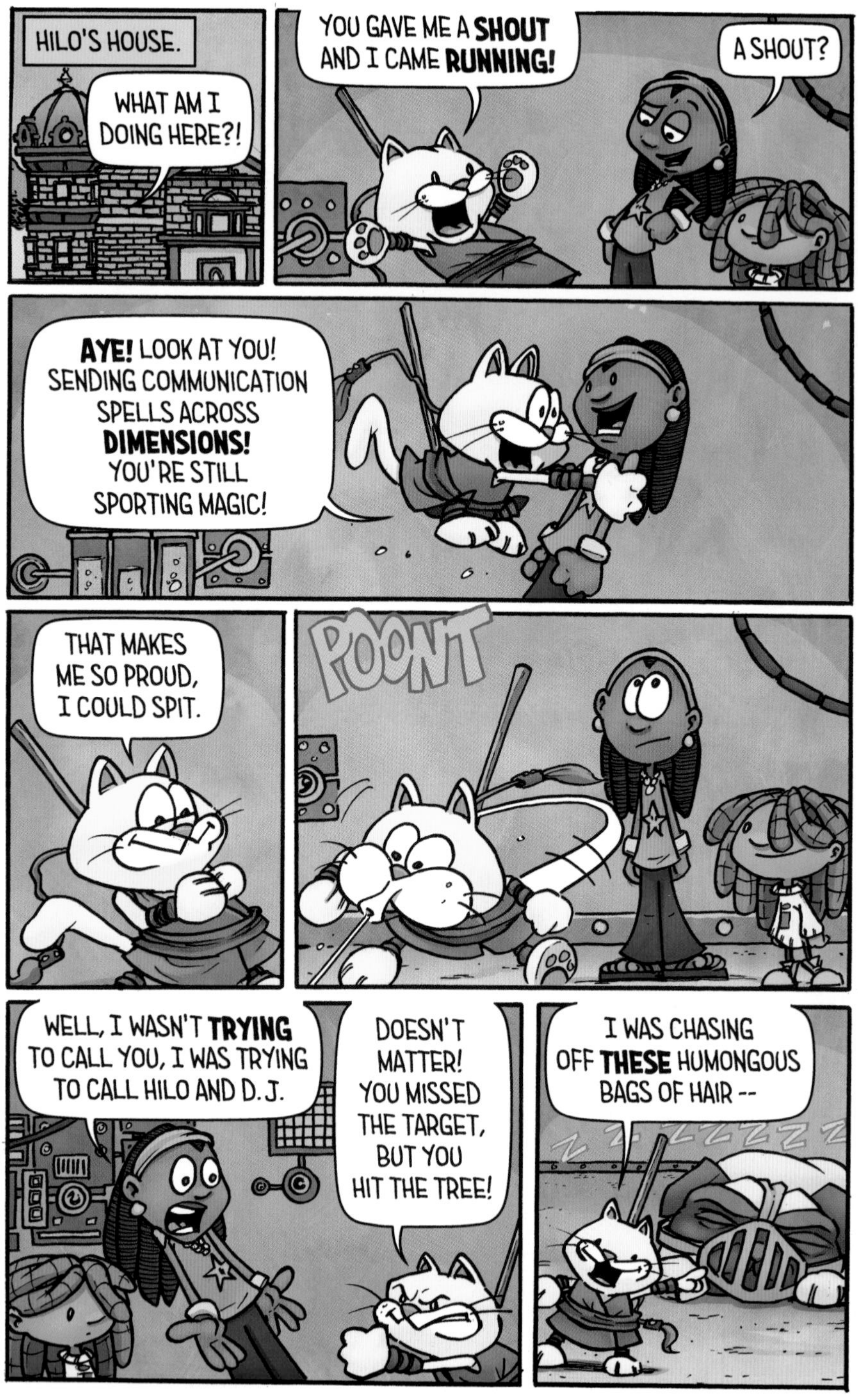
HILO'S HOUSE.
WHAT AM I DOING HERE?!
YOU GAVE ME A **SHOUT** AND I CAME **RUNNING!**
A SHOUT?
AYE! LOOK AT YOU! SENDING COMMUNICATION SPELLS ACROSS **DIMENSIONS!** YOU'RE STILL SPORTING MAGIC!
THAT MAKES ME SO PROUD, I COULD SPIT.
POONT
WELL, I WASN'T **TRYING** TO CALL YOU, I WAS TRYING TO CALL HILO AND D.J.
DOESN'T MATTER! YOU MISSED THE TARGET, BUT YOU HIT THE TREE!
I WAS CHASING OFF **THESE** HUMONGOUS BAGS OF HAIR --
Z Z Z Z Z Z Z Z Z

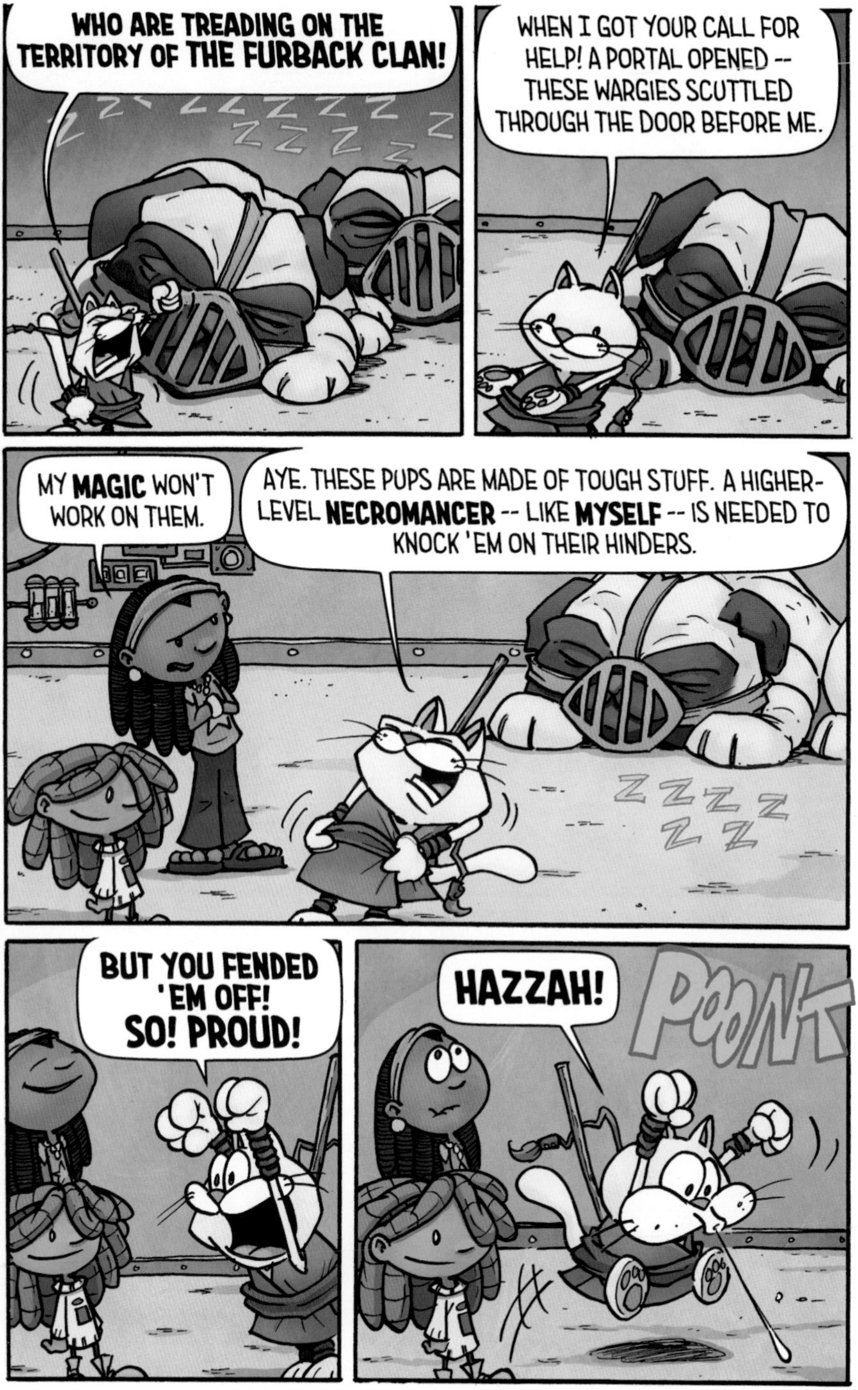
WHO ARE TREADING ON THE TERRITORY OF THE FURBACK CLAN!
WHEN I GOT YOUR CALL FOR HELP! A PORTAL OPENED -- THESE WARGIES SCUTTLED THROUGH THE DOOR BEFORE ME.
MY MAGIC WON'T WORK ON THEM.
AYE. THESE PUPS ARE MADE OF TOUGH STUFF. A HIGHER-LEVEL NECROMANCER -- LIKE MYSELF -- IS NEEDED TO KNOCK 'EM ON THEIR HINDERS.
BUT YOU FENDED 'EM OFF! SO! PROUD!
HAZZAH!
POONK

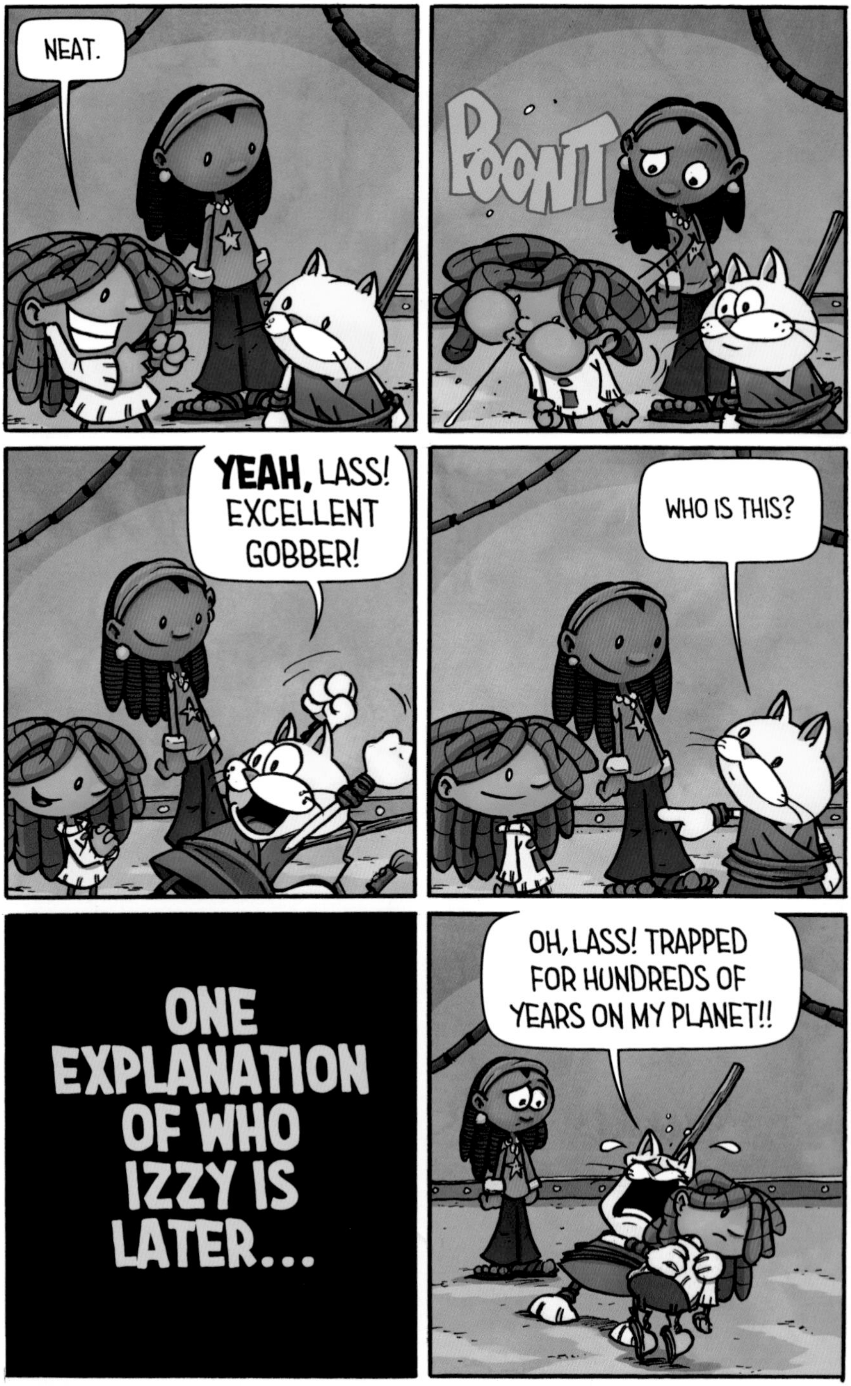
NEAT.
BOONT
YEAH, LASS! EXCELLENT GOBBER!
WHO IS THIS?
ONE EXPLANATION OF WHO IZZY IS LATER...
OH, LASS! TRAPPED FOR HUNDREDS OF YEARS ON MY PLANET!!

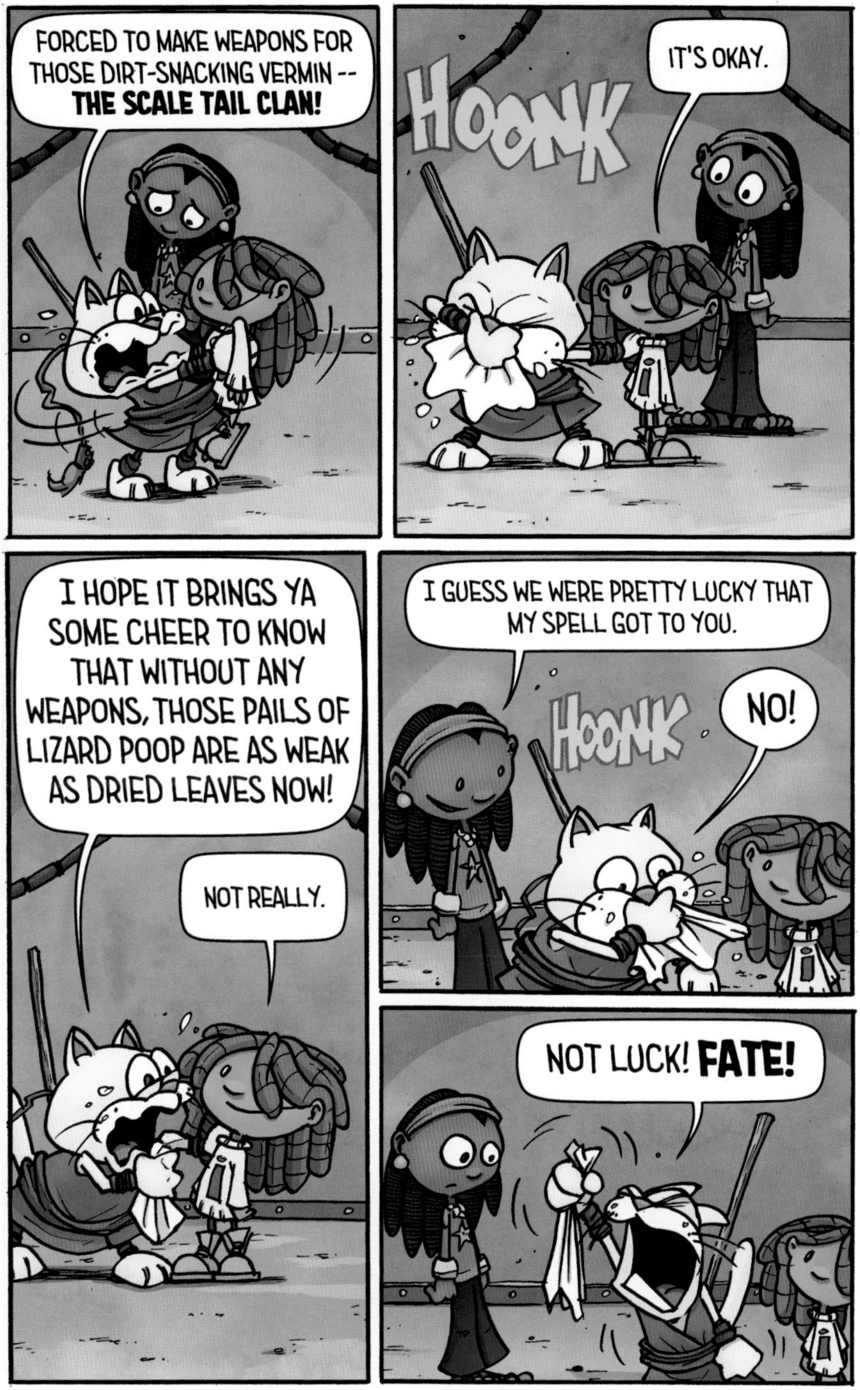
FORCED TO MAKE WEAPONS FOR THOSE DIRT-SNACKING VERMIN -- **THE SCALE TAIL CLAN!**
HOONK
IT'S OKAY.
I HOPE IT BRINGS YA SOME CHEER TO KNOW THAT WITHOUT ANY WEAPONS, THOSE PAILS OF LIZARD POOP ARE AS WEAK AS DRIED LEAVES NOW!
NOT REALLY.
I GUESS WE WERE PRETTY LUCKY THAT MY SPELL GOT TO YOU.
HOONK
NO!
NOT LUCK! **FATE!**

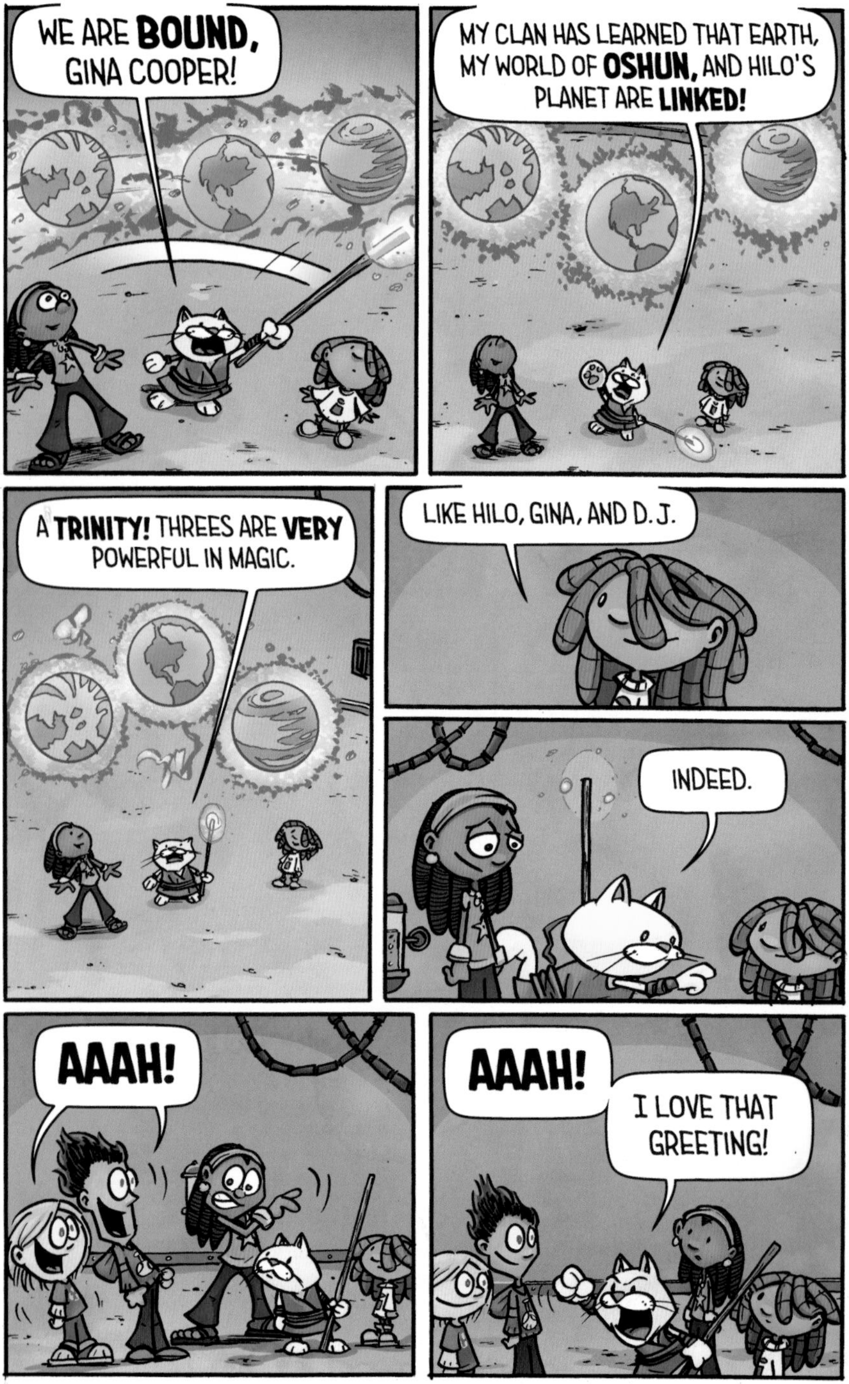
WE ARE BOUND, GINA COOPER!
MY CLAN HAS LEARNED THAT EARTH, MY WORLD OF OSHUN, AND HILO'S PLANET ARE LINKED!
A TRINITY! THREES ARE VERY POWERFUL IN MAGIC.
LIKE HILO, GINA, AND D. J.
INDEED.
AAAH!
AAAH!
I LOVE THAT GREETING!

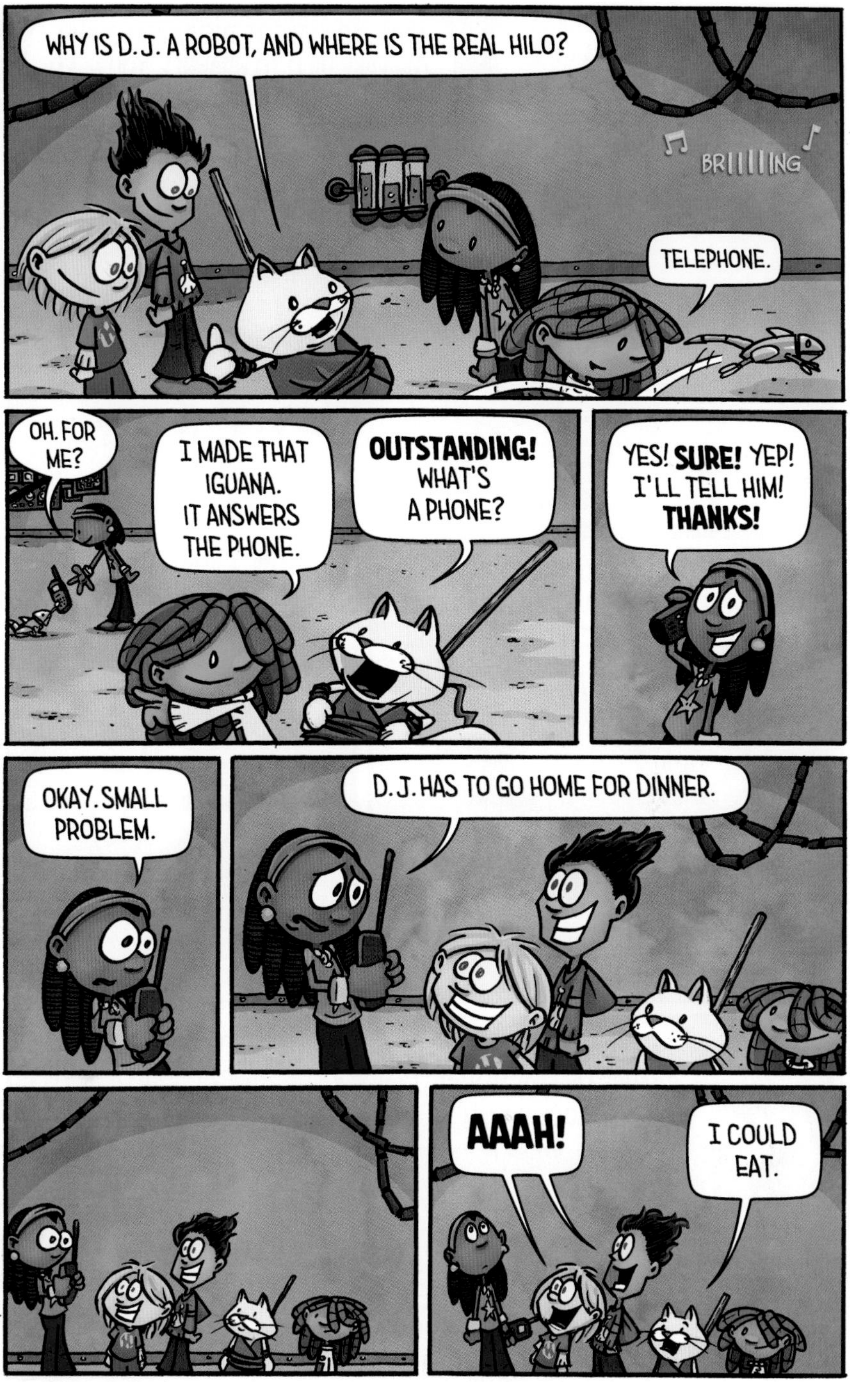

WHY IS D. J. A ROBOT, AND WHERE IS THE REAL HILO?
BRIIIIING
TELEPHONE.
OH. FOR ME?
I MADE THAT IGUANA. IT ANSWERS THE PHONE.
OUTSTANDING! WHAT'S A PHONE?
YES! SURE! YEP! I'LL TELL HIM! THANKS!
OKAY. SMALL PROBLEM.
D. J. HAS TO GO HOME FOR DINNER.
AAAH!
I COULD EAT.

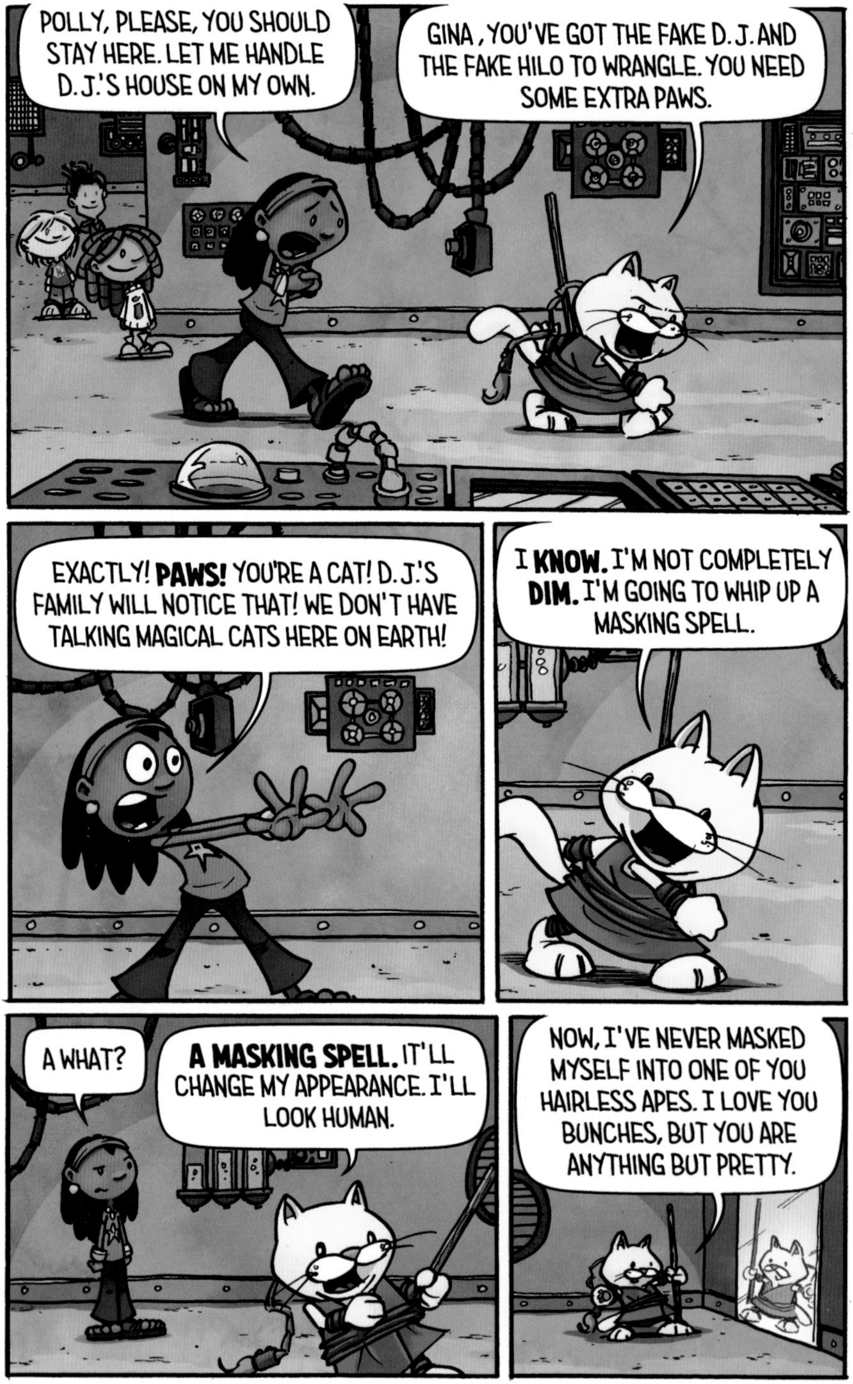
POLLY, PLEASE, YOU SHOULD STAY HERE. LET ME HANDLE D.J.'S HOUSE ON MY OWN.
GINA, YOU'VE GOT THE FAKE D.J. AND THE FAKE HILO TO WRANGLE. YOU NEED SOME EXTRA PAWS.
EXACTLY! PAWS! YOU'RE A CAT! D.J.'S FAMILY WILL NOTICE THAT! WE DON'T HAVE TALKING MAGICAL CATS HERE ON EARTH!
I KNOW. I'M NOT COMPLETELY DIM. I'M GOING TO WHIP UP A MASKING SPELL.
A WHAT?
A MASKING SPELL. IT'LL CHANGE MY APPEARANCE. I'LL LOOK HUMAN.
NOW, I'VE NEVER MASKED MYSELF INTO ONE OF YOU HAIRLESS APES. I LOVE YOU BUNCHES, BUT YOU ARE ANYTHING BUT PRETTY.

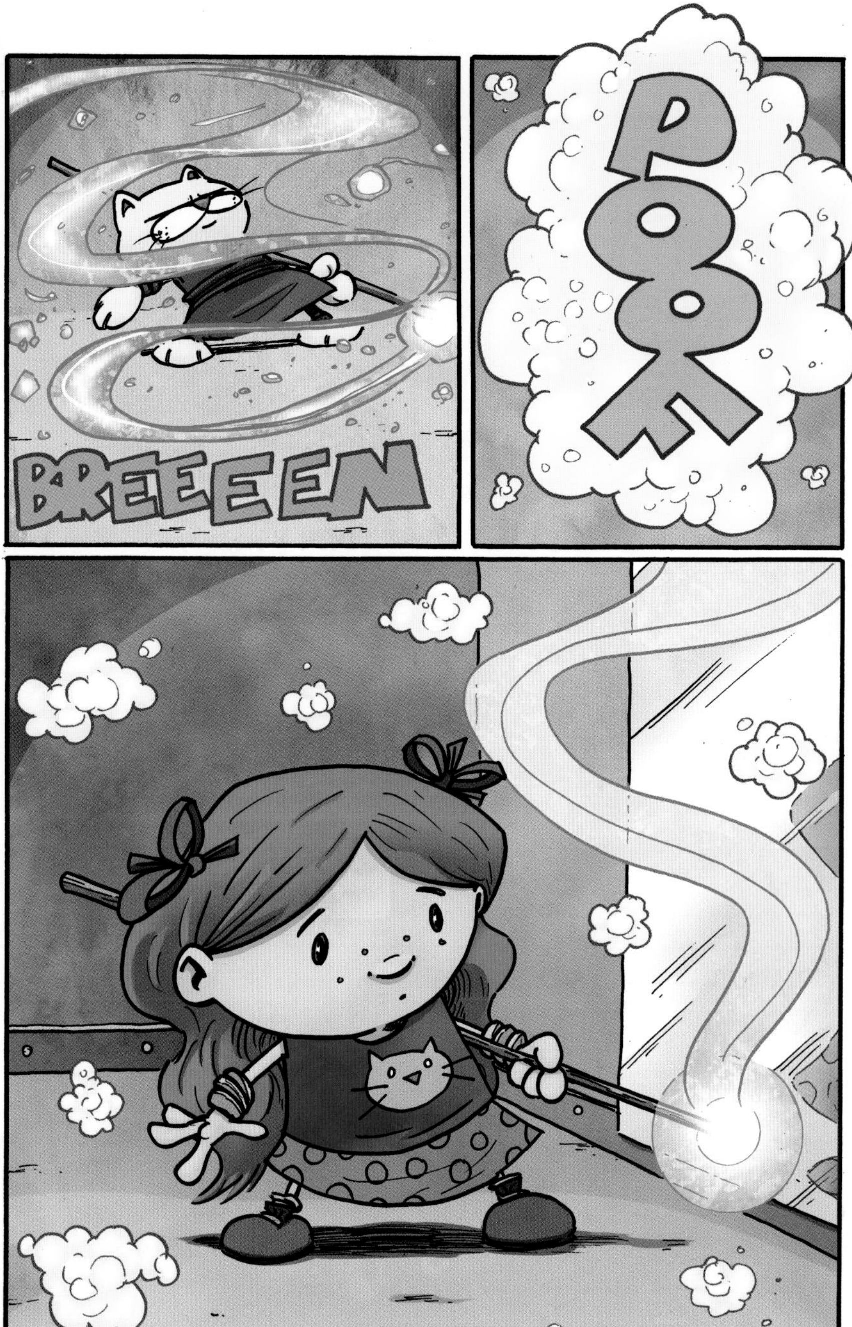
BREEEEN
POOF

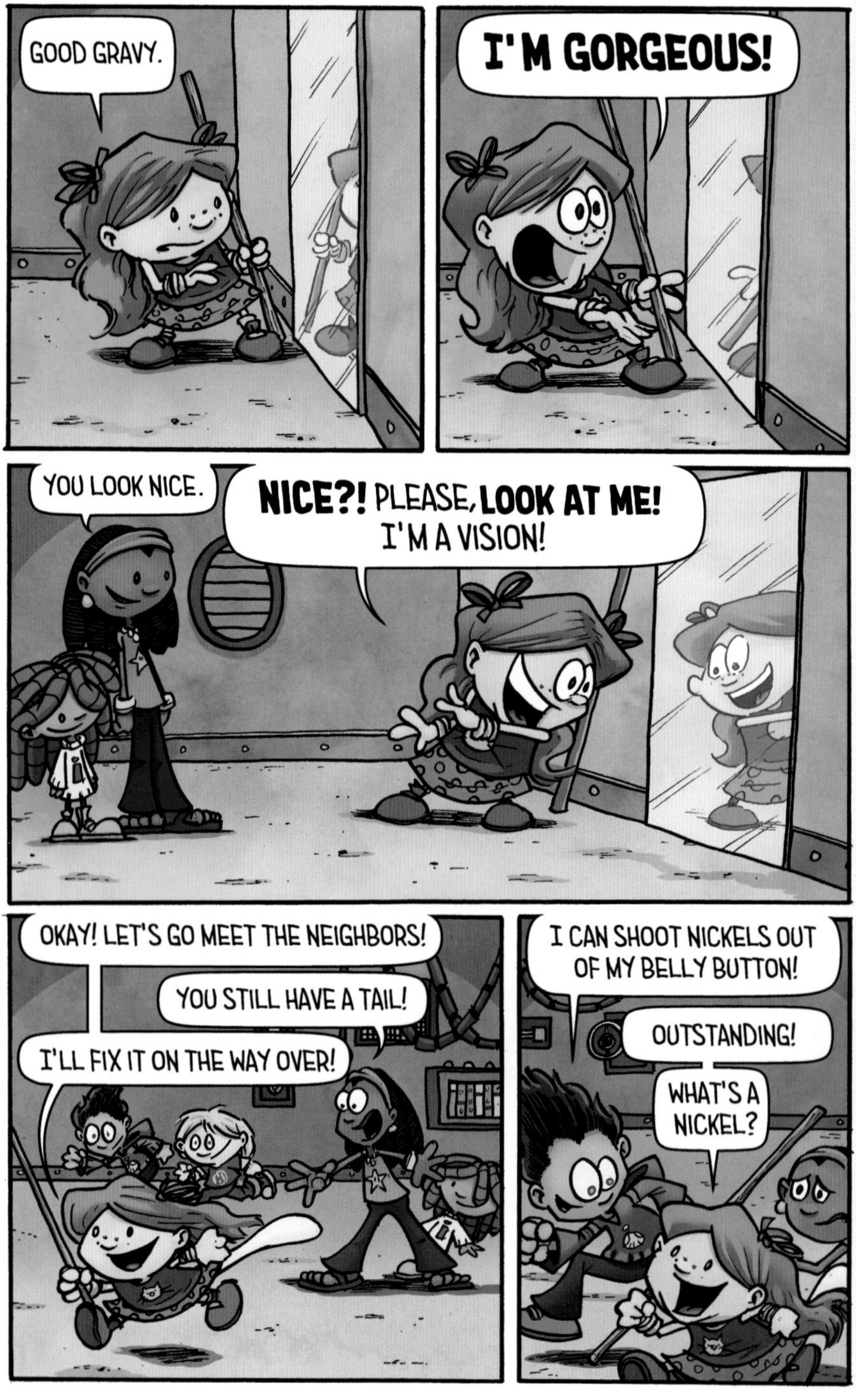
GOOD GRAVY.
I'M GORGEOUS!
YOU LOOK NICE.
NICE?! PLEASE, LOOK AT ME! I'M A VISION!
OKAY! LET'S GO MEET THE NEIGHBORS!
YOU STILL HAVE A TAIL!
I'LL FIX IT ON THE WAY OVER!
I CAN SHOOT NICKELS OUT OF MY BELLY BUTTON!
OUTSTANDING!
WHAT'S A NICKEL?

CHAPTER 6

IN THE DARK

WHAT DO YOU MEAN, "THE TECH IS GONE"?
THE TECHNOLOGY IS **GONE.**
LOOK AT THIS PLACE!

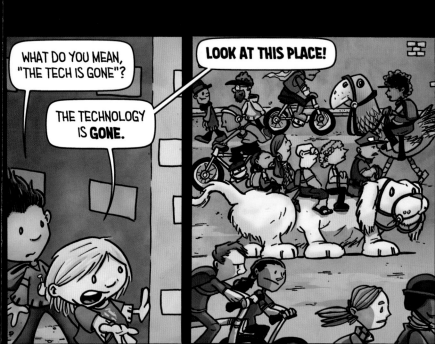

NO ROBOTS.

IT'S LIKE SOMEONE TURNED IT ALL OFF.

C'MON! I JUST REMEMBERED SOMETHING.

WHA --

AAAAAAAAH!

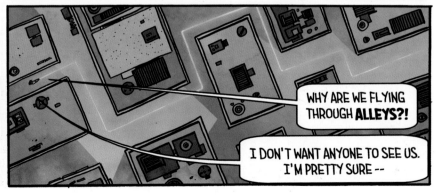

WHY ARE WE FLYING THROUGH **ALLEYS**?!

I DON'T WANT ANYONE TO SEE US. I'M PRETTY SURE --

76

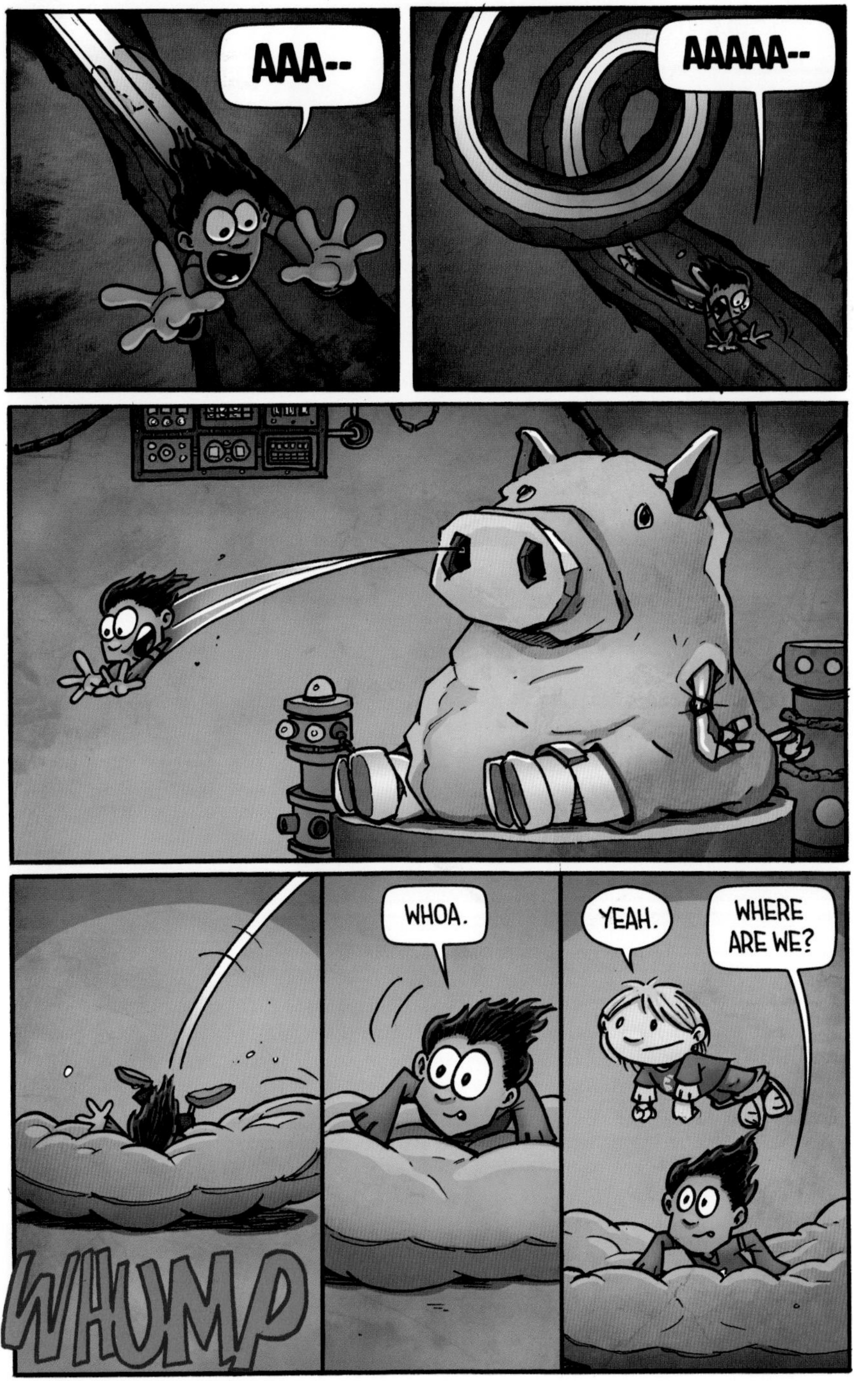
AAA--
AAAAA--
WHUMP
WHOA.
YEAH.
WHERE ARE WE?

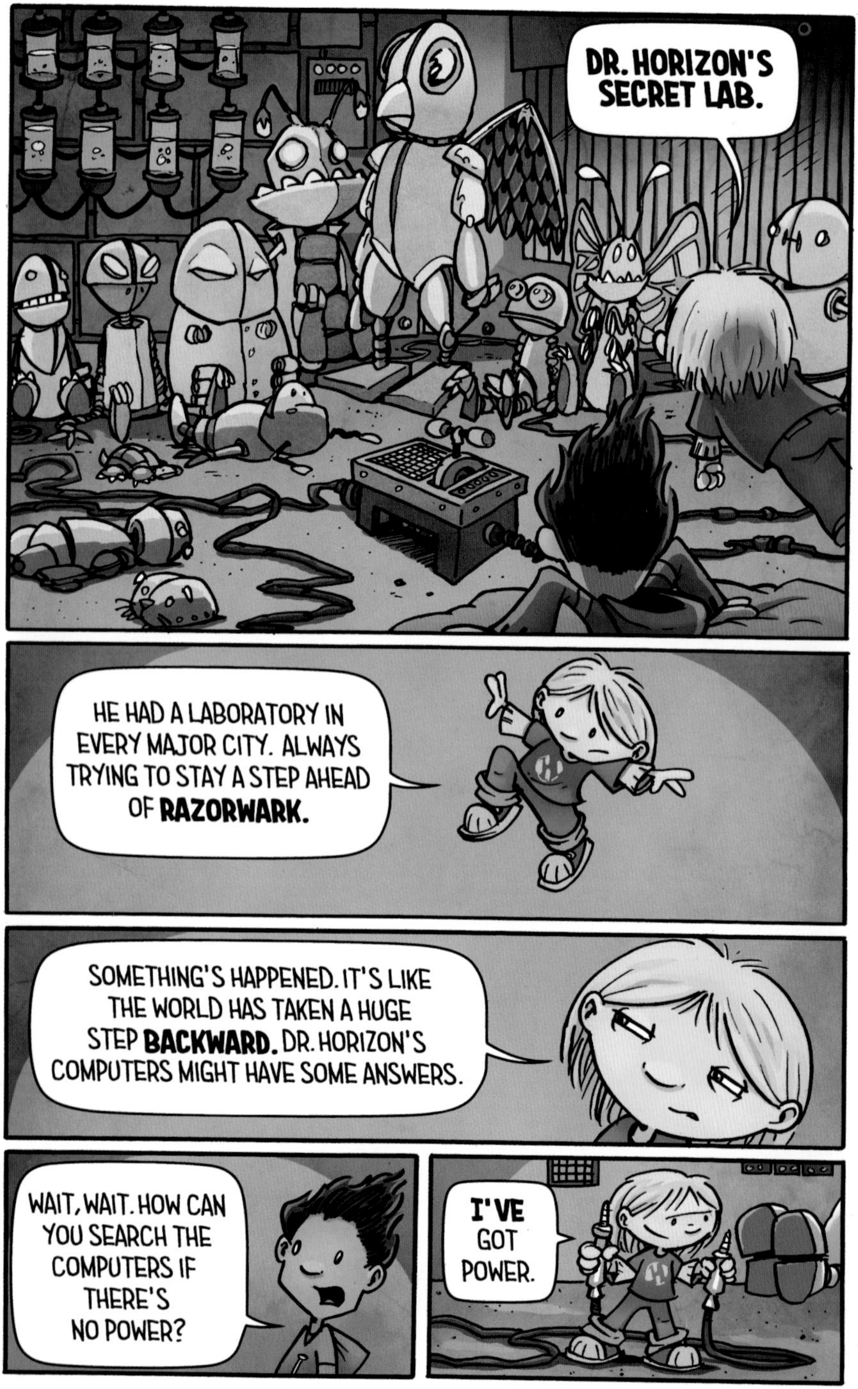
DR. HORIZON'S SECRET LAB.
HE HAD A LABORATORY IN EVERY MAJOR CITY. ALWAYS TRYING TO STAY A STEP AHEAD OF **RAZORWARK.**
SOMETHING'S HAPPENED. IT'S LIKE THE WORLD HAS TAKEN A HUGE STEP **BACKWARD.** DR. HORIZON'S COMPUTERS MIGHT HAVE SOME ANSWERS.
WAIT, WAIT. HOW CAN YOU SEARCH THE COMPUTERS IF THERE'S NO POWER?
I'VE GOT POWER.

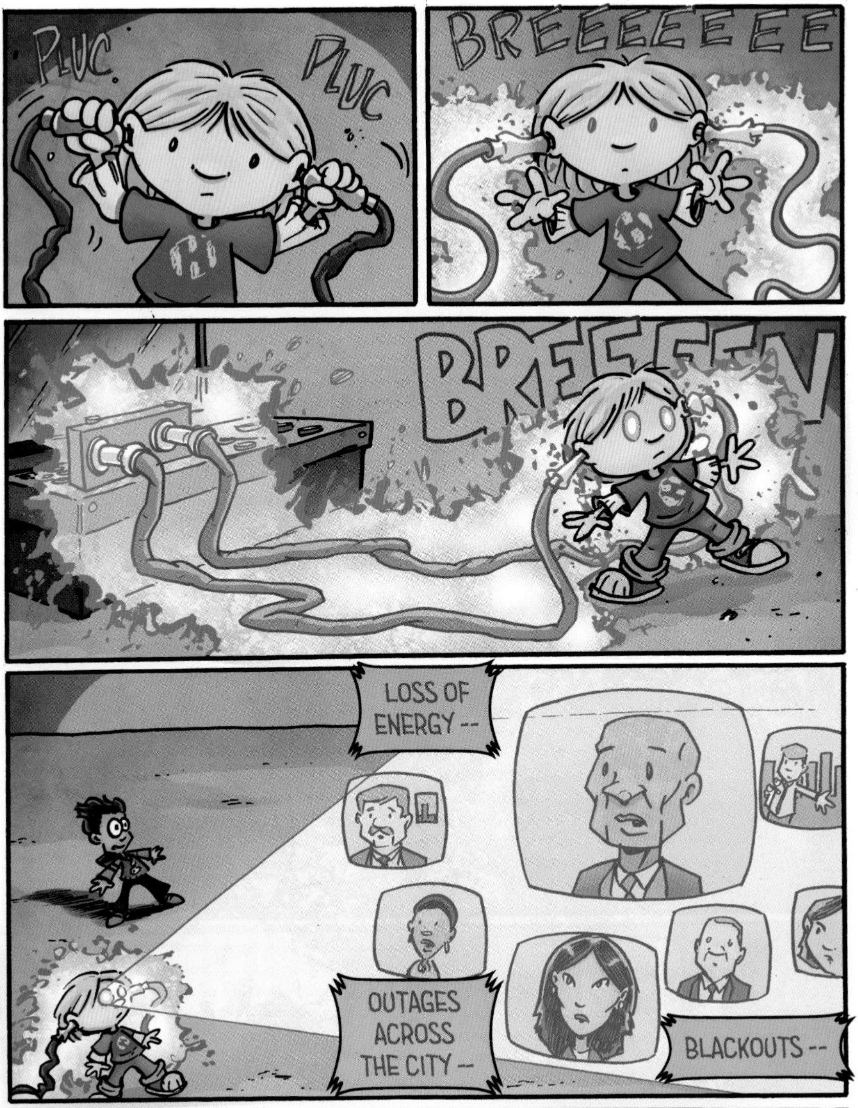
PLUC
PLUC
BREEEEEEEE
BREEEEN
LOSS OF ENERGY --
OUTAGES ACROSS THE CITY --
BLACKOUTS --
REPORTS IN MOST MAJOR CITIES OF INCREASING POWER OUTAGES. THOUSANDS HAVE BEEN LITERALLY LEFT IN THE DARK --

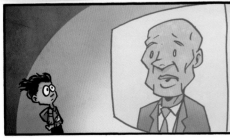

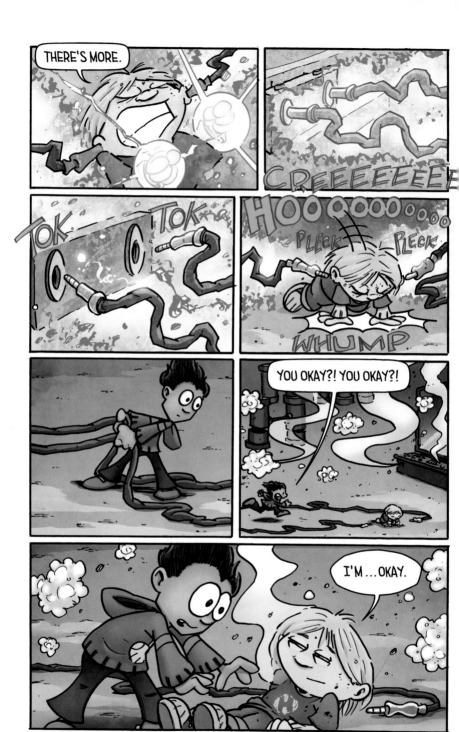

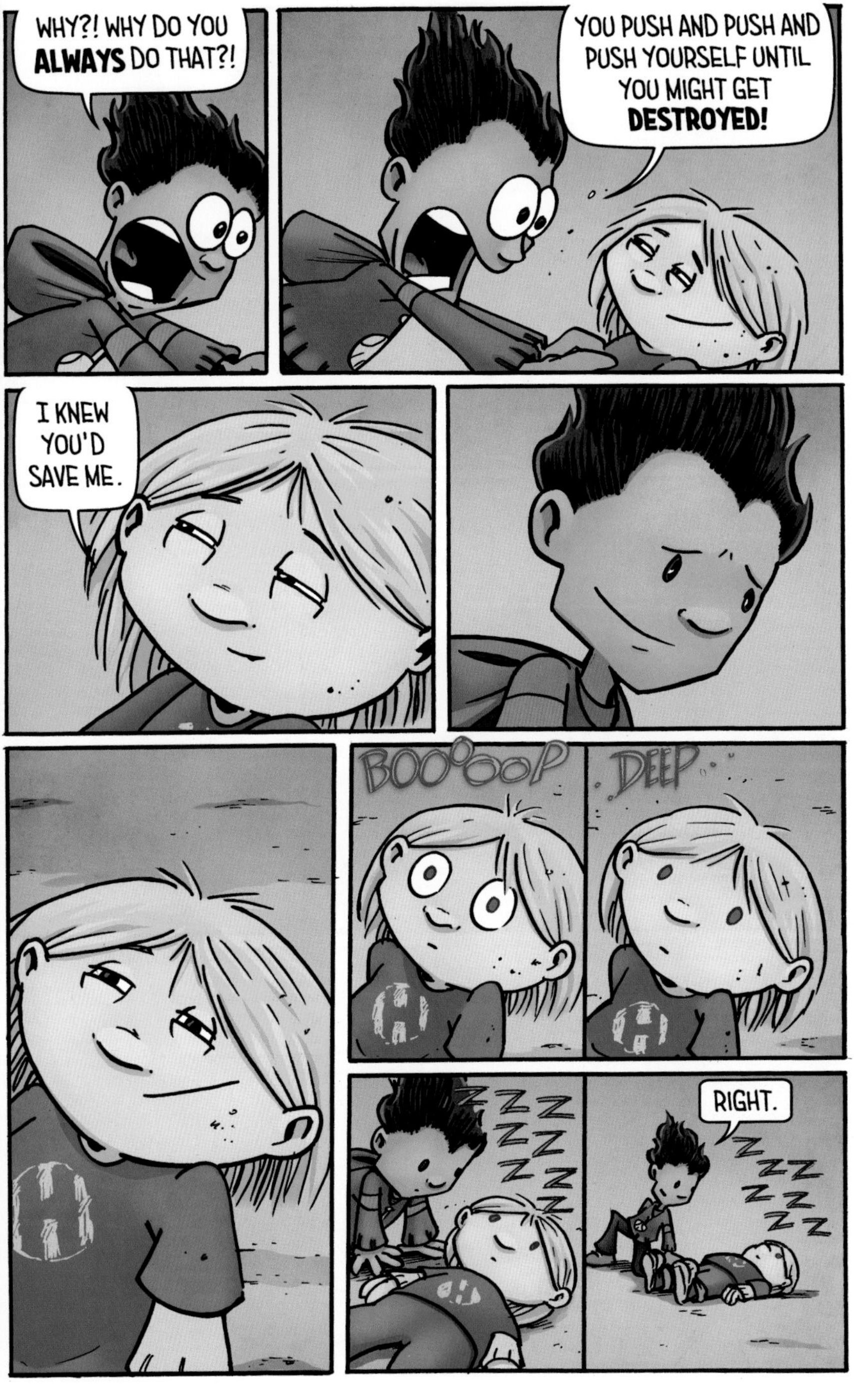
WHY?! WHY DO YOU **ALWAYS** DO THAT?!
YOU PUSH AND PUSH AND PUSH YOURSELF UNTIL YOU MIGHT GET **DESTROYED!**
I KNEW YOU'D SAVE ME.
BOOOOOP
DEEP
RIGHT.

A SEARCH OF EVERY PRIVATE PERSONAL COMPUTER, MEDICAL RECORD, SECURITY CAMERA, SCHOOLS --

CHECK **EVERY** FILE AND COMPUTER DATABASE ON **EARTH?**

THIS "BOY" FLIES, FIRES LASERS FROM HIS HANDS, AND -- OH YEAH --

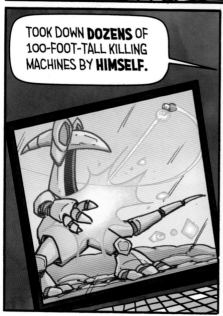

TOOK DOWN **DOZENS** OF 100-FOOT-TALL KILLING MACHINES BY **HIMSELF.**

HE'S AN ENTIRE **ARMY** IN SHORT PANTS.

WE'VE NEVER SEEN **ANYTHING** MORE DANGEROUS ...

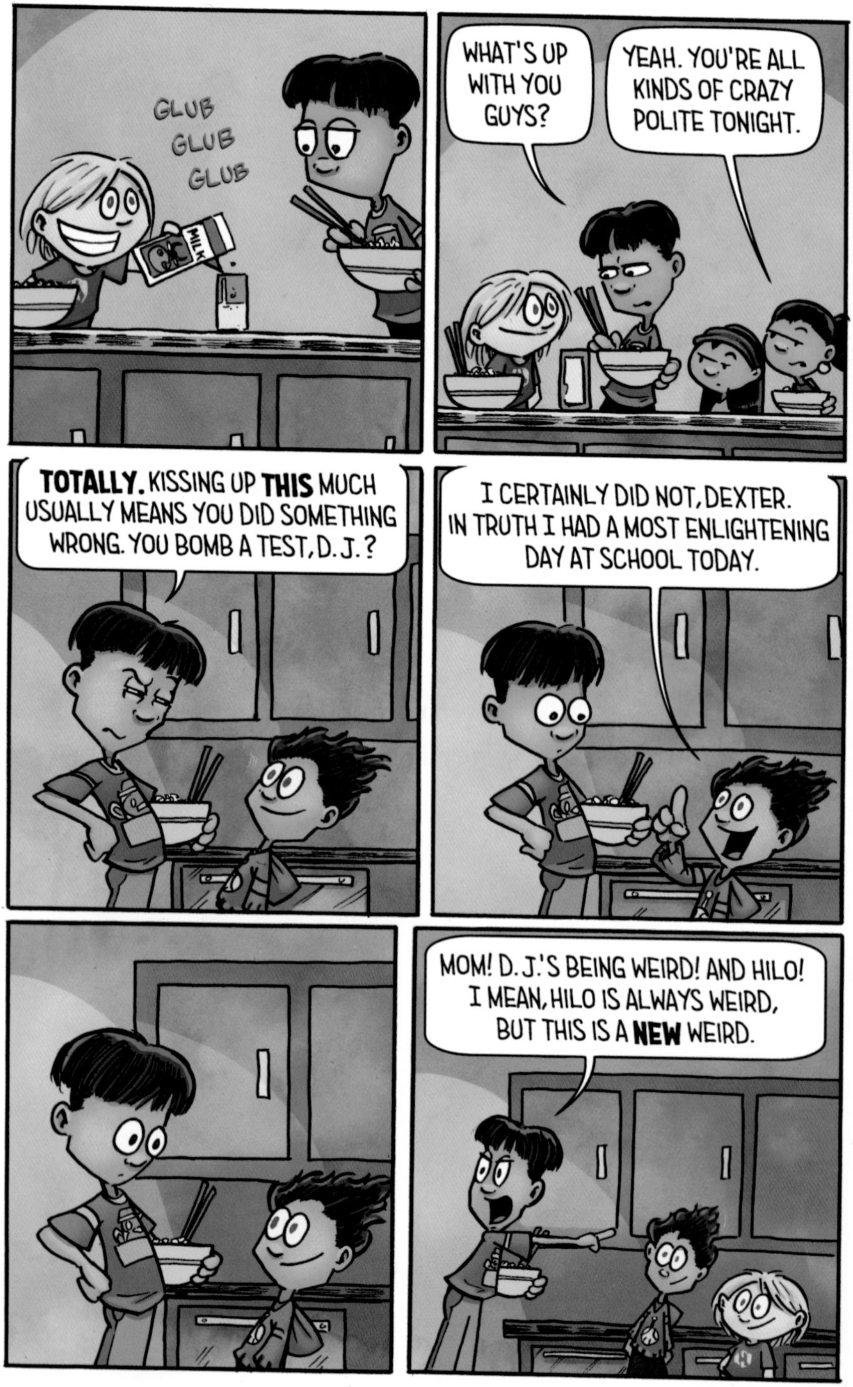
GLUB
GLUB
GLUB
MILK
WHAT'S UP WITH YOU GUYS?
YEAH. YOU'RE ALL KINDS OF CRAZY POLITE TONIGHT.
TOTALLY. KISSING UP THIS MUCH USUALLY MEANS YOU DID SOMETHING WRONG. YOU BOMB A TEST, D. J.?
I CERTAINLY DID NOT, DEXTER. IN TRUTH I HAD A MOST ENLIGHTENING DAY AT SCHOOL TODAY.
MOM! D. J.'S BEING WEIRD! AND HILO! I MEAN, HILO IS ALWAYS WEIRD, BUT THIS IS A NEW WEIRD.

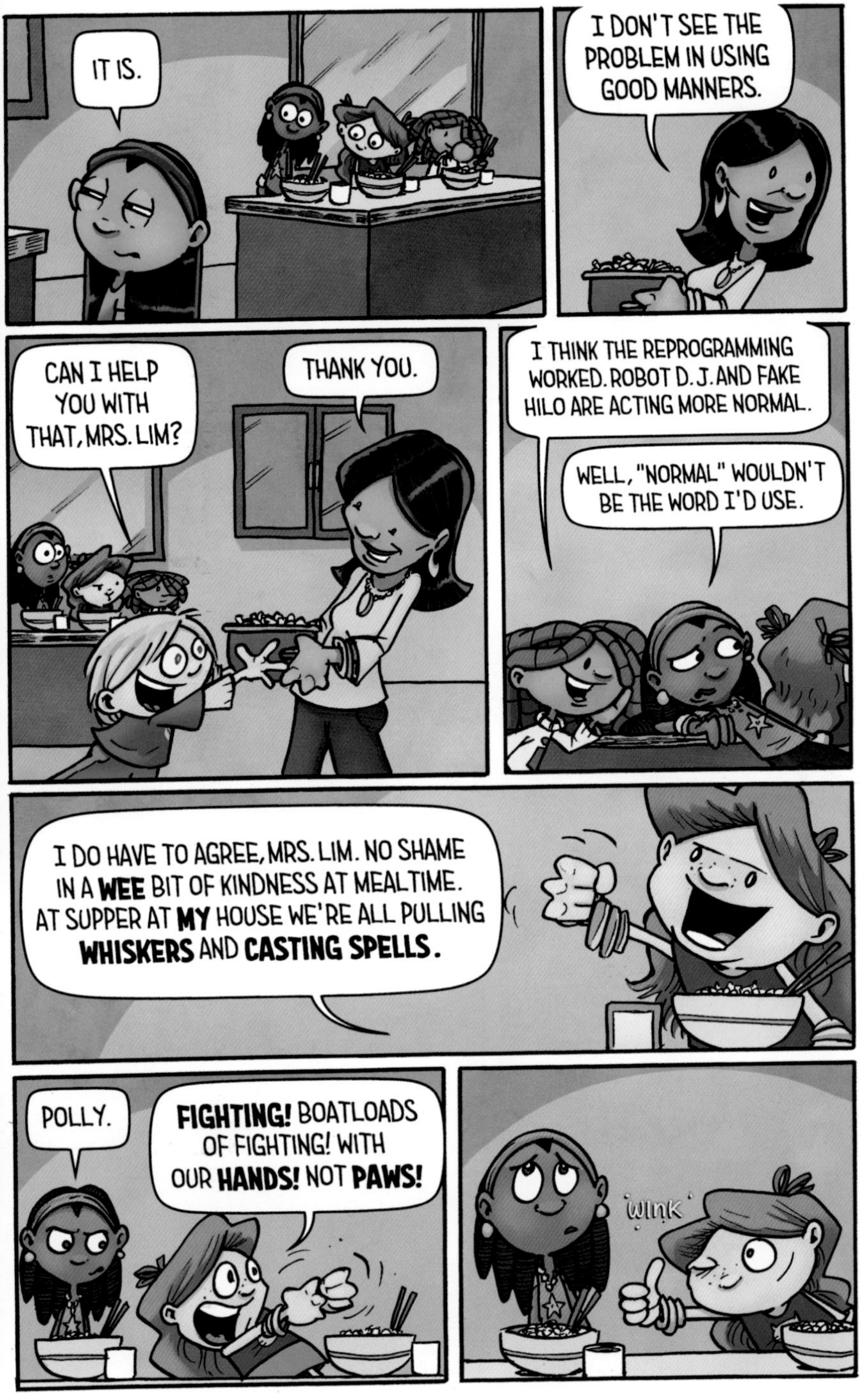
IT IS.
I DON'T SEE THE PROBLEM IN USING GOOD MANNERS.
CAN I HELP YOU WITH THAT, MRS. LIM?
THANK YOU.
I THINK THE REPROGRAMMING WORKED. ROBOT D. J. AND FAKE HILO ARE ACTING MORE NORMAL.
WELL, "NORMAL" WOULDN'T BE THE WORD I'D USE.
I DO HAVE TO AGREE, MRS. LIM. NO SHAME IN A WEE BIT OF KINDNESS AT MEALTIME. AT SUPPER AT MY HOUSE WE'RE ALL PULLING WHISKERS AND CASTING SPELLS.
POLLY.
FIGHTING! BOATLOADS OF FIGHTING! WITH OUR HANDS! NOT PAWS!
WINK

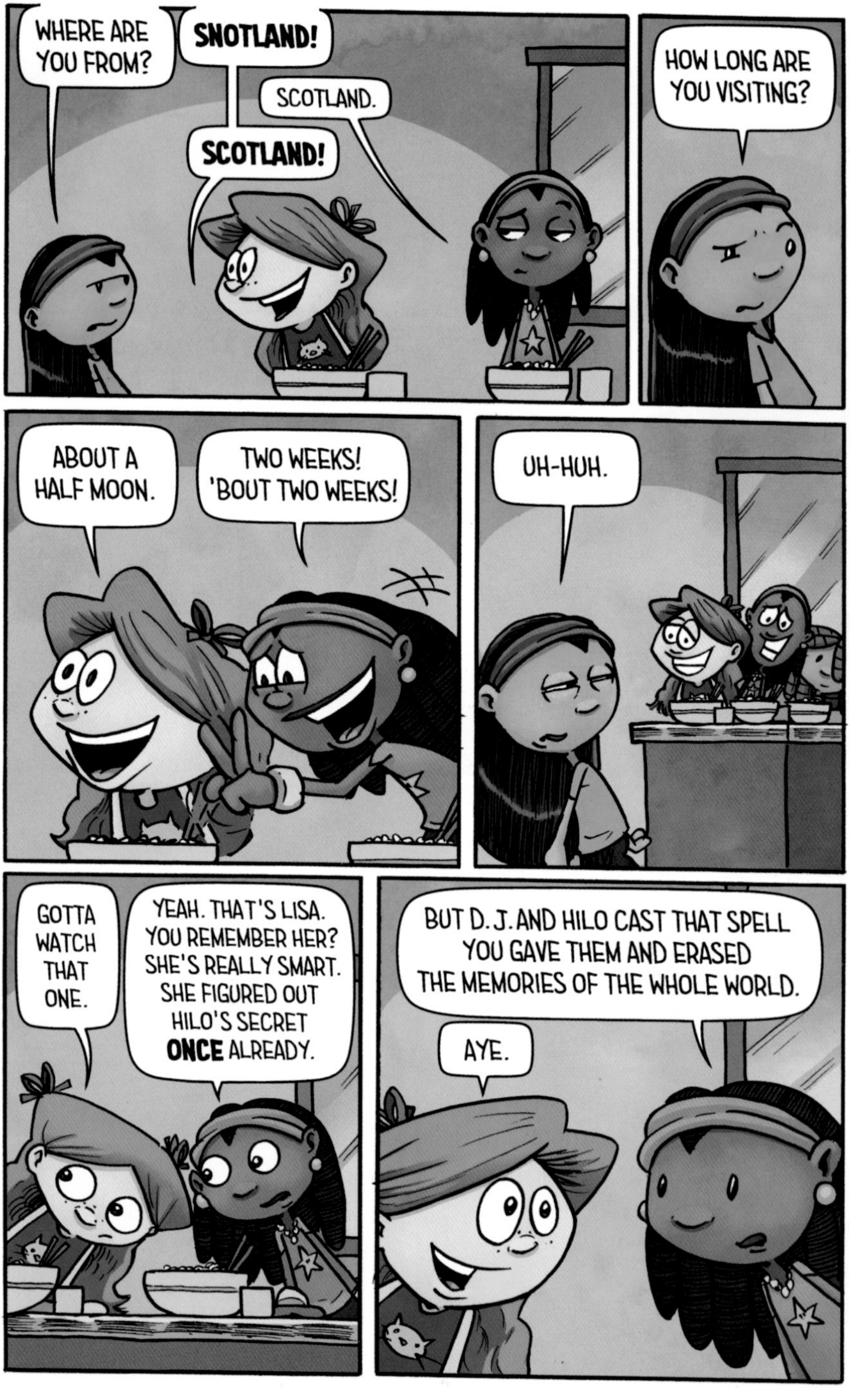
WHERE ARE YOU FROM?
SNOTLAND!
SCOTLAND.
SCOTLAND!
HOW LONG ARE YOU VISITING?
ABOUT A HALF MOON.
TWO WEEKS! 'BOUT TWO WEEKS!
UH-HUH.
GOTTA WATCH THAT ONE.
YEAH. THAT'S LISA. YOU REMEMBER HER? SHE'S REALLY SMART. SHE FIGURED OUT HILO'S SECRET **ONCE** ALREADY.
BUT D. J. AND HILO CAST THAT SPELL YOU GAVE THEM AND ERASED THE MEMORIES OF THE WHOLE WORLD.
AYE.

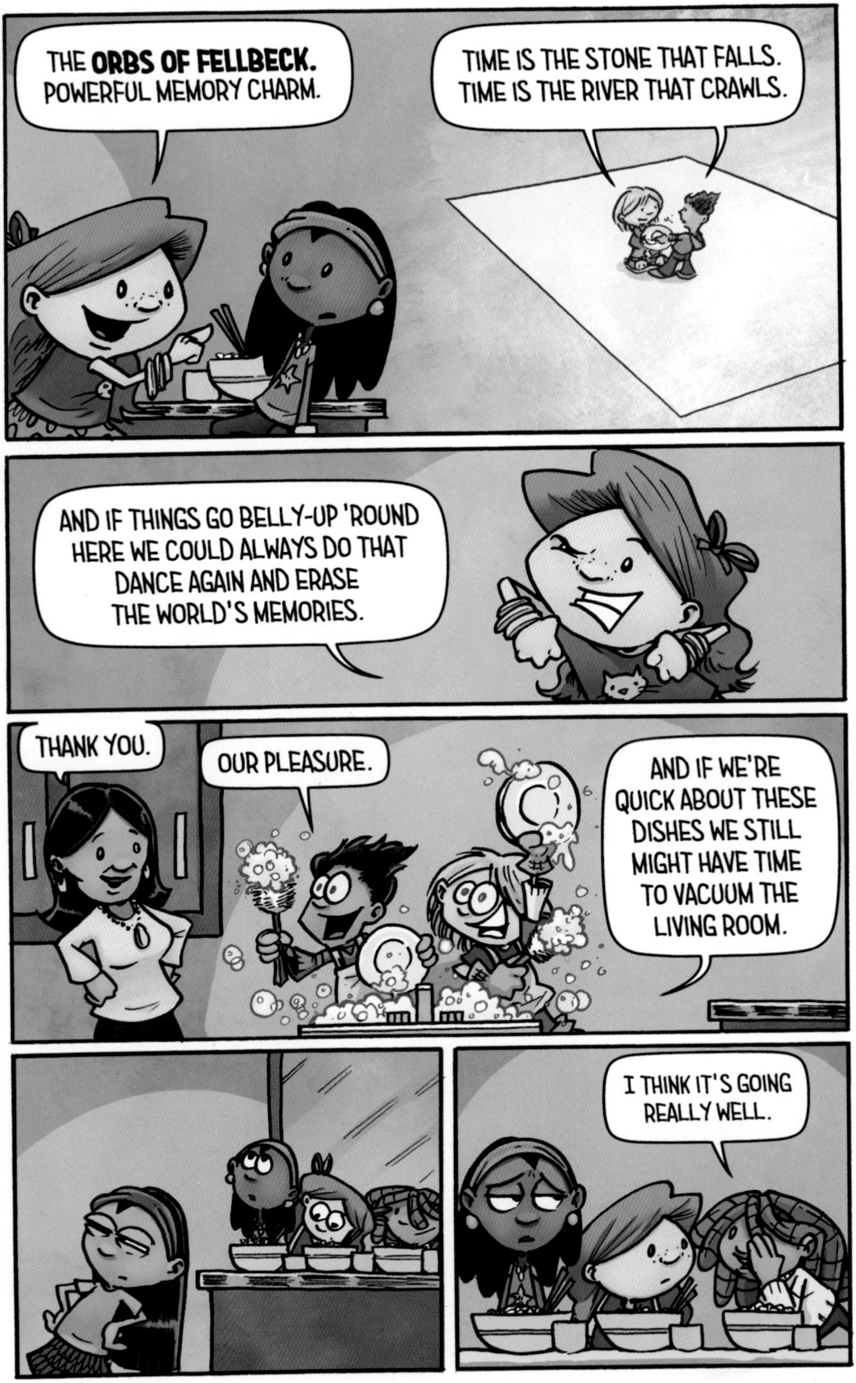
THE **ORBS OF FELLBECK.** POWERFUL MEMORY CHARM.
TIME IS THE STONE THAT FALLS. TIME IS THE RIVER THAT CRAWLS.
AND IF THINGS GO BELLY-UP 'ROUND HERE WE COULD ALWAYS DO THAT DANCE AGAIN AND ERASE THE WORLD'S MEMORIES.
THANK YOU.
OUR PLEASURE.
AND IF WE'RE QUICK ABOUT THESE DISHES WE STILL MIGHT HAVE TIME TO VACUUM THE LIVING ROOM.
I THINK IT'S GOING REALLY WELL.

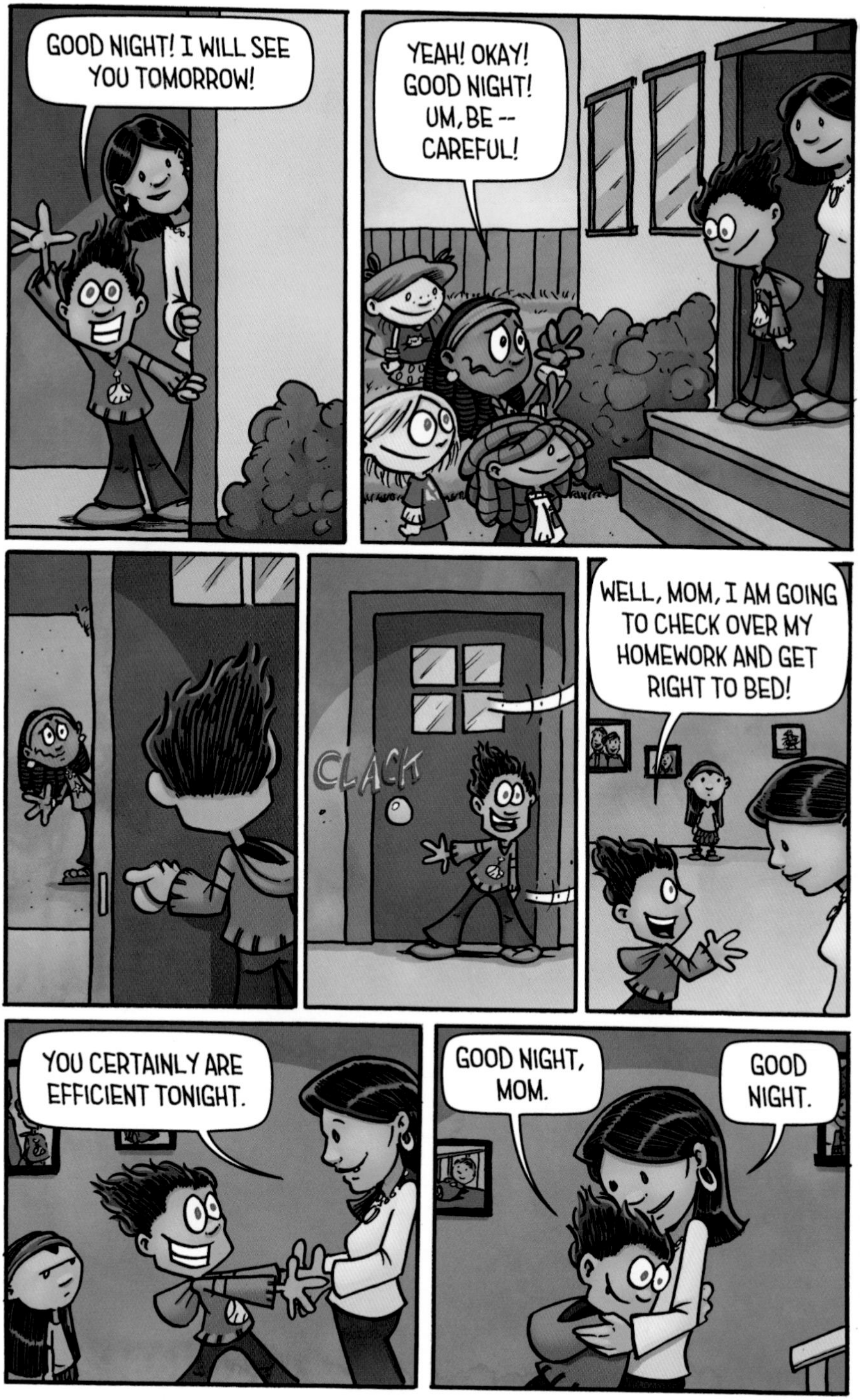
GOOD NIGHT! I WILL SEE YOU TOMORROW!
YEAH! OKAY! GOOD NIGHT! UM, BE -- CAREFUL!
CLACK
WELL, MOM, I AM GOING TO CHECK OVER MY HOMEWORK AND GET RIGHT TO BED!
YOU CERTAINLY ARE EFFICIENT TONIGHT.
GOOD NIGHT, MOM.
GOOD NIGHT.

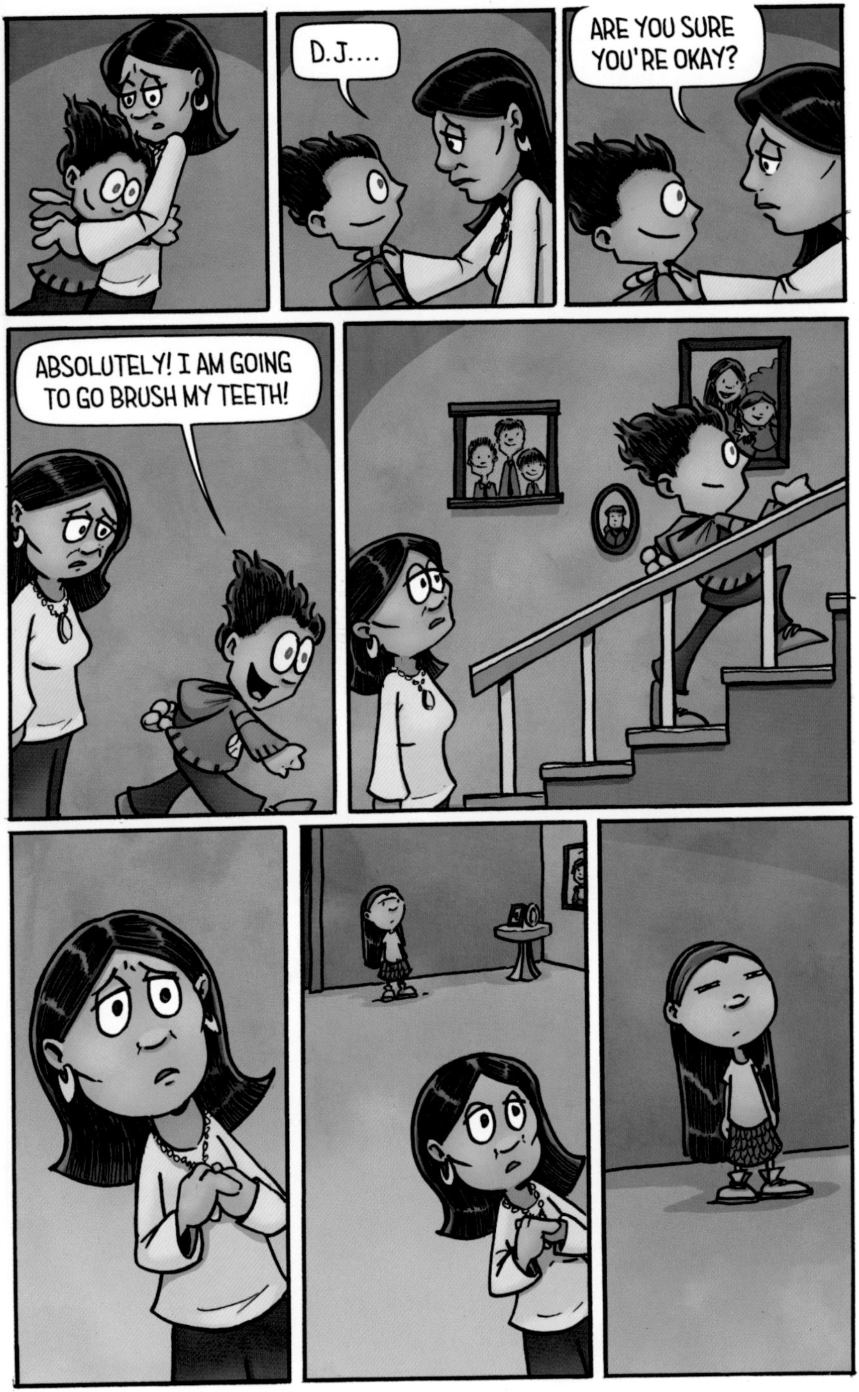

D.J....
ARE YOU SURE YOU'RE OKAY?
ABSOLUTELY! I AM GOING TO GO BRUSH MY TEETH!

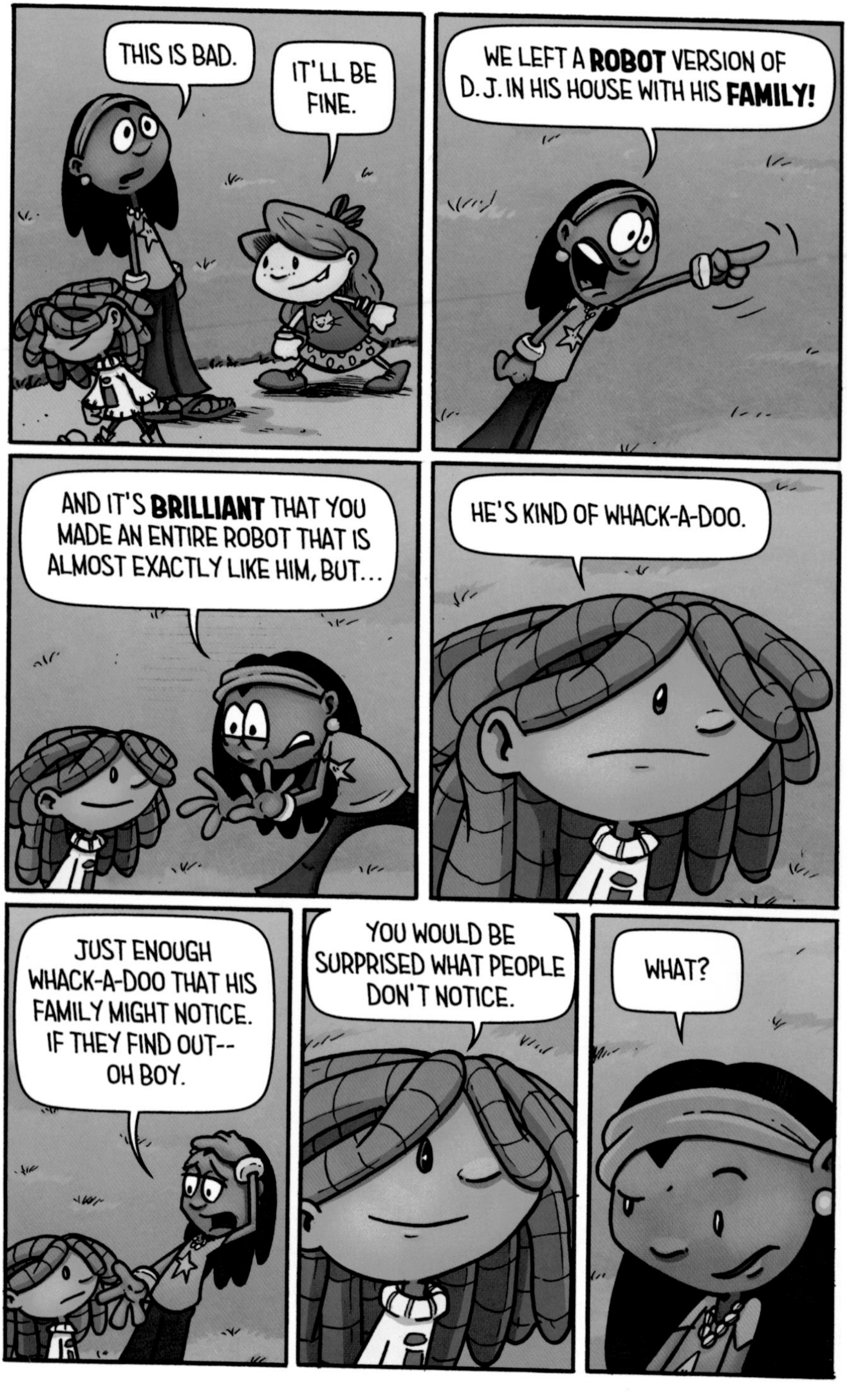
THIS IS BAD.
IT'LL BE FINE.
WE LEFT A **ROBOT** VERSION OF D.J. IN HIS HOUSE WITH HIS **FAMILY!**
AND IT'S **BRILLIANT** THAT YOU MADE AN ENTIRE ROBOT THAT IS ALMOST EXACTLY LIKE HIM, BUT...
HE'S KIND OF WHACK-A-DOO.
JUST ENOUGH WHACK-A-DOO THAT HIS FAMILY MIGHT NOTICE. IF THEY FIND OUT-- OH BOY.
YOU WOULD BE SURPRISED WHAT PEOPLE DON'T NOTICE.
WHAT?

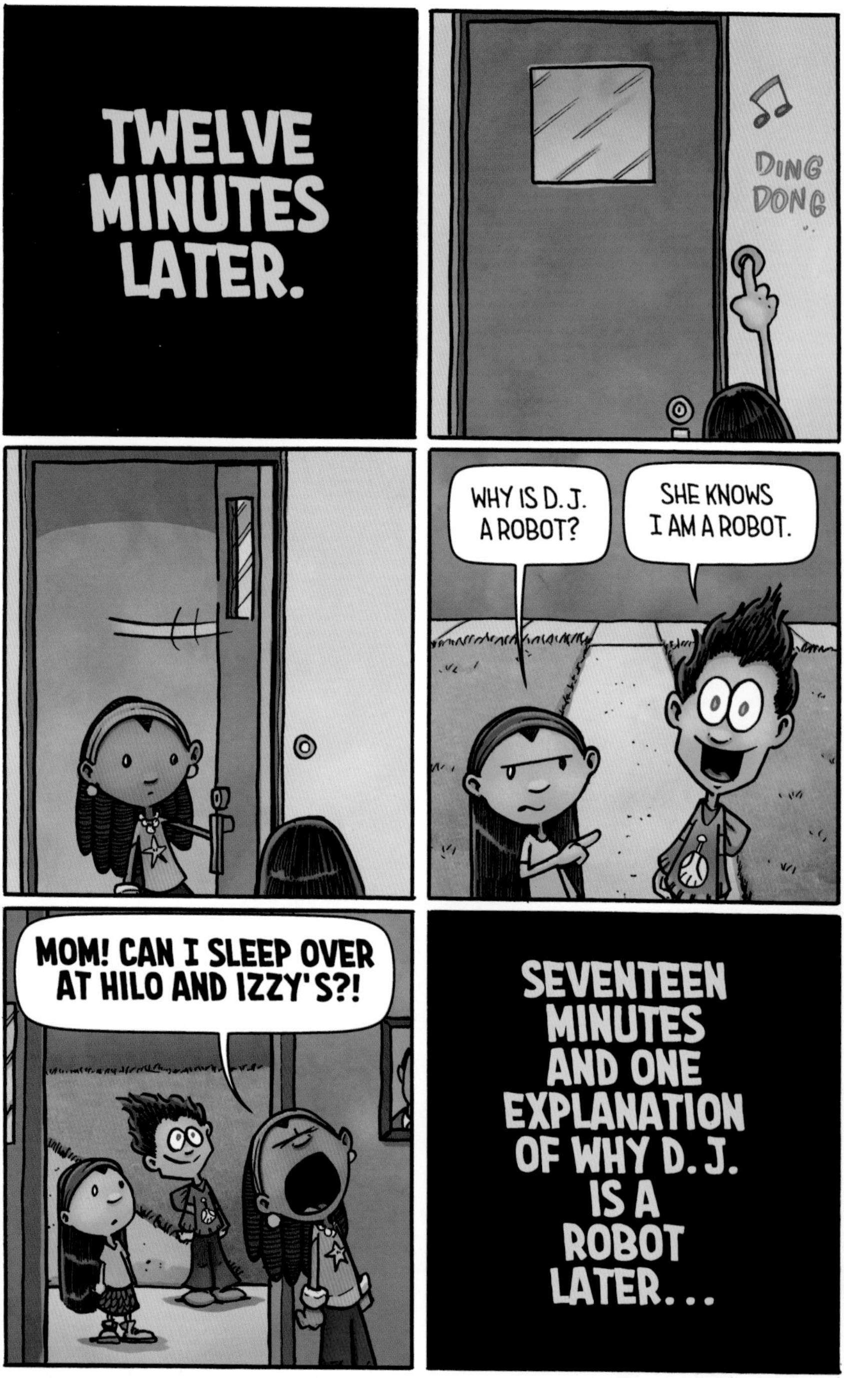
TWELVE MINUTES LATER.
DING DONG
WHY IS D. J. A ROBOT?
SHE KNOWS I AM A ROBOT.
MOM! CAN I SLEEP OVER AT HILO AND IZZY'S?!
SEVENTEEN MINUTES AND ONE EXPLANATION OF WHY D. J. IS A ROBOT LATER. . .

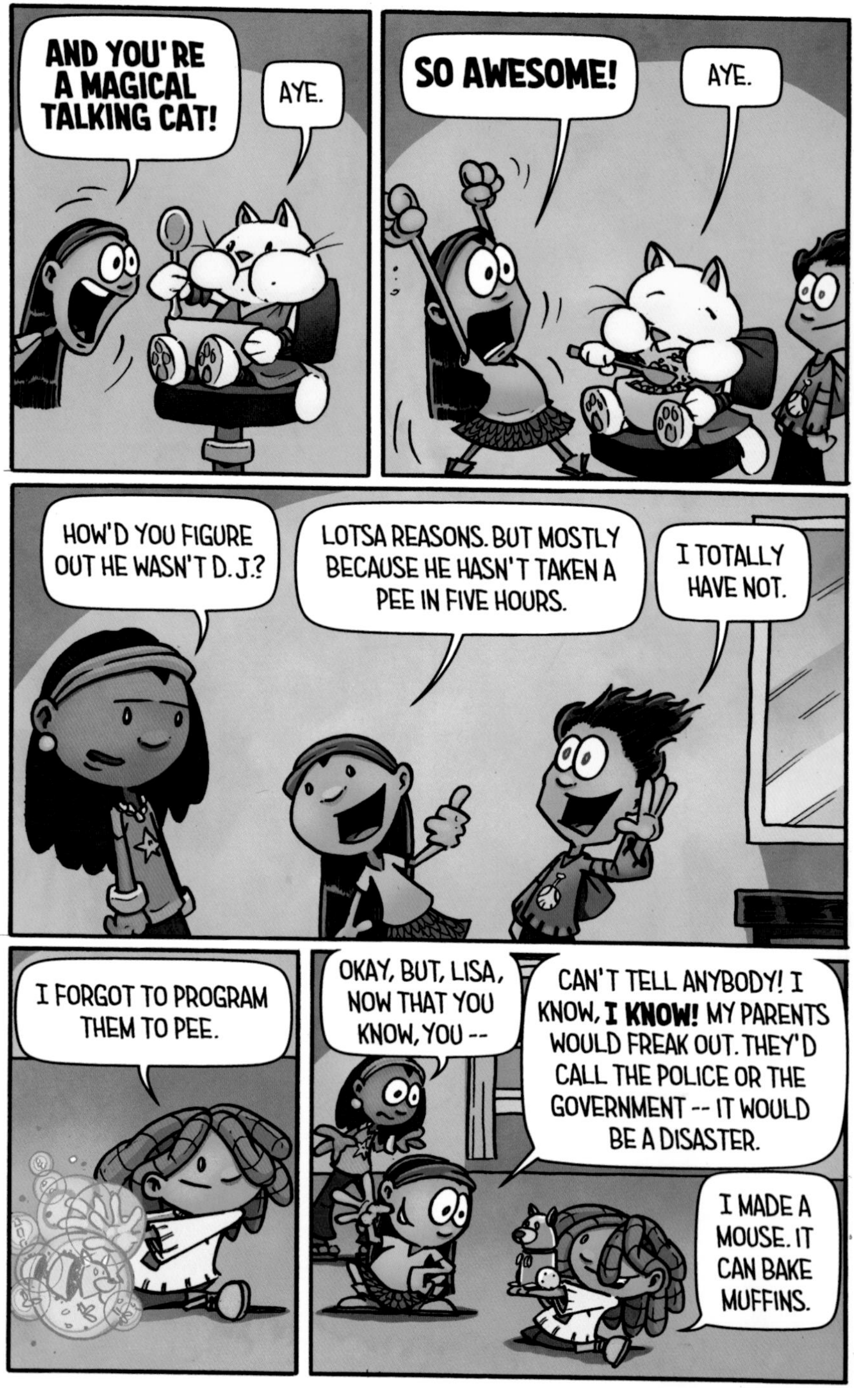
AND YOU'RE A MAGICAL TALKING CAT!
AYE.
SO AWESOME!
AYE.
HOW'D YOU FIGURE OUT HE WASN'T D.J.?
LOTSA REASONS. BUT MOSTLY BECAUSE HE HASN'T TAKEN A PEE IN FIVE HOURS.
I TOTALLY HAVE NOT.
I FORGOT TO PROGRAM THEM TO PEE.
OKAY, BUT, LISA, NOW THAT YOU KNOW, YOU --
CAN'T TELL ANYBODY! I KNOW, **I KNOW!** MY PARENTS WOULD FREAK OUT. THEY'D CALL THE POLICE OR THE GOVERNMENT -- IT WOULD BE A DISASTER.
I MADE A MOUSE. IT CAN BAKE MUFFINS.

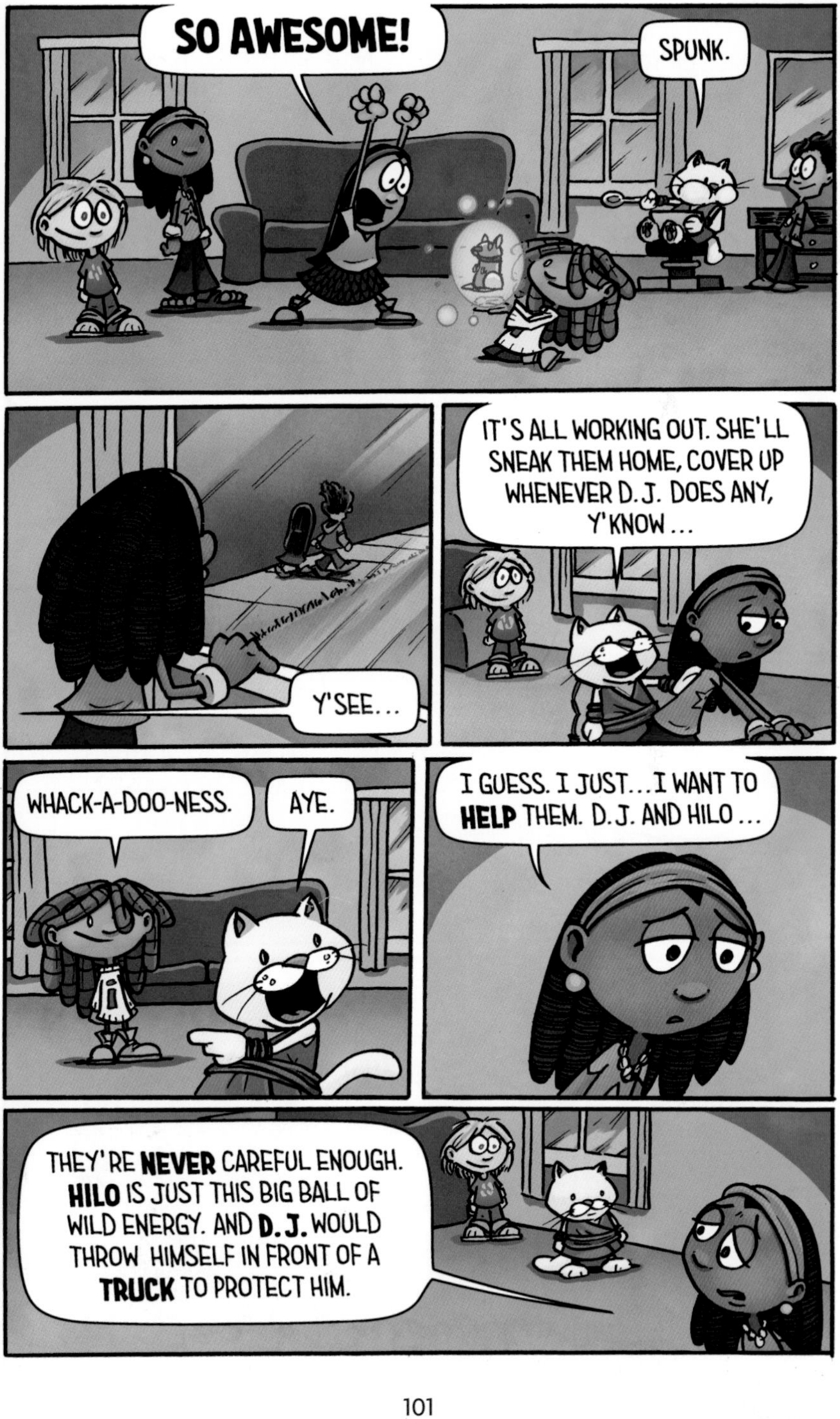
SO AWESOME!
SPUNK.
Y'SEE...
IT'S ALL WORKING OUT. SHE'LL SNEAK THEM HOME, COVER UP WHENEVER D. J. DOES ANY, Y'KNOW ...
WHACK-A-DOO-NESS.
AYE.
I GUESS. I JUST... I WANT TO HELP THEM. D. J. AND HILO ...
THEY'RE NEVER CAREFUL ENOUGH. HILO IS JUST THIS BIG BALL OF WILD ENERGY. AND D. J. WOULD THROW HIMSELF IN FRONT OF A TRUCK TO PROTECT HIM.

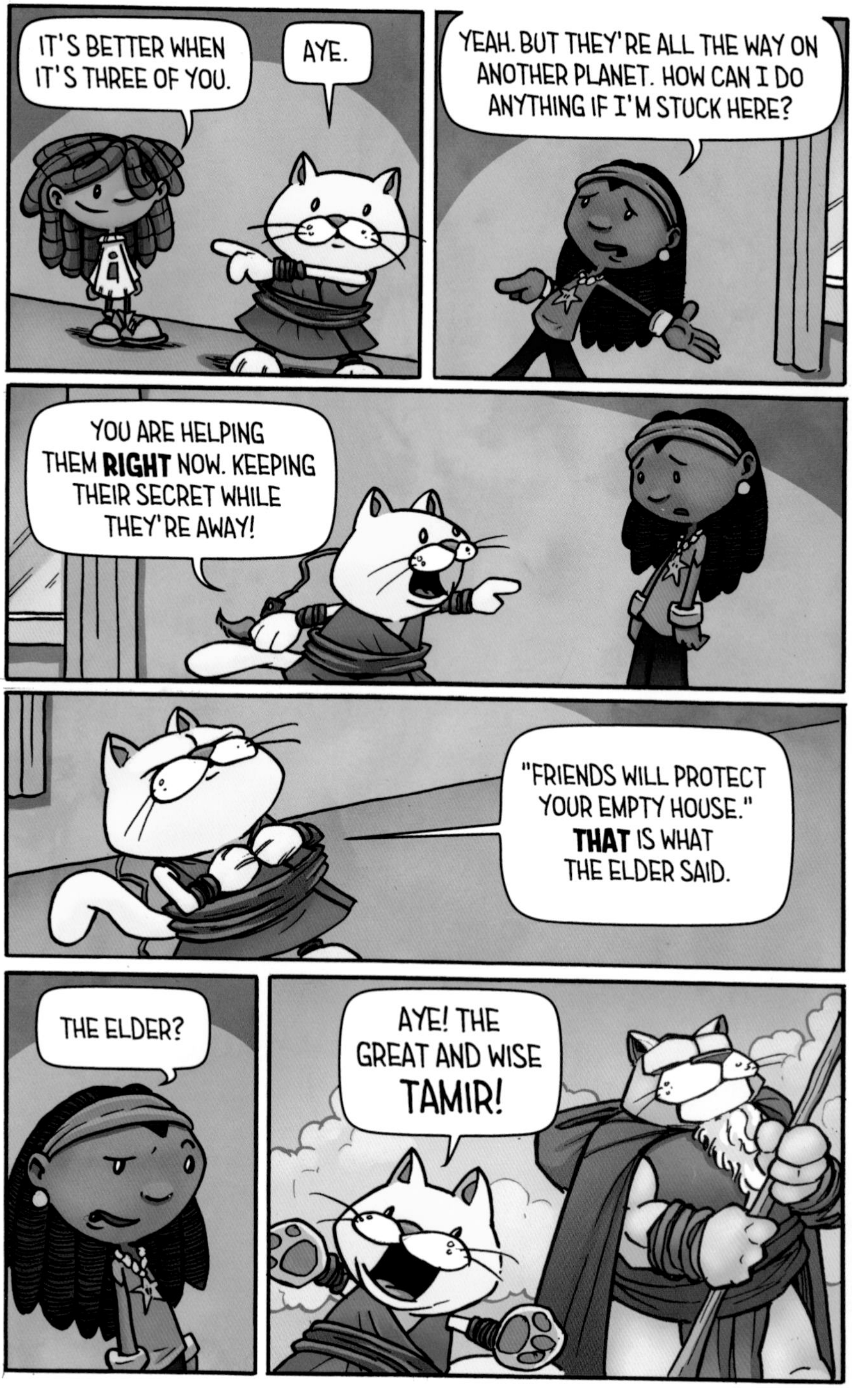
IT'S BETTER WHEN IT'S THREE OF YOU.
AYE.
YEAH. BUT THEY'RE ALL THE WAY ON ANOTHER PLANET. HOW CAN I DO ANYTHING IF I'M STUCK HERE?
YOU ARE HELPING THEM **RIGHT** NOW. KEEPING THEIR SECRET WHILE THEY'RE AWAY!
"FRIENDS WILL PROTECT YOUR EMPTY HOUSE." **THAT** IS WHAT THE ELDER SAID.
THE ELDER?
AYE! THE GREAT AND WISE **TAMIR!**

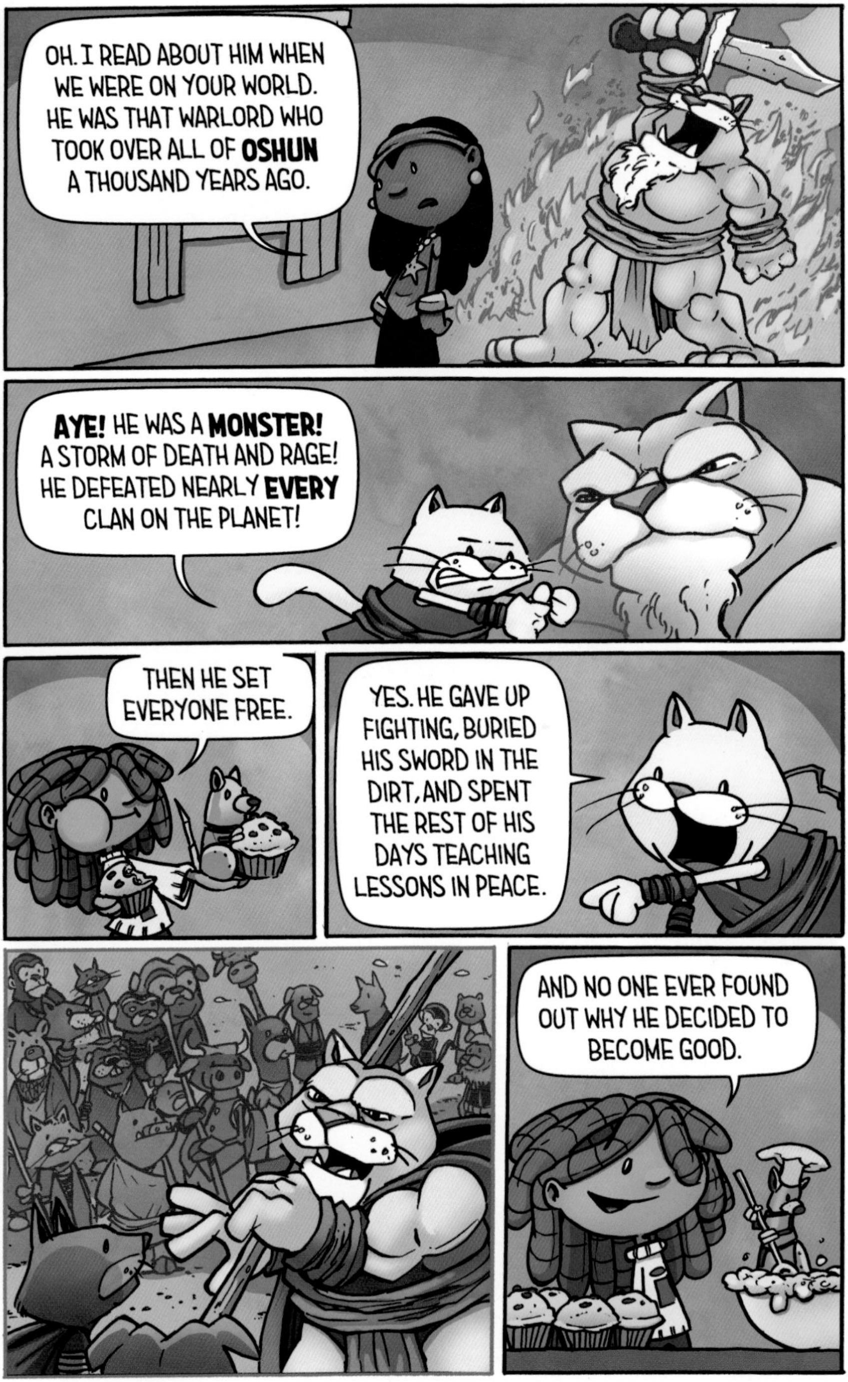
OH. I READ ABOUT HIM WHEN WE WERE ON YOUR WORLD. HE WAS THAT WARLORD WHO TOOK OVER ALL OF OSHUN A THOUSAND YEARS AGO.
AYE! HE WAS A MONSTER! A STORM OF DEATH AND RAGE! HE DEFEATED NEARLY EVERY CLAN ON THE PLANET!
THEN HE SET EVERYONE FREE.
YES. HE GAVE UP FIGHTING, BURIED HIS SWORD IN THE DIRT, AND SPENT THE REST OF HIS DAYS TEACHING LESSONS IN PEACE.
AND NO ONE EVER FOUND OUT WHY HE DECIDED TO BECOME GOOD.

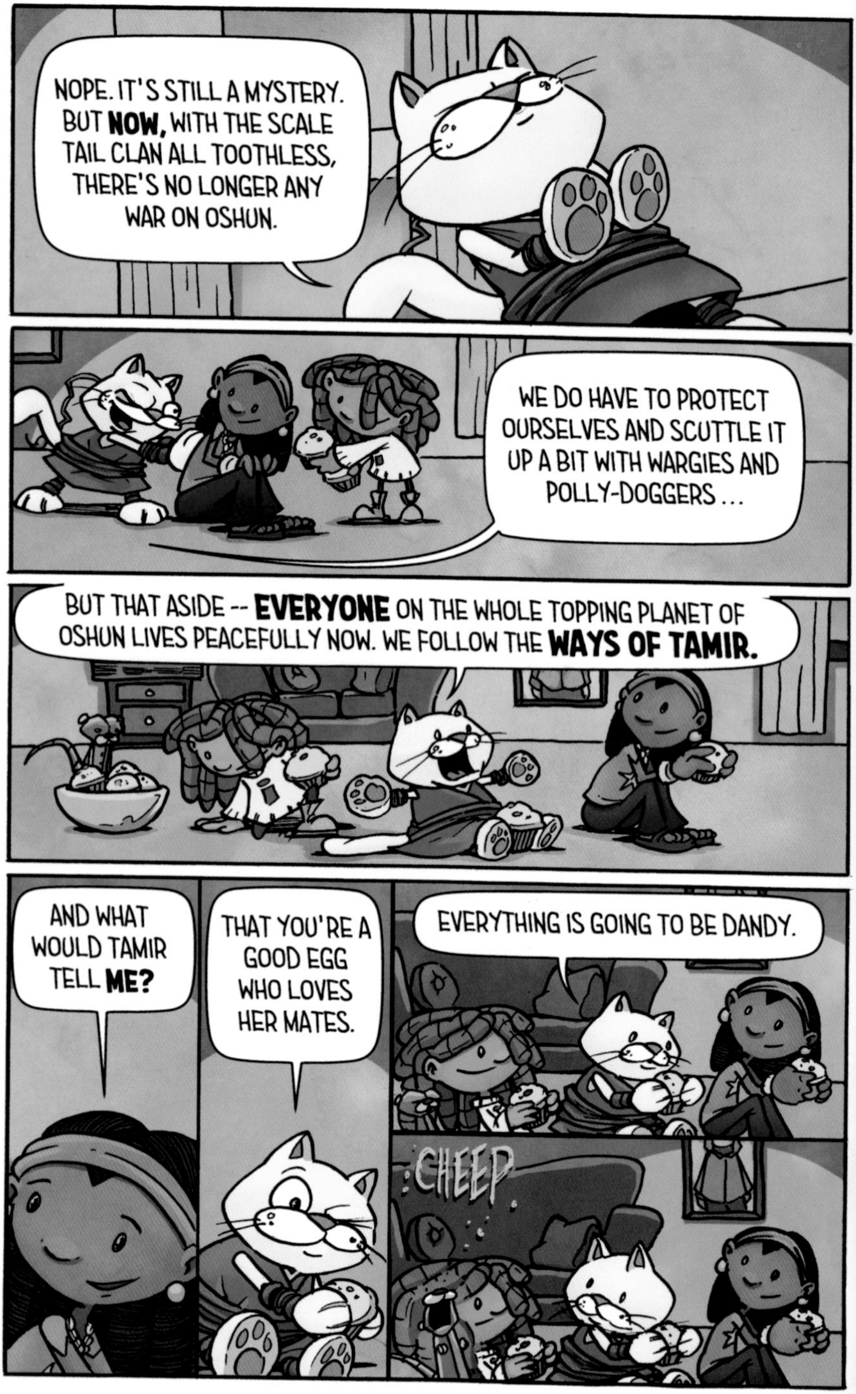

NOPE. IT'S STILL A MYSTERY. BUT NOW, WITH THE SCALE TAIL CLAN ALL TOOTHLESS, THERE'S NO LONGER ANY WAR ON OSHUN.
WE DO HAVE TO PROTECT OURSELVES AND SCUTTLE IT UP A BIT WITH WARGIES AND POLLY-DOGGERS ...
BUT THAT ASIDE -- EVERYONE ON THE WHOLE TOPPING PLANET OF OSHUN LIVES PEACEFULLY NOW. WE FOLLOW THE WAYS OF TAMIR.
AND WHAT WOULD TAMIR TELL ME?
THAT YOU'RE A GOOD EGG WHO LOVES HER MATES.
EVERYTHING IS GOING TO BE DANDY.
CHEEP

CHAPTER 7

DANDY

JANNUS.
SO IT GOES
TOUGH COOKIES

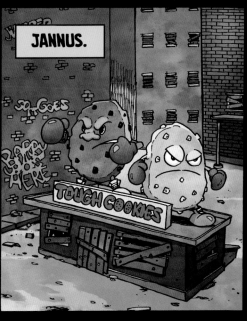

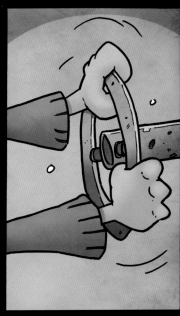

106

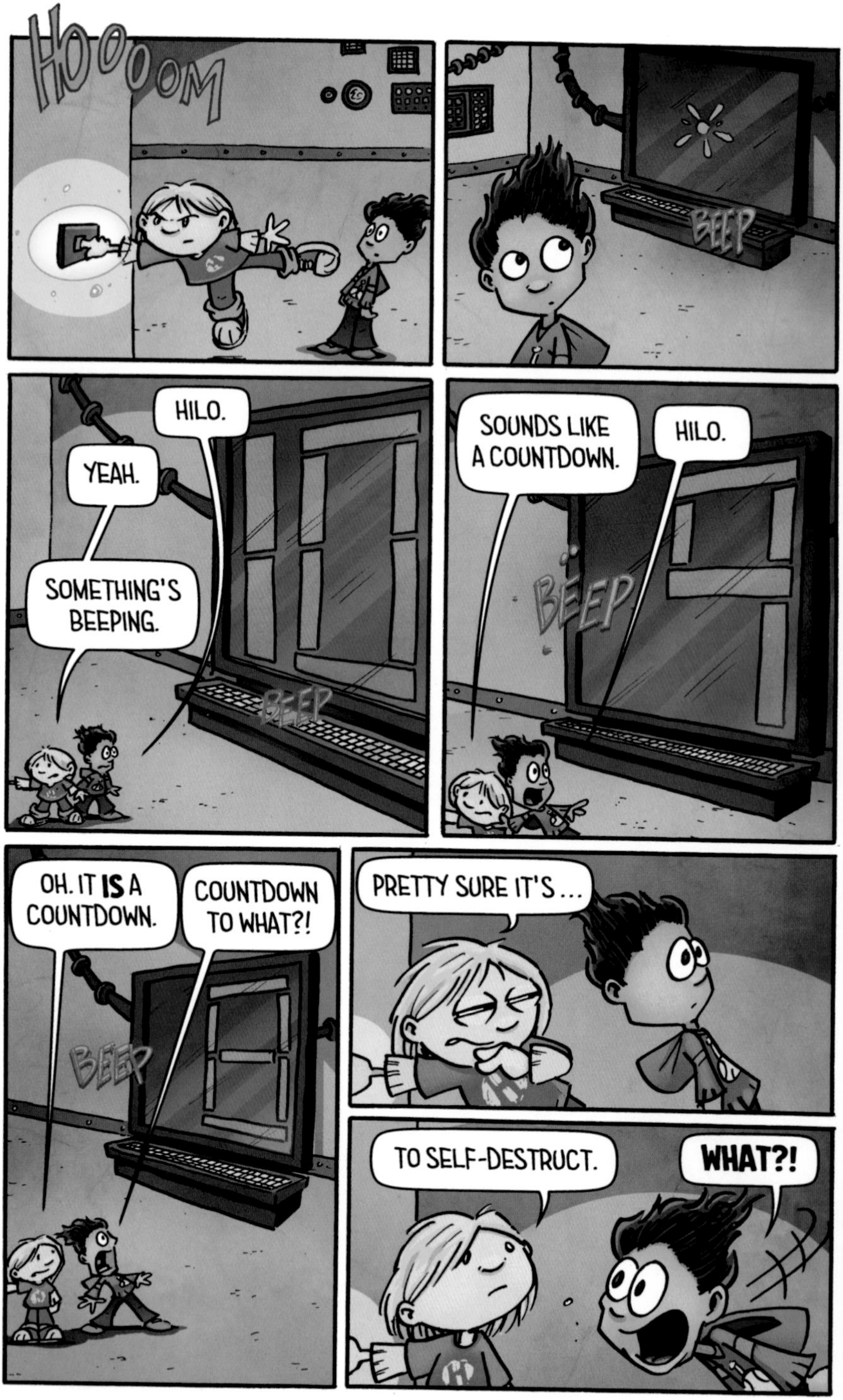
HOOOOM
BEEP
HILO.
YEAH.
SOMETHING'S BEEPING.
BEEP
SOUNDS LIKE A COUNTDOWN.
HILO.
BEEP
OH. IT **IS** A COUNTDOWN.
COUNTDOWN TO WHAT?!
BEEP
PRETTY SURE IT'S . . .
TO SELF-DESTRUCT.
WHAT?!

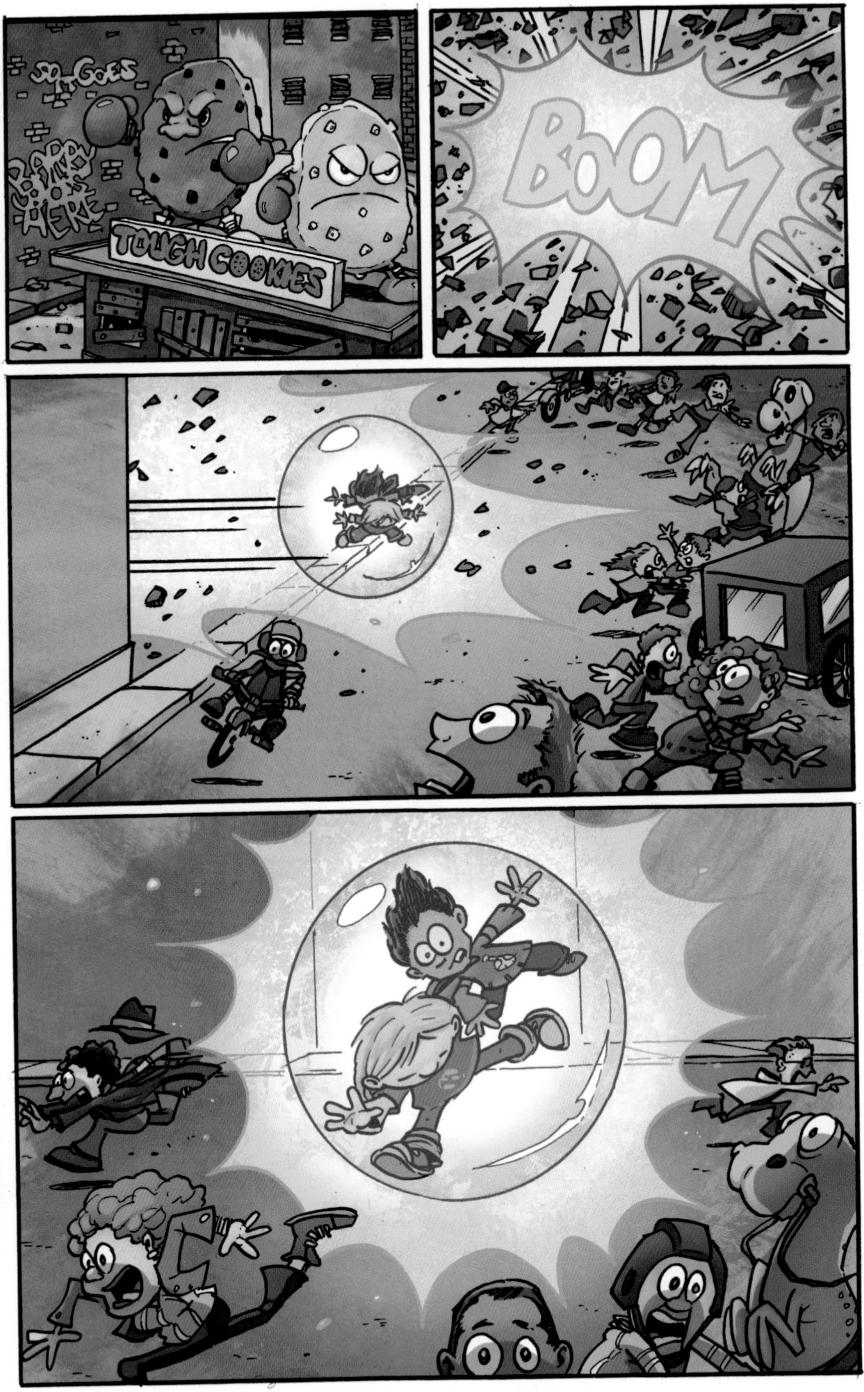
TOUGH COOKIES
BOOM

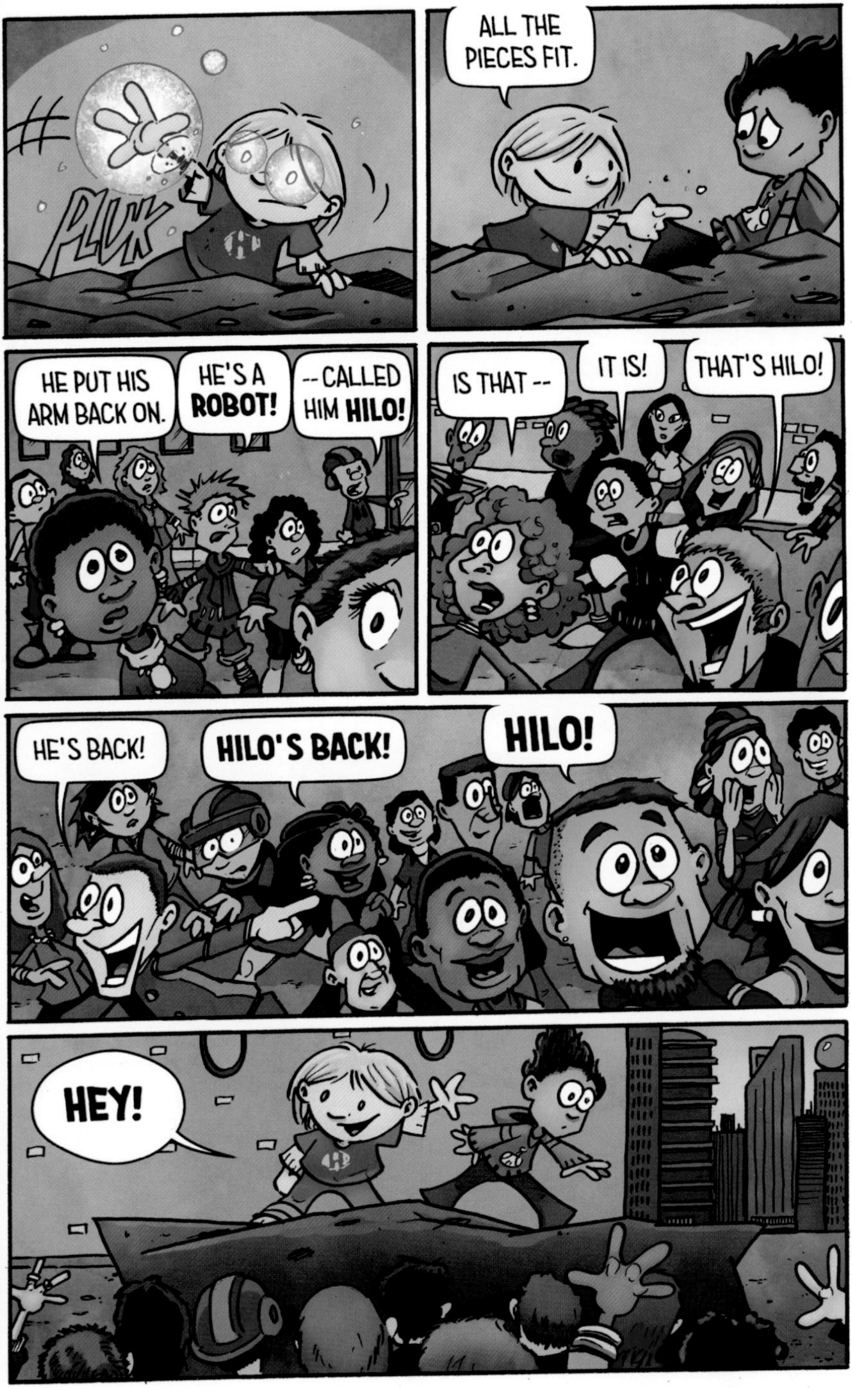
PLUK
ALL THE PIECES FIT.
HE PUT HIS ARM BACK ON.
HE'S A ROBOT!
-- CALLED HIM HILO!
IS THAT --
IT IS!
THAT'S HILO!
HE'S BACK!
HILO'S BACK!
HILO!
HEY!

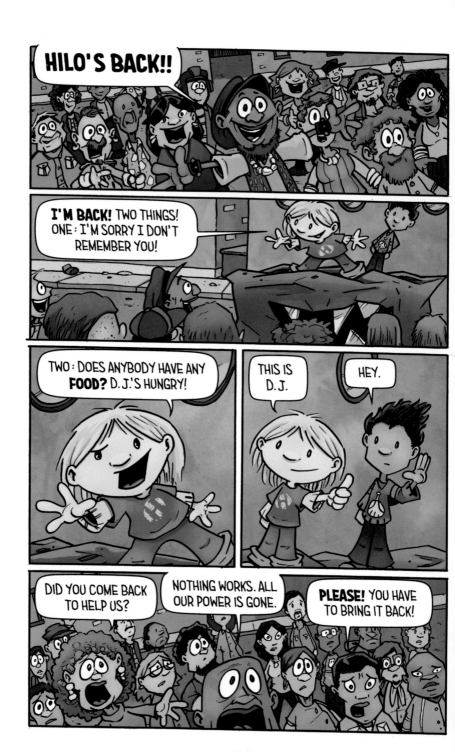

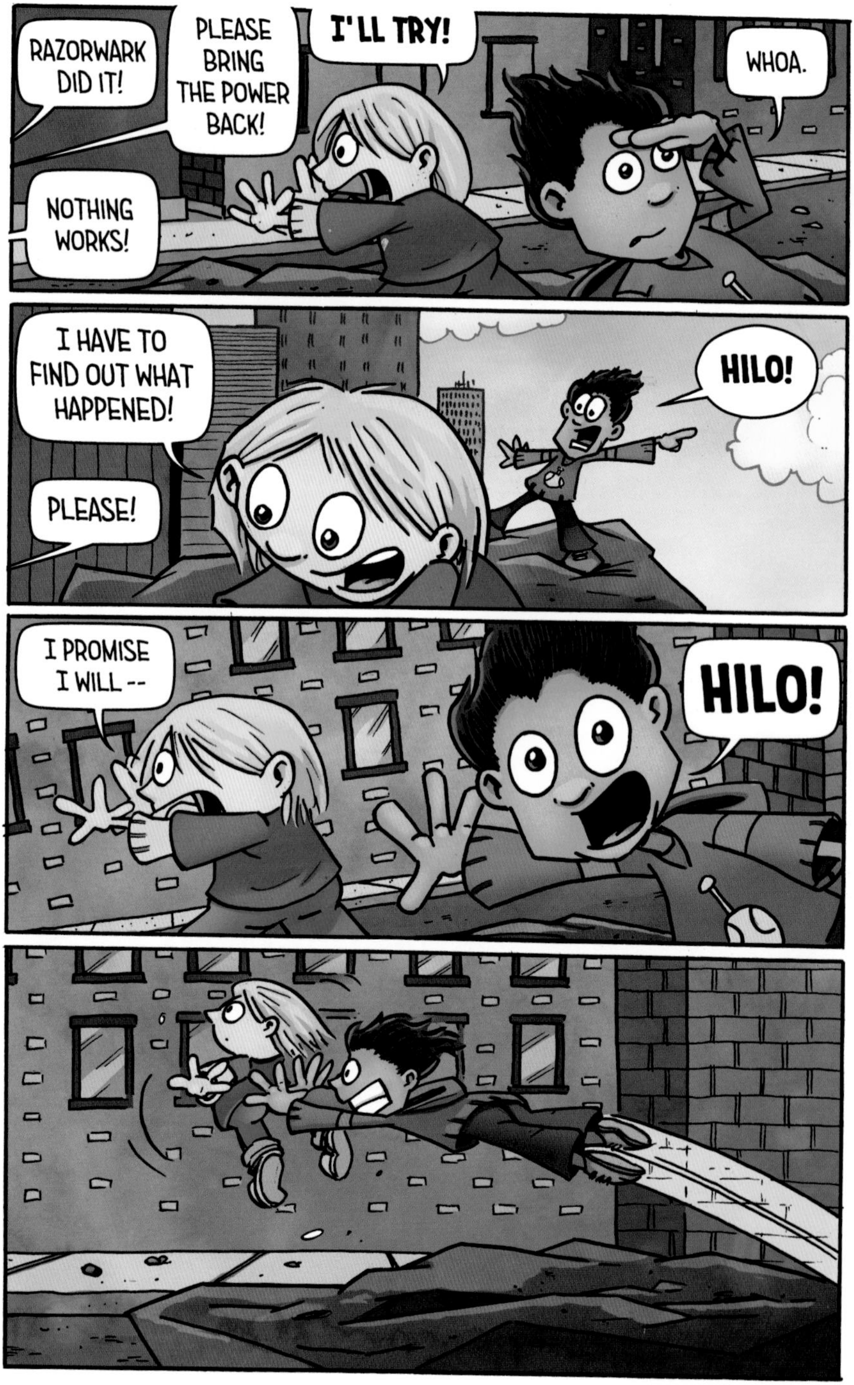
RAZORWARK DID IT!
NOTHING WORKS!
PLEASE BRING THE POWER BACK!
I'LL TRY!
WHOA.
I HAVE TO FIND OUT WHAT HAPPENED!
PLEASE!
HILO!
I PROMISE I WILL --
HILO!

CHAPTER 8

PERMANENT RECORD

HILO'S HOUSE.
HELLO THERE!
HOW ARE YOU?

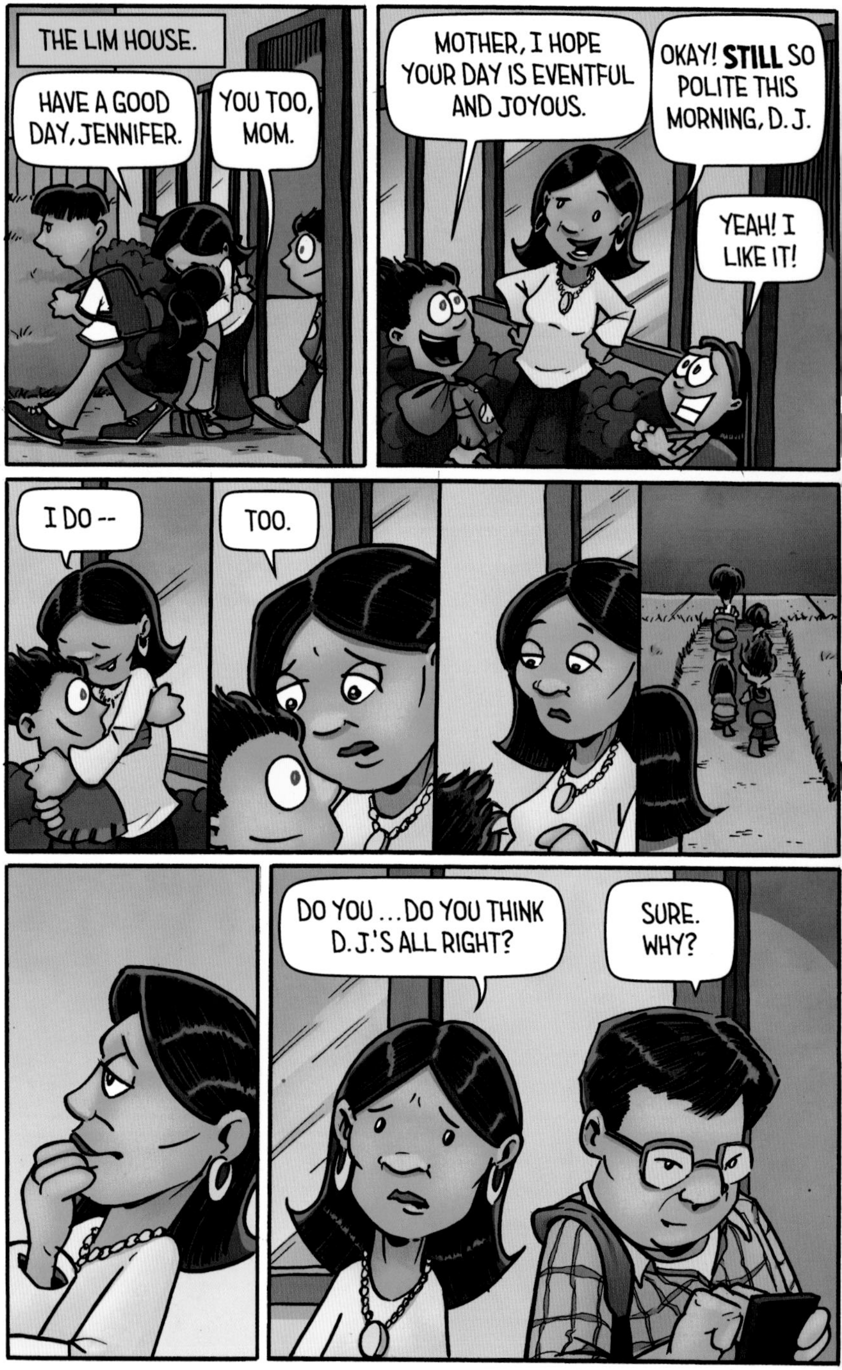
THE LIM HOUSE.
HAVE A GOOD DAY, JENNIFER.
YOU TOO, MOM.
MOTHER, I HOPE YOUR DAY IS EVENTFUL AND JOYOUS.
OKAY! **STILL** SO POLITE THIS MORNING, D. J.
YEAH! I LIKE IT!
I DO --
TOO.
DO YOU ... DO YOU THINK D. J.'S ALL RIGHT?
SURE. WHY?

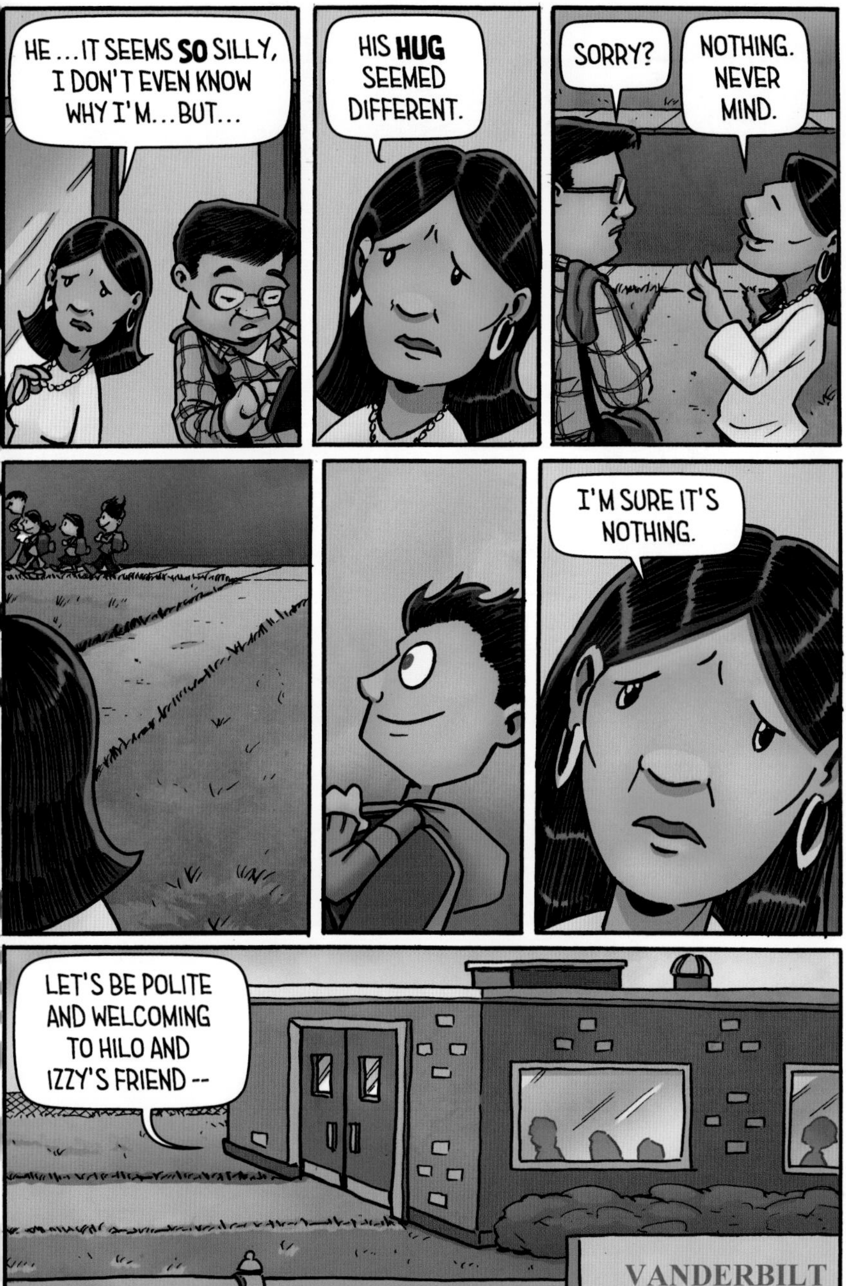
HE . . . IT SEEMS **SO** SILLY, I DON'T EVEN KNOW WHY I'M. . . BUT. . .
HIS **HUG** SEEMED DIFFERENT.
SORRY?
NOTHING. NEVER MIND.
I'M SURE IT'S NOTHING.
LET'S BE POLITE AND WELCOMING TO HILO AND IZZY'S FRIEND --
VANDERBILT ELEMENTARY SCHOOL

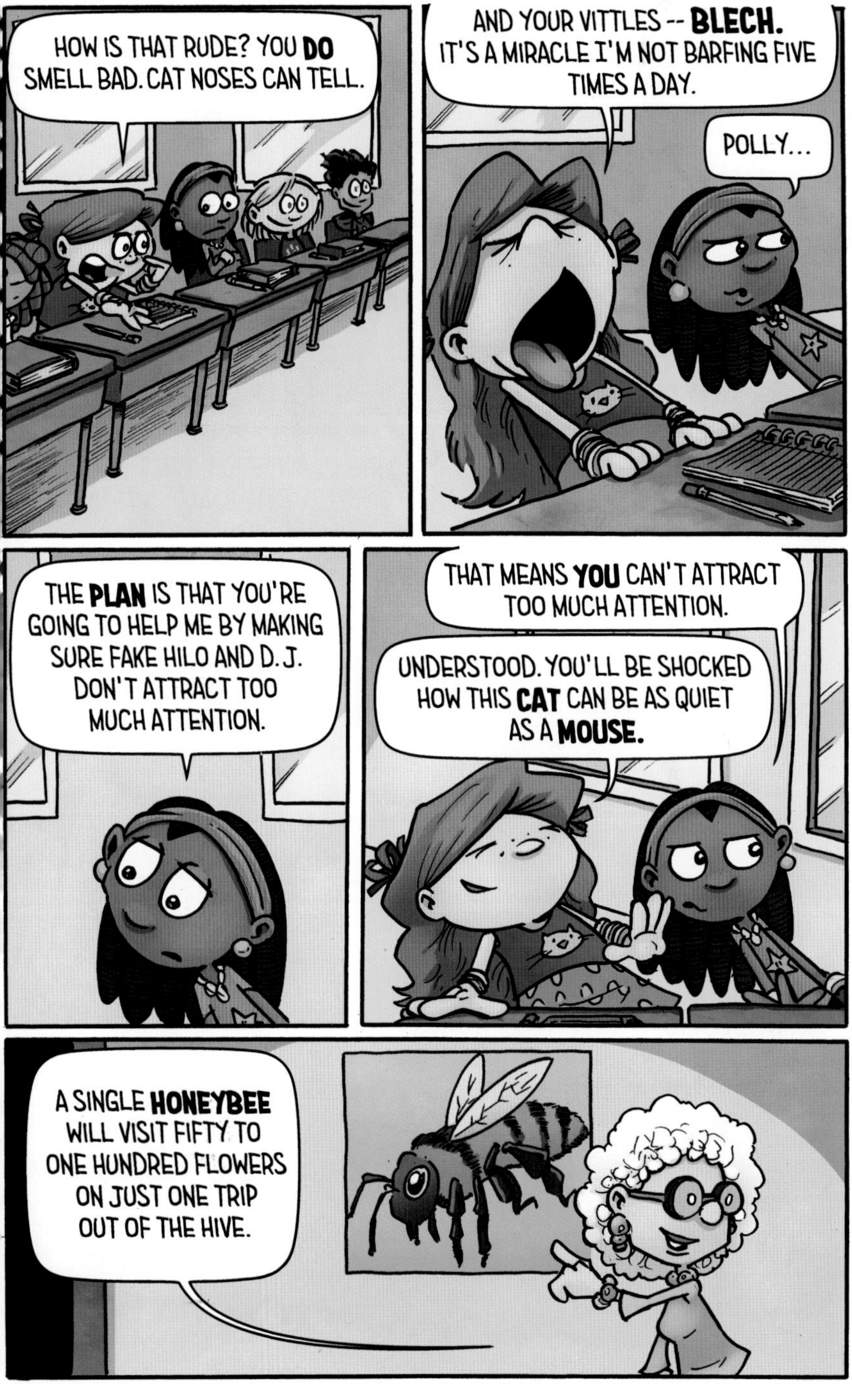
HOW IS THAT RUDE? YOU **DO** SMELL BAD. CAT NOSES CAN TELL.
AND YOUR VITTLES -- **BLECH.** IT'S A MIRACLE I'M NOT BARFING FIVE TIMES A DAY.
POLLY...
THE **PLAN** IS THAT YOU'RE GOING TO HELP ME BY MAKING SURE FAKE HILO AND D. J. DON'T ATTRACT TOO MUCH ATTENTION.
THAT MEANS **YOU** CAN'T ATTRACT TOO MUCH ATTENTION.
UNDERSTOOD. YOU'LL BE SHOCKED HOW THIS **CAT** CAN BE AS QUIET AS A **MOUSE.**
A SINGLE **HONEYBEE** WILL VISIT FIFTY TO ONE HUNDRED FLOWERS ON JUST ONE TRIP OUT OF THE HIVE.

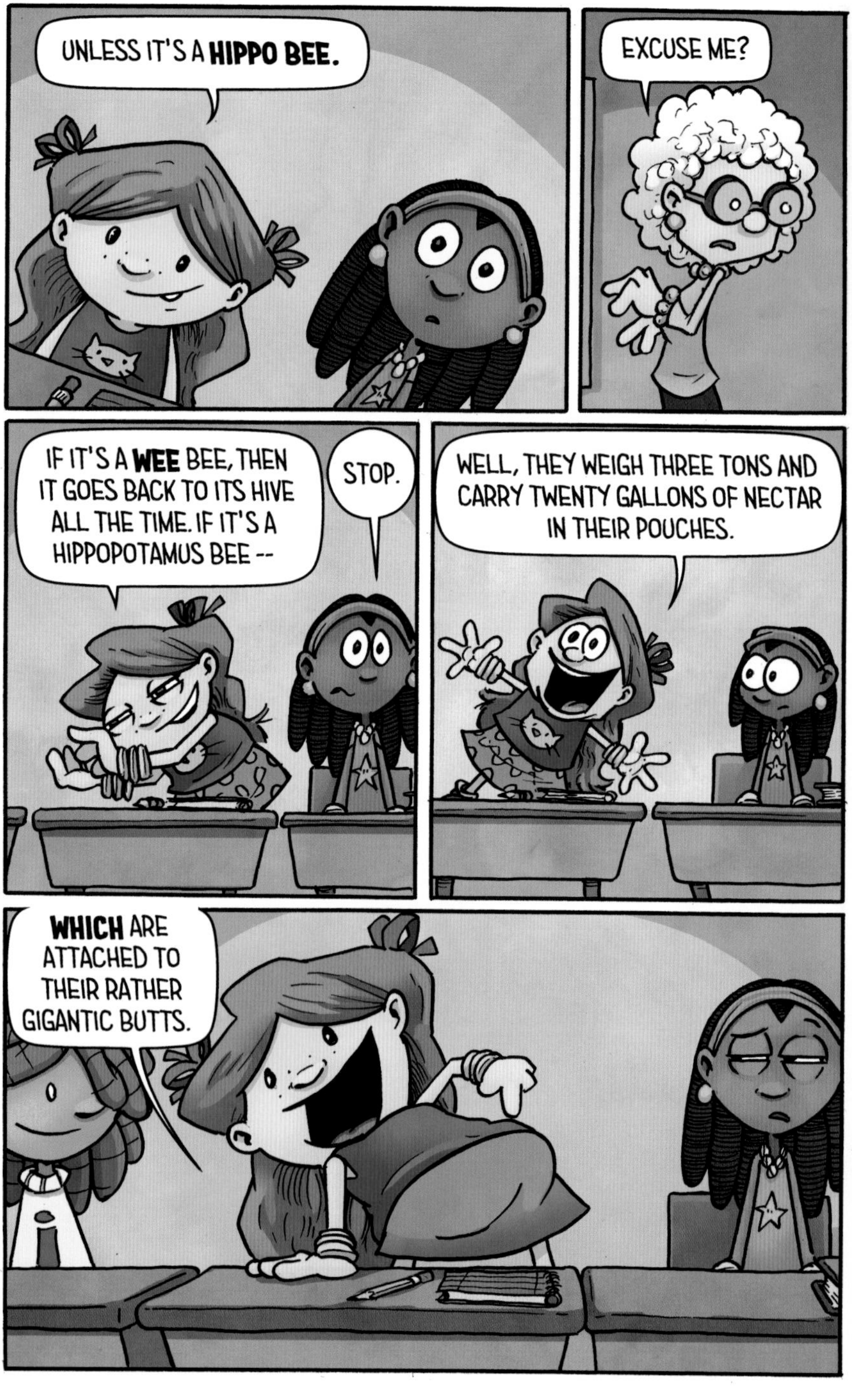
UNLESS IT'S A **HIPPO BEE.**
EXCUSE ME?
IF IT'S A **WEE** BEE, THEN IT GOES BACK TO ITS HIVE ALL THE TIME. IF IT'S A HIPPOPOTAMUS BEE --
STOP.
WELL, THEY WEIGH THREE TONS AND CARRY TWENTY GALLONS OF NECTAR IN THEIR POUCHES.
WHICH ARE ATTACHED TO THEIR RATHER GIGANTIC BUTTS.

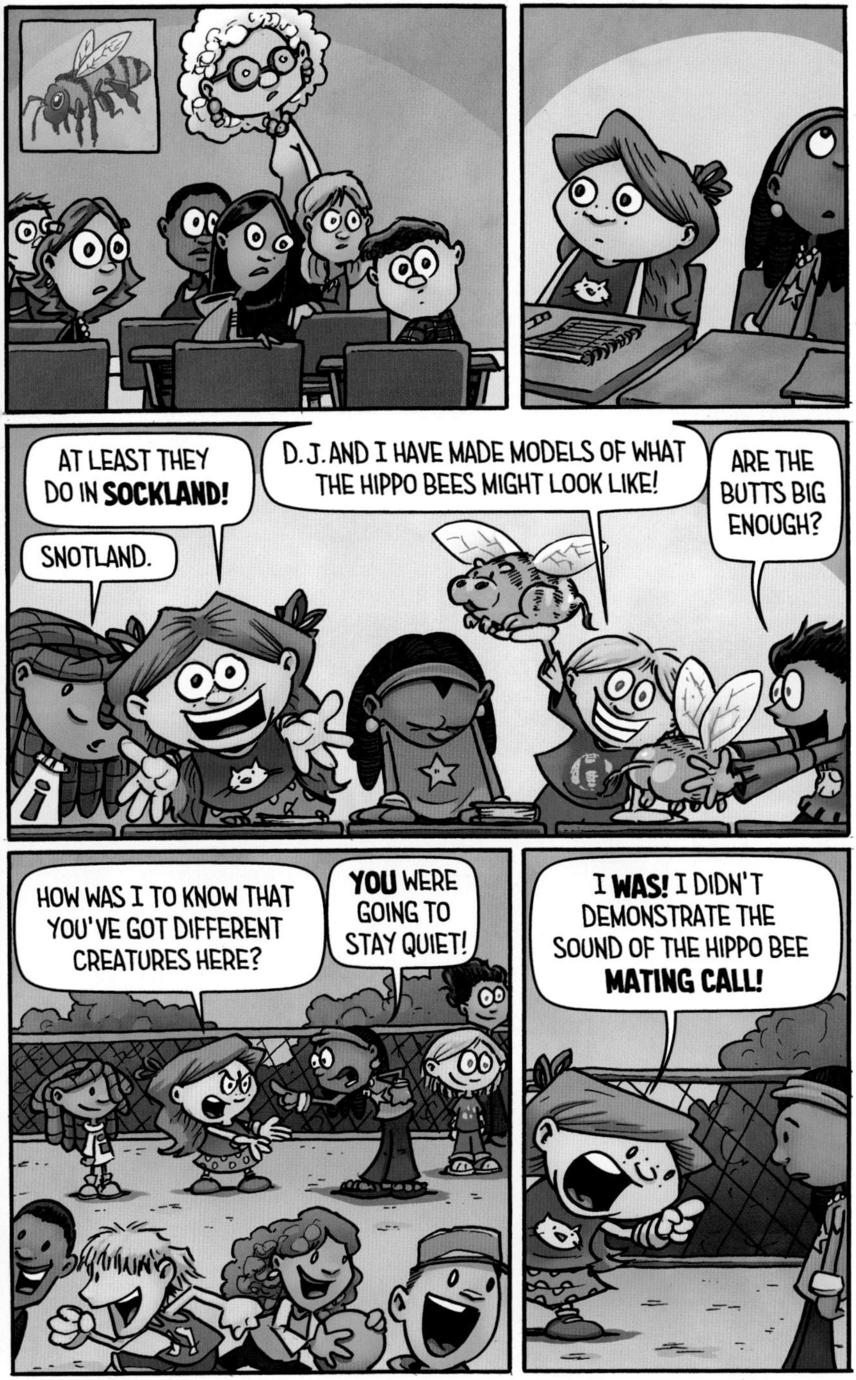

AT LEAST THEY DO IN **SOCKLAND!**
SNOTLAND.
D.J. AND I HAVE MADE MODELS OF WHAT THE HIPPO BEES MIGHT LOOK LIKE!
ARE THE BUTTS BIG ENOUGH?
HOW WAS I TO KNOW THAT YOU'VE GOT DIFFERENT CREATURES HERE?
YOU WERE GOING TO STAY QUIET!
I **WAS!** I DIDN'T DEMONSTRATE THE SOUND OF THE HIPPO BEE **MATING CALL!**

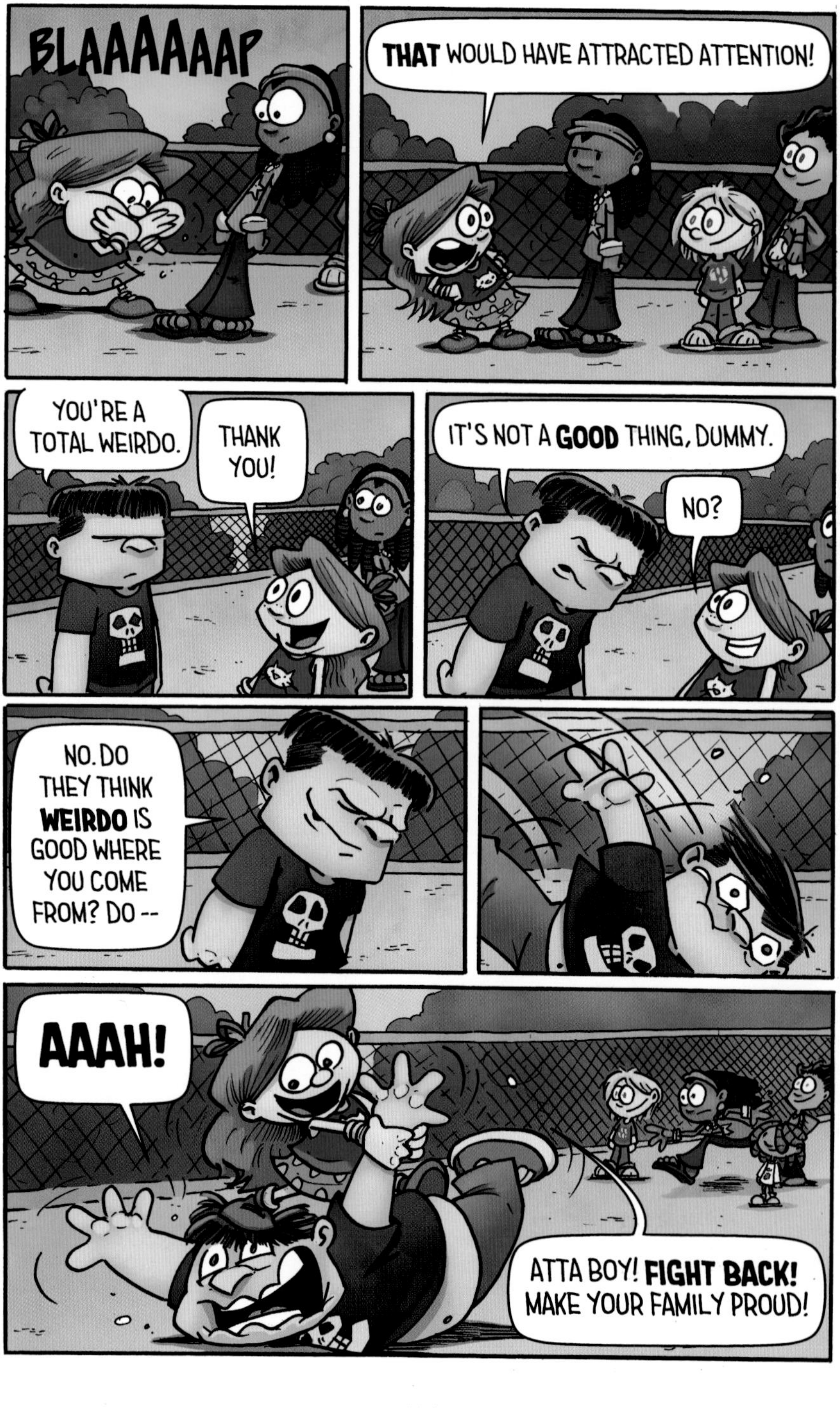
BLAAAAAAP
THAT WOULD HAVE ATTRACTED ATTENTION!
YOU'RE A TOTAL WEIRDO.
THANK YOU!
IT'S NOT A GOOD THING, DUMMY.
NO?
NO. DO THEY THINK WEIRDO IS GOOD WHERE YOU COME FROM? DO --
AAAH!
ATTA BOY! FIGHT BACK! MAKE YOUR FAMILY PROUD!

127

MY FOOD SMELLS GROSS?! YOU SHOULD TAKE A WHIFF OF THAT SLOP YOU CALL A MEAL WITH **MY** SNORTER! YOU'LL HORK UP AN **OCEAN,** LADDIE.

PRINICPAL'S OFFICE.

YOU ARE ALL **THIS** FAR AWAY FROM HAVING A REPORT IN YOUR **PERMANENT RECORDS!**

OUTSTANDING!

SO NOT OUTSTANDING.

MY BAD. I CAN'T STAND HAIR PULLING.

131

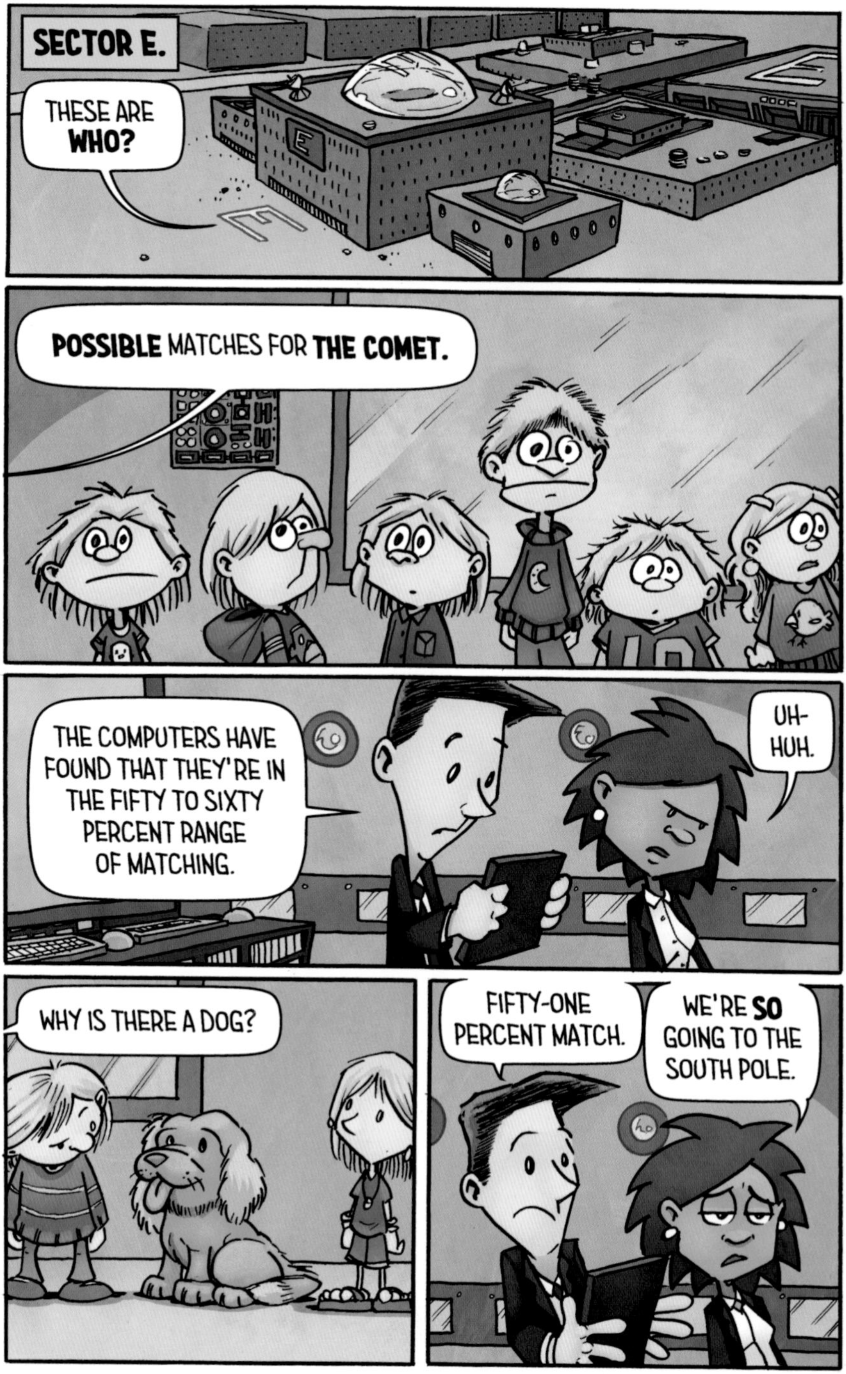
SECTOR E.
THESE ARE WHO?
POSSIBLE MATCHES FOR THE COMET.
THE COMPUTERS HAVE FOUND THAT THEY'RE IN THE FIFTY TO SIXTY PERCENT RANGE OF MATCHING.
UH-HUH.
WHY IS THERE A DOG?
FIFTY-ONE PERCENT MATCH.
WE'RE SO GOING TO THE SOUTH POLE.

CHAPTER 9

BLOODMOON AND LIGHT

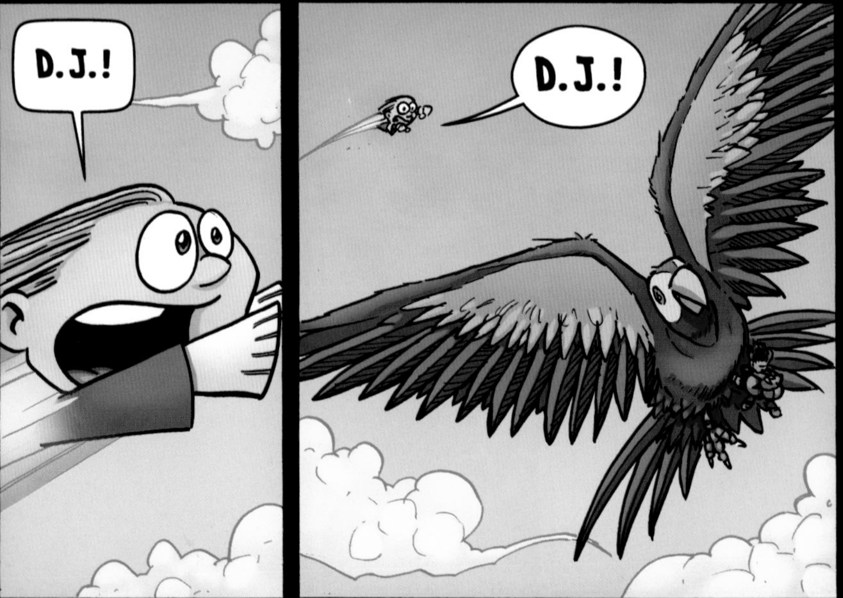
D.J.!
D.J.!

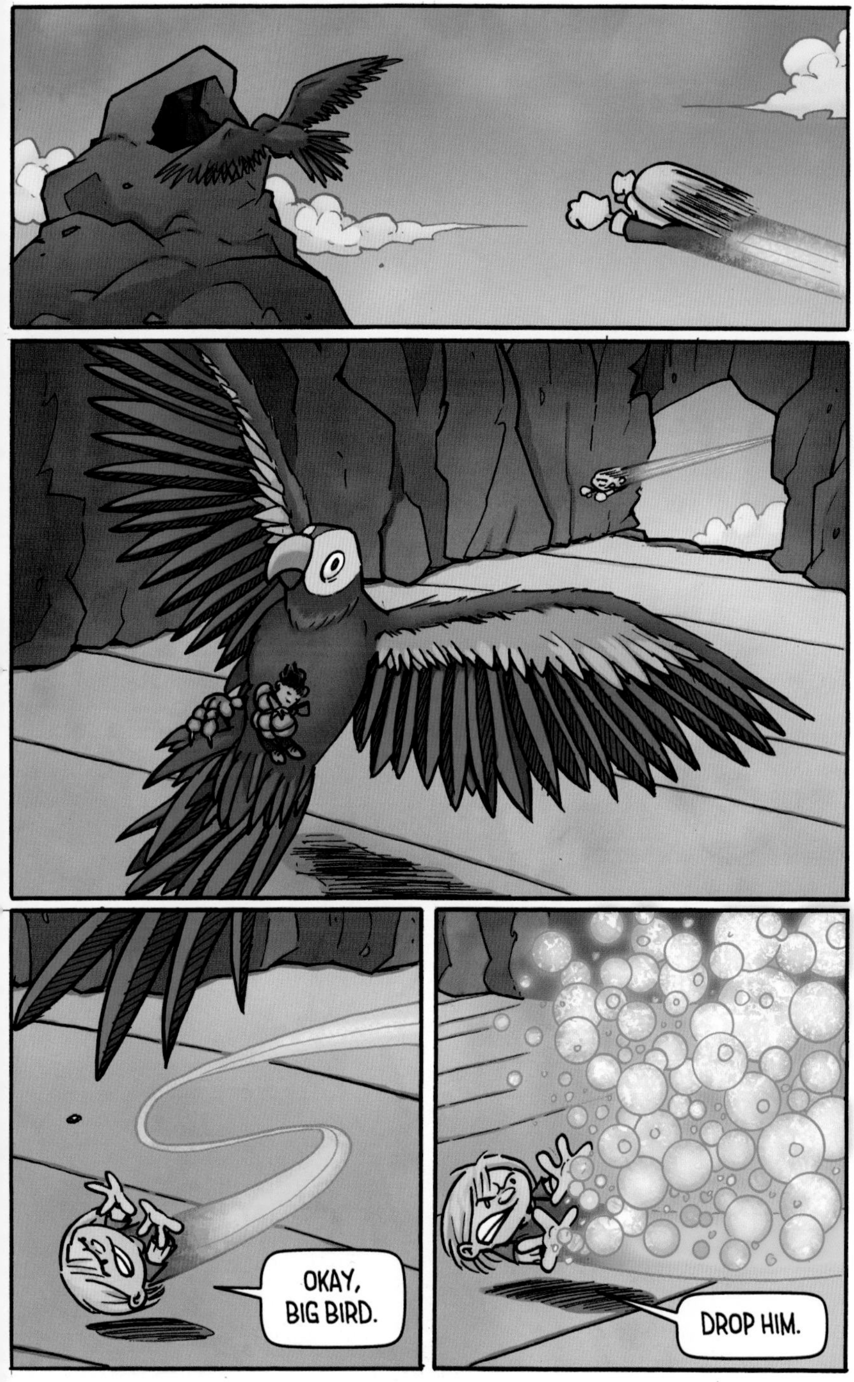
OKAY, BIG BIRD.
DROP HIM.

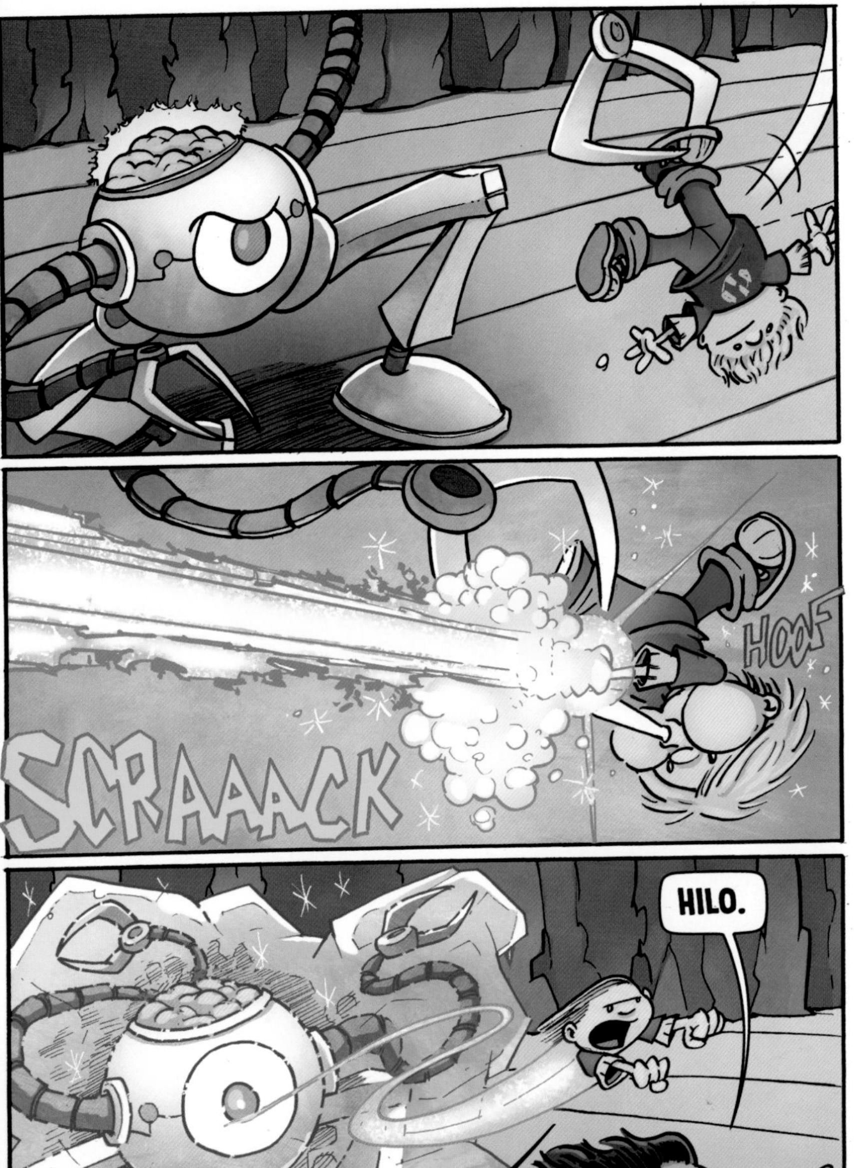
HOOF
SCRAAACK
HILO.
I SEE 'EM!

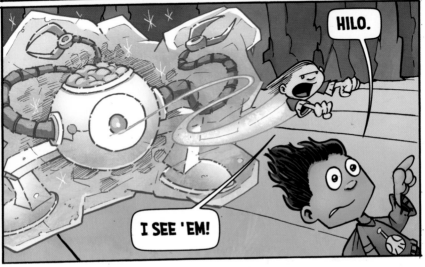

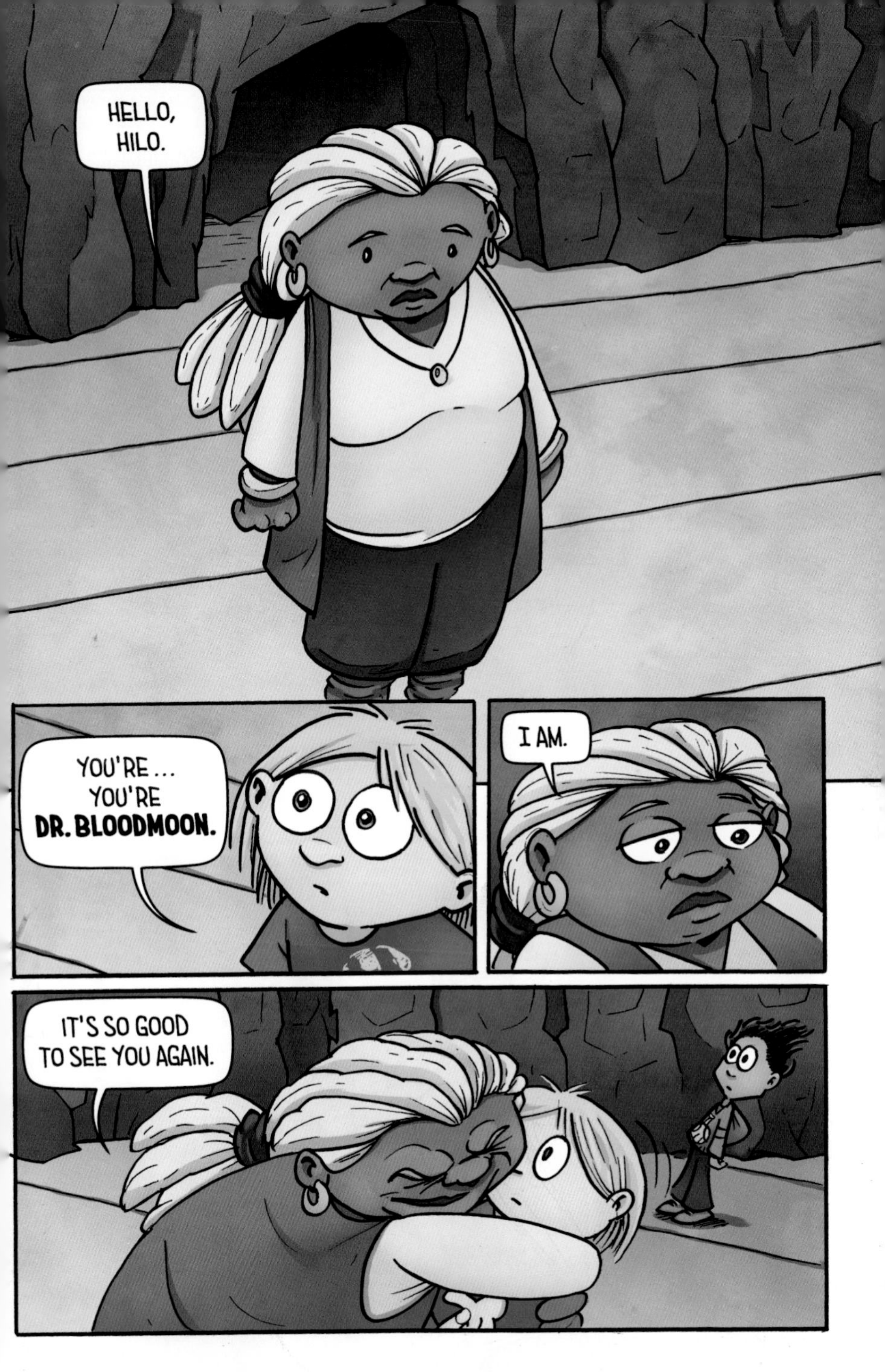
HELLO, HILO.
YOU'RE... YOU'RE **DR. BLOODMOON.**
I AM.
IT'S SO GOOD TO SEE YOU AGAIN.

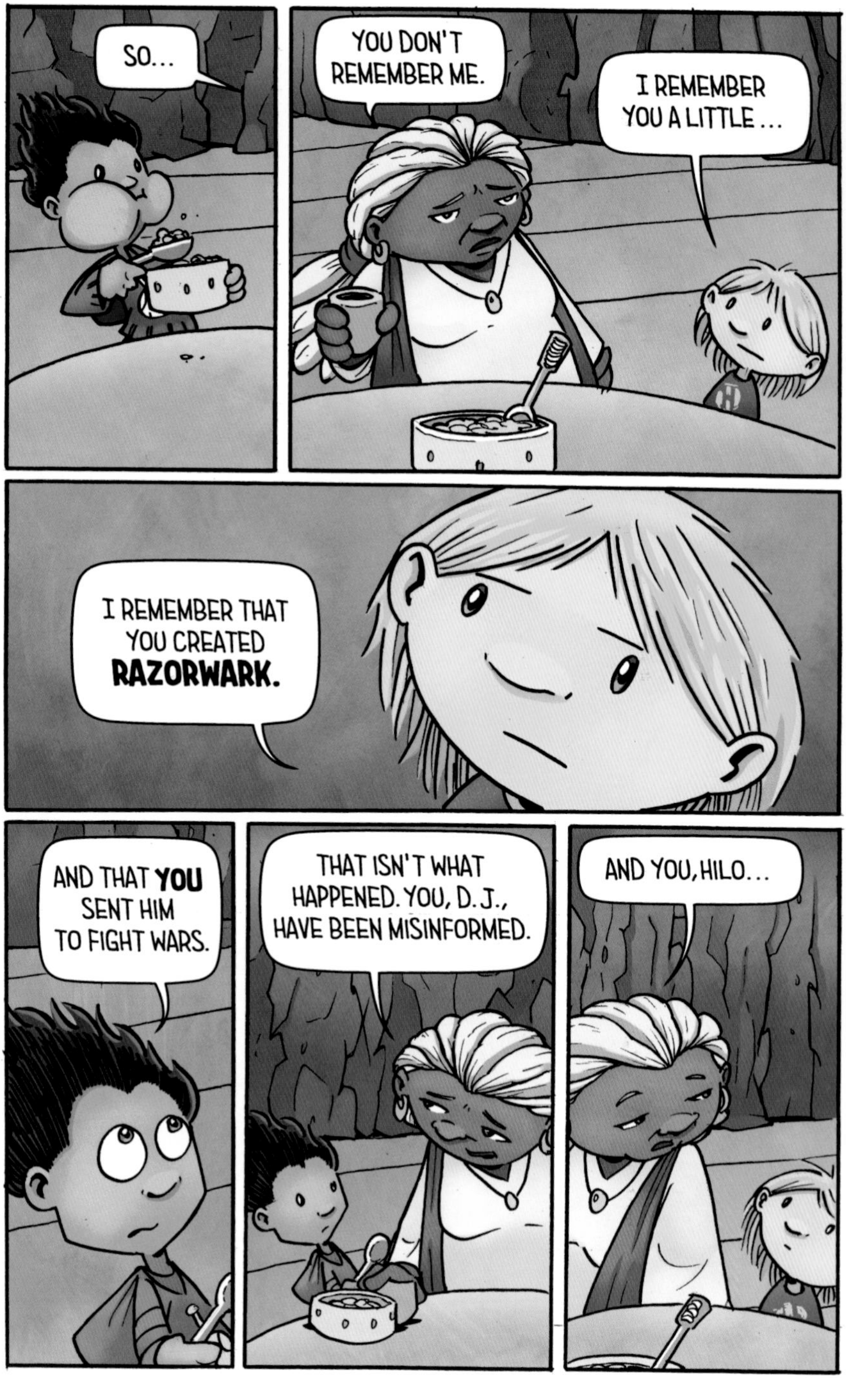
SO...
YOU DON'T REMEMBER ME.
I REMEMBER YOU A LITTLE...
I REMEMBER THAT YOU CREATED **RAZORWARK.**
AND THAT **YOU** SENT HIM TO FIGHT WARS.
THAT ISN'T WHAT HAPPENED. YOU, D. J., HAVE BEEN MISINFORMED.
AND YOU, HILO...

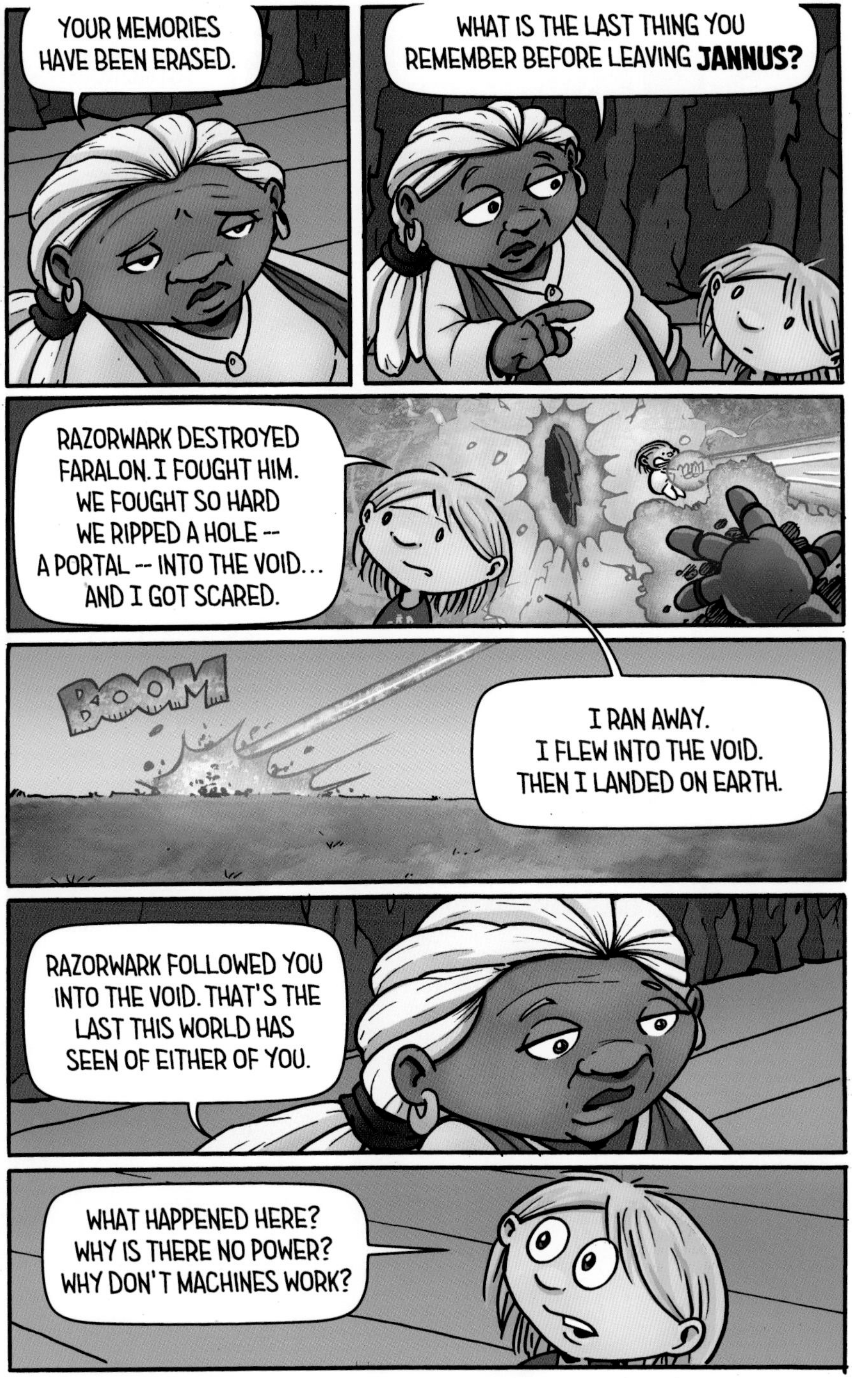
YOUR MEMORIES HAVE BEEN ERASED.
WHAT IS THE LAST THING YOU REMEMBER BEFORE LEAVING **JANNUS?**
RAZORWARK DESTROYED FARALON. I FOUGHT HIM. WE FOUGHT SO HARD WE RIPPED A HOLE -- A PORTAL -- INTO THE VOID... AND I GOT SCARED.
BOOM
I RAN AWAY. I FLEW INTO THE VOID. THEN I LANDED ON EARTH.
RAZORWARK FOLLOWED YOU INTO THE VOID. THAT'S THE LAST THIS WORLD HAS SEEN OF EITHER OF YOU.
WHAT HAPPENED HERE? WHY IS THERE NO POWER? WHY DON'T MACHINES WORK?

EXCEPT HERS.

THESE ARE YOUR ROBOTS, RIGHT?

YES. MY MACHINES STILL WORK.

LET ME TELL YOU WHAT YOU HAVE FORGOTTEN.

I AM **CONSTANCE BLOODMOON**, THE LEADING ROBOTIC SCIENTIST IN THE WORLD.

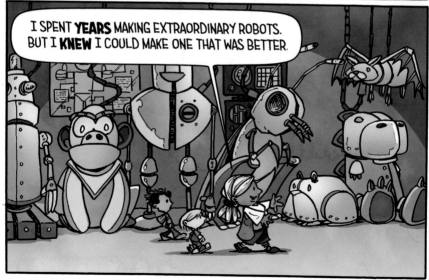

I SPENT **YEARS** MAKING EXTRAORDINARY ROBOTS. BUT I **KNEW** I COULD MAKE ONE THAT WAS BETTER.

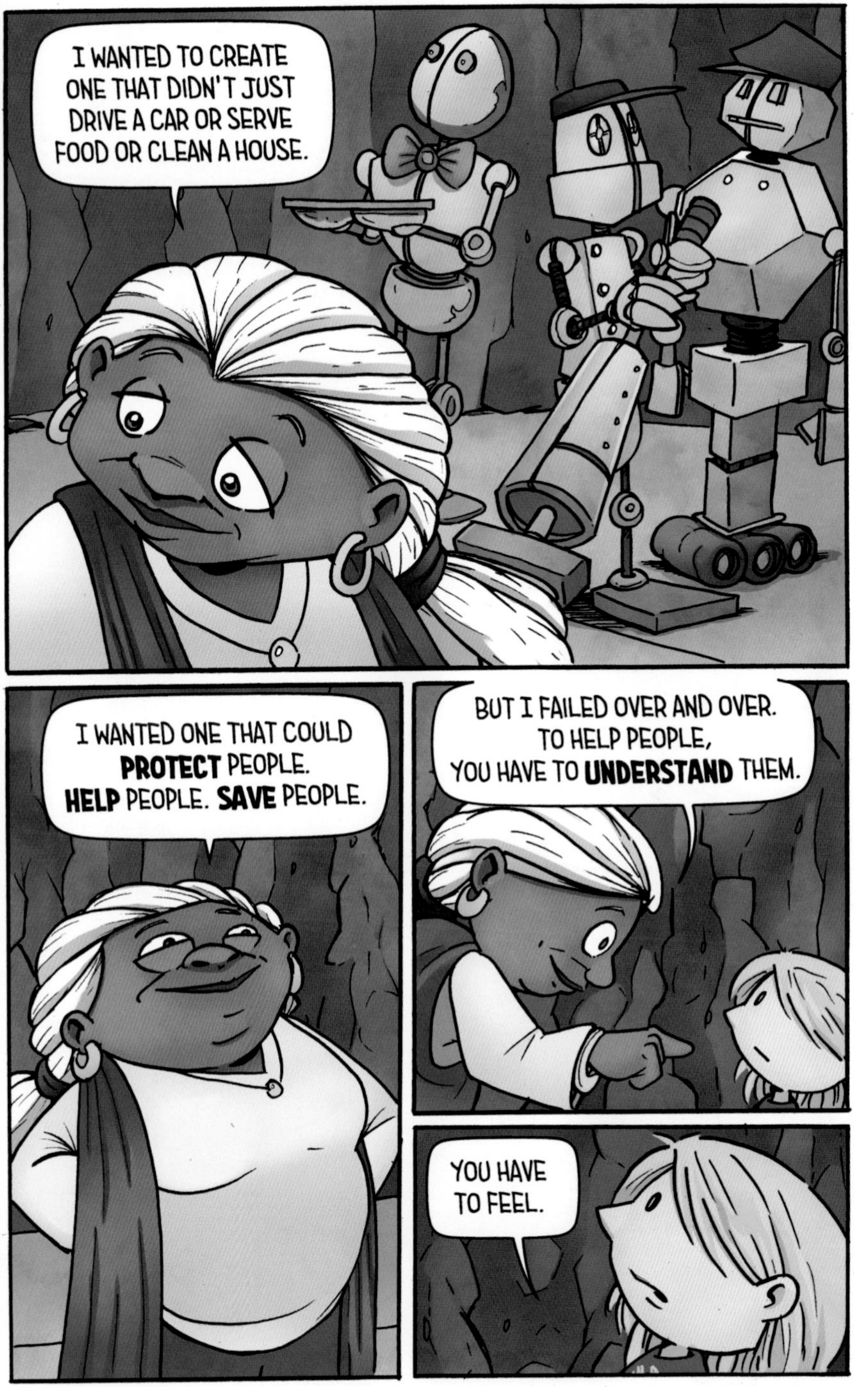
I WANTED TO CREATE ONE THAT DIDN'T JUST DRIVE A CAR OR SERVE FOOD OR CLEAN A HOUSE.
I WANTED ONE THAT COULD **PROTECT** PEOPLE. **HELP** PEOPLE. **SAVE** PEOPLE.
BUT I FAILED OVER AND OVER. TO HELP PEOPLE, YOU HAVE TO **UNDERSTAND** THEM.
YOU HAVE TO FEEL.

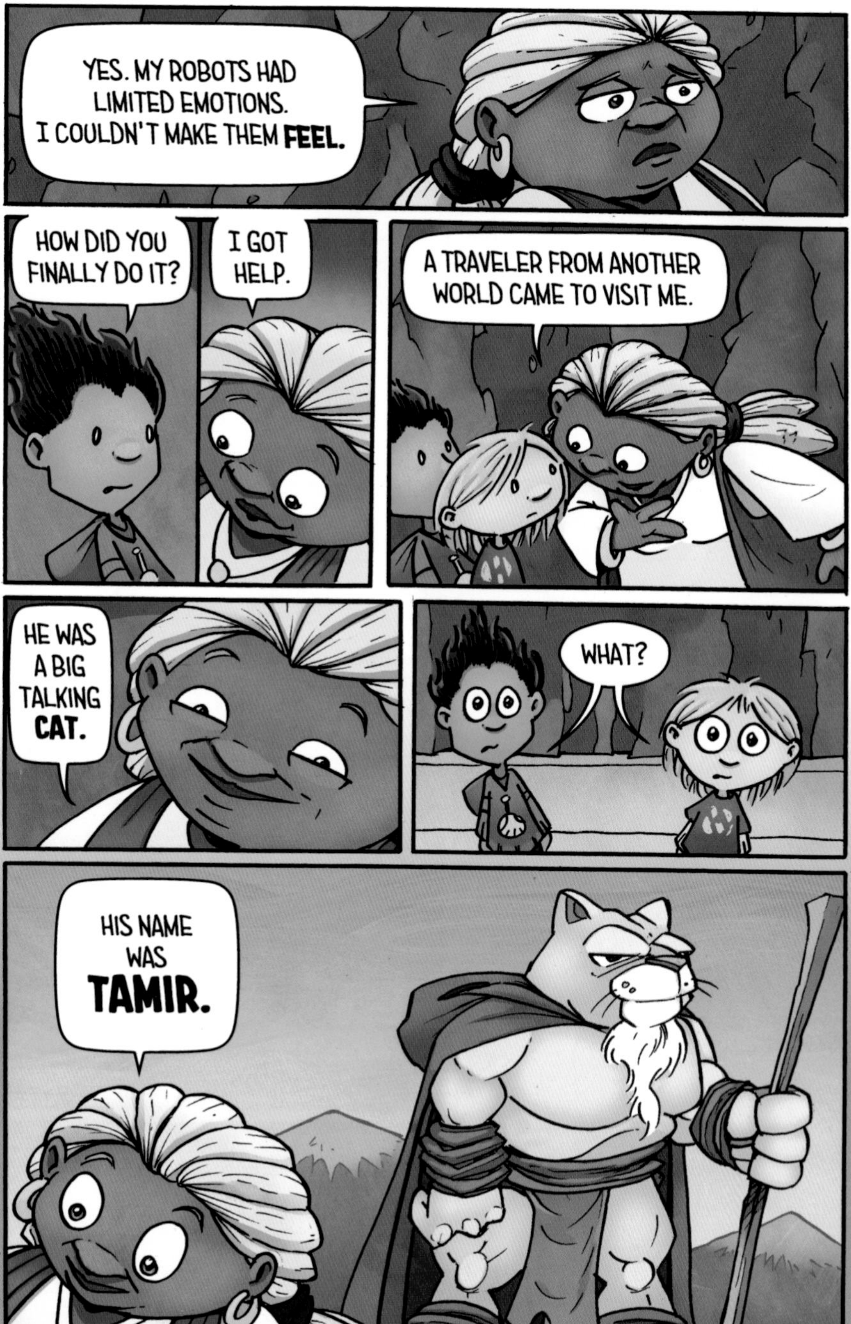
YES. MY ROBOTS HAD LIMITED EMOTIONS. I COULDN'T MAKE THEM **FEEL.**
HOW DID YOU FINALLY DO IT?
I GOT HELP.
A TRAVELER FROM ANOTHER WORLD CAME TO VISIT ME.
HE WAS A BIG TALKING **CAT.**
WHAT?
HIS NAME WAS **TAMIR.**

MY ARMY HAD JUST DEFEATED THE WILLOW TRIBE OF MOUNT FATUM. THEY WERE A RESILIENT BUT ULTIMATELY SIMPLE PEOPLE.

THEY MOSTLY DWELLED WITHIN THEIR MOUNTAIN, WHICH SHOULD'VE BEEN **FAR** TOO COLD TO LIVE IN.

BUT WHEN WE VENTURED IN, WE WERE BATHED IN SUCH WARMTH. SUCH A COMFORTING HEAT.

I ALONE SEARCHED FOR THE SOURCE OF THIS HEAT, AND WHEN I FOUND IT...

I DISCOVERED SO MUCH **MORE** THAN A SOLUTION TO THE COLD.

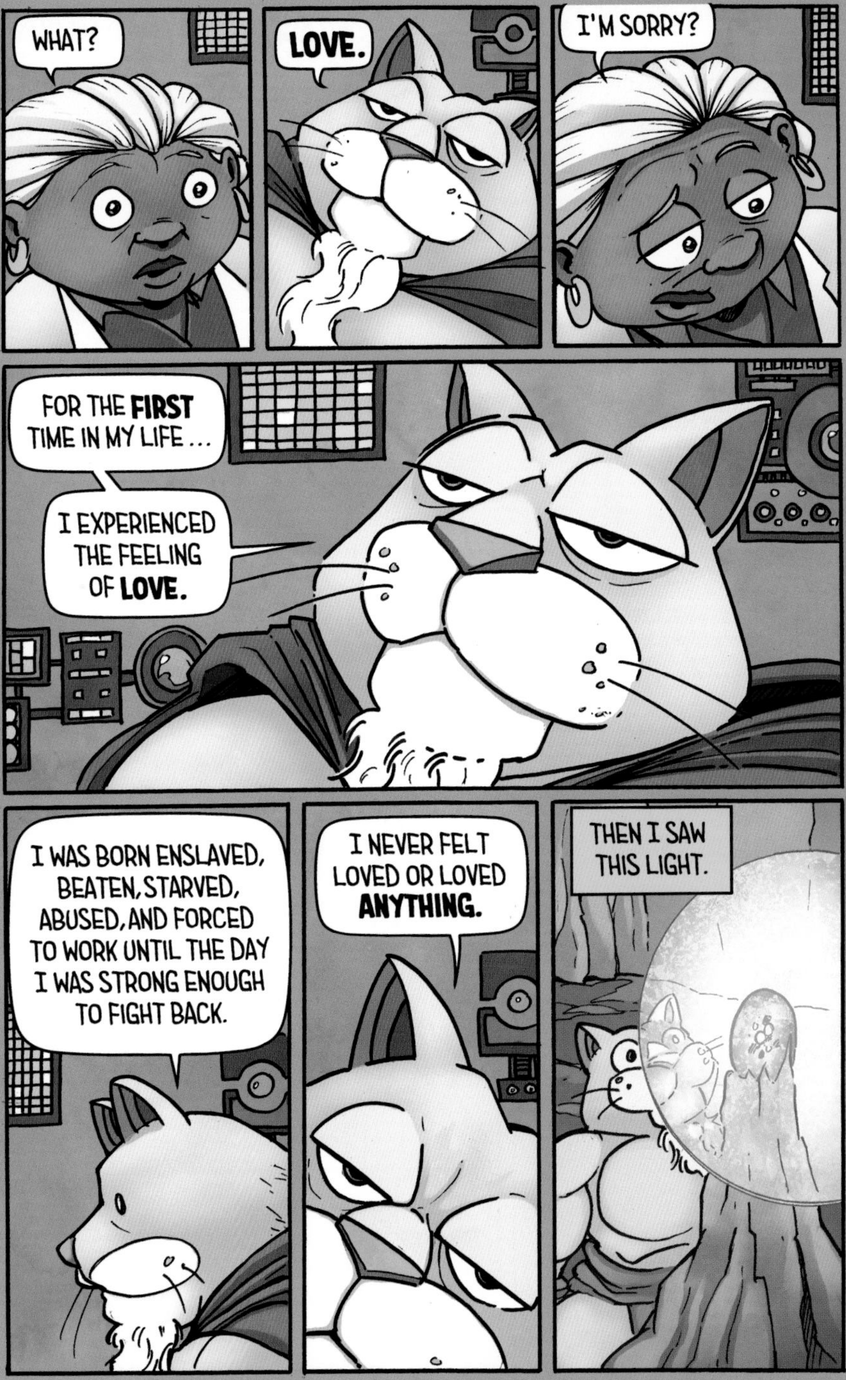
WHAT?
LOVE.
I'M SORRY?
FOR THE FIRST TIME IN MY LIFE . . .
I EXPERIENCED THE FEELING OF LOVE.
I WAS BORN ENSLAVED, BEATEN, STARVED, ABUSED, AND FORCED TO WORK UNTIL THE DAY I WAS STRONG ENOUGH TO FIGHT BACK.
I NEVER FELT LOVED OR LOVED ANYTHING.
THEN I SAW THIS LIGHT.

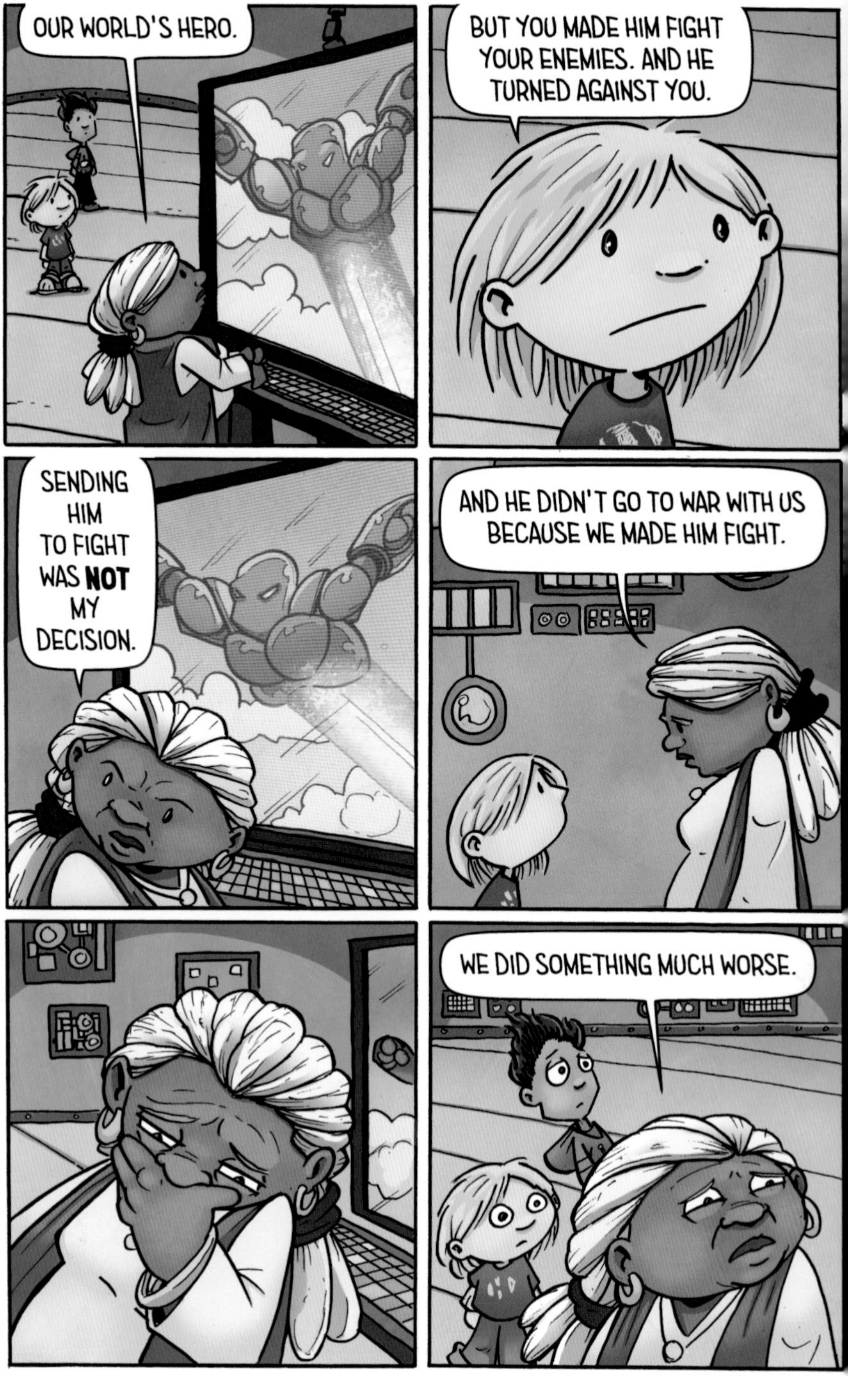
OUR WORLD'S HERO.
BUT YOU MADE HIM FIGHT YOUR ENEMIES. AND HE TURNED AGAINST YOU.
SENDING HIM TO FIGHT WAS **NOT** MY DECISION.
AND HE DIDN'T GO TO WAR WITH US BECAUSE WE MADE HIM FIGHT.
WE DID SOMETHING MUCH WORSE.

CHAPTER 10

THEN EVERYTHING WENT WRONG

FIGHTING! AT SCHOOL! ALL DAY!
YES!
WE HAD TO PROTECT IZZY AND POLLY!
I DON'T NEED PROTECTING.
I WAS OKAY TOO.

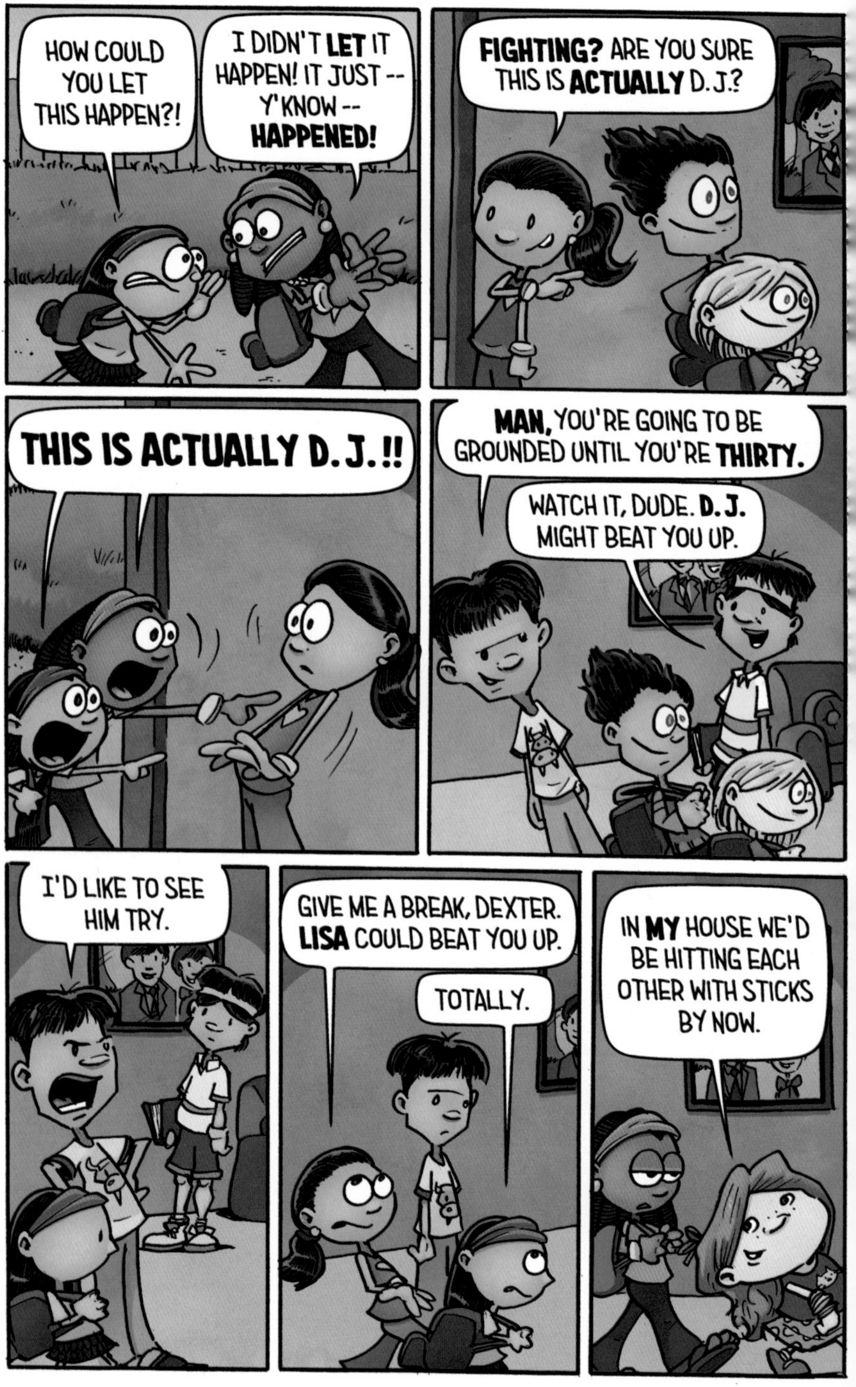
HOW COULD YOU LET THIS HAPPEN?!
I DIDN'T LET IT HAPPEN! IT JUST -- Y'KNOW -- HAPPENED!
FIGHTING? ARE YOU SURE THIS IS ACTUALLY D.J.?
THIS IS ACTUALLY D.J.!!
MAN, YOU'RE GOING TO BE GROUNDED UNTIL YOU'RE THIRTY.
WATCH IT, DUDE. D.J. MIGHT BEAT YOU UP.
I'D LIKE TO SEE HIM TRY.
GIVE ME A BREAK, DEXTER. LISA COULD BEAT YOU UP.
TOTALLY.
IN MY HOUSE WE'D BE HITTING EACH OTHER WITH STICKS BY NOW.

YOU THREE NEED TO GO HOME. **NOW.** GINA, YOUR MOTHER IS WAITING FOR YOU. IZZY, HILO -- YOUR **UNCLE TROUT,** WELL, HE KEEPS TALKING ABOUT BARBECUE, BUT YOU SHOULD GO HOME.

SIGH.

I AM JUST SO DISAPPOINTED IN **ALL** OF YOU.

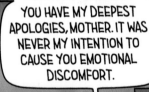

YOU HAVE MY DEEPEST APOLOGIES, MOTHER. IT WAS NEVER MY INTENTION TO CAUSE YOU EMOTIONAL DISCOMFORT.

DANIEL.

WHAT'S WRONG?

NOTHING AT ALL, MOM.

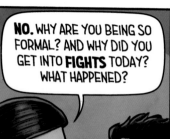

NO. WHY ARE YOU BEING SO FORMAL? AND WHY DID YOU GET INTO **FIGHTS** TODAY? WHAT HAPPENED?

THIS ISN'T YOU.

IT'S GOING TO BE OKAY, MRS. LIM. YOU'LL SEE.

I'LL **SEE**?

THINGS COME TOGETHER. LIKE GINA, HILO, AND D.J. I KNOW IT SEEMS WEIRD... BUT I PROMISE...

THE PIECES WILL FIT.

IZZY, I DON'T KNOW WHAT YOU MEAN.

MOM?

OH. I HAVE TO GO.

BEEP

MOM.

157

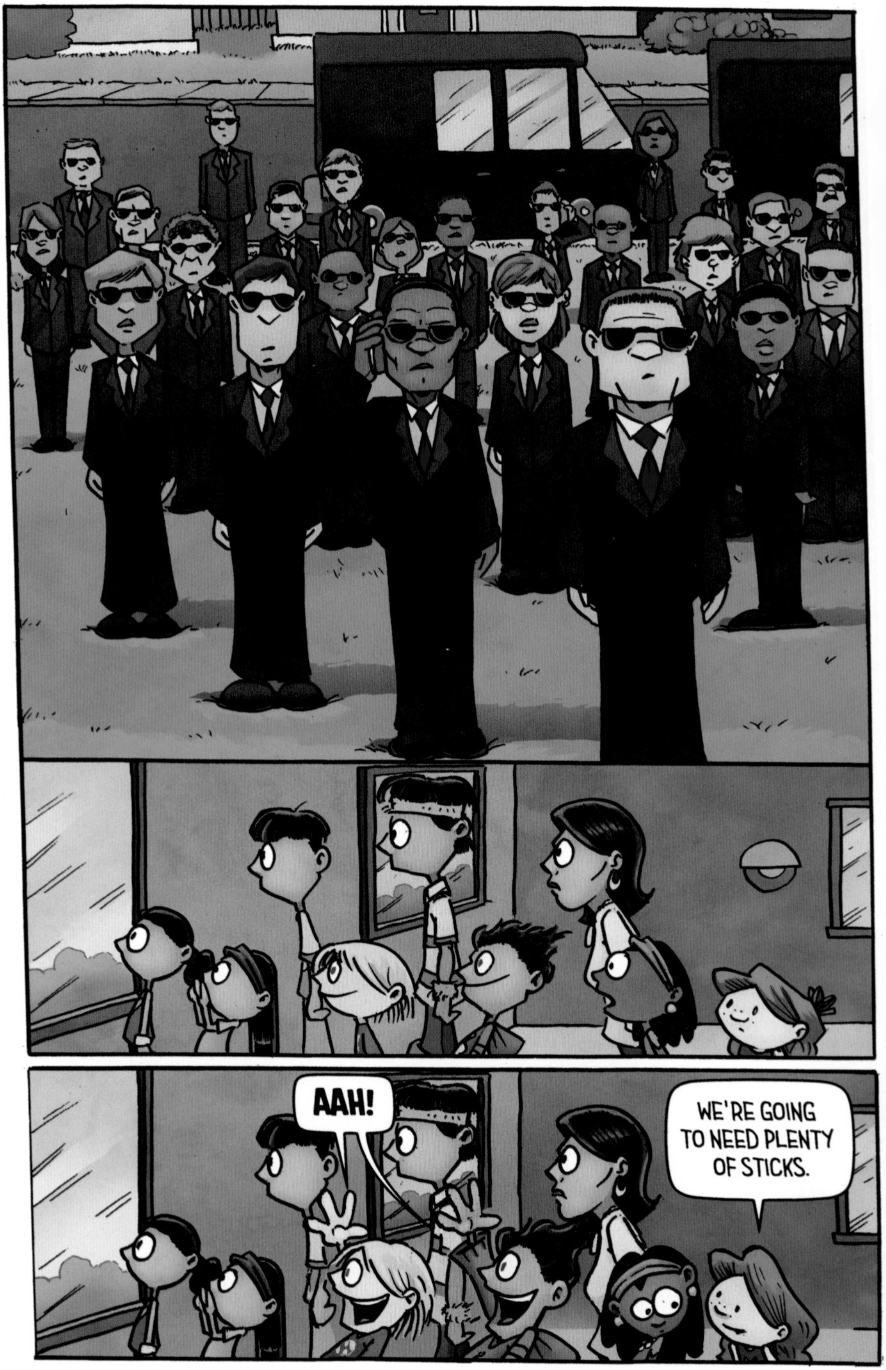
AAH!
WE'RE GOING TO NEED PLENTY OF STICKS.

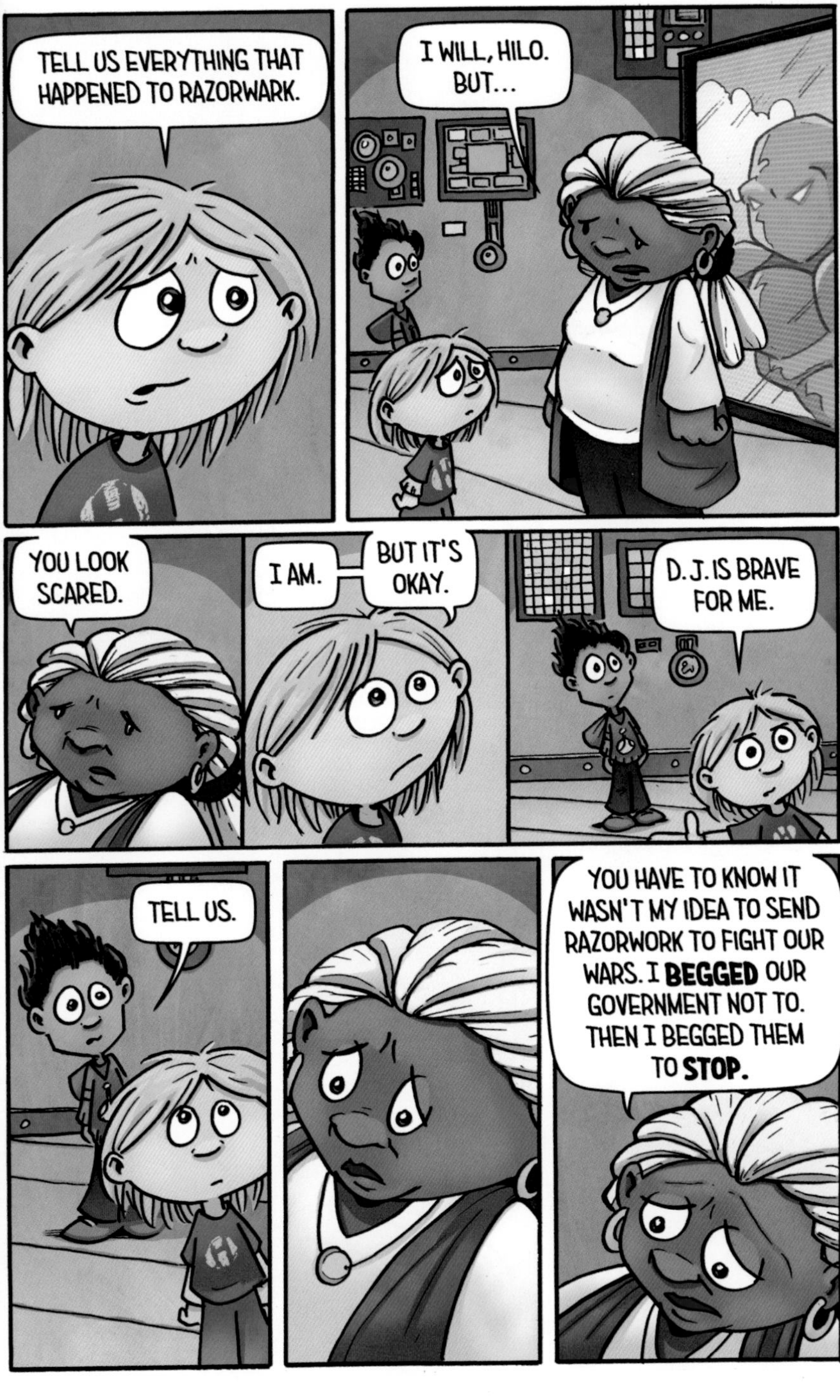
TELL US EVERYTHING THAT HAPPENED TO RAZORWARK.
I WILL, HILO. BUT...
YOU LOOK SCARED.
I AM.
BUT IT'S OKAY.
D.J. IS BRAVE FOR ME.
TELL US.
YOU HAVE TO KNOW IT WASN'T MY IDEA TO SEND RAZORWORK TO FIGHT OUR WARS. I **BEGGED** OUR GOVERNMENT NOT TO. THEN I BEGGED THEM TO **STOP.**

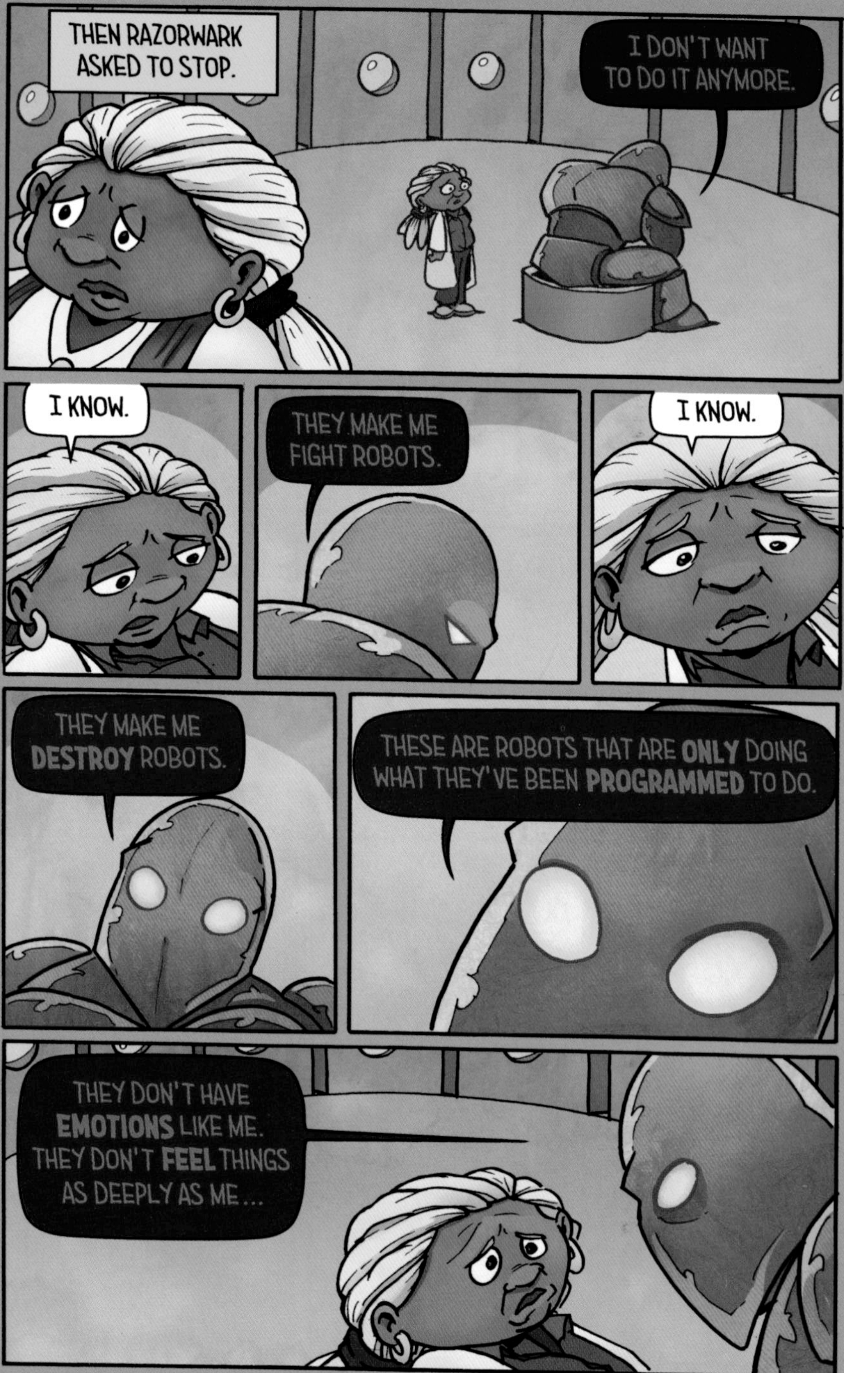
THEN RAZORWARK ASKED TO STOP.
I DON'T WANT TO DO IT ANYMORE.
I KNOW.
THEY MAKE ME FIGHT ROBOTS.
I KNOW.
THEY MAKE ME DESTROY ROBOTS.
THESE ARE ROBOTS THAT ARE ONLY DOING WHAT THEY'VE BEEN PROGRAMMED TO DO.
THEY DON'T HAVE EMOTIONS LIKE ME. THEY DON'T FEEL THINGS AS DEEPLY AS ME...

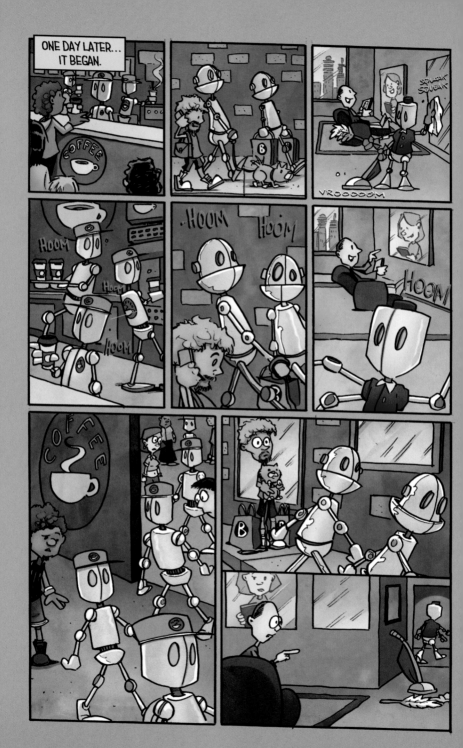

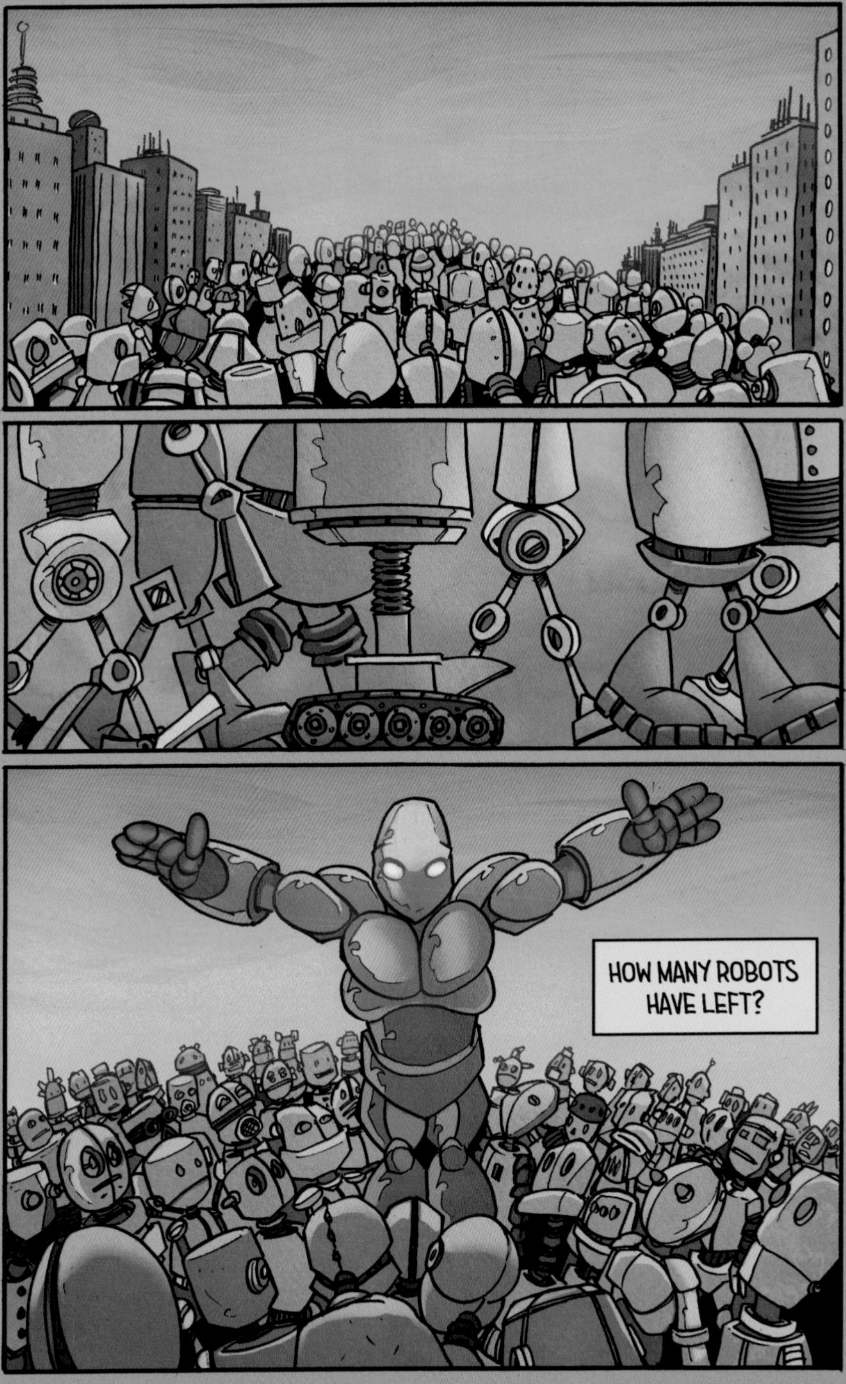
HOW MANY ROBOTS HAVE LEFT?

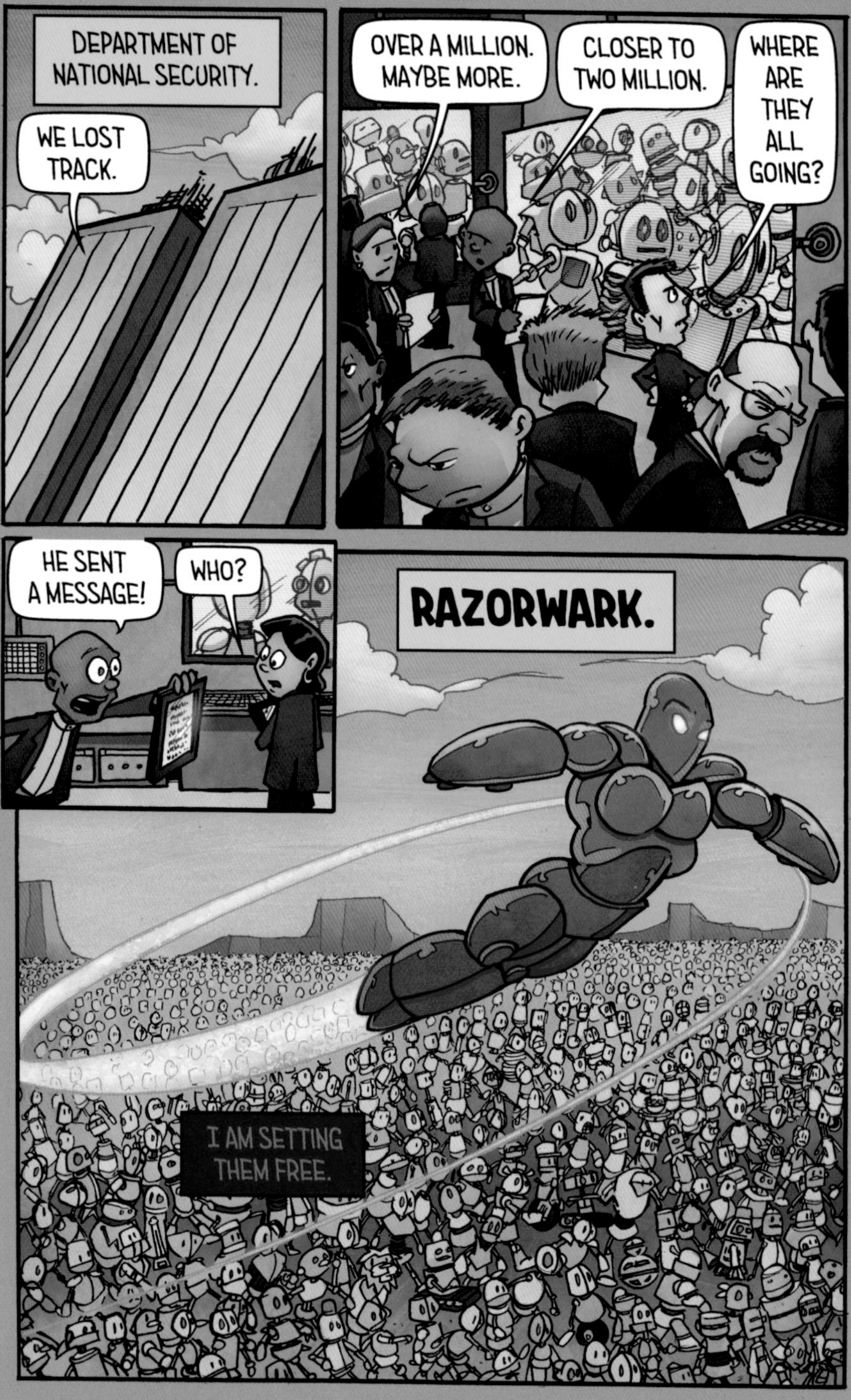
DEPARTMENT OF NATIONAL SECURITY.
WE LOST TRACK.
OVER A MILLION. MAYBE MORE.
CLOSER TO TWO MILLION.
WHERE ARE THEY ALL GOING?
HE SENT A MESSAGE!
WHO?
RAZORWARK.
I AM SETTING THEM FREE.

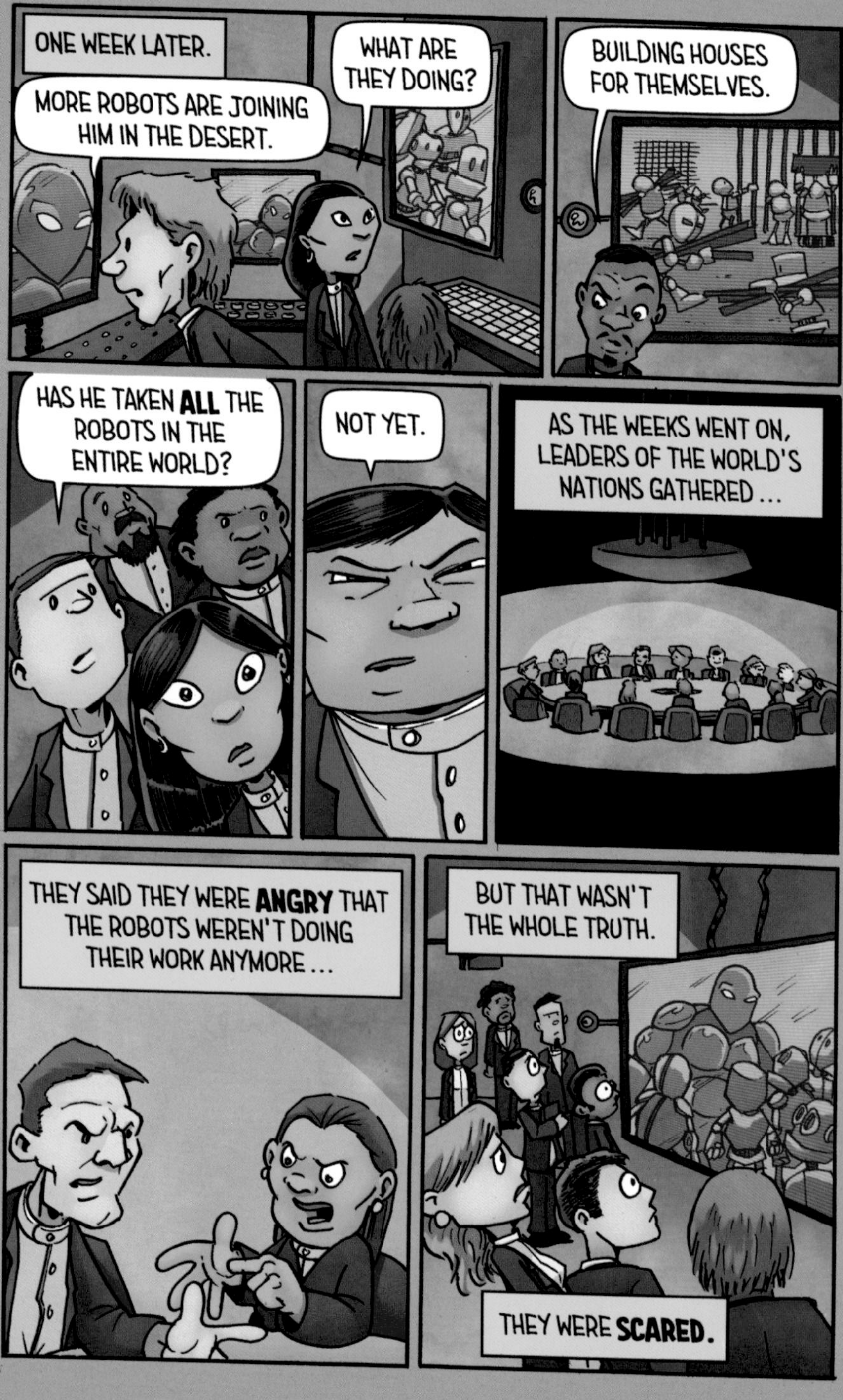
ONE WEEK LATER.
MORE ROBOTS ARE JOINING HIM IN THE DESERT.
WHAT ARE THEY DOING?
BUILDING HOUSES FOR THEMSELVES.
HAS HE TAKEN ALL THE ROBOTS IN THE ENTIRE WORLD?
NOT YET.
AS THE WEEKS WENT ON, LEADERS OF THE WORLD'S NATIONS GATHERED ...
THEY SAID THEY WERE ANGRY THAT THE ROBOTS WEREN'T DOING THEIR WORK ANYMORE ...
BUT THAT WASN'T THE WHOLE TRUTH.
THEY WERE SCARED.

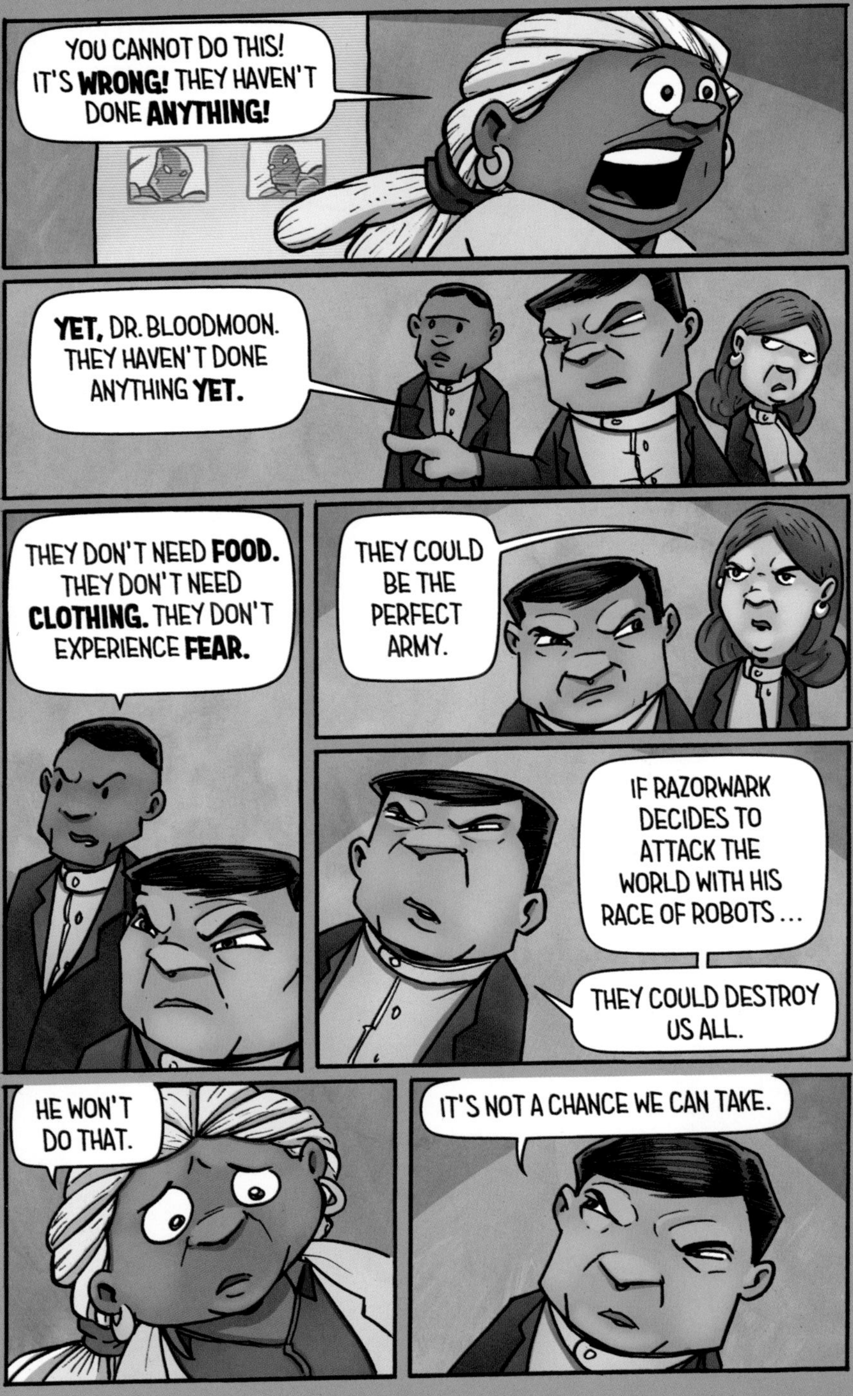
YOU CANNOT DO THIS! IT'S **WRONG!** THEY HAVEN'T DONE **ANYTHING!**
YET, DR. BLOODMOON. THEY HAVEN'T DONE ANYTHING **YET.**
THEY DON'T NEED **FOOD.** THEY DON'T NEED **CLOTHING.** THEY DON'T EXPERIENCE **FEAR.**
THEY COULD BE THE PERFECT ARMY.
IF RAZORWARK DECIDES TO ATTACK THE WORLD WITH HIS RACE OF ROBOTS ...
THEY COULD DESTROY US ALL.
HE WON'T DO THAT.
IT'S NOT A CHANCE WE CAN TAKE.

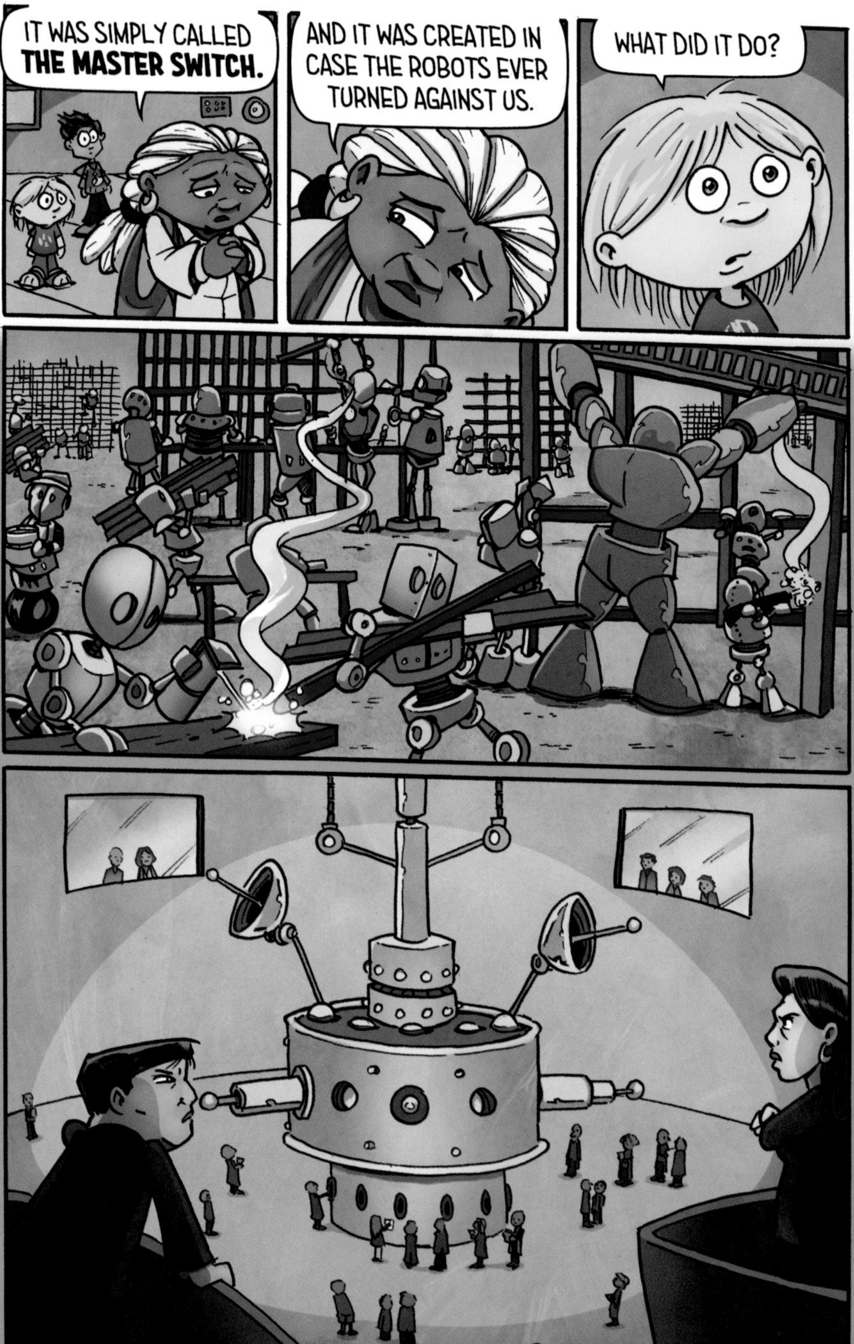
IT WAS SIMPLY CALLED **THE MASTER SWITCH.**
AND IT WAS CREATED IN CASE THE ROBOTS EVER TURNED AGAINST US.
WHAT DID IT DO?

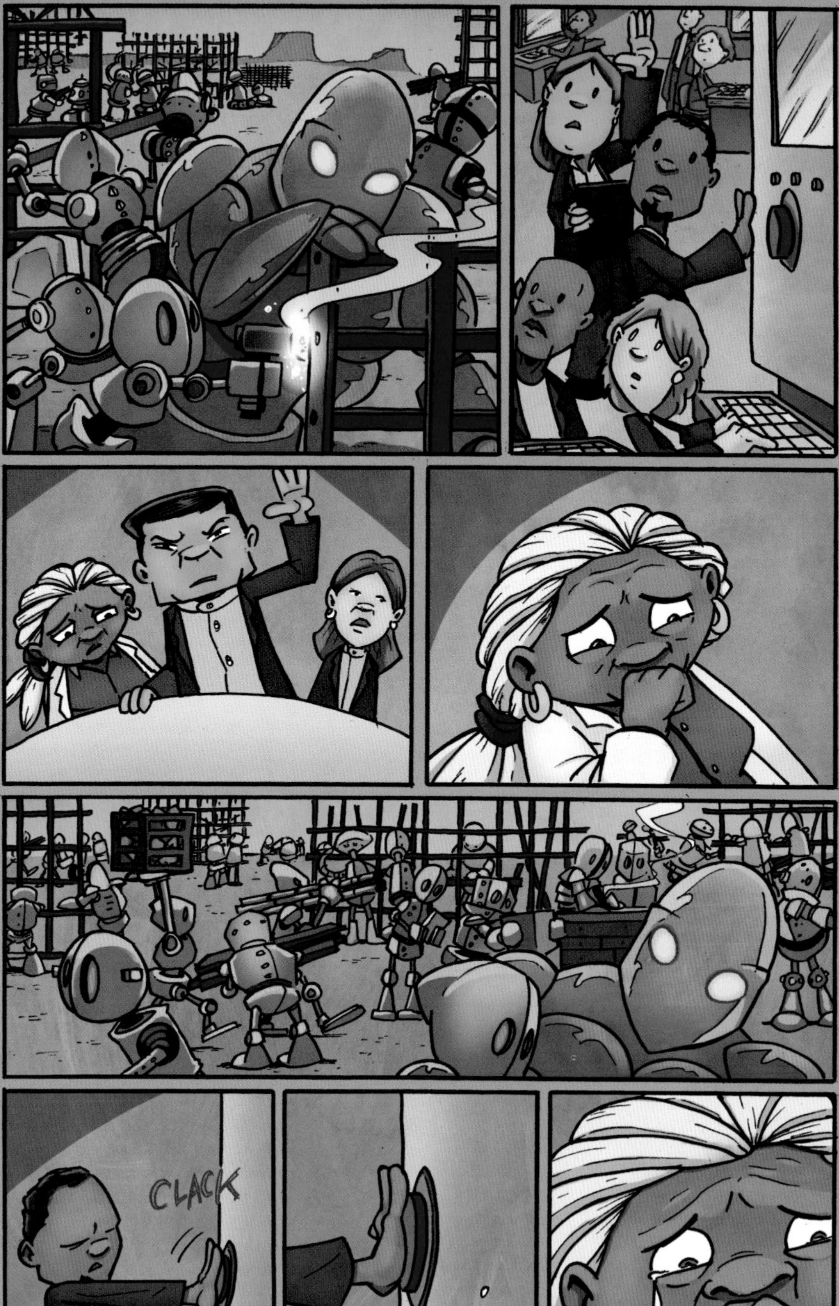
CLACK
BEEP

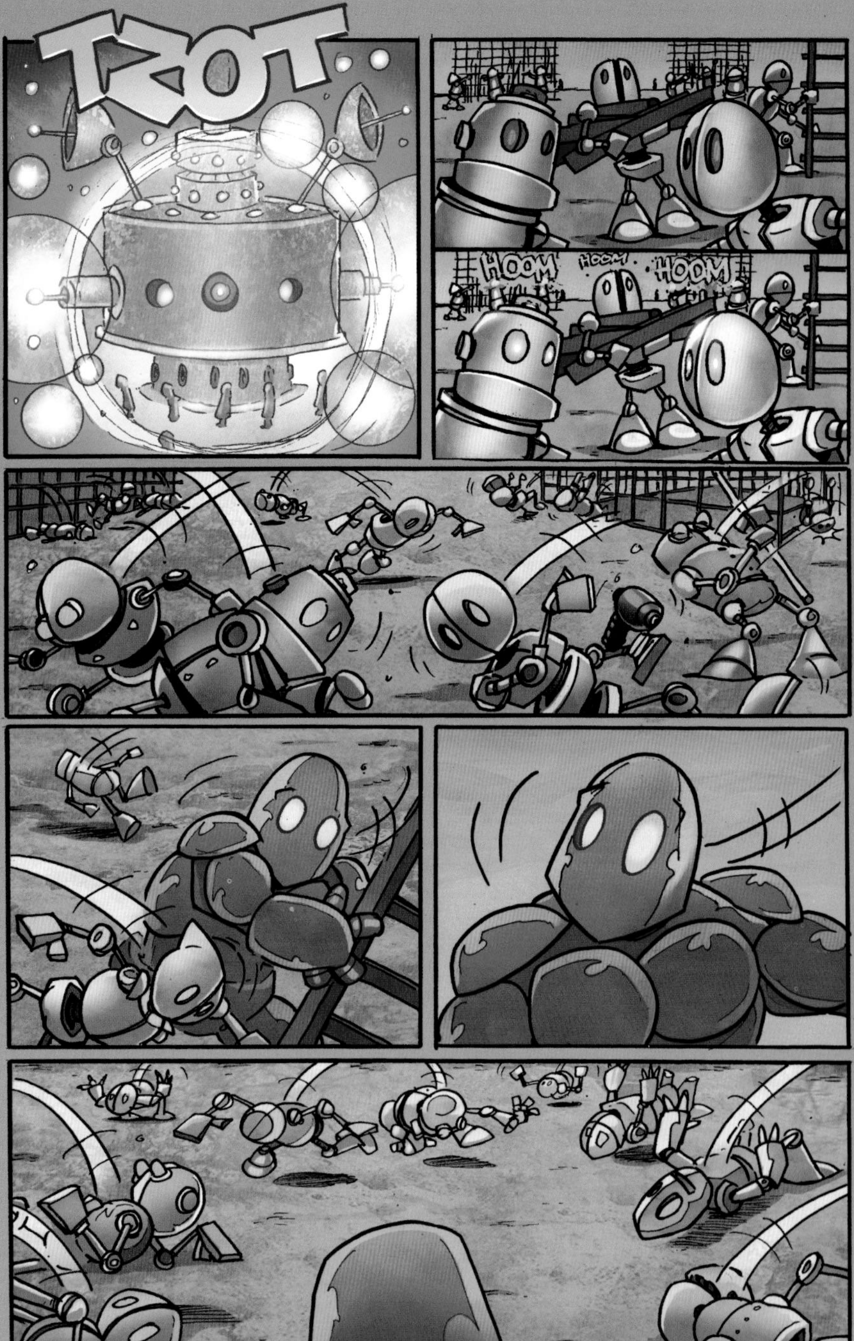
TROT
HOOM
HOOM
HOOM

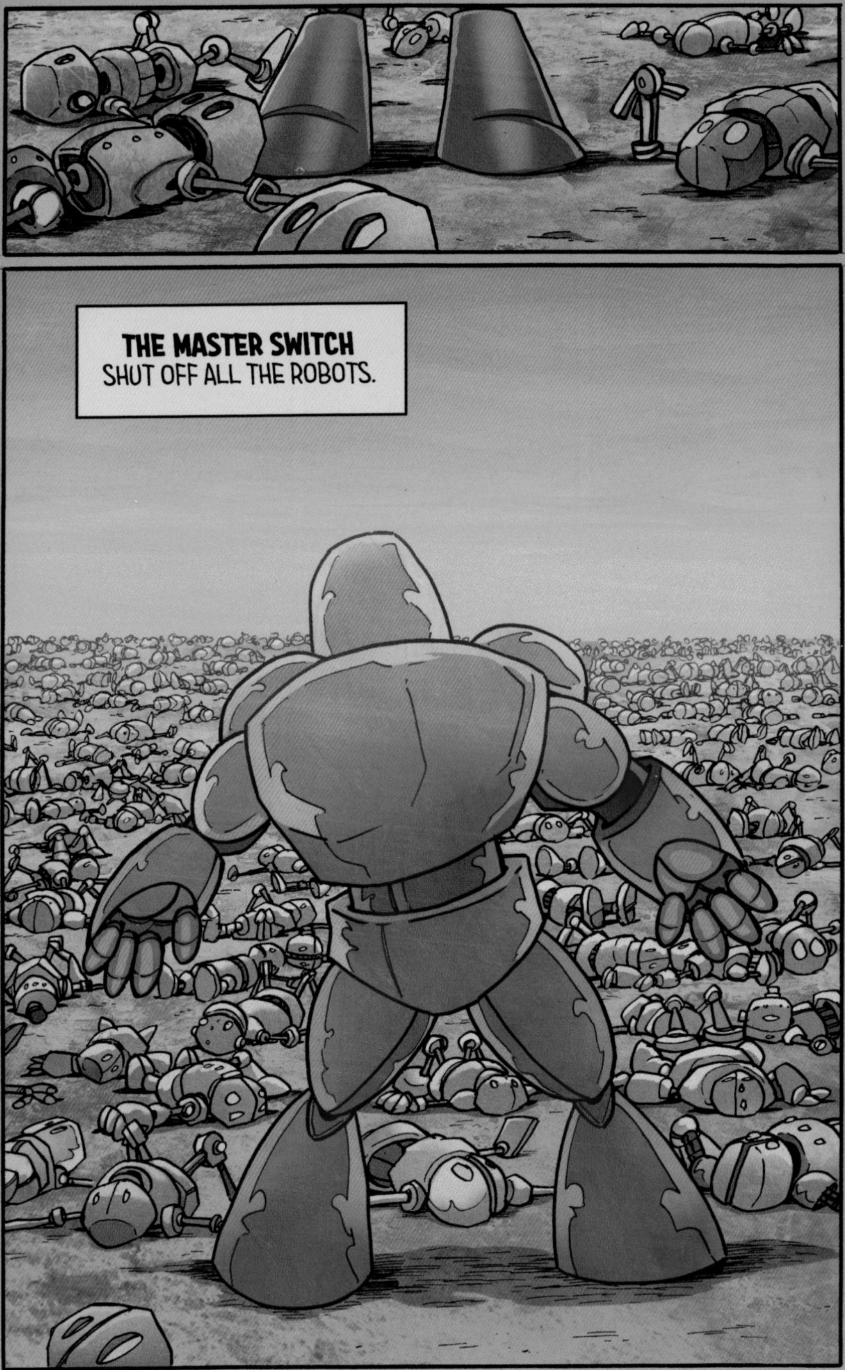
THE MASTER SWITCH
SHUT OFF ALL THE ROBOTS.

HE DESTROYED **SEVEN** ROBOT FACTORIES IN ONE DAY.

HIS MESSAGE WAS CLEAR.

NO MORE!

THAT WAS WHY HE WENT TO WAR WITH US.

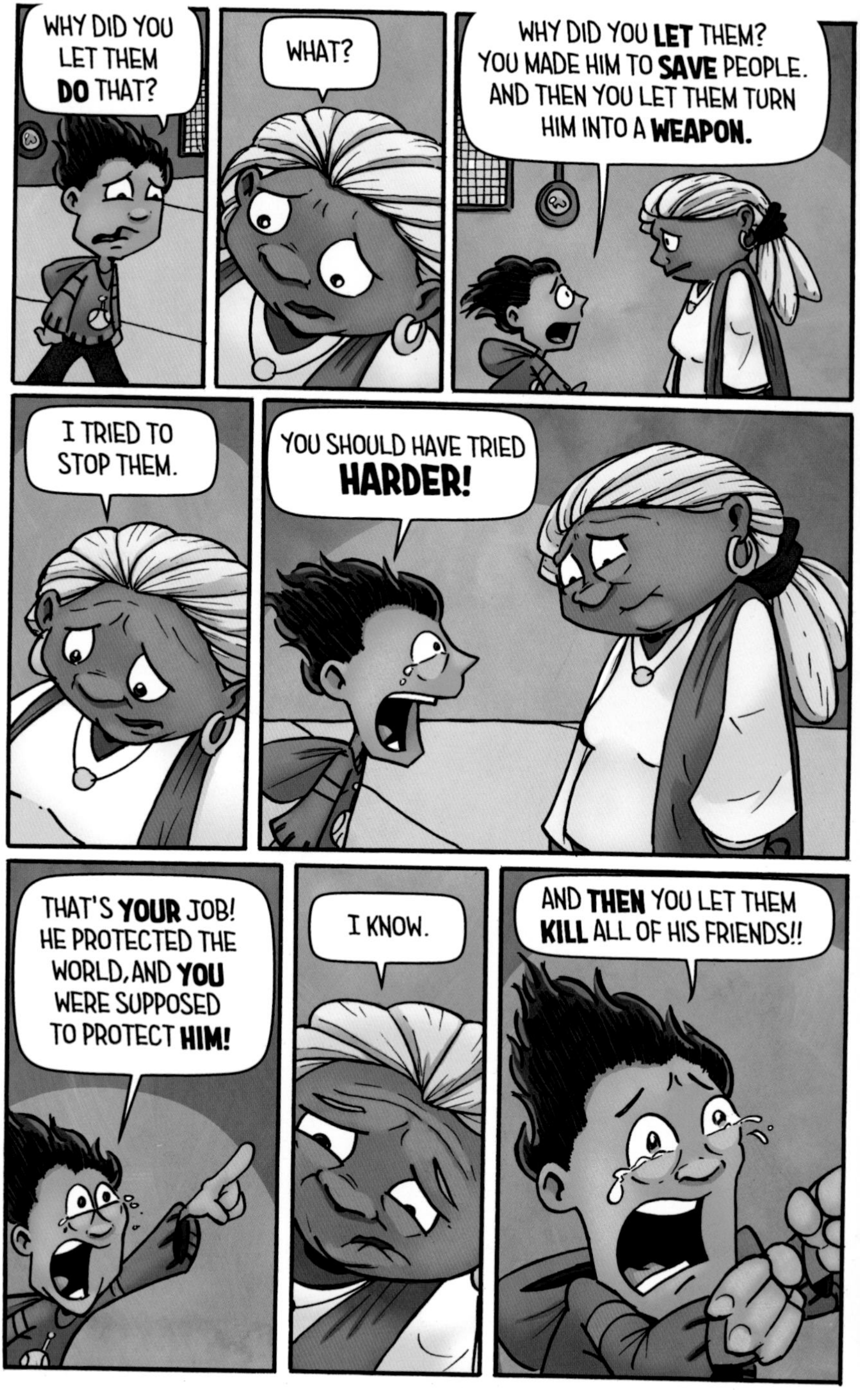
WHY DID YOU LET THEM **DO** THAT?
WHAT?
WHY DID YOU **LET** THEM? YOU MADE HIM TO **SAVE** PEOPLE. AND THEN YOU LET THEM TURN HIM INTO A **WEAPON.**
I TRIED TO STOP THEM.
YOU SHOULD HAVE TRIED **HARDER!**
THAT'S **YOUR** JOB! HE PROTECTED THE WORLD, AND **YOU** WERE SUPPOSED TO PROTECT **HIM!**
I KNOW.
AND **THEN** YOU LET THEM **KILL** ALL OF HIS FRIENDS!!

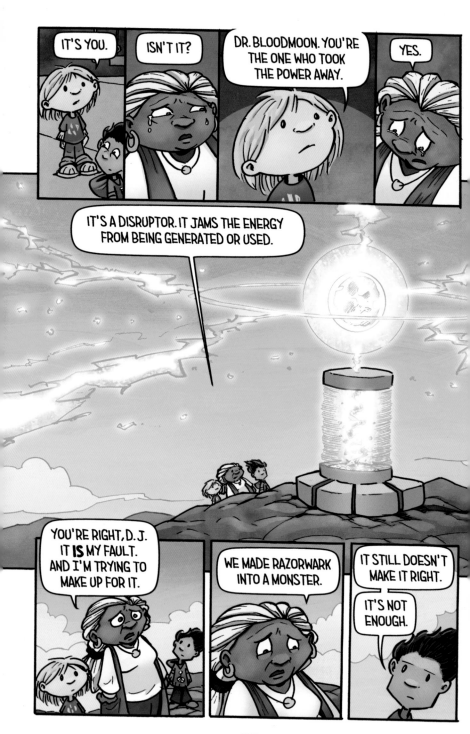

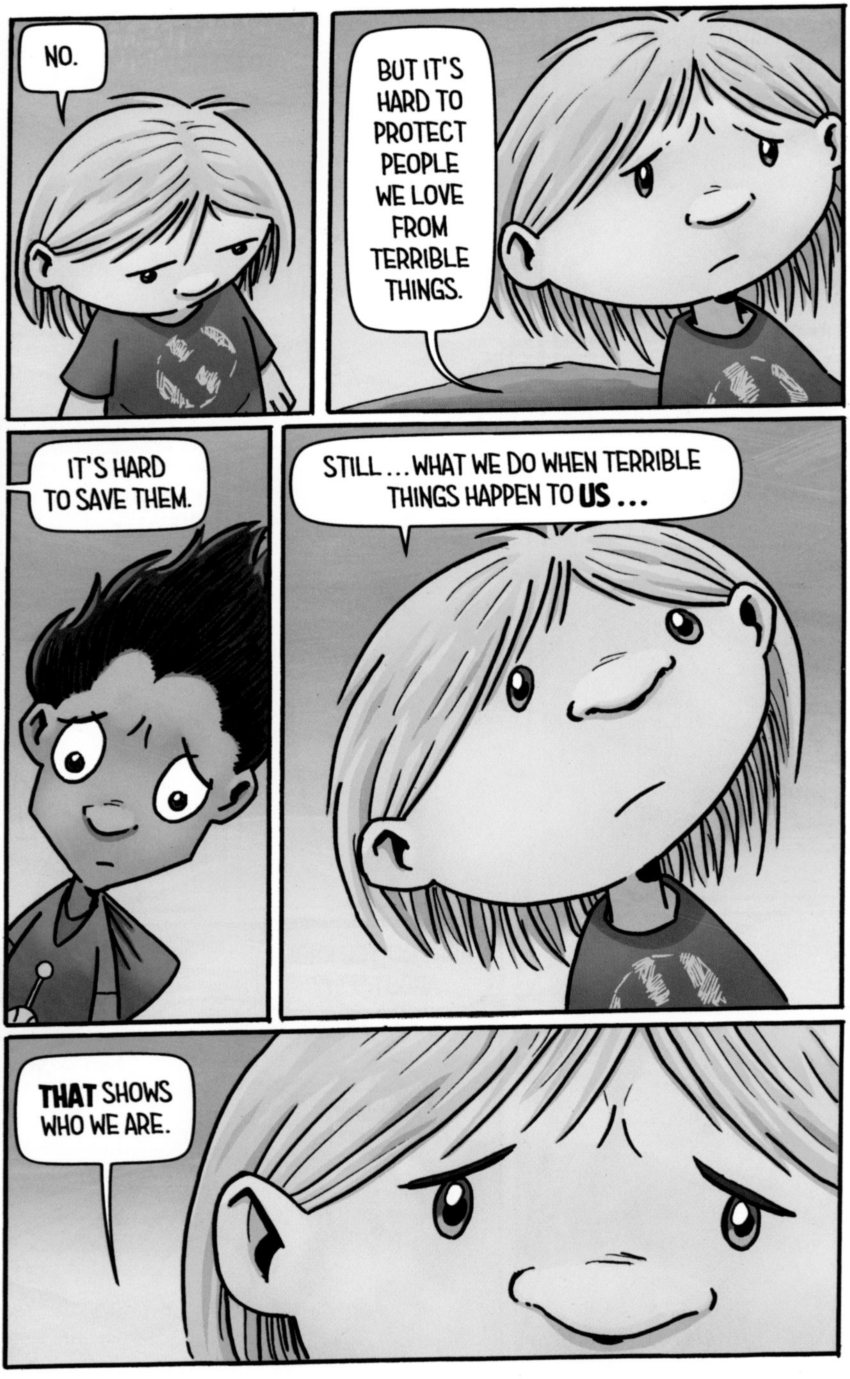
NO.
BUT IT'S HARD TO PROTECT PEOPLE WE LOVE FROM TERRIBLE THINGS.
IT'S HARD TO SAVE THEM.
STILL ... WHAT WE DO WHEN TERRIBLE THINGS HAPPEN TO **US** ...
THAT SHOWS WHO WE ARE.

CHAPTER

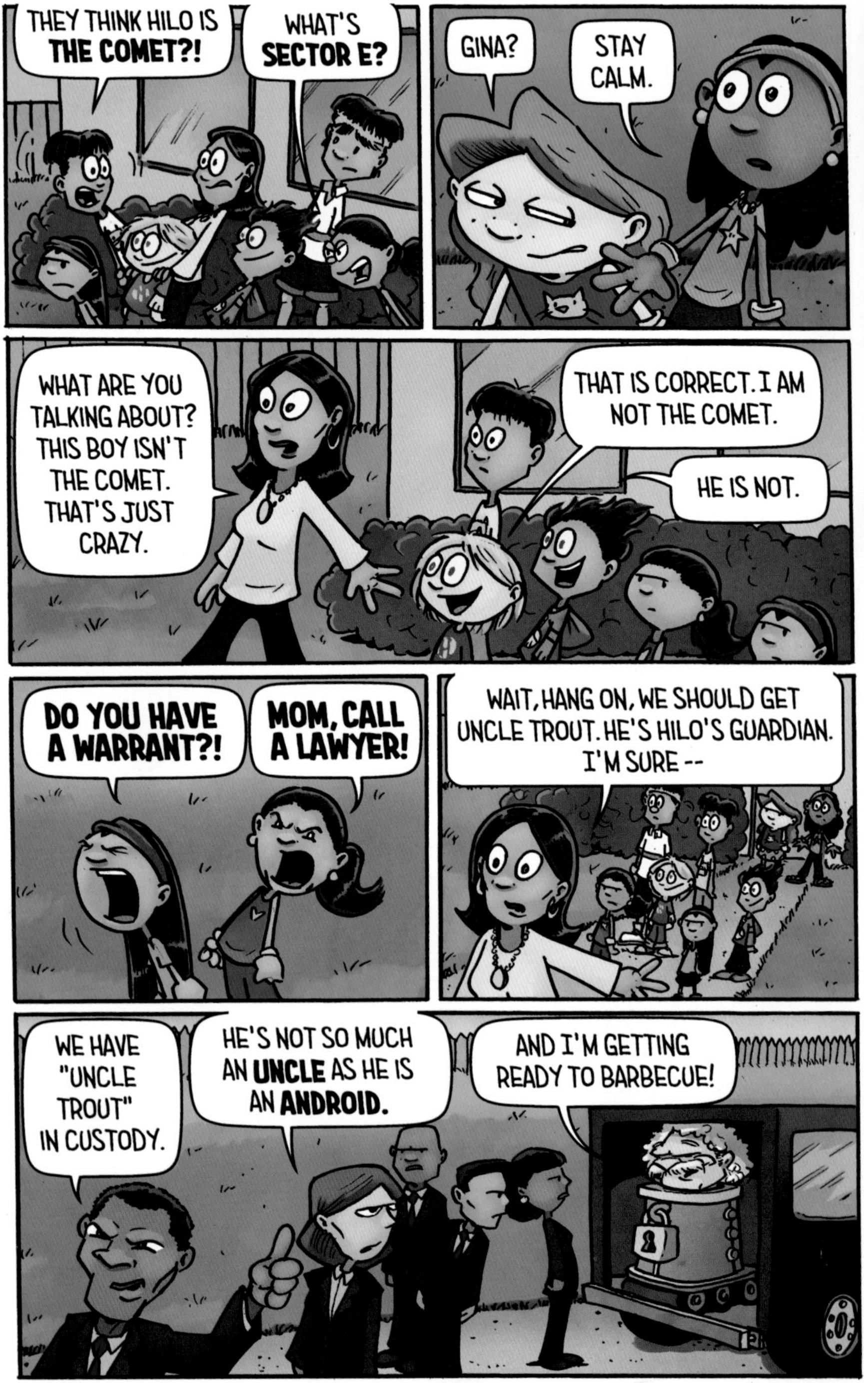
THEY THINK HILO IS **THE COMET?!**
WHAT'S **SECTOR E?**
GINA?
STAY CALM.
WHAT ARE YOU TALKING ABOUT? THIS BOY ISN'T THE COMET. THAT'S JUST CRAZY.
THAT IS CORRECT. I AM NOT THE COMET.
HE IS NOT.
DO YOU HAVE A WARRANT?!
MOM, CALL A LAWYER!
WAIT, HANG ON, WE SHOULD GET UNCLE TROUT. HE'S HILO'S GUARDIAN. I'M SURE --
WE HAVE "UNCLE TROUT" IN CUSTODY.
HE'S NOT SO MUCH AN **UNCLE** AS HE IS AN **ANDROID.**
AND I'M GETTING READY TO BARBECUE!

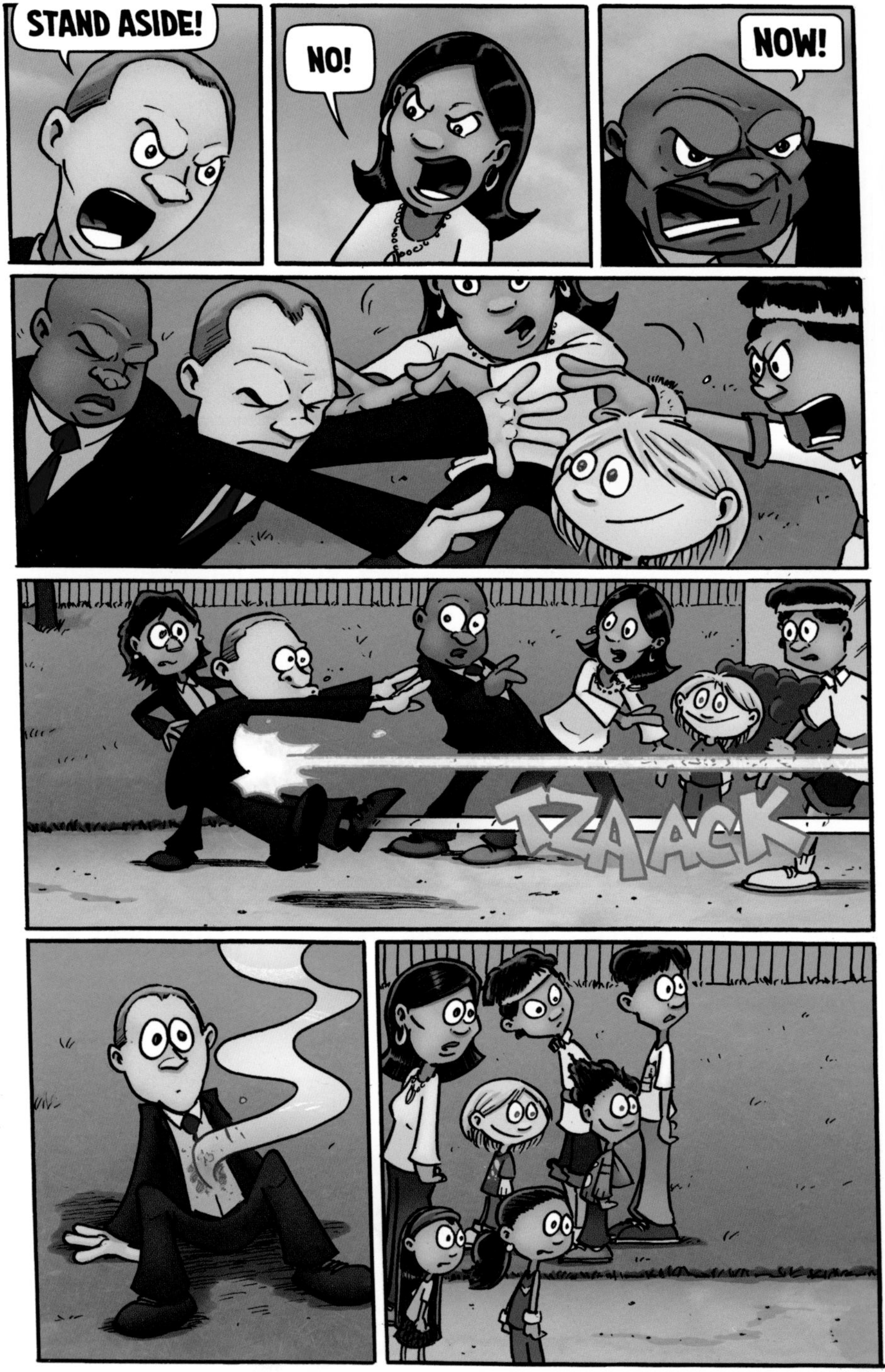
STAND ASIDE!
NO!
NOW!
TZAACK

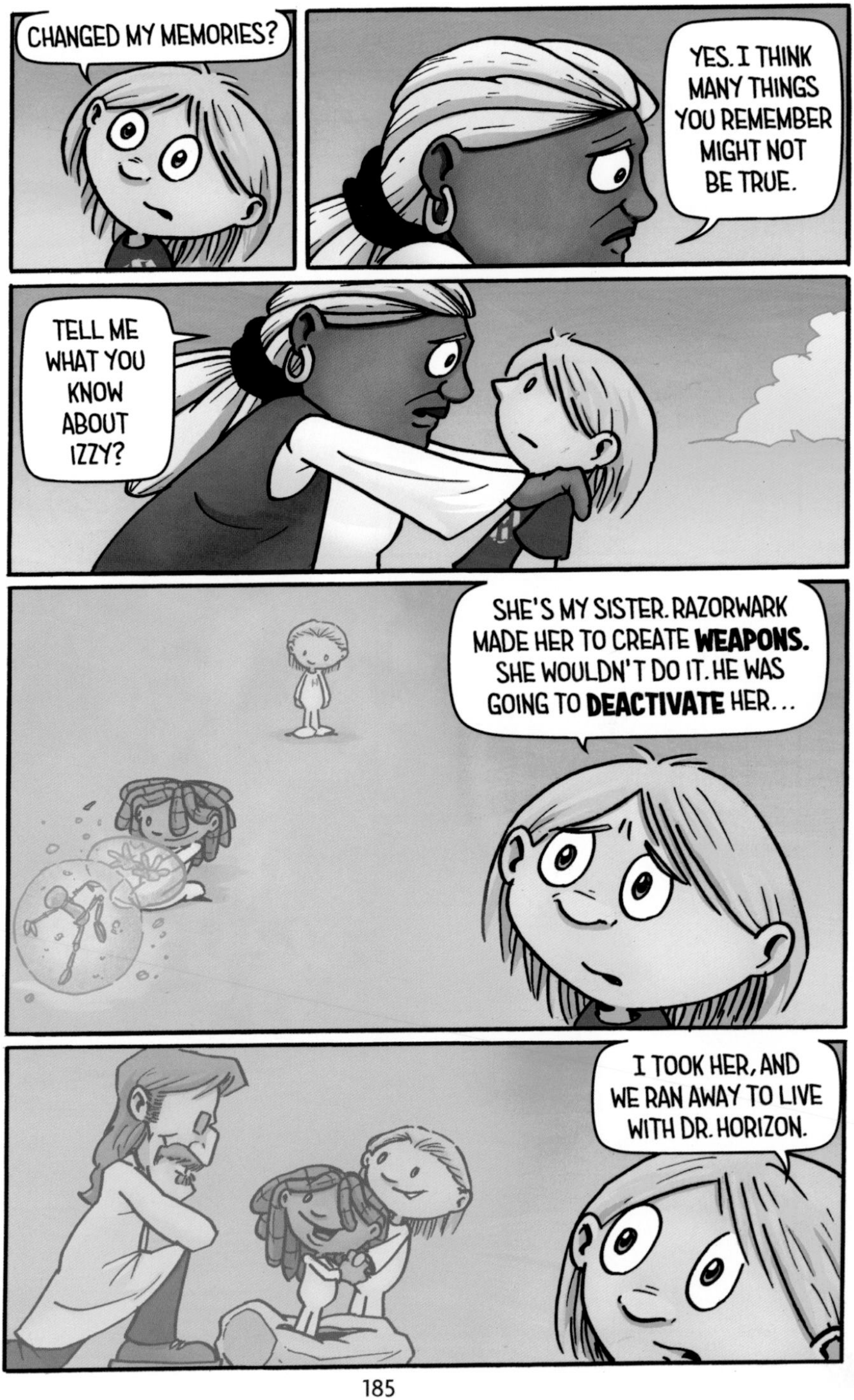
CHANGED MY MEMORIES?
YES. I THINK MANY THINGS YOU REMEMBER MIGHT NOT BE TRUE.
TELL ME WHAT YOU KNOW ABOUT IZZY?
SHE'S MY SISTER. RAZORWARK MADE HER TO CREATE **WEAPONS.** SHE WOULDN'T DO IT. HE WAS GOING TO **DEACTIVATE** HER...
I TOOK HER, AND WE RAN AWAY TO LIVE WITH DR. HORIZON.

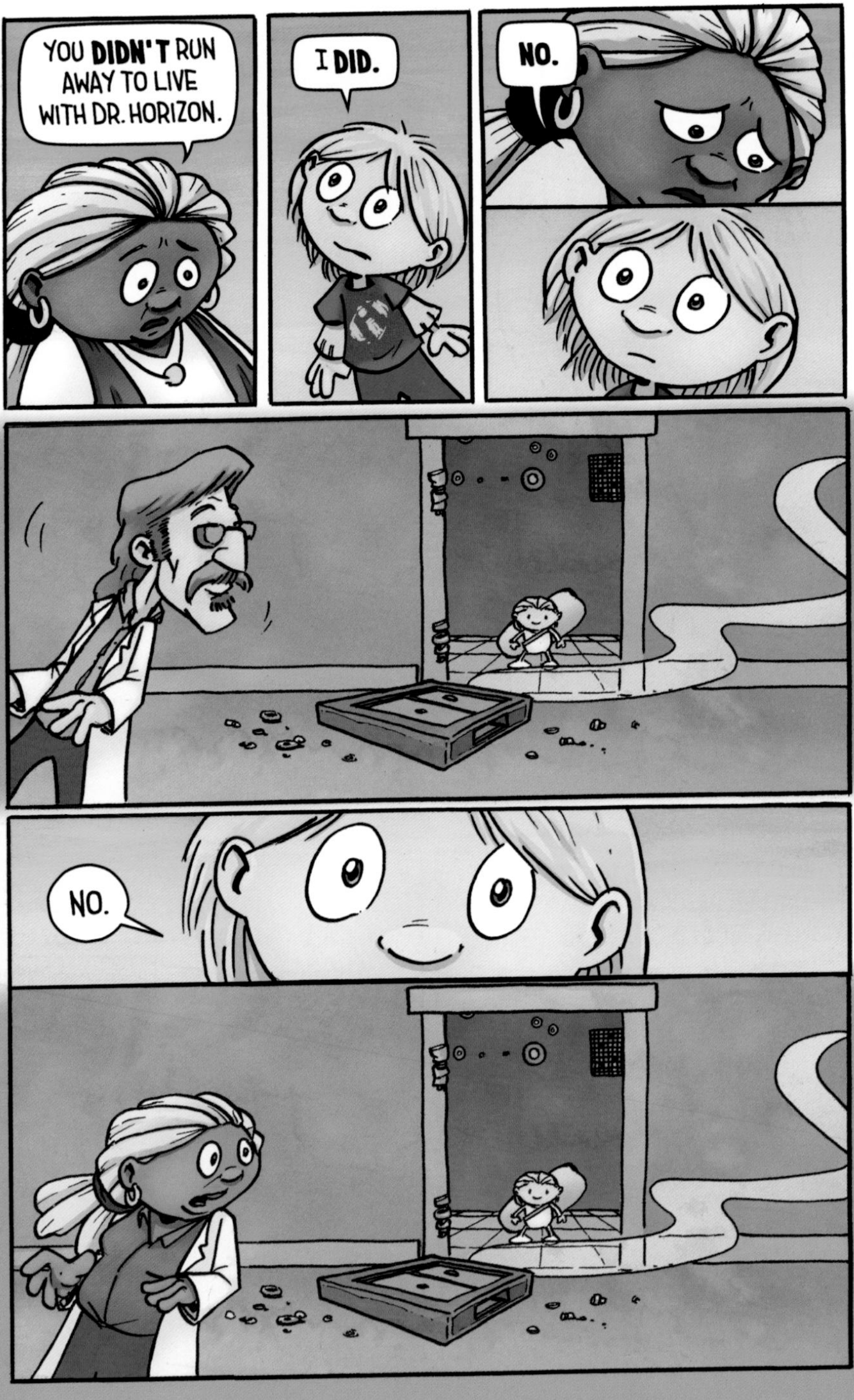
YOU DIDN'T RUN AWAY TO LIVE WITH DR. HORIZON.
I DID.
NO.
NO.

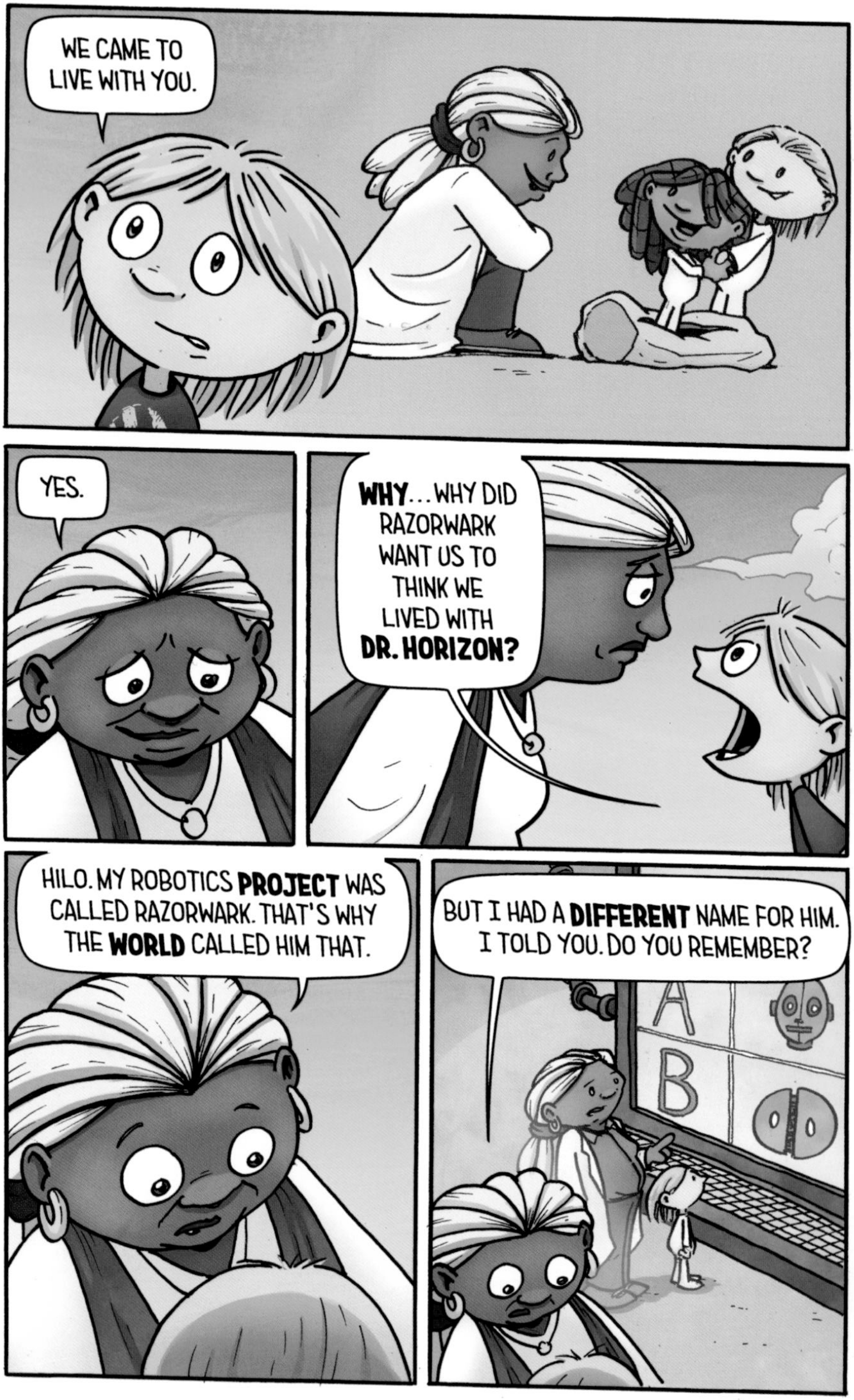
WE CAME TO LIVE WITH YOU.
YES.
WHY... WHY DID RAZORWARK WANT US TO THINK WE LIVED WITH DR. HORIZON?
HILO. MY ROBOTICS PROJECT WAS CALLED RAZORWARK. THAT'S WHY THE WORLD CALLED HIM THAT.
BUT I HAD A DIFFERENT NAME FOR HIM. I TOLD YOU. DO YOU REMEMBER?
A
B

IT TOOK **EIGHT** TRIES TO MAKE HIM.

JUST LIKE YOU.

I...REMEMBER.

HILO? WHAT IS IT? WHAT DO YOU REMEMBER?

HIS NAME.

189

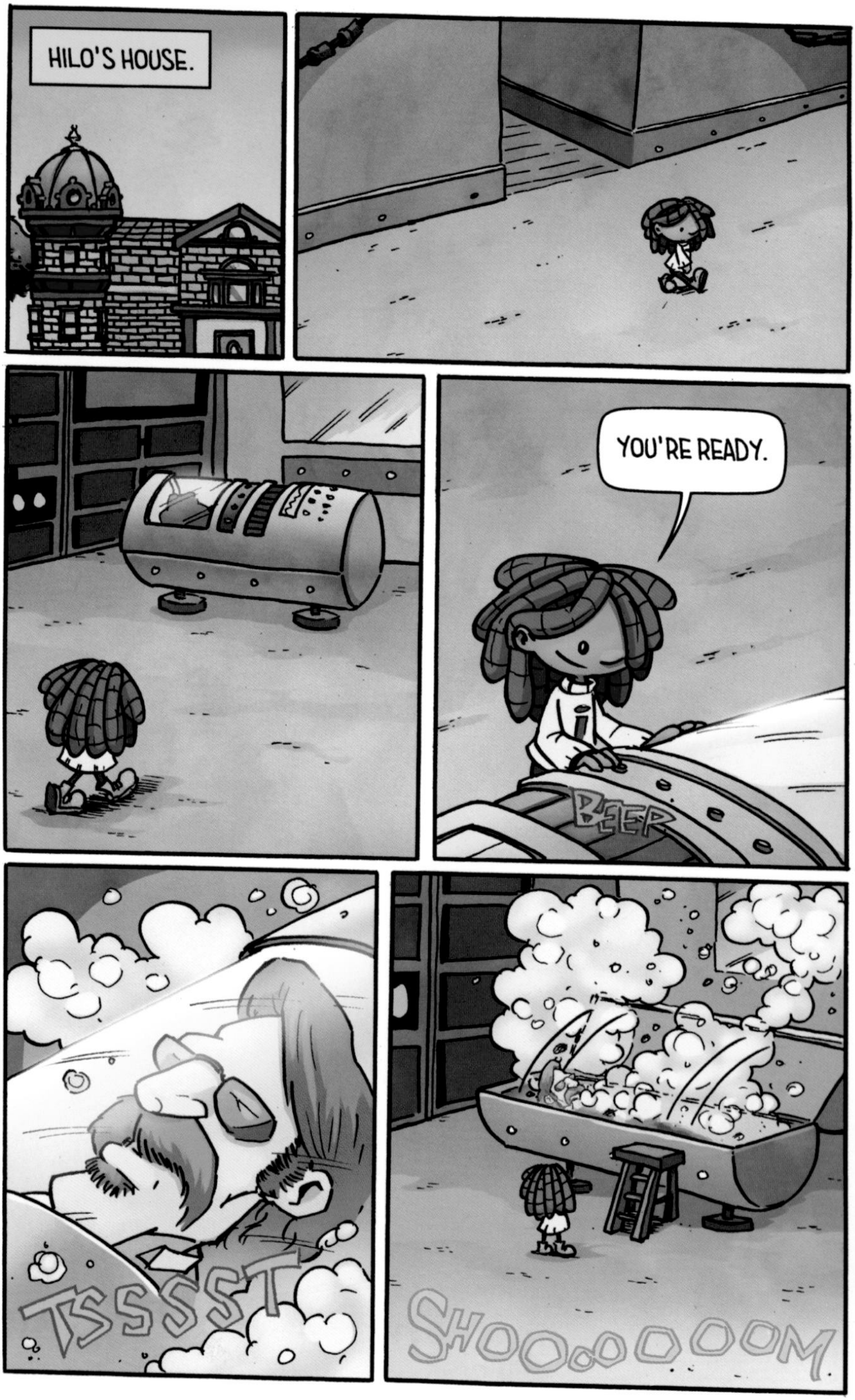
HILO'S HOUSE.
YOU'RE READY.
BEEP
TSSSST
SHOOoOOOOM

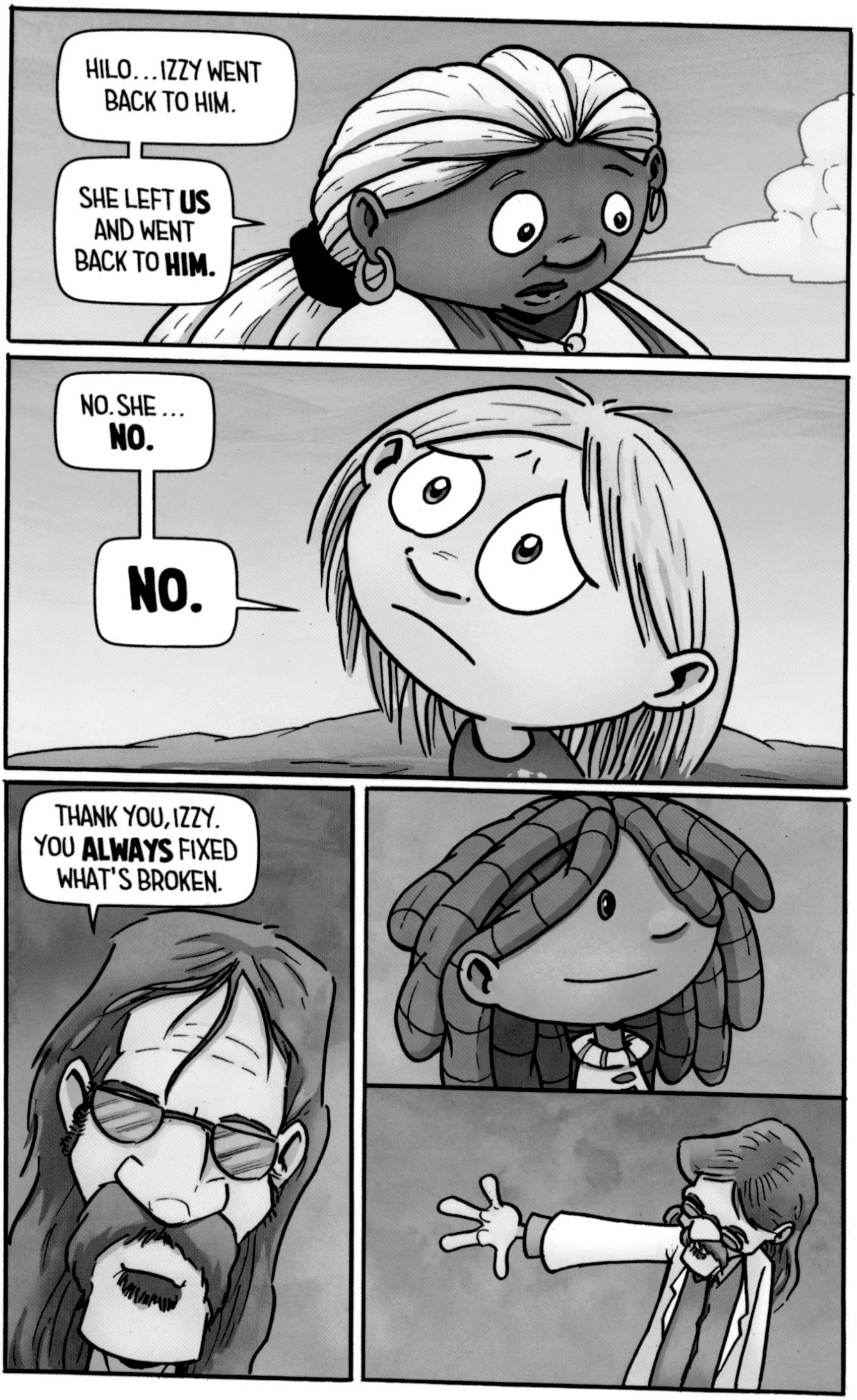
HILO... IZZY WENT BACK TO HIM.
SHE LEFT **US** AND WENT BACK TO **HIM.**
NO. SHE... **NO.**
NO.
THANK YOU, IZZY. YOU **ALWAYS** FIXED WHAT'S BROKEN.

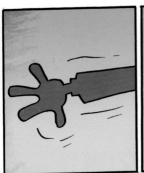

HILO! WHAT IS IT?!

I REMEMBER RAZORWARK'S NAME.

HORIZON.

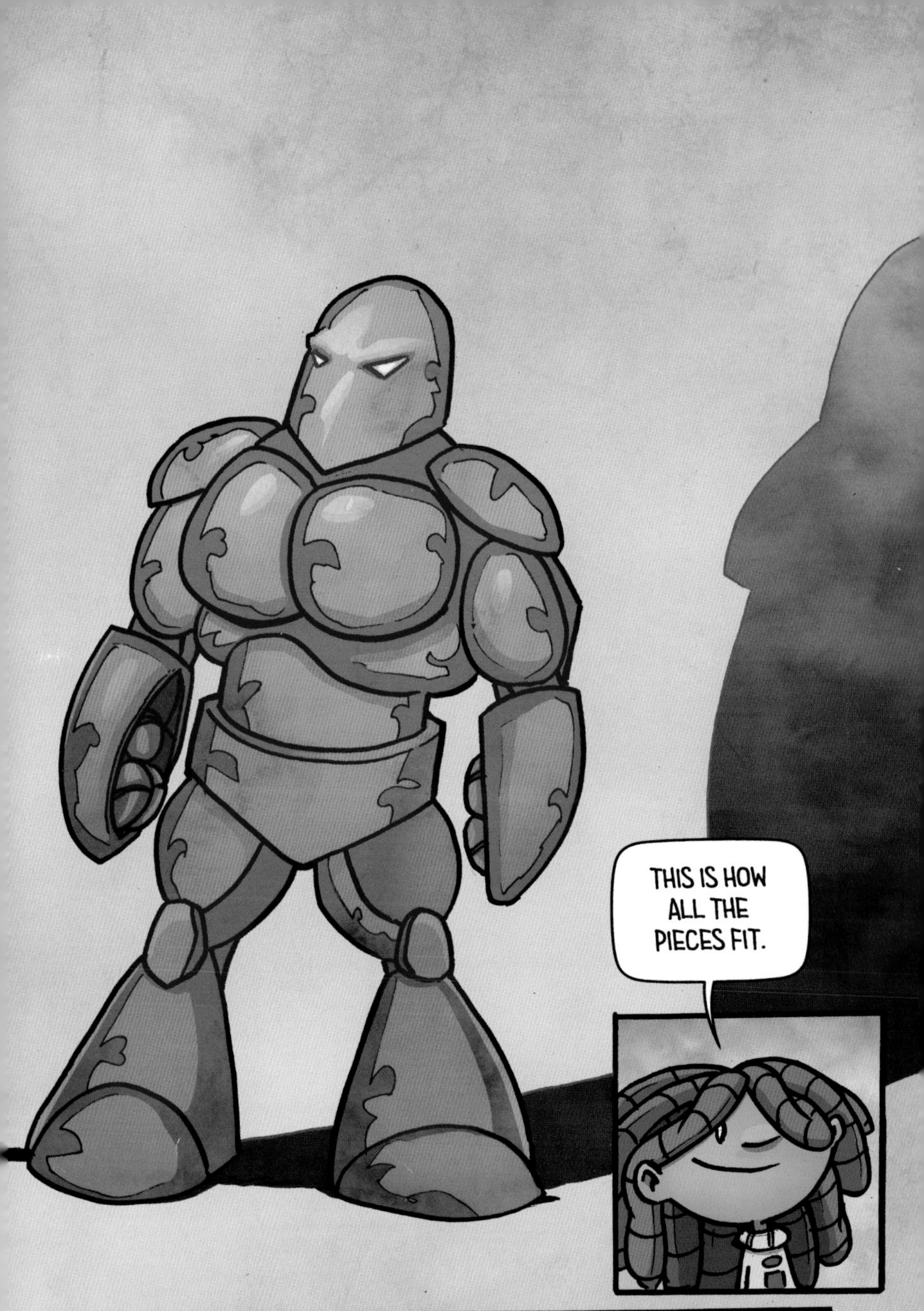
THIS IS HOW ALL THE PIECES FIT.

END OF BOOK FIVE

QUESTIONS WILL BE ANSWERED
MYSTERIES WILL BE REVEALED

HiLo
BOOK 6
ALL THE PIECES FIT

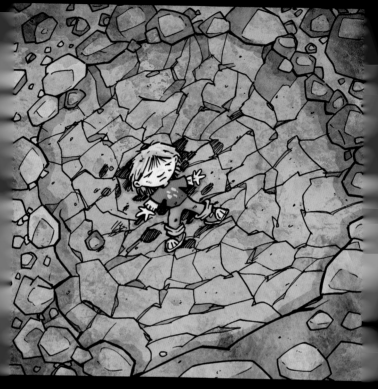

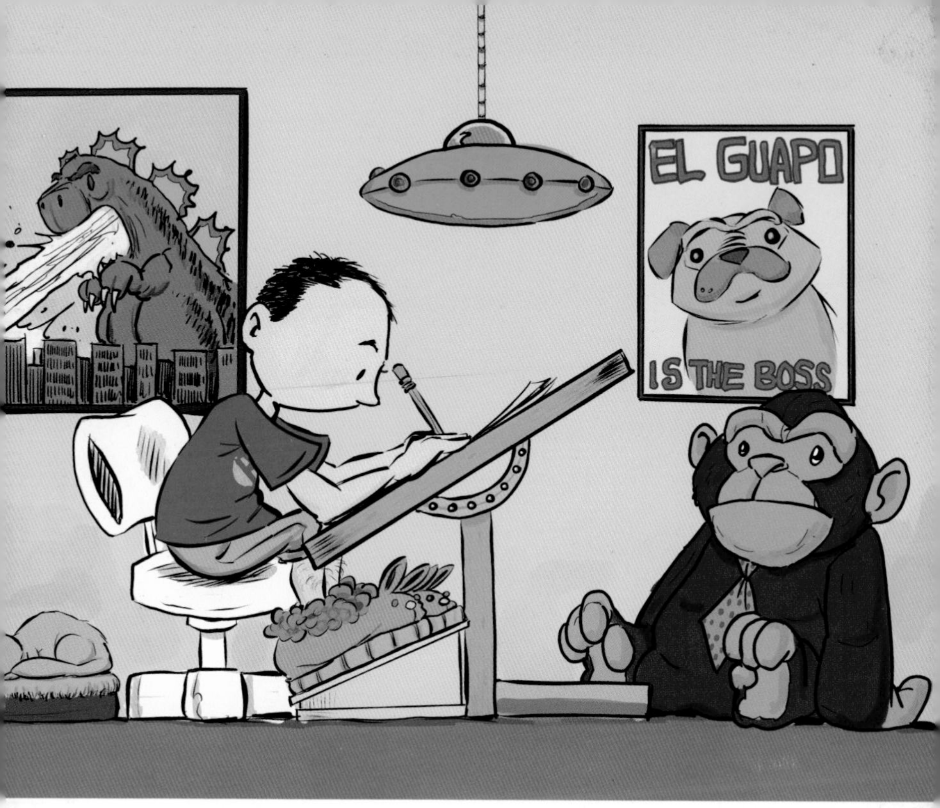
EL GUAPO
IS THE BOSS

JUDD WINICK is the creator of the award-winning, **New York Times** bestselling Hilo series. Judd grew up on Long Island with a healthy diet of doodling, **X-Men** comics, the newspaper strip **Bloom County**, and **Looney Tunes**. Today, he lives in San Francisco with his wife, Pam Ling; their two kids; their cat, Chaka; and far too many action figures and vinyl toys for a normal adult. Judd created the Cartoon Network series **Juniper Lee**; has written issues of superhero comics, including Batman, Green Lantern, and Green Arrow; and was a cast member of MTV's **The Real World: San Francisco**. Judd is also the author of the highly acclaimed graphic novel **Pedro and Me**, about his **Real World** roommate and friend, AIDS activist Pedro Zamora. Visit Judd and Hilo online at juddspillowfort.com or find him on Twitter at @JuddWinick.

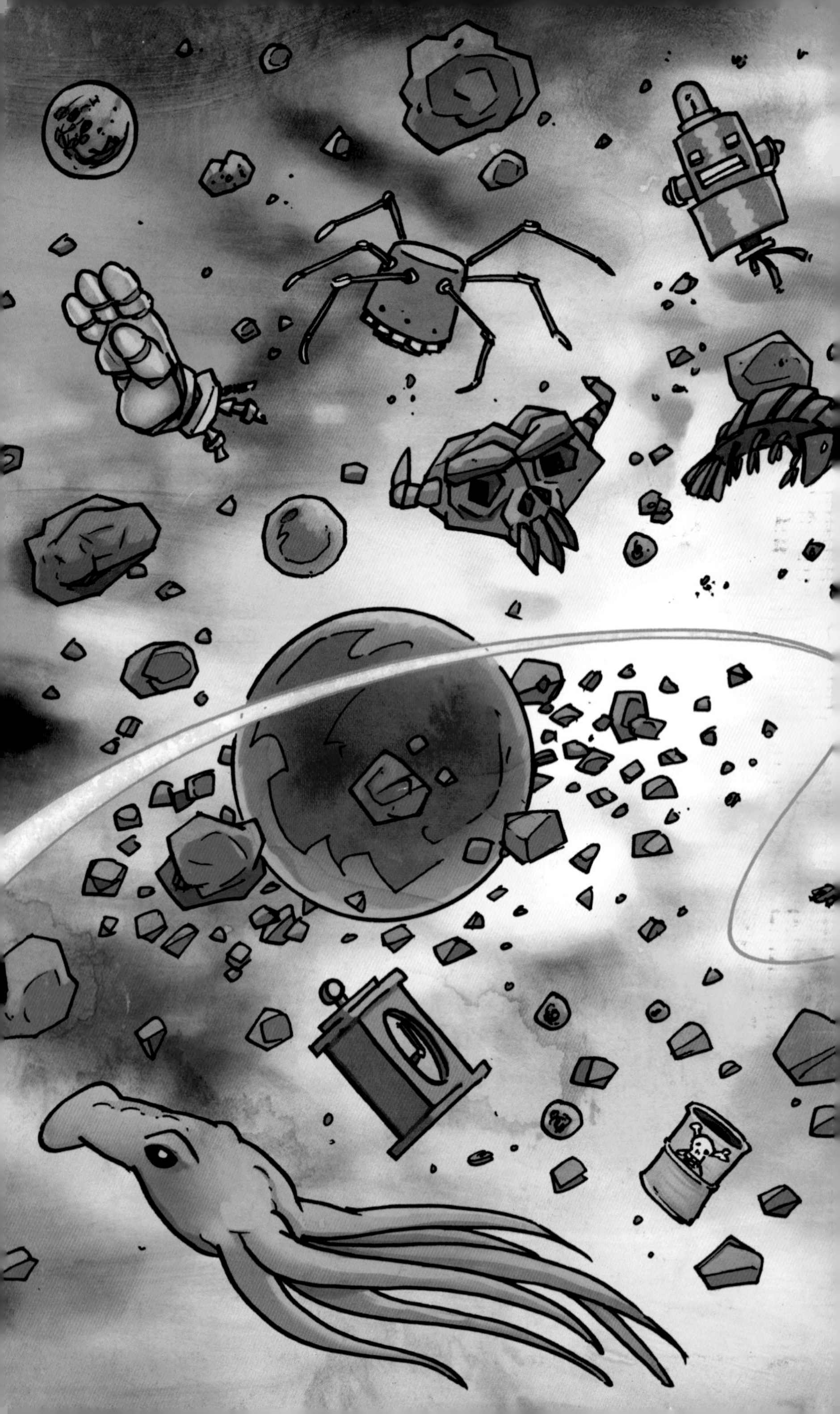